HOW TO PICK UP WOMEN WITH A DRUNK SPACE NINJA

THE ADVENTURES OF DUKE LAGRANGE, BOOK I

JAY KEY

OTHER BOOKS IN THE ADVENTURES OF DUKE LAGRANGE

BY JAY KEY

How to Pick Up Women with a Drunk Space Ninja

(Book I)

How to Win at Pit Fighting with a Drunk Space Ninja

(Book II)

How to Save the Universe with a Drunk Space Ninja

(Book III)

How to Battle Giant Monsters with a Drunk Space Ninja

(Book IV)

The Adventures of Duke LaGrange Omnibus, Volume I: The Collected Adventures (Books I-III)

For Shelley, the universe's most patient and understanding space ninja.

Anything without a cost isn't worth having.

QUEEN JOE

CHAPTER 1

CYBORG JOE'S

A NINJA CAN BE QUITE *handy when he isn't drunk off his ass.*

The crowd slowly poured into Cyborg Joe's Grill N' Go & the Why Not Saloon—voted the loudest bar in the galaxy for the past twelve cycles and home to the MechaBurger 8000, a treat that kills twenty-three percent of the life forms that try to digest it. Duke LaGrange clicked his fingers against the uneven wooden bar top and stared into a slightly dirtier-than-it-should-be glass containing just a small remnant of golden Glyptodian ale. The bounty hunter shook his head as his mind raced to solutions for his quandary. How was he alone and all of these other life forms, if they wanted to call themselves that, were lining up their prospects for the evening? He concluded that he had just grown too damn accustomed to the tried-and-true method of luring in intoxicated females with his sidekick's conversation-starter party tricks, most of which included an element of sword play and damage to the bar. It had to be. Regardless, this evening Duke knew he would have to revise his strategy or give up and join his masked friend on the barroom floor. And Cyborg Joe's wasn't known for having the cleanest floors.

"You know, Duke, you need to move your companion. That area of the floor is reserved for tonight's musical act," said the barkeep as she wiped down some sullied glass goblets imprecisely.

"Who's the act?"

"The Trampling Death Robots." She held the glassware to the light to examine its cleanliness.

"Any good?"

"Well, that depends. Do you like loud explosions and large objects crashing to the floor?"

"I'm not into the performance arts. Can they work around him?"

"I wouldn't advise it."

"Fair enough, Queen, I'll grab him. Nothing better to do, I suppose," the bounty hunter replied in a sullen tone.

"Alright, LaGrange. Hold up. Lay it on me. What's with the pouting?"

"Huh?"

"Look, you've frequented my little watering hole more than I care to recall—but, through all of the time that you've graced us at Joe's with your presence, I've come to know Duke LaGrange quite well. In fact, it's amazing what you can learn by pouring a man's drinks for as long as I have."

"I really don't know what you're talking about. Everything's fine. Great. Grand. Hunky dory, even."

Duke lobbed a forced smile in the Queen's general direction. She countered. All things considered, a snarky glance was getting off easy with someone like the Queen. No one really knew much about the Queen outside of a few key details: she was quite possibly the most powerful sentient being in the galaxy, she was a damn good bartender, and she was the only one that could control the portals that made Cyborg Joe's one of the most frequented establishments by space travelers from every sector. Portals connecting destinations in the universe and allowing intergalactic travel were by no means unique, that's how most spacecraft got from point A to point B. But portals so small and controllable that they could transport individual beings without ripping them to shreds at the atomic level just simply didn't exist. Except at Joe's. These portals also made it a key point of interest for the government du jour. Scholars quipped that the reason that there hadn't been a universal governing body for eons was because the Queen refused to give her endorsement to any one system of rule. There was always someone or something trying to unite the planets—dictators, religious groups, military coups, you name it —but none managed to stabilize for more than a moment. The universe wasn't in anarchy, though some individual worlds subscribed to that political arrangement—everyone just did their own thing. It was a system that received general approval.

Her age was also a point of debate amongst patrons of Joe's. She joked that she was old enough to have dated the single-celled organisms that were the very genesis of life. For some reason, Duke believed it. It just made sense to him.

Outside of those well-known characteristics, she was a complete mystery. No home world. No rumors or memories or accounts of a time before Cyborg Joe's. Not so much as a single eyewitness testimony of her existence outside of the bar itself. Even her name—"Queen Joe"—was just the product of legions of guests associating her with their favorite drinking locale. No one really thought her name was Joe—but it made everyone feel good. She never fought it.

"Duke, I know your typical game—hell, I've seen your game for going on ten cycles. The whole bounty-hunter-by-day, playboy-by-night gig isn't exactly new in these parts. It's just that you play the part with such conviction. I don't see anything resembling conviction tonight. So what's going on? Mazilda Cloax again?"

"Seriously, Queen. I really think that..."

"Duke, for the sake of all that's right in this galaxy! You haven't even hit on me tonight!"

The bounty hunter, like most beings with the gift of sight, found Queen Joe attractive—very attractive, at that—but not even he had the audacity to engage her seriously with amorous intent. His flirtations had become almost a fixed prelude for ordering a drink at the bar. The Queen even told him once that she stored a few of his best lines somewhere deep in her memory as she felt they might one day be useful to another patron of Joe's, and only in the direst of situations.

"I'm sorry, you're off on this one, Queen."

She bent down to grab a bottle of Erontian saké behind the bar. Duke's eyes migrated southward and lingered.

"At least I know that you're not entirely broken."

"Sorry. Habit."

"So, talk straight to me. What's with the 'woe is me' shtick? Maybe I can help."

The bounty hunter inhaled deeply, exhaled slowly.

"Queen, well, it's quite—" he stumbled over his words uncharacteristically. "—embarrassing."

"You know good and well, Duke, that all I ask for in my clientele is that they show tolerance; understand that beauty comes in many forms; and pay me properly if they choose to use one of my portals. That's it. In return, I promise them a place in which they can unload their grievances without fear of condemnation, meet members of a new species or two, and enjoy a well-made martini. You've definitely met a 'friend' or two under my roof—and you've imbibed your weight in martinis. Now I think it's time that you let me know what's wrong and unload those grievances."

"Fine."

Duke paused, each of his thoughts waging a war against the others. The "shoulds" had a slight upper hand on the "should nots."

"I've lost *it*," Duke cried out. His admission dissolved a

tightness in the pit of his stomach that he likened to a prisoner finally succumbing to cycles of torture.

"What exactly do you mean by 'it'?" Queen Joe questioned cautiously.

"You know… 'it.'" Duke let out an audible sigh. "My talent. My power. My mojo. My 'it.'"

"You can't hit on women anymore?"

"Not successfully."

The Queen turned away from the bounty hunter.

"Are you laughing? I thought this was a place where you could unload without condemnation?"

The Queen didn't respond but reached down and unlocked a small cabinet. She pulled out a dusty, transparent vessel containing darkened liquid the color of toasted caramel. *Earth whisky.* She slung two small glasses on the bar; one slid toward the bounty hunter and stopped just short of the bar's edge. Duke plucked it off the bar top and planted it before the Queen. She topped off both glasses in the potent liquor.

"To misplaced mojo!"

They both downed their drinks. The Queen refilled them as soon as they hit the wooden bar top.

"And finding it again," she said, finishing her two-part toast.

The whisky hit the back of Duke's tongue and immediately warmed his very being.

"Duke, I'm sorry, but I don't think that I can help you with your lady troubles—"

"I figured."

"Though maybe the whisky can. In fact, there isn't much that a little whisky can't fix."

Duke pondered this for a second and didn't disagree.

"However, I do have an opportunity for you. It might be the thing you're looking for to get your mind off of your current quandry."

"An opportunity? Queen, you've never asked me to track

someone down for you—I'm honored. My 'bounty hunter slash playboy' billing always lists bounty hunter first, ya' know—I'm quite good."

"This certain opportunity falls outside of your current job description. It's a bit bigger in scope, I'm afraid."

"Go on."

Queen Joe pointed across the stage to the wall on the east side of the building. It was battered and beaten as if an entire armada had released a heavy concentration of hate upon its stone-like façade. Duke was familiar with this wall—in fact, all of the patrons, first-timers and regulars alike, were familiar with this wall. He surveyed the slender door frames that spanned the entirety of the barrier. Each frame surrounded an ornate door—all of them quite distinct.

"The portal doors?"

"No, not *my* portals. Over there. Beyond them, in the far corner."

Duke noticed it for the first time; tucked behind the portals, in the center of a recessed area hidden within the few shadows that escaped the glow of Cyborg Joe's neon advertisements. The bright beams danced erratically, crackling and sizzling.

"Another doorway? When did that happen? Where did it come from? Those wild lights shooting out of the opening are quite trippy though—nice touch."

"That gateway appeared without my consent a few days ago. The others I can control, for the most part—however, when I showed up to the bar today, this mess had ripped through the wall. We did our best to board it up but it's hard to not notice."

"Any ideas?"

"I don't know. It's been some time since I left Kelt or even the bar, so I get most of my adventures secondhand through those that stumble in here. I was curious if you had seen or heard about anything like this."

"I got nothing. I'm up the proverbial creek without a paddle... or even a boat. Though if I stare at it any longer I'm going to feel like I'm messed up on some Gheo'to Morphio root. Freaky."

"My final conclusion was that it's a dimensional tear similar to my other doors—but far more unstable. After examining it, I feel it leads somewhere."

"So it *is* a portal."

"I think so. However, my intuition tells me that it's not the sort of portal that leads to a happy field of lollipops. There's a negative energy; not necessarily evil—but negative."

"So what's this opportunity about? I'm assuming it has something to do with the door."

"Yes. I'm extremely worried about this intrusion. It isn't sitting right with me—and now some of the patrons are starting to not only notice it, but ask questions too. Questions that I can't answer. Cyborg Joe's doesn't *allow* questions that I can't answer. This is very unsettling."

"So, the opportunity?"

"Here it is. If you can successfully find out why this tear is occurring in my bar and get rid of it—I'll give you access to my portals. Free of charge. For the next cycle. No questions asked. No reservations needed. Unlimited use. Needless to say, I've never offered this type of deal before."

Duke paused. "Why me? Because I'm depressed about losing my mojo?"

"No—but if you think about it, becoming the first person ever to be granted unlimited access to the portals—free of charge—can only help your reputation. I win, you win."

"That is, if I don't get obliterated by this pissed-off dimensional door."

"True. But I have faith in you, Duke LaGrange. I won't ask any questions about what you plan on doing or how you plan on doing it. Your methods are to your own design. Just as long as that thing is gone."

"How about another shot of that Earth whisky and I'll think about it. When can I give you my answer?"

"Tonight. If I'm not serving, tell Earl to track me down. I really hope you consider it."

Duke pounded the next glassful of whisky.

"Tonight... I can do that. I think I'm gonna see if this whisky is helping with my problem, first. I would prefer to get back on track without risking my life trying to exterminate an unhinged inter-dimensional anomaly."

"Do what you need to do. However, my offer will expire at the end of the night. Try not to get into trouble, Duke. This is not an offer that you will see again."

"One last question. Can Ishiro'shea come with me?"

"Of course. And you *do* realize that he is still on the floor?"

"Thanks for the reminder, Queen. Those damn ninja side-kicks—can't live with 'em, can't keep 'em from rendering themselves unconscious on overpriced beer. Am I right?"

Joe smirked. "Overpriced beer?"

"You know what I mean," the bounty hunter stammered. "C'mon, Queen—it was just a joke."

She responded only with an enigmatic smile—equal parts playful banter and genuine offense—and effortlessly tossed her rag to an approaching armor-shelled Glyptodian barkeep named Earl.

"I'll let you know by tonight," Duke replied as the Queen locked up the Earth whisky, "even though this little venture could come at a hefty cost!"

"Anything without a cost isn't worth having."

She disappeared into the rapidly burgeoning crowd of Cyborg Joe's.

CHAPTER 2

THREE-HEADED ICE WOMBATS

T HE BOUNTY HUNTER SAT STARING at eight feet of hulking Glyptodian.

"Hey Earl."

"Greetings, Mr. LaGrange. Welcome back to Cyborg Joe's. Can I be of any assistance in relation to your alcohol consumption or culinary desires?"

Earl was very capable behind the bar and had been employed at Joe's for as long as Duke could remember. Earl's coat carried only a trace of its once brown hue; now it shone mostly silver—in fact, Duke couldn't recall a time when the large biped appeared "young." The Queen once told him that she felt Earl added much-needed sophistication and class to her operation. Duke was aligned with that statement—though, in his travels, manners were never high on the list of requirements when choosing a place to knock back a few refreshments. Duke liked Earl but found him overly formal and a substantial downgrade in appearance from the Queen, so he decided it was the perfect time to go fetch Ishiro'shea.

"I'm okay right now, Earl. Just a little ninja retrieval on the to-do list."

"Sounds exhilarating, Mr. LaGrange. If you need anything, don't hesitate to ask. And give my regards to Mr. Ishiro'shea. When he awakens from his rest, that is."

Duke spun around on the stool, which gave a shrieking whine produced by a lifetime sans upkeep. As he headed over to his passed-out sidekick his attention was diverted by the high-pitched giggles of two young female humanoids. They appeared uninterested in the advances of two heavy-set humanoids adorned in tactical gear and looking very serious. *Military attempts to take over the universe must be in season. When will they ever learn?* Almost involuntarily, Duke performed a lightning-quick scan of the two female targets to make sure that they had at least two limbs and no more than three eyes. He wasn't picky but did have some standards. The pair possessed figures that Duke found instantly appealing. He particularly appreciated, at least aesthetically, the airtight polymerized chloroprene body suits that both females wore— jet black and with no discernible markings of any kind. His imagination was aroused by the question of where certain parts of their anatomy began and ended. *How did they get those damn things on,* he thought to himself, *and how do I get them off? I have a few minutes before the Robots go on—I'm sure Ishiro will be fine. Anyways, I need to test drive this whisky before I get back to the Queen with an answer about her little opportunity.*

"Ladies. Can I buy you both a drink?"

His line was met with more giggles and the batting of electric violet eyelashes—or at least, they were close enough to eyelashes. Any new adventure—especially one involving unknown dimensional tears—could wait a bit longer. *Tonight is saved.*

"If you don't know already, I happen to be Duke LaGrange..."

He waited for a sign of recognition. When it didn't come,

he continued, "Adventurer. Trailblazer. Poet. A true man of the universe."

"Is that so, handsome?" retorted one of the females, followed by even more giggles. Her voice was surprisingly confident and possessed an almost soothing quality. However, she let the last syllable of each word dangle until she started the next. And that damn giggling never stopped. "This is my best girlfriend and fourth cousin on my quasi-aunt's side, Arlut. You can call me Turla, sugar. On Hilteria, it means 'very generous.'"

The corners of Duke's mouth shot upward in a sly grin. His voice, already deeper than most upright humanoids, lowered even further to become the velvety tones of an experienced seducer. "There is nothing I love more than a charitable soul."

After the third round of especially fiery Glyptodian Summer Ale, Duke launched into his adventurous tales of capturing the scum of the cosmos with nothing more than his wits and bare hands. His overly embellished accounts of danger and heroism were interrupted only by the thunderous explosions of the Trampling Death Robots that echoed through the cavernous dimensions of the bar—its ceilings as tall as a Quibbian erecto-varmint.

"So there I was on Tardasio 7 staring down a rabid, blood-sucking, three-headed ice wombat. He had just killed the entire staff of Sol's Bail Bonds-O-Rama and was headed for a local petting zoo," Duke said.

The two magenta-skinned females oohed and aahed in tandem at every exaggerated piece of the chronicle. They never missed an opportunity to bat those purple eyelash things.

"Now remember, ladies, I had just captured an entire gang of speed cycle assassins before lunch and was quite the worse for wear—but there was no way that I was going to let this demon beast get away with eating my benefactors." A bit of honesty somehow managed to slip through his defenses.

"What'd you say, hun? Benefactors?" asked Arlut.

Luckily, the Trampling Death Robots hit the crescendo of "I Want to Smash You, My Binary Baby" and Duke's delicate game of romance was preserved.

"I'm sorry, my beautiful belles," he replied with faux annoyance. "I was saying... there was no way that I was going to let this raging, maniacal demon beast get away with eating the poor, innocent, sweet, young orphans visiting the local children's petting farm." Emphasis on *orphans*.

Flawless recovery. He was also proud of his ability to augment his description with even more adjectives that were neither necessary nor true. *The whisky must be working*.

"Duke, honey, you're simply amazing."

The bounty hunter did not shy away from the praise.

"And utterly gorgeous. Are you sure you aren't lawfully bound to something?"

Turla's flirtations overwhelmed her companion's attempts. She was the alpha flirter.

Duke's chin raised triumphantly.

"My beautiful Turla, I am now and have always been lawfully bound to my oath of protecting the innocent, defending the peace, fighting for the freedom of all that deserve it, and honoring my home—the proud colony of Nova Texas. But maybe, just maybe, I have been waiting for someone equally as amazing to stroll into my life."

Duke thought he might have overstepped the bounds into the realm of low-budget romance films; luckily, the Hilterian ate it up, as so many had before her.

This was the all-too-familiar homestretch. Duke was a hunter and his prey was wounded. He extended his hefty and calloused—yet comforting—hand and gently covered Turla's delicate digits that dangled from a perfectly circular palm that resembled glowing porcelain. He tilted his well-worn stone-colored Stetson so that his glare could pierce her defenses. *Kill time.* The intoxicated laughter morphed abruptly into a longing gaze that immobilized Turla. Even though his brown eyes were locked into the deep smoky obsidian of his conquest's, Duke could sense that Arlut—or as Duke christened her in his head, "Option B"—was growing increasingly jealous. Being his second choice would pierce her inebriation with a jolt of sobriety and Duke knew it. *Can't have that—not when the finish line is in sight.* Duke was well aware, from combing the vast unknown of the universe as the most infamous bounty hunter playboy of the last fifteen cycles, how to guarantee that a night of spoils would not be sabotaged by a really pissed off best friend. He decided to pick up the pace.

"Babe, how about we get outta—"

"Turla, I'm tired," interjected Arlut in a pouty tenor.

"I want to hear more stories from Duke," Turla snapped back emphatically. There was an implied "go away."

The purple visors attached to her eyelids fluttered rapidly and the back of her cranium pulsated, showcasing that she was ready for some mature recreation.

"Turla!" shrieked Duke's newest archenemy.

His autopilot set in. Unfortunately.

"Have you ever seen someone cut off their own head?" he directed at Arlut.

One of the more reliable lines in the world of misdirection.

"My friend would like to show you..."

Both females looked perplexed as Duke's words seemed to fade into the dense stagnant air of the bar. His eyes peered around, hoping to land on his emerald-clad sword-wielding Irish-Japanese cohort, who had a mastery of warding away potential killjoys like Arlut. Duke recalled the hundreds of instances in which he had used that asinine phrase and how he never needed to wait for Ishiro'shea to leap into action. It was the split-second sleight of hand that had allowed Duke to leave with "Option A" on countless occasions. By the time the victim typically collected themselves enough to respond to the bounty hunter's answerless riddle and fully take in the fact that a stout martial artist decked out in a bright green *shinobi shozoku* appeared seemingly out of nowhere, Duke had escaped with the top prize. When the victim had discovered she had been hoodwinked and turned back to address Ishiro'shea, the ninja would vanish. He was a ninja, after all. However, at this moment, Duke was ninja-less.

The Trampling Death Robots cacophonous guitar solo filled every pocket of breathable air at Cyborg Joe's—and triggered Duke's cognitive functions instantaneously.

Holy hedgehogs! Ishiro'shea! Damn this whisky.

Duke shouted to himself in a fit of sudden awareness, "Trampling Death Robots!"

A vision crept into his head of a messy puddle of squashed ninja. *And for what? A night of bright pink ecstasy with the faint undertones of average beer? Ishiro'shea probably wouldn't consider that a good enough reason.*

The bounty hunter started for the stage but was quickly halted by Turla's tight grip.

"Duke, honey, your friend would like to show us what?"

"What friend?" interjected Arlut. "I don't see any friend. I told you, Turla! I knew he was a lying sack of..."

"Shut up, Arlut!"

The Beta Hilterian cowered.

"Duke, now what were you saying?"

"Sorry ladies, I must attend to something kinda important."

Duke felt Turla's grip tightening.

"More important than me, sweetie?"

He writhed his hand out of the slightly moistened clutch of the Hilterian and tried to think of a clever, if not a bit flirtatious, response. He dug deep—but came up empty.

"I'll call you."

The next sensations that Duke felt were the simultaneous

four-digit slap across his right cheek and the showering of Glyptodian Summer Ale all over his face. He cleared the booze from his eyes just in time for one last glance at the polymerized chloroprene-clad package of sensuality that he was letting slip through his fingers.

Okay, focus. Find Ishiro. But damn, those bodies. Focus. Yeah, those bodies.

CHAPTER 3

THE WRATH OF SPRINKLES

T HE BOUNTY HUNTER RACED TO the stage floor where the Trampling Death Robots were about to begin their opus—a power ballad trilogy known as "Moonlight Over the Squashed Bones of Puny Beings, Parts I–III in E Flat"— and he hurled himself onto a table of animated Jungafallowians who were each clanking their two heads together with reckless aggression. The Trampling Death Robots were huge on Jungafallow III though, oddly enough, on Jungafallow IV they topped the planet's most wanted criminals list. Either way, they were in demand.

Upon his clean landing, Duke studied the performance area, his eyes darting with the speed and accuracy of lasers. He saw the Trampling Death Robots. He saw their devotees gathered around them, attempting to make the loudest sounds that their individual anatomies would permit. He did *not* see any flattened remains of an intoxicated assassin. *Is he really that good a ninja that he could have vanished postmortem?* Duke hated to admit it, but he was actually considering that hypothesis. Moments after he had come to terms with Ishiro'shea as a zombie magician, he caught a glimpse of what appeared to be a lime green comet. As his focus steadied in on the speedy Ishiro'shea—now stationary—he noticed that his musical instrument of choice was an ancient Earth katana. In the known universe, there were many types of swords, daggers, rapiers, blades, sabers, cutlasses, scimitars, and knives— but none of them doubled as a guitar.

He seems to be having fun and no one seems to mind; no reason to interject, I guess. If anything, this should be entertaining, Duke thought.

As Duke watched his partner in crime—well, his partner in stopping crime (in most cases)—wail away alongside the Trampling Death Robots, he took a seat next to a pair of two-headed Jungafallowians and an anthropomorphic musk ox.

"Hello there," the musk ox bellowed quite formally, "my name is Lilly and I come from one of the moons of Gartosh."

Duke did not reciprocate the niceties. Lilly seemed accustomed to being ignored.

The bounty hunter didn't really care for the explosion-centric rhythms of what constituted popular music in this area of the galaxy; however, even he couldn't deny the energy that the band generated. In fact, he even caught himself tapping the soles of his boots to the melodic tones of plasma grenades being detonated. There was no debate that the band had a really, really good percussion section.

As the sentient mechanical rock stars crushed both the stage and the occasional security guard, it became apparent to Duke that they were, in fact, not aware of the sword-wielding assassin dashing feverishly amongst them. As they smashed and crushed and kaboomed, Ishiro'shea added to each pounding roar a circular whip of his arm across the invisible strings of his katana-guitar. Duke hoped that the Trampling Death Robots would just play on without noticing his enigmatic green sidekick but, as in so many cases, the alcohol outpointed the ninja. Ishiro'shea, who had perfected not only agility and nimbleness but also the ability to remain unseen in broad daylight, stumbled like a toddler trying to navigate through a field of tripwire in a rainforest. He crashed violently into the frontman of the Robots. Duke, while not knowledgeable in the realm of music, recognized the mechanical goliath immediately—mostly from wanted posters and the best cosmic gossip rags available. It was the infamous Sprinkles. *Damn.* Ishiro'shea managed to fall sword-first into the thigh plate of the raging lead singer and detonation specialist, who was known more for his destruction of hotel properties than for his lyrical genius.

The music screeched to a sudden halt. With Ishiro'shea still gripping his katana, Sprinkles grabbed the ninja's shoulder with his well-constructed human-like left hand. Duke didn't know the true origins of the Trampling Death Robots or which assembly-line conveyor belt they had fallen off—but he did not doubt the craftsmanship of their mysterious creators. *Neither did Ishiro'shea's right shoulder*, the bounty hunter concluded. Ishiro'shea was paralyzed in the restrictive grasp. Sprinkles' right arm possessed less of a hand and more of a blunt instrument of obliteration. Extending from a thick silver gauntlet was a 900-pound (give or take) hammer that would make Thor embarrassed for toting a mere plexor in comparison. The robot slowly lifted his right arm upwards and into kill position. Ishiro'shea's bloodshot eyes remained half closed. *It has to be a pretty good night on the sauce to fail to react to your impending death by an extremely heavy hammer.* Nonetheless, Ishiro'shea —now held immobile by Sprinkles' hand—drifted into an alcohol-induced sleep. Sprinkles didn't seem to notice his adversary's narcolepsy and was more focused on the continued extension of his right arm. Sprinkles was a showman.

Duke's right hand fell to his hip and to the handle of his laser revolver. Even after a night of flirting, Earth whisky, and Glyptodian brew, he could place a shot from his laser revolver between the eyes of a pygmy hamster, blindfolded (not that blindfolding the hamster makes the shot anymore difficult). *Sprinkles will be a dead robot before he has a chance to drop that hammer on the skull of my inebriated lil' buddy*, thought Duke. And if a blast from his trusted pulse pistol—fabricated to appear like a vintage laser revolver for that more romantic feel—wasn't enough to take down the behemoth, there was always Ol' Betsy. Betsy was an out-of-date, out-of-production Widowmaker sonic shotgun that had been used during the settlement of the colony planet of Nova Texas. It had been the first firearm to harness the power of hydroxy re-gen explosion technology, now used in the majority of handheld weaponry in the galaxy, including Duke's pulse pistol. If hydrogen and oxygen particles were within a light year from the gun, it could generate the proper combination to create exploding projectiles. There was never a need to reload or, more importantly, worry about what color ammunition strap clashes with the user's favorite warmongering ensemble. Newer models sported elegant ammo—Betsy, not so much. What she lacked in sophistication and design, she made up for in pure noise. When Betsy sang, people listened. As much as Ishiro'shea was his sidekick and most trusted confidant, it was hard to tell if Duke LaGrange ever cared for anything more than he did Ol' Betsy.

It was known by all travelers in this part of the universe, Duke included, that Cyborg Joe's had really great drink specials and a better-than-average karaoke night, but even more so, it was known for its criminally loose firearm policy. This made it a hot spot for the criminally loose of mind. It was also why Ol' Betsy was resting nicely in Duke's custom-made Ootrelian tanned leather back holster without drawing even the faintest of regard from the other patrons. The one-sided staring match between Sprinkles and Ishiro'shea seemed to last for eons as Duke awaited the next move. His fingers twitched ever so slightly across the titanium butt of his revolver. His eyes fixated on the optical visor of the angered musician—in a situation such as this he always anticipated the next move by reading eyes (or a well-crafted mechanical vision apparatus). A less experienced man would have been nervous, but this was not a new position for Duke and his Irish-Japanese companion.

The robotic musician waited for the drunken stage crasher to make the first move. Time passed slowly and nothing happened. After all, Ishiro'shea was asleep. Duke could sense that Sprinkles was losing his patience and was concerned that his street cred as a bad mutha' was slipping—it might appear as though he was going to show mercy. The silence was broken by a few inebriated calls from the back of the bar.

"Wuss!"

"Poser!"

"Hack!"

"You can't even stop a squirrel monkey!"

These insults appeared to shake the metal performer. When a loyal Jungafallowian questioned his robotic manhood, Duke saw him snap. Sprinkles' cerebral processor sparked and his visor tinged a deep red. Just as Duke assumed, the eyes told the story.

The Queen's opportunity isn't looking like such a bad deal at the moment.

A loud crash rang through Cyborg Joe's. It was the sound that a penguin makes when you put it in a blender and then drop it on a landmine.

Sprinkles dropped the ninja and his hammer fell from attack position.

Duke was standing on the top of the table, drawing the bewildered stares of the two Jungafallowians and Lilly, the anthropomorphic musk ox from one of the moons of Gartosh. The Trampling Death Robot frontman glared directly at the Stetson-wearing humanoid with his firearm in plain sight. But it wasn't the laser revolver that he held firmly in his hand—it was Ol' Betsy, smoke still curling from the barrel. The shotgun pointed not at the musical goliath but at the ceiling of Cyborg Joe's.

Hopefully that broke the tension.

Duke figured that Sprinkles didn't really want to kill Ishiro'shea; however, not killing him would be detrimental to his reputation and, thus, his musical career—and he needed a way to divert the focus away from this powder keg. Of course, there was always the possibility of the explosion triggering the robot to drop the hammer instinctively, in the process creating the galaxy's first ninja pancake. Luckily for all involved, Duke's lightning-quick psychoanalysis was spot on. He gambled—and the early returns were favorable.

"Okay, Mr. Sprinkles, let's all calm down. I'm not here to cause any trouble," Duke said with diplomatic caution. "I'm deeply sorry for interrupting your transcendent set—as is my intoxicated friend, there. And I am sure he would be apologizing profoundly if he was, ya' know, awake. How about I just pick him up, we'll go on our merry way, and you can continue to entertain your legions of fans here at this fine establishment? Sound good?"

Sprinkles inched closer to the bounty hunter. His eyes sparkled an intense shade of contempt. *No deal, I guess.*

"We can be civil about this quite insignificant imbroglio. And, with all due respect, I don't think you want to have a chat with Betsy here."

Duke aimed the wide-mouthed firearm at the oncoming musician. He continued to try to reason: "I can see you're a bit upset. I get it, believe me I do—but there's no need to cause another scene."

Sprinkles continued to approach, his metallic frame convulsing to the point that it almost appeared organic and elastic.

A second crash!

The robot halted. The bounty hunter dropped the barrel of his shotgun. They both looked around Joe's in unison. *A Jungafallowian? That big musk ox chick?*

Duke saw what constituted a sly grin on Sprinkles' mechanical mug. He looked up.

Looks like this is not going to be my night, the bounty hunter thought.

The loud crash manifested itself in the form of fragments falling from the ceiling. The rapid descent was slowed—albeit not to the point of no longer being life-threateningly dangerous—by the bounty hunter's headwear. The debris knocked Duke from his feet and he collapsed amidst a pile of ceiling rubble, splintered table shards, and sticky puddles of spilled Glyptodian brew.

CHAPTER 4

THE GOOEY BITS

DUKE WASN'T SURE QUITE HOW much time had elapsed; he opened his eyes and stared up at Lilly and four angry Jungafallowian faces.

That could've been a lot worse.

"He's alive," moaned the Gartoshian beast. "Everyone! The odd-looking primate with the interesting choice in evening wear is alive."

Duke awaited audible sighs of relief from the patrons of Joe's—he heard nothing, resulting in a slight bruising of his ego.

"Wait a damn minute. Who are you to be calling me odd-looking?" he muttered hazily.

"Shut up! You ruined the show, you moron," interjected one of the heads of the larger Jungafallowian.

"No one messes with the almighty Sprinkles and gets away with it," barked the other head in a slightly sinister tone.

"Damn skippy."

Duke recognized that voice. Cold. Robotic. Tone deaf. Sprinkles. *Guess the ceiling missed him.*

He sat up and tried to focus on the approaching mecha-nized madman. His concentration bounced around erratically from the throbbing pain in his skull to the blurred pair of Sprinkleses that wouldn't stand still long enough to merge back into one another. And Betsy wasn't within reach. He quickly grabbed the laser revolver but his disorientation from the falling ceiling debris certainly wasn't going away. *50–50 chance.*

Just as Sprinkles was mere strides from Duke, a green flash pounced up like an Erontian River Camelcat and landed firmly in a strike position with katana raised. Ishiro'shea stood resolutely between his cohort and the performer. He held his sword in his right hand parallel to his shoulders at eye level. The blade glistened with reflections of the neon that covered the walls. His stance suggested the alertness of a person that had never downed even the slightest drop of firewater—a remarkable trait in which Duke knew Ishiro'shea took pride.

Defending his partner—that's why he's the best sidekick in the business.

Ishiro'shea, without moving any other part of his body, made eye contact with his longtime friend. Duke gave him a shaky thumbs-up from within his tomb of fallen debris. The ninja glanced at Sprinkles, his eyes smoldering to the point of being able to boil water. It was quite easy to see that Ishiro'shea didn't appreciate the singer's manner—looking all guilty and up to no good. He knew that Ishiro felt confident in his gut, no matter how much of it was filled with fermented grain. *Cycles of being placed in precarious situations with me will do that to you. Hey, we have fun,* Duke reasoned.

The ninja's strike was lightning fast. Sparks and metal shrapnel exploded from Sprinkles' titanium chest and abdomen—the blow would have halved most sentient beings, but it was a mere annoyance for the multiton, multiplatinum artist. Sprinkles retaliated with a hammer strike that narrowly missed the stealthy and now very much sober martial artist. The thunderous crash of the hammer into the floor of Cyborg Joe's caused the onlookers to cover their ears (or whatever they used to hear) and left Duke wondering if Earl was already reviewing Cyborg Joe's insurance policy. Sprinkles struggled to remove the head of the hammer from the divot in the flooring; this was the opening that Ishiro'shea needed in order to thrust his katana straight into the optical visor of his adversary. As the blade pierced the lens, the sizzle of skewered circuitry resonated throughout the bar. Duke noticed a hint of sadness and regret in the giant musician's pulsating vision apparatus. Ishiro'shea plunged his sword directly through the glass-like eye. It was a sight worthy of pity—one of the most recognizable figures in robotic explosion rock flailing in agony, one hand stuck four feet into the sweat- and booze-covered stage floor while the other hand grasped at what was left of his optical visor plate as bursts of sparks and smoke escaped through his fingers. But Duke had no time for pity.

The remaining Trampling Death Robots stood momentarily frozen as this diminutive menace rendered their charismatic and controversial lead singer immobile; but they soon collected themselves in an attempt to extinguish the career wrecker. The three bandmates charged Ishiro'shea, their instruments doubling as weapons, bent on sending him to that great dojo in the sky. They encircled Ishiro'shea and took turns at trying to decapitate him. One swung his Panatynian Earblaster guitar with reckless abandon. Another swatted inelegantly with his signature 14-string Grevlon Electro-Bass. Another jabbed rapidly with his iron drumsticks, trying to skewer the dwarfed combatant. Ishiro'shea parried each oncoming strike and dashed his way around the three attackers.

"You doing okay, little buddy?"

Ishiro mirrored Duke's thumbs-up from moments earlier as he continued his masterful ballet of devastation.

"Thought so. How about we head out of here? You're sober now, and I've got a massive headache—that usually means that we've worn out our welcome."

Though he was effectively toying with his opponents, Ishiro'shea was still preoccupied fighting off the angry mechanical musicians and making sure he didn't get a Panatynian Earblaster to the skull.

Duke stood up and grabbed Betsy. *Okay, time to shut these guys up and end this mess. I have to get back to the Queen with an answer about this damn door.* He aimed the gun at the bassist of the Robots, Doug (Model 8). *I never understood the bass guitar.*

Before he could fire, there was a firm tap on his shoulder.

He spun around. Standing in front of him was one of the Jungafallowians—the larger of the two, armed with a wooden shard from the broken table and a sharp steak knife. *That might break the skin.*

"You aren't going to get away with this, human."

I can't be done in by booze, bad music, poor roof maintenance, and low quality cutlery.

Duke felt a firm tug on his biceps and realized very quickly that he was pinned up against something. He inhaled deeply and realized that the "something" was the other Jungafallowian. *Hard to mistake that smell of rotting meatloaf smothered in expired mayonnaise.*

"You're dead, human. Nobody does that to the Robots," a slithery voice hissed from behind.

Duke struggled but the Jungafallowian, even though he was the smaller of the two, had a grip that was unbreakable.

"Where should I stab him, Flakka-Grog? I can't remember where the gooey bits are on humans."

A duo of cream-colored reptilian heads on muscular neck stems slowly peered around either side of Duke. Both sets of red eyes scanned the bounty hunter meticulously. *Creepy.* Duke noticed Ol' Betsy resting on the floor, out of reach; his revolver rested firmly in his holster—but his arms weren't going anywhere if the Jungafallowian had any say.

"Flakka, do you think we stab him in here?" the head known as Grog whispered as he glared at Duke's chest.

"Oh no, Grog—I think we should have Orbo-Terg stab him here." Flakka's snout touched the bounty hunter's left ear. "Humans can't survive losing this part, I don't think."

"How about you let go of me, your friend can drop the knife, and we can talk this through?" pleaded the bounty hunter.

"Just like you wanted to talk it through with Sprinkles?" asked the scaly Flakka-Grog. "You will pay for what you did, fleshy."

"Can I stab him yet?" barked both of the larger Jungafallowian's heads in unison. "Revenge for Sprinkles! Revenge for the Robots!"

The barbaric alien pumped his oversized fist in the air. Duke noticed, for the first time, that the T-shirt Orbo-Terg wore was for the Trampling Death Robot's "Four Faces of Death Galactic Tour" and, emblazoned on the black fabric, were the faces of the four band members. Duke's life hung in the balance of four much uglier faces. Regardless, he appreciated the symbolism.

"Orbo-Terg, calm down. We want to make sure this primate suffers for what he's done to Sprinkles," hissed Flakka. It was clear to Duke that Orbo-Terg was the physically superior of the two; however, Flakka-Grog pulled the strings.

"Yes, he's committed the ultimate sin against the Holy One—we need to do more than merely kill him," continued Grog.

"Hurry up and decide!"

"Okay, we definitely think we should stick him here."

The long neck supporting the Flakka head curved around and nodded toward the human's midsection.

"There?"

"No, lower—between his legs. Under that ridiculous ornament."

"Ridiculous? My buckle? What are you talking—oh wait, where are you going to stab me?"

"There!" grunted one of the heads of Orbo-Terg as he pointed a knobby finger at an area of Duke's anatomy that the bounty hunter held in high esteem. The Jungafallowian coughed up a laugh from deep in his innards.

"C'mon guys, no need to stab me there—I mean, I have plenty of other good parts. I promise they will hurt a lot more."

"Is that right, human? No, no, I think we are going to stick to our plan."

Duke struggled, but it was futile; he was held almost inert in the powerful grip of Flakka-Grog. *I am about to get castrated by a smelly two-headed metal junkie all because I was distracted by some cheap floozies. Screw symbolism.*

Duke kicked his legs frantically in an attempt to prevent Orbo-Terg's impending charge.

"Hold still!"

"So you can stab me? Yeah, I'll get on that."

"Flakka-Grog, make him hold still!" Terg shouted in a borderline temper tantrum.

A thick stump of a leg wrapped around Duke from behind, limiting the bounty hunter's movements even more. *This bastard is strong.*

"Stab him!"

Orbo-Terg charged knife first.

Duke closed his eyes, awaiting a pain that he was not prepared to endure. He felt a gust of wind surge across his stubbled face and heard a loud thud a few paces away.

He opened his eyes. Orbo-Terg was curled up on the barroom floor—out cold. Lilly stood over him, thin-lipped with nostrils flared and breathing heavily. Her hands remained clenched in boulder-sized fists.

Duke was thrown to the ground ferociously by the Jungafallowian; he scrambled to grab Betsy. The two-headed beast rushed toward the Gartoshian female but Lilly about-faced before the sinister reptiloid could get on top of her. She lowered her massive cranium and lunged headfirst at her attacker. Duke heard the Jungafallowian's sternum crack. From his seated position on the floor, clutching his prized shotgun, he noticed Flakka-Grog stumble backwards.

"No, no, no, no..."

He immediately found himself sandwiched between the floor and the limp and odorous body of Flakka-Grog.

"Get this—oh my god, it smells so bad!"

"Let me help," proclaimed a booming voice, twice as deep as Duke's and as full-bodied as the richest of Noctdaryan wines.

In one swift yank, the anthropomorphic musk ox easily winched up the Jungafallowian corpse with one massive three-fingered hand, then dropped it beside the recovering bounty hunter. Duke remembered scorning the fem-beast at the table, only moments ago.

"Thanks?"

"I see that you're confused, Mr. Human."

"You could say that. Don't get me wrong, lady, I'm glad you saved me—but why? I wasn't overly 'interested' earlier." Duke dusted Jungafallowian grime from his clothes.

"That's okay. I wasn't offended by your silence—I just assumed you were too ignorant to understand anything more than simple language. I mean, you don't look overly intelligent."

"Insult aside, thank you. But why risk your life to save me from those moronic rock nuts?"

"Oh, Mr. Human. No matter how discourteous your gesture might have been—what those two uncouth reprobates said to me was beyond heinous. After you caused your scene with the ceiling tiles and started your little tiff with that robotic bandleader, I decided to be the better being and exit the situation—no need to engage with those lower life forms. Then, of course, I saw them about to impale you with a steak knife—*my* steak knife, no less—and I felt obligated to punish those two and, in turn, save you."

"A moral crusader, huh? Well, thank you, Lilly. It was Lilly, right?"

"Good memory."

Duke made it to his feet and extended his hand.

"I hope that I can return the favor someday."

"I hope that won't be necessary. But your cute friend appears to need your help."

Holy hedgehogs! Ishiro'shea!

The bounty hunter turned around and saw his cohort still countering every blow from the three members of the Trampling Death Robots—at least, the ones without an appendage lodged into the floor. But he was tiring visibly. Even the most skilled martial artist has his physical limits.

"Enough of this garbage," the bounty hunter muttered to himself as he aimed.

KURGHUFFINSHOBEPOW! (BOOM! never really captured the true sound.)

The bassist of the Trampling Death Robots dropped to the floor. He had a hole in his chest the size of an exceptionally large ice wombat. Ol' Betsy was angry. The other two froze and then attended to their second fallen comrade of the night. Amidst the turmoil on the stage, Ishiro'shea stealthily made his way over to Duke.

"Ishiro, what took you so long with those guys? I would have thought..."

Ishiro'shea gave Duke an expression that the bounty hunter interpreted as *Shut up, you conceited redneck. I was fighting for my life while you managed to get pinned by a piece of ceiling tile.* At least, that's how Duke interpreted it.

"This has not been my night. Long story. Let's just say that I'm lucky that I'm only half as big of a jerk as those two idiots over there." Duke pointed to the unconscious Orbo-Terg and Flakka-Grog. "Thanks again, Lilly."

The Gartoshian gave him a blasé wave from across the bar as she pushed through a cluster of military conspirators and entered the ladies' room. Ishiro'shea looked confused as he tried to catch his breath.

"*Really* long story."

Ishiro'shea responded with a lengthy eye roll.

"Oh, but hey—I do have some news. The Queen gave us a crack at a small opportunity. Could be exciting."

The ninja halted. Duke knew what his partner was thinking.

"No, a *legitimate* opportunity. Nothing impossible. Seriously. You don't believe me?"

The masked man shook his head with undisguised incredulity.

"Fine. Follow me."

They headed to the bar, ignoring the chaos that they had—in large part—caused.

"Greetings, sirs," Earl said as they approached. "How may I help you? I see that you have had quite the eventful evening here at Joe's."

"Earl, can you fetch Queenie, please?"

"I'm right here," came a voice from behind the bar. Queen Joe rose elegantly from a crouched position near where she kept the pricier bottles of happiness.

"Startled me there, Queen. Anyways, please tell Ishiro'shea about our opportunity."

"Ah yes, what we discussed earlier, I presume?"

"Yes, ma'am," Duke said with a smirk.

"If you could've solved my problem regarding an unknown and seemingly uncontrollable astral anomaly that was creeping into my bar—I would've given you both access to my portals free of charge."

"See, Ishiro! I told you—wait—'could've'?"

"I'm sorry, Duke. The 'portal' is gone. Sometime between you hitting on those Hilterians and getting crushed by the ceiling, it left. No wild portal, no free portal card. Sorry."

"You've got to be kidding me? This is really not my night. Any chance for another shot of that whisky, at least?"

Ishiro'shea seemed reenergized at the thought.

"Guys, I'm not so sure that this is the time to be drinking. I mean, for one thing—you did a number on my bar tonight. More than usual. I'm not overly happy about that. You also seriously injured two members of one of our biggest musical draws—during their performance, no less. Oh yeah, and you shot a hole in my roof."

"So, you're telling me that we probably aren't going to get another shot of whisky?"

"Turn around."

Duke could see the Trampling Death Robots starting to collect themselves—and repair themselves. *They're gonna be pissed.* Flakka-Grog wiggled around a bit. *Damnit, he's not dead?* He could sense the crowd getting louder and bolder. *If they riot, I'm public enemy* numero uno.

"We'll just take the bill, if it's all the same to you, your Highness."

"We can settle later. I would probably just leave before things get to a point where even I can't help you."

"Thanks. Much obliged."

Duke and Ishiro'shea headed for the exit opposite the stage.

"At least you got your 'it' back, Duke!" shouted the Queen.

"Good point! I might hit up those Hilterians next time we're in town!"

The bounty hunter stumbled over what appeared to be a black polymerized chloroprene suit clinging to a magenta-skinned body. It was motionless. In its perfectly circular palm was a half-eaten MechaBurger 8000.

Okay, maybe I won't, Duke thought to himself as he and Ishiro'shea exited the bar.

CHAPTER 5

THE BEEPS AND BLINKS OF
SPACE TRAVEL

"TONIGHT WAS KINDA CRAZY, HUH?"

Ishiro'shea did not respond to Duke. In fact, he accelerated the speed of his march towards the parking area.

"Slow down, bud. Are you mad at me? Or are you just trying to get as far away as possible from what's brewing inside the bar?"

The rumbling from inside Cyborg Joe's continued to intensify.

"Fine. I'm sorry for leaving you on the floor—and choosing to hit on those Hilterians; but you can't blame me for your ill-fated attempt to join the band. And I didn't force you to puncture Sprinkles' eye with your sword. You gotta cut me some slack there, Ishiro."

Still the ninja did not respond; he kept his hurried pace.

"Oh yeah, sorry for the whole table thing, too. I didn't mean to leave you fending off those robots—I was truly in a bit of a predicament myself."

Once again, the ninja did not respond. But Duke was not surprised by Ishiro'shea's lack of reaction—in fact, Ishiro'shea hadn't said much of anything since he took his vow of silence upon graduation from the College of Cohorts, Consorts, Co-Conspirators, and Other Assorted Sidekick Types many cycles ago. He was the Salutatorian. Duke and Ishiro'shea had a partnership solidified by more than simple words and pats on the back. They didn't need to communicate in the traditional sense; they had true bonding experiences. Real friendship-forging stuff. However, Duke was quickly realizing that he, at present, was bonding more with his own guilt than with his sword-wielding colleague.

"Can you even imagine what we could've done with unlimited access to those portals?"

Duke LaGrange and his silent sidekick stared up at the *Deus Ex Machina*, or at least the parts of her that towered over the other ships parked at the loading dock. She was an old ship, but she was *their* ship, twice the size of Cyborg Joe's and twice the alcohol consumption. She looked as if she came off of the same assembly line as Ol' Betsy. She was loud and weathered and battle-tested; she possessed nothing new, sleek, or sexy—she encompassed the phrase "they don't make 'em like that anymore" in both the positive and negative connotations. It was without a doubt that ecological regulations were ignored to produce such a spacecraft. She was a priceless relic to half of those that laid eyes on her and a worthless pile of junk to the other half—she was art. Duke and Ishiro'shea loved the *Deus Ex Machina*—no matter the pickle they were in, no matter how impossible a solution seemed, no matter if they backed themselves into a corner with no plausible manner in which to escape—she always bailed them out.

"Mr. LaGrange, your keys," exclaimed the Glyptodian valet at the loading dock.

"Thank you, my good man," Duke responded as he took the keys from his furry grasp.

The valet held out his hand for the customary tip. Duke paused at the sight of the extended arm and upright palm. He then slammed his hand down, probably bruising the Glyptodian's metacarpus.

"Alright, son! Stay in school."

The valet appeared to be caught off guard, then seemed agitated. Duke launched himself down the loading dock until he reached the *Deus Ex Machina*.

"Come on, Ishiro'shea—we need to book it before those pissed-off patrons figure out that we vamoosed."

As Ishiro'shea patted the young Glyptodian on the shoulder and flipped him some monetary units, Duke yelled out, "My tip wasn't good enough?"

Ishiro'shea rapidly made his way to the parking spot just as Duke was opening the hydraulic hatch on the left side of the massive ship. For such a large ship, the entry hatch was quite confined. The door closed with the noisy clang of a dropped pot on a ceramic floor and the elevator shot them up towards the bridge. It was only a ten second climb but those ten seconds contained the same maddening elevator Muzak that was installed the day that Duke acquired the ship during a rousing game of No-Limit Nova Texan Strip Skeeball. It had been fifteen cycles of the same melody; fifteen cycles of that same earworm-planting monstrosity.

"I'm going to install a new song in this damned thing. I mean it this time. I've had it!" Duke barked.

Ishiro remained silent.

The door slid open with a nails-on-a-chalkboard screech to reveal the austere bridge of the *Deus Ex Machina*.

"Seriously, I mean it. I'm thinking the Nova Texas Planetary Anthem. How about that, huh?"

Ishiro'shea ignored the statement and approached the main control panel. It mirrored the appearance of the ship, in that it was oversized and underwhelming to the eye. A bit long in the tooth for a modern onboard controls system, but it still worked for the majority of the time. With speed befitting a ninja, Ishiro'shea's dexterous digits poked and prodded the luminescent buttons of the panel. Duke loved the beeps and blinks of space travel.

The bounty hunter made his way up to a raised platform in the geometric center of the bridge. There, in all of its glory, was his captain's chair. His leathery throne. The most comfortable place to rest one's tired body in the whole of the known universe. Over the cycles of use, the chair had formed around the shape of Duke's backside—he took pride in knowing that this piece of furniture was now customized for his needs. He kicked up his feet along the surrounding rail as he sank into the warmth of his favorite seat. His headache started to dissipate, his eyes closed, and he took in a deep, long breath. As he approached a moment of true bliss, he broke in and out of muddled song.

Hail Nova Texas, a beauty under the sun,
It gets hotter than Hell,
For which it ain't much fun,
But we have cacti and critters and fried meats on-the-go,
Don't tell us what to do 'cause we have our shotguns in tow...

...and we don't have sex with our livestock.

He petered out. "Yep, definitely gonna make this the new elevator tune."

Duke had almost forgotten about the damage that he had caused back at Joe's and was about to drift off into a long overdue nap, until the familiar rattling of *Deus Ex Machina*'s shell signified takeoff. The ship departed the loading dock with a clamoring "see ya' later" to Kelt, then headed into the vast playground of space.

"Where to, Ishiro? Anywhere tickle your fancy?" Duke asked with a slight yawn.

Ishiro'shea pressed a few buttons and swiped his right hand quickly over a holopad. It glimmered. Immediately, the large view screen at the front of the bridge appeared above the control panel. The split-panel view screen showed both the actual space in front of the ship, and also a more technical interface with all of the scanning data, systems status checks, and other miscellaneous bits of information needed to keep a spacecraft flying. Front-and-center on the dashboard, the long-range scanner results were materializing.

"Not a lot of traffic in this sector right now, is there? Okay, want to bounce on over to Oscavia? I think we have a few free massages from those triplets that we helped out—remember? I'm pretty sure that we need to collect on that. Two for me, one for you."

The ninja's glare was icy.

"One for me, one for you—flip for the third?"

Ishiro'shea repositioned the long-range scanners to examine the area to the right of the vessel. More blinks and beeps. He didn't acknowledge Duke's suggestion.

"Okay, no to the Oscavian Caves. Want to do some work? We can make it to Tardasio 7 in no time and see what Sol has cookin'—sound good?"

Suddenly, something appeared on the scanner. The icon on the interface was that of a spacecraft. But it was big. Really big.

"What in Nova Texas is that?"

Ishiro'shea's hands were working at a speed that Duke had never seen before. *He must be pretty curious as well.*

"It looks like... like... a school bus? At least we didn't fire on 'em. That would've been messy. On to Sol's."

Duke relaxed back into his chair and tilted his hat over his eyes. In a matter of seconds, he was startled by a slap on his shoulder. It was as firm as frozen peanut brittle. *How did he get up here without me knowing? Oh yeah, he's a ninja.*

The ninja pointed towards the screen.

"You've got to be kidding me. That's no ordinary school bus!"

The goliath ship continued on a course straight towards

the *Deus Ex Machina*. It engulfed the view screen. Upon it, dead center in crudely applied stencil work, were the words:

TRAMPLING DEATH ROBOTS FAN CLUB & ATTACK SQUAD, JUNGAFALLOW III CHAPTER.

"I guess we're gonna get to finish that scuffle after all. Let's get in position, little buddy."

CHAPTER 6

BUTTONS WHERE THERE WEREN'T NO BUTTONS

THE SHIP DWARFED THE *DEUS Ex Machina* in the same manner that a peanut is dwarfed by a macadamia nut—if the macadamia nut is the size of a high school gymnasium.

"Ishiro, patch me in."

The ninja swiftly darted over to the far left side of the control panel and began to input digits with rapid-fire precision. After a few moments, he threw his hands up in frustration.

"Not answering our hail? See if you can override."

The ninja worked with speedy aggression.

"Hurry... hurry... they're firing up their weapons. And not to add any more pressure or anything, but they've got an Ootrelian star cannon."

Ishiro paused momentarily. The Ootrelian star cannon was one of the most deadly weapons in the known universe.

"I thought those were outlawed," said Duke, mostly to himself.

Ishiro'shea threw his thumb up.

"Excellent, little buddy."

Duke cleared his throat and began.

"My name is Duke LaGrange. Adventurer. Trailblazer. Poet. A true man of the universe. And I'm sure that this is just a big mix up."

Silence. Then a small crackle of interference.

"Mr. LaGrange. It is nice to finally meet. Your reputation precedes you."

"And who are you?"

"You have indeed put some of my closest friends away for long periods of time," the voice said, ignoring Duke's question. "You're probably the eighth or ninth most decorated and respected bounty hunter in this sector."

"Eighth or ninth? I would like to meet the other seven. I'm..."

"However," the voice interrupted, "I am afraid that you are severely overmatched and outclassed this time. Your folksy charm and overactive libido will not save you. I will take pleasure in knowing that I was the one responsible for ending your life. The Robots and my fellow brothers must be avenged. Plain and simple."

Word travels fast.

"Mister, I am afraid it is *you* that's run out of luck."

"You and your ego amuse me, LaGrange. Your systems, if they are working properly that is, have probably detected the fact that I have an Ootrelian star cannon. Your dilapidated ship won't withstand one direct hit. On top of that, my other armaments are immeasurably more advanced than anything on your floating junk heap."

"I think you underestimate us. Which is surprising for a school bus driver." Duke knew it was obvious he was bluffing. "But indulge me: to whom must I credit for finally putting me out to pasture?"

"I am Prince Korzo-Tapor of Jungafallow III."

Duke muted communication.

"Hey Ishiro, I thought there was a revolt against his government and he was hung? Double-looped noose and all."

The ninja motioned that he could not confirm the incident.

"You are probably thinking that I was killed in the Not So Great Revolt of 4392?" the voice said.

"Never crossed my mind."

"Needless to say that I was not. And I have taken back what is rightfully mine—Jungafallow III. With the help of the loyal and proud members of the Trampling Death Robots Fan Club, of course."

They really are loyal.

"But alas, I must end this autobiographical interlude," a distinctly different voice said.

Must be the other head.

"Only a fool could think that they could take out Duke LaGrange with a school bus full of fanboys."

"I am not a fool and this is no school bus. In fact, its design is what allowed us to approach without any suspicion. So, who's the fool, Mr. LaGrange?"

As the prince spoke, the interstellar school bus decloaked and a boxy Jungafallowian Fighter materialized. The only two characteristics that remained consistent were the Ootrelian star cannon and the fan club stenciling.

"So how did you survive the revolt, your highness? Or is it highnesses? What is the proper way to greet dual-craniumed royalty?"

"Mr. LaGrange, you are simply stalling now—and I am sure that your mute comrade is planning some sort of chicanery as we speak. I hear he is the brains of your outfit."

Duke noticed Ishiro'shea's smile beneath his mask.

"You're right, your Royal Scumbag, I *was* stalling. My old floating junk heap managed to lock on its tractor beam undetected. More advanced, my ass."

"Tractor beam?" the prince laughed. "LaGrange, it really was a pleasure to meet you. But now, you must die."

"Go, Ishiro'shea!"

Ishiro'shea redirected the tractor beam onto the Ootrelian star cannon in a narrowed field of pure concentrated power. The *Deus Ex Machina* descended with a jarring jerk. An explosion engulfed the front of the larger spacecraft. The star cannon was ripped off like a dirty bandage. Clearly, the cannon had been a custom after-market addition to the ship, so there was no gaping hole left where the weapon had been—the innards were completely guarded. This was unfortunate for Duke and Ishiro'shea.

"What were you saying about a star cannon? You might be the one with the ego problem, o great exalted ones. I think it's now a bit more of an even playing field, as they say."

"Well played."

The poise and lack of emotion—traits not common among the prince's species—made Duke quite uneasy.

"Commander, I'm ready to engage with the rest of our artillery," hissed another, decidedly more Jungafallowian voice.

"Proceed, Lieutenant."

"Rest of their artillery?" asked Duke, directing his query to Ishiro.

The gigantic vessel roared with a thunderous salvo of weapons. Duke stood on the bridge as the ship unleashed a round of fury that he knew was likely the last thing that he would see in this lifetime.

"Brace for impact, little buddy."

The *Deus* was rocked.

"And now for the final blow to the mildly famous Duke LaGrange," Korzo-Tapor's voice echoed over the speakers.

"Mildly?" Duke smirked.

The sizzles of frying wires and the clangs and cracks of failing infrastructure throughout the doomed ship redirected his focus to Ishiro'shea.

"It's been a real pleasure," Duke said solemnly as he

tipped the brim of his hat in the direction of his friend. "Didn't think this was how it was going to end."

Ishiro'shea continued to plug away at the control panel. He turned around and gave his longtime companion a simple wink.

The *Deus Ex Machina* was overwhelmed by the Jungafallowian artillery barrage. Explosions consumed the aging shuttle. Its crippled body fell limp as it began to float away against the infinite tapestry of space.

"Well, that wasn't fun."

Duke tried to lift himself up into the captain's chair, while ignoring some very serious bruising.

The emerald-clad swordsman slowly made his way back to the control panel. He looked around and touched different parts of the control panel tenderly, presumably checking on the welfare of the systems. Groggily, he extended his thumb, signaling that the unit was in working order, then he collapsed with a plop onto his chair stationed at the control panel.

The *Deus'* view screen was still functional. To Duke's surprise, Prince Korzo-Tapor and his mega-ship were nowhere to be seen.

"How in Nova Texas did we survive that? I'm not *that* lucky."

Ishiro'shea pointed to the far right side of the controls. A plastic dome-like hatch had been smashed, revealing a clownish red button.

"What the hell is that?"

Ishiro'shea shrugged.

"I've spent the last fifteen cycles on this ship and I've never seen that thing. Giant buttons just don't spring out of nowhere!"

A look of realization overcame Ishiro'shea's face.

"You got something?"

The ninja pointed to his right thigh. Part of his green *shinobi shozoku* was torn and shards of broken glass gracefully clung on to his hip.

"That explains *how* the glass was broken. But where'd it come from? Do we have a manual or something?"

Duke knew Ishiro was thinking something along the lines of "Are you serious?" But being a good sidekick—Salutatorian-worthy, in fact—he searched for the manual. He unlocked a drawer under some newly exposed circuitry from the attack and pulled out a dusty tome covered in filth and grime. Duke grabbed it and read aloud:

"*Owner's Manual for the* Deus Ex Machina: *You Must Be in Pretty Deep, Volume I*," Duke began. "They aren't wrong about that."

"'Foreword.' 'Chapter One: Getting to Know Your Ship.' 'Chapter Two: Taking Off amidst Intergalactic War.' Wow, they don't waste any time." He continued to scan the table of contents.

"Got it! 'Chapter Eleven: Buttons.' 'Section Three: Buttons Where There Weren't No Buttons.' Pages 283 through 284."

Duke thumbed to the pages in question.

"'You probably have noticed by now that the *Deus Ex Machina* has pulled you out of some real jams, huh? Well, that isn't the half of it,'" Duke read. "'The *Deus Ex Machina* is equipped to instantly birth survival tech when recognizing a situation in which there is no way to possibly escape. It's quite convenient when you are backed into that proverbial corner with no hope for continuing your adventure. Some discerning thinkers call it a big "cop-out" but they can kiss our collective asses. Love, the builders of the *Deus Ex Machina*.'"

The entire next page was an image of a furry creature clinging to a wire above a pit of ravenous serpents; a word bubble above the struggling fuzzball enclosed the phrase: "Persevere. It will all work out." The two companions looked at each other. "I'm guessing that's supposed to offer some encouragement. But is it encouragement for the little hairy guy clinging to the wire? Or those snakes anxiously awaiting their dinner?"

Duke then noticed the small print below and continued, "P.S. Always push the big red button."

Sound advice.

"Well, that explains it," Duke rejoiced. "I guess, at the last moment, the ol' girl became the proud mama of some new anti-Jungafallowian shielding. That explanation works for me. You good?"

Ishiro'shea nodded hesitantly.

"Remind me to thank the builders if we ever meet 'em."

It's best not to question mysterious red buttons that save your life, Duke concluded.

"Okay, since we have that sorted out, we need to go bring those bastards to justice."

Ishiro pointed to the barely functioning control panel. The maroon light signifying their tracking device was blinking rapidly.

"Ishiro'shea! You genius! You sent out a tracker as we were being blown into oblivion? *That* is why you were Salutatorian."

The emerald-clad ninja smiled under his mask for the second time. *I guess a little recognition does go a long way.*

"There's no way that they would even think to scan for trackers—they probably just assumed we were scrambling to get our shields up. Remind me to give you a raise. We can split the bounty, 70–30."

Ishiro'shea's smile dissipated.

"Ok, fine, 51–49. The usual. We have no time to lose; let's see if we can make up ground pronto. Did the ship happen to evolve a better engine?"

Ishiro shook his head.

"Worth a try. Let's go. I can't wait to see the prince's face—or is it princes'? I'm not really sure; I mean with the two heads but one body and all. Can you imagine that day in grammar school when you have to learn plural possessives? That could get ugly, real quick."

The bounty hunter seemed to snap back into his original thought.

"I can't wait to see him *or* them when we show up—two badass ghosts with vengeance on their mind. This is going to be epic, little buddy."

Ishiro set a course out of what should have been the site of major wreckage and their untimely deaths—but with some noticeable caution.

He should be more excited. Oh wait, I guess we need a plan or something; we are still a bit of an underdog, militarily-speaking. Unplanned vengeance usually ends poorly.

"Don't worry, Ishiro, I have an idea," Duke bluffed.

The *Deus Ex Machina* halted suddenly.

"Hey, what's with the brakes?"

Before the ninja could respond, though he wouldn't have even if there was time, a light overwhelmed the bridge—brighter than the Jungafallowian attack, but a lot quieter. The bounty hunters covered their eyes involuntarily as the illumination permeated the ship. With his forearm draped over his eyes, Duke gingerly opened one eye to a squint.

"Holy hedgehogs! Try to patch into the Queen... now."

Ishiro did as Duke requested.

"Hello, thank you for calling Cyborg Joe's Grill N' Go & the Why Not Saloon, home of the MechaBurger 8000. I'm Earl; how may I be of assistance on this fine evening?"

"Earl! This is Duke—put the Queen on the phone! Now!"

"Mr. LaGrange, it is truly a pleasure to speak to you again—"

"Earl! For the love of all that you hold dear, put the Queen on—I don't have much time. It's about her uninvited portal friend—and our recent opportunity."

"Mr. LaGrange, if I recall—the unknown astral entity disappeared earlier today and has not returned. I believe the Queen has terminated her previous offer based on these circumstances. I am truly sorry. Is there anything else that I can help you with?"

"You hairy Glyptodian bastard! Tell the Queen that I'm looking right down its bright red gullet as we speak; not too far from the Keltian atmosphere. I think she might want to know."

"You do make a valid point, Mr. LaGrange. I will seek her out with unrivaled haste. Do you mind if I place you on hold briefly?"

"Yes, I mind, Earl!"

"Thank you."

"No, I said, I do mind—"

The hold music interrupted and chimed away, a ringing annoyance that was meant to keep telemarketers at bay. The Queen's assumption was that if the blood-sucking reprobates could withstand an hour or so of agonizing high-pitched musical aggravation, they earned a few minutes of her time.

"Duke, Earl tells me that you have something to share with me. Proceed, by all means."

The Queen's voice was a refreshing interlude to the hold music.

"I wanted to revisit our proposed deal, Queen. It appears that your unknown portal buddy is back—and it doesn't look happy to see us."

"Interesting."

"Interesting? So is it back on? Will you hold up your end of the bargain if we venture to the other side?"

"Duke, I'm—"

A crimson tsunami of the most intense illumination hit the bridge of the *Deus Ex Machina*. Duke and the sure-footed

Ishiro'shea hit the ground unceremoniously. The beams were more than simple light—and they rattled the ship to its core.

"What was that, Queen? You broke up," Duke shouted from the floor. "Yes or no? Do we have a deal?"

The Queen responded but a barrage of noises—whizzes, whirls, and a few mini-explosions for good measure—overwhelmed her voice.

Then everything went black.

CHAPTER 7

BORING OLD SPACE

THE HULL OF THE *DEUS Ex Machina* rumbled like the stomach of a ravenous yak, then mellowed to a slight murmur. Amber sparks danced about the control panel, intermingling with sporadic puffs of willowy smoke emitting from the mangled metal and pulverized plastic. The cabin's lighting system flickered as the onboard emergency systems tried to put out fires that had risen up in various locations on the ship's bridge. Alarms sounded as the craft tried to self-diagnose a catalog of ills all at the same time. Many things were happening inside the *Deus Ex Machina*, but Duke LaGrange was even more curious as to what was happening outside.

"Any chance of getting the view screen up?" Duke said solemnly as he stepped over what appeared to be a piece of the main panel. "I want to have some idea of where this son of a bitch dropped us off."

Ishiro'shea sat Zen-like amidst flashes and smoldering electronics. He clearly was more prepared to handle portal travel—especially one that had an unknown destination.

"Diagnosis?"

Ishiro'shea popped up with the same display of energy that he had showcased during his jam session with the Trampling

Death Robots. With a single downward motion, he struck the impaired main panel with a forceful *shuto-uchi*. The view screen fizzled—and then resumed its bright, shiny high-definition glory.

"Thank you. That's a new one."

Ishiro bowed.

"Holy hedgehogs, there's nothing out there. Looks like our favorite portal is gone too—so I guess that's a win. I was half expecting to be dropped into an intergalactic shootout or the stomach of some moon-sized cosmic zebra. We are just in... boring old space. Seems like a lot of trouble to gobble us up and spit us out in the celestial boondocks. Something doesn't make sense. Or maybe there was a glitch in the portal. I mean, there wasn't even an in-flight film. Portal travel isn't what it used to be."

Ishiro's expression led Duke to believe that he shared the same uneasiness about how anticlimactic the whole situation had been.

"Any chance we get the auto-nav back up? Another one of your karate chops?"

The stout ninja pointed aggressively at the tattered remains of a helm. He shook his head with noticeable pessimism.

"That bad, huh?"

Ishiro then began to repeatedly jab his finger in the air—pointing to the view screen.

Duke cringed.

"You want me to fly this manually? It's been more cycles than I care to recall since I actually had to drive."

The ninja did not yield; he continued to point.

Damnit.

Ishiro sat down and started to clear away as much debris as possible from the control station. Most of the fires were out by now. Duke knew Ishiro was more than capable at the helm of the *Deus*; however, Duke also knew that he was better. Even rusty, he was better.

"Fine. Let's see if we can figure out where we are—and if we can get back. Maybe the Queen will give us something for reporting that the portal leads to absolutely nowhere of consequence. You know, she could sell access on the black market—I'm sure someone would pay to send his enemy to an exile complete with a horrific death by boredom. And now that death by boredom has been officially outlawed in most sectors, it should fetch a pretty penny."

Duke sat down at the helm. *This has been a long time.* He wiped away a bit more of the accumulated debris and let out a long, drawn-out sigh. The ninja swiftly positioned himself in the vacant seat beside him.

"Well, crap." Duke shrugged. "Should we go left or right?"

Ishiro'shea pointed directly ahead.

"Straight it is, partner, straight it is."

The ship rattled and flexed its inflexible bits as it made its way into manual drive for the first time in many cycles. It jerked ferociously.

"Whoa, simmer down now. Easy does it."

Duke noticed his loyal companion appeared uncomfortable.

"Hey now, Ishiro. This was your idea, remember? I got it under control. Just like breakin' in a new horse," Duke said with a slightly exaggerated accent. "Easy, easy." He had never broken in a horse.

The *Deus Ex Machina* steadied and gradually accelerated into open space.

"Any chance we can get the other systems back up and running, Ishiro? I don't mind driving the girl but it would be nice to get some comm, in case we actually encounter something out here. We might want to strike up a conversation, after all."

The ninja went to work on the panel, seeming somewhat optimistic. Duke smiled.

"Seriously, there is *nothing* out here. I don't recognize the star patterns at all. They're entirely different than any that we've encountered—in any sector. Maybe the ship will think this is one of those 'backed into a corner' moments and spontaneously produce a star map for us."

Ishiro ignored Duke's far-fetched hope.

"A boy can dream, right?"

The *Deus Ex Machina* pushed on. The star patterns became no more recognizable to the displaced bounty hunter.

***

"Cheers!"

Ishiro'shea grabbed the beer and inhaled it. Duke cranked back his head and poured the sweet nectar of Glyptodia down his throat. He repeated this a few more times.

"Don't worry. I drive better after a few drinks."

Ishiro responded with a thumbs-up, then slugged another Erontian brew. And then another. And another. He then proceeded to the alcohol storage and dissemination unit. He reached down and pulled out a bottle of ancient Earth saké, regarded as possessing slightly higher quality than its Erontian cousin, and fetching a higher price.

"Buddy! Hey now! That's the bottle we, uh, relieved from that archeological pirate that we busted. Are you sure this is the special occasion to make you want to open it? You know what? To hell with it! From aimlessly piloting our ship in unknown and uncharted space to finding a probably dead-end planet that we'll spend our dying days on, it sounds like a special occasion to me. I've definitely never done it before. Cheers, hombre!"

The ninja removed his katana and swung it down upon the bottle with a silent precision. The glass did not shatter but the top inch of the bottle fell on the bar counter—introducing a rich aroma of fermented rice to the atmosphere of the bridge.

"Well done."

Ishiro'shea pulled his mask down to under his chin, hoisted the bottle skyward, and rotated the exposed bottleneck towards his open mouth. The liquid sparkled as it left the bottle and flowed ceaselessly into Ishiro's throat. Duke nearly choked on his beer.

"C'mon man! Don't hog the juice. Save some for me."

Duke shot out of his chair and stumbled towards his partner. The ship jolted abruptly. Duke lost his balance and hit the floor. Ishiro started to laugh, but the *Deus* kangarooed again and he fell on his posterior—without spilling a single drop of saké, however.

"Holy hedgehogs, I forgot—I'm driving this thing, right?"

Ishiro responded with a lazier thumbs-up.

"But I *really* want some of that saké. Choices, choices."

The ninja shook his head and pointed toward the helm.

"Oh, you think I should get back to driving, huh?"

The ninja repeated his headshake-and-point routine.

"Ishiro, c'mon, man, buddy, pal. I just want one shot before it's gone. We're best friends; why are you being such a bastard?"

Ishiro stood woozily and extended the bottle to his long-time companion.

"Thanks, little buddy. Cheers to us and finding our way. Our way *somewhere*."

Duke held the bottle aloft but was swiftly robbed of his balance due to the ship tipping again. The saké bottle crashed to the floor and shattered.

"No! The saké —"

Duke fell to his knees and tried to lap up the remaining liquid pooled on the ground. It was not his most shining moment. The ship violently rolled to starboard. Duke was thrown from the floor into the wall.

"Eyes *off* the prize, Duke," he said to himself. "Getting back to the controls."

Ishiro appeared a bit more focused and found his way back to the panel before Duke.

"Ok, let's wrangle this gal in."

The *Deus* rocked and rolled, herked and jerked, and did some stuff that would make a roller coaster vomit.

"I got it, I got it. Steady... steady."

The ship stabilized.

"How was the saké, jerk?"

Ishiro smirked.

"Look out the view screen! How long were we drinking?"

Duke aimed the newly-steadied ship at the planet—now much larger in the view screen—with a gradual, almost calming, acceleration.

"Get a load of that. It appears to be almost all water except for those two landmasses. They're connected. Looks like a giant upright dumbbell. I know we can't scan for life or tech or anything worthwhile—but maybe we can get a bit closer to see if we can identify a city or something."

The silent ninja nodded in agreement.

The *Deus* crept closer to the planetary body.

"I really hope it's not a planet of primitives. I can't stand primitives. Terrible conversation and nine out of ten haven't mastered brewing yet. And the women are so shaggy."

The hull rattled.

"Brace for some turbulence. Entering a stronger portion of the planet's gravitational pull."

Ishiro buckled his seat belt.

"What the—? Since when did we get seat belts? Where's mine?"

The ship rocked again. Duke and his seat parted ways.

"Damnit."

He climbed back into his chair and feverishly searched for his buckle without success.

"Fitting. Let's see if I can settle her down."

The view screen was now completely engulfed by the planet with the odd-shaped continent front and center. Ishiro pointed to the heart of the southern landmass.

"I see it, buddy. A city. Doesn't look like a megalopolis, but definitely civilization. Oh look, there's another one on the top half. And a few more sprinkled in. Maybe this isn't some deserted wasteland. Any ideas?"

Ishiro'shea shook his head.

"There seems to be a bit more cover around the first one. I think it makes the most sense. We have to chance it, right? Thoughts? Alternative ideas?"

The ninja seemed to agree.

Duke manually input a final descent and landing sequence into the tattered remains of the control panel.

"No chance the scanners will be up soon, huh? Let's hope this Podunk planetoid has an atmosphere suitable for two handsome bounty hunters with a boatload of questions."

The *Deus Ex Machina* broke through the outer atmosphere.

CHAPTER 8
SOUFFLÉS

"**I** REALLY DO HATE THIS music."

Ishiro'shea said nothing, as per usual.

"I also hate thinking that this will be the last thing we hear before we die. The place looks habitable enough from the bridge but without working instruments on the ship, it could be toxic land, for all we know. And what a time to leave the exploration enviro-suits at the dry cleaners! Anyways, if I haven't told you before, little buddy..."

Ishiro'shea looked up at his dear companion.

"...if this is the end... it's been a hell of a ride!"

The ninja nodded.

The elevator pinged as it hit the floor of the entryway hatch; the door swung open wildly, inviting the planet in for an atmospheric tea party. Duke and Ishiro held their breaths.

The Nova Texan counted down on his fingers. Three... two... one. The duo stepped out onto the grass-covered ground and took in the atmosphere of this new world.

Duke began to choke immediately. He fell to the ground, hacking and convulsing. Ishiro'shea stood above him, his eyes wide. And not choking.

"The air is so—clean. I hate it!"

The bounty hunter made it to his knees and eventually stood with the wobbly legs of a newborn giraffe. He clutched the supporting arm of his lifelong friend.

"Thanks, Ishiro," he hacked. "This is going to take some getting used to. I need a smoke. There has to be *some* pollution somewhere. Tell me there's some pollution somewhere."

His companion did not respond. In fact, he looked as if he enjoyed the change.

"It'll support us, at least," he continued between coughs, "despite this major headache."

Ishiro'shea inhaled even deeper and exhaled with a look of enjoyment.

Asshole, thought Duke.

"Do you think our parking job is good enough?" Duke pivoted to see the *Deus* expertly tucked away in a small patch of vegetation. He only counted four trees that had been severed in half by the hulking mass of the ship. He always strived to be eco-friendly.

"Let's hope these folks can help us out—and they don't find the *Deus*. I don't think my lungs can stand this planet longer than a few hours."

The ninja rolled his eyes.

"How can you stand this?" Duke wheezed. "Fine, maybe I won't die from it—but at least let me adjust to it. You know how long it's been since I've taken in something so damned clean?"

Ishiro'shea ignored the question—*probably doesn't know either*, concluded Duke—and started to head towards the city.

"By my best estimation, we're a few miles away. I'm hoping they can give us something useful."

They left the lush foliage that had served as their landing pad and started the trek across the grassy plain. It was a simple place, very different to the harsh deserts of Nova Texas, or the urban chaos of Kelt, or the dank labyrinths of Erontia, or the caramel sky-piercing mountains of Oscavia.

And very different to the alcohol-induced bedlam of Cyborg Joe's.

The bounty hunters had been walking for less than an hour before Duke was able to see the outskirts of the city on the horizon. It was becoming much brighter and Duke was finally adjusting to the atmosphere. As they closed in, they could make out huts and other unsophisticated single-story dwellings.

"Primitives. As if this day couldn't get any worse, we've landed amongst some backwards aboriginals that probably haven't figured out basic plumbing or electricity or quantum-time manipulation. Or soufflés."

Duke knew soufflés were often perfected after a civilization had mastered quantum-time manipulation—and ninety percent of all major civilizations never made it to the "Soufflé Stage." So he didn't hold that one against them.

"I'm sure these furry cavemen are either going to charge us with bloodlust and uncontrolled aggression—or they're going to worship us as gods. Just in case, let's be ready for both."

Duke tapped the butt of his revolver, double-checking it was there. He didn't need to do the same for Betsy; he could feel her on his back. Ishiro'shea flashed his katana. Duke liked that.

"What are you thinking, Ishiro? Stroll in nonchalantly? Sneak around and try to get into the city center undetected? It does appear to be a bit more advanced than this dump and, I'm sure, more likely to provide some answers."

Ishiro'shea aimed his finger at an area about a ship's length from the outermost hut—here the grass was twice as tall with pockets of messy, dense bushes. The thicker undergrowth extended well beyond the primitive homestead and appeared to end at the foot of the walled township.

"Think that's good enough cover to circumnavigate this outpost?"

Ishiro was already in stealth position and darting towards the hedges.

"I forgot. You're a ninja," Duke chided himself. "Wait up!"

The two blended in with the flora and eased their way around the settlement. They encountered no one and no thing in the fields. The two sat, entirely concealed from any potential lookouts from the village, and peered through an opening in the foliage.

"Where is everyone? We are literally a stone's toss away from this joint and I don't see a soul anywhere. Deserted? Raided? Nah, not enough dead bodies."

Ishiro thumped Duke's shoulder. He rested his cheek on clasped hands.

"Not the worst idea, Ishiro. Maybe their species is nocturnal. Remember the nightfolk of Ruddia Gophp? Those cats were spooky. And their cats were even spookier."

Ishiro motioned a slicing movement with his hand, signaling decapitation.

"Spooky and messy."

"As much as I want to know about where all these hut dwellers are—which is absolutely not at all—I think our answers are gonna be right over there."

Duke nodded in the direction of the city center.

"Let's keep moving."

The ornate doors appeared to stretch to the sky. There was no other way to enter the walled city, at least none that were easily identifiable to Duke.

"I dig the design. Imposing but artful."

Ishiro'shea nodded.

"Maybe those village folk moved inside here and didn't bother to knock down their old homes. This *would* be an upgrade, ya' know. Although, not the most functional, if you think about it. You spend the dough building these giant walls but don't have a single sentry tower? Not real thinkers, it seems; unless this joint was designed to keep people in—not out."

The emerald-clad ninja gave a look that suggested he agreed with that assumption.

"I guess we knock, amigo?"

Ishiro ignored him and began to inspect the door meticulously, gently testing the façade for any weaknesses or clues. He crouched down and started to follow along the base of the wall for a few yards.

"No time for that, Ishiro."

Duke raised his right hand and struck the behemoth doors purposefully. A ringing thud vibrated out from the door—as loud as anything from the Trampling Death Robots' holiday album.

Ishiro quickly returned to Duke's side and slapped him on the shoulder. *Oh, he's pissed.*

"What? We didn't have time to sneak in. I want answers now—and maybe we've got a chance to get out of this godforsaken fresh air!"

Ishiro feverishly signaled in multiple directions with an angry jabbing motion.

Maybe we should have chatted first.

"Ishiro, look at this place. A fairly basic structure with a rinky-dink village in its shadows. How dangerous can it be? When we were scooting around in the bushes, I just kept thinking about how these primitives are probably going to be more scared of us than we are of them."

Duke's friend simply shook his head as the bounty hunter tried to rationalize his hasty decision.

"Seriously, buddy. Listen—we know they aren't advanced and they obviously aren't paying too close attention to us. They were too stupid to know that they should have some lookout posts along their wall. The more I think of it, my guess is that they finally discovered how to build something stronger than a wooden hut a few cycles ago—and moved the whole family in here. Nothing more, nothing less. Just another entry on the long list of primitive, backwoods, who-gives-a-damn planets."

Ishiro pointed at the intricate metalwork adorning the oversized gates.

"Okay, maybe they didn't *just* discover how to build these —apparently, they have *some* skill. But, I think you're giving them too much credit. Look, they didn't even send out a welcoming party—"

Duke's gabbling was halted by a thunderous groan. The doors began to swing inward at a deliberate pace. The noise reminded Duke of the moans of Joe's patrons after consuming a MechaBurger 8000.

"Why, hello there," chimed a high-pitched voice. The 'hello' was elongated and seemed never to end. It was an unusually cheery tone.

CHAPTER 9

THE THING ABOUT ORBS

OUT FROM THE SHADOWS OF the doors appeared the deliverer of the jovial greeting. He was humanoid, but unusually gaunt; his drab blue skin clung to his skeletal frame. His quasi-ellipsoid face was as emaciated as his body, and hung slightly out in front of his chest; it was connected to a thin neck that jutted out from between his shoulders. His circular, murky eyes were devoid of pupils.

"I can assure you, my fine fellows, we are not stupid nor 'backwoods'—as you call it. Nor are we dangerous. It does appear, however, that I *am* your official welcoming party. I'm afraid that we don't have many visitors here; thus, we don't spend too much time on preparing formal greetings and the like."

As he came farther into the light, the cylindrical headgear balanced atop his cranium reflected the sun's rays. It stood as tall as his narrow face was long, and was studded with petite blue jewels; they matched a single stone of similar color affixed squarely to his chin.

We have an over-accessorizer, thought Duke.

"That's okay," Duke said.

"Oh, I apologize again, my handsome visitors!"

He's quite the chipper one. But it's obvious he has keen observation skills.

"As you have probably noticed, I'm a bit rusty at this hospitality thing. Let me introduce myself, my new friends. I am High Priest Vernglet Wip, a proud member of the Order of the Orb, and appointed steward of this modest municipality in which you now find yourself. The gates of Dre'en are open and we are humbled by your presence." The last phrase was uttered with an attempt at a more grandiose announcement.

Vernglet Wip knelt down with a simple bow, steadying himself against his gilded walking staff resting in his right hand. The jeweled chains dripping from his decorative breastplate rattled and jingled. Small spheres of gold hung from each chain, mirroring the larger sphere atop his staff.

"Where are we, exactly?"

"You are at the gates of the city known as Dre'en."

"I don't mean to be rude, but this joint wasn't on our itinerary. Can you tell us what... um, planet... we're on?"

Vernglet paused for a moment. An uneven smile crept across his face.

"You have found your way to Neprius—and Neprius welcomes you."

"Neprius, huh? Never heard of it."

"Oh, you don't say? I can't say that I'm shocked, my ruggedly adorable off-worlder," chirped Vernglet. "Like I said, we don't get a lot of visitors to our beautiful home. Truly a shame, I suppose."

"Yeah, it doesn't look too bad—but this air... You gotta do something about this air."

"Is it not to your liking?"

"It's borderline toxic to my kind," responded Duke.

Ishiro'shea shook his head.

"Interesting. What exactly is your kind?"

Duke began to answer but the priest cut him off.

"Please forgive me. I have been entirely rude and offensive. What is your kind—what are you thinking, Vernglet? You know better than that," he muttered to himself. His voice quivered as if he expected to be tortured for his hosting faux pas. "I should've asked you the required questions that a respectable host extends to his guests. What are your names? Where do you visit us from? Tell me all about yourselves. Please."

Once again, Duke's retort was interrupted by the slightly feminine tone of their one-man welcoming party.

"I am so rude again! We are just standing here at the gate—come in, come see the city of Dre'en—the southern jewel of Neprius. I hope you like it!"

What an odd person. Duke glanced over at Ishiro and noticed that the ninja was diligently scanning every visible nook and cranny. The bounty hunter had known him long enough to tell that he was feeling skeptical about Dre'en—and possibly about High Priest Vernglet Wip.

"As we make our way in from the gates, you will see the road directly in front of us—yes? That leads straight into the heart of Dre'en and the Altar House of the Orb. I must admit, if I'm being honest—and we are honest people here on Neprius—there isn't much to write home about for quite some time if we travel this path to the center. I hope that you can withstand our toxic air, my lovely friend. However, it will give us time to get more acquainted. Then, we can enjoy the marvels of our quaint town."

The trio started down the uneven path. The priest's prediction had been accurate—to the left and the right of the road, for as far as they could see, was nothing but dense forest. Duke noticed that Ishiro continued to examine their surroundings—never focusing on the road for more than a second at a time. Duke was impressed with the road itself—despite its wildly irregular stonework, the tops of each individual rock were polished to an almost mirror-like quality. But they weren't slippery. *I'm guessing the lady Neprians don't wear a lot of skirts.*

"So friends, as we were about to get to earlier, what are your names and where do you visit us from?"

"My name is Duke LaGrange," the bounty hunter decreed boastfully; his chest puffed out. "Adventurer. Trailblazer. Poet. A true man of the universe."

"Oh, is that so? I can see it. Definitely can see that. Very impressive."

"This is my longtime friend and trusted sidekick, Ishiro'shea."

"Hello, there Ishiro'shea, sidekick to the great Duke LaGrange."

Ishiro bowed. Vernglet mimicked the movement to reciprocate the greeting.

"Don't worry, Ishiro doesn't say much."

"And why is that? Does his species lack the ability to speak?"

"Vow of silence."

"Then, Mr. Ishiro'shea, I commend you on this solemn vow of vocal condemnation. As the High Priest of the Order of the Orb, I too know about commitment. But tell me, travelers, where did you come from—and why did you choose our world as a place to visit?"

"The universe is our home," Duke retorted. Only he knew that the line was plagiarized from a Willie's World of Galactic Winnebagos television ad. ("The universe is our home, so make it yours... Now with flushing toilets compatible with up to 85 species!")

"Interesting."

"Our work takes us to many planets, and we've been doing it for so long that our birthplaces are almost a distant memory. Our ship back there is the closest thing we have to a home. But, if you must know, the story of yours truly started many cycles ago on a rugged, yet embracing, rock known as Nova Texas."

"I see many similarities already between you and this Nova Texas in which you speak."

Duke soaked in the unwarranted praise.

"Ishiro'shea is from a place known as Earth."

"Earth, you say? Interesting."

"Heard of it?"

"Um, no," Vernglet hesitated. "I don't think so. Yes, definitely a 'no.'"

"Well, you nailed the best way to describe Earth. 'Interesting.'"

"Do you not visit this Earth much? What do they have there that makes it so intriguing?"

"Wars, mostly."

"But do they have great crops that reach to the sky?" Vernglet asked somewhat dramatically, with his arms reaching upward.

Peculiar question.

"Um, sure there are crops—I think. There used to be, at least. Not sure if they reach to the sky—but what do I know? Ishiro? You know anything about giant crops from living on Earth?"

Ishiro shrugged.

"Why do you ask?"

"Oh, just curious. I was a farmer before I joined the priesthood and I like to know that there are places out there with bountiful harvests for all. I apologize for sidetracking the conversation. So why did you two assuredly unrivaled cosmic explorers choose to come to Neprius?"

"Ya' know, Vern—" Duke caught himself. "Can I call you Vern?"

"Whatever suits the great Duke LaGrange."

Out of the corner of his eye, Duke caught Ishiro shaking his head at the compliments being heaped upon him.

"We didn't quite *choose* to come to Neprius."

"Interesting."

I knew he was going to say that.

"It was more that we hitched a ride, you could say."

"Hitched a ride? What do you mean?"

"We actually were hoping that you could help us out with this? We essentially were gobbled up by a giant red star blob—and it conveniently dropped us off on your front doorstep."

The priest paused as if to collect his thoughts.

"Can you describe this 'star blob'?"

"Sure. It first appeared in one of our favorite bars—"

"In a bar? As in a place to consume beverages and to partake in assorted merriment?"

"Yes, a bar. And yeah, it was much smaller then but kept trying to break in through the wall, but Queen Joe—she's the proprietor of the joint—said it decided to stop bugging her about the time that Ishiro and I left."

Duke noticed the Neprian's increased concentration.

"Then Ishiro and I had some business dealings with some Jungafallowians—"

"Jungafallowians?"

"Smelly creatures. Terrible taste in music. They are of no consequence."

"Did these Jungafallowians send this 'thing' to kill you?"

"Oh no, they're way too moronic for that. But once we parted ways with these Jungafallowians—"

Ishiro snorted at Duke's choice of words to describe their encounter with Prince Korzo-Tapor.

"—our little astral friend resurfaced. And he wasn't so little."

"What did you do?"

"We didn't do much. We *couldn't* do much. We held on as tight as we could as he swallowed us whole."

"This is quite—"

"Let me guess: interesting?"

"I'm sorry, I will think of another word to use in its place,"
Vernglet said with an apologetic curtsy.

"Just messing with ya', Vern. But, in a blink of an eye, we
were deposited, ship and all, in the friendly neighborhood we
now know as Neprius."

"Wow, quite an interesting—I mean, fascinating
—journey."

"So, Ishiro and I were kinda hoping that someone here
might know what this is all about. Why would this unknown
disturbance in space want to plop anyone or anything down in
your general vicinity?"

"I am afraid that I am unaware of any such disturbances.
When we get to the center of Dre'en, I can ask some of my
colleagues. We have a few priests that concentrate on all things
in the sky and space. They might be of better assistance."

"Can't hurt," replied Duke, though his tone was tinged
with pessimism. "Anyways Vern, we've talked enough about
ourselves. Tell us about Neprius. And Dre'en. And your fascination with orbs."

"My new comrade, it is not a fascination with orbs—it is a
fascination with *the* Orb."

"*The* Orb?"

"Yes. The Orb That Controls Everything and Must Be
Respected."

Neprius is in dire need of a good advertising agency,
thought Duke.

"It is the reason for our being, our salvation, and our
progression. Our leader and our savior is the almighty Orbius,
the Orbmaster of the Orb That Controls Everything and Must
Be Respected."

"Orbius?"

"Yes, the Orbmaster of the Orb."

"Redundancy aside, what does that actually mean? This
might shock you but Orbmaster is not a common occupation in
most parts of the universe."

"Orbius is the Orbmaster of The Orb, the Sultan of the Sphere, the Guardian of the Globe, He Who Controls the Orb that Controls Everything and Must Be Respected. He is our savior."

"So is that what he puts on his business card?"

High Priest Vernglet Wip did not laugh.

CHAPTER 10

A LIBRARY WITH LESS SEX

THE VIEW FROM THE WINDOW framed the town square of Dre'en. The sun was setting; nightfall was imminent, but a few shafts of radiant orange peeked from behind the buildings. The square itself was actually almost circular, with the center plaza made of the same polished stone as the road into Dre'en. At the rear of the cul-de-sac an ornate set of steps led up to an equally ornate door of a single unornamented tower, stark and plain. The dour building and its indulgent entrance seemed an unhappy marriage. Two Neprians—clothed in the same manner as Vernglet—stood guard outside. More nondescript buildings of muddy stone and auburn timber encircled the court, punctuated only by the single road. Rising from behind the structures was the continuation of the wall where Duke LaGrange and Ishiro'shea had met Vernglet Wip.

"My friends, is this accommodation up to your standards? I know you have traveled to many exotic and, no doubt, luxurious lands with opulent lodgings; I hope that you will not be disgusted with our quaint room. The view of the heart of Dre'en is the best that we have."

"It'll do, Vern," said Duke as he peered out onto the arcade. "This is the southern jewel of Neprius, eh?"

"Why yes, Mr. LaGrange."

"Doesn't seem to be a whole lot of folks. Where's the foot traffic? The hustle and bustle? The actual Neprians? I mean, since Ishiro and I met ya', we've strolled through ninety percent of Dre'en on that road and have only seen you—and those two guards out there standing next to that interesting-lookin' door. See Vern, now you got me saying 'interesting.'"

"Ah, yes, Mr. LaGrange. That 'interesting' door is the entrance to our most beloved building—the Altar House of the Orb. And, believe me, you will meet many of our lovely residents. It happens to be a day of work for many of us, and clergymen like myself are busy preparing for our evening services."

"What about the villages that we passed before we came into the city? They looked as if they'd been recently abandoned."

"Oh, no, I assure you—they are not abandoned. The villagers are working."

"All of them?"

"Yes, all of them. And they tend to be shy."

"Do they all work together?"

"I almost forgot—you said you wanted to discuss the red 'blob' with our star scholars, yes? I will arrange an appointment first thing in the morning with our leading minds. You will be impressed with their celestial knowledge. If there is anyone on Neprius that can provide you some direction or insight that relates to your cosmic query, it will be one of our scholars here in Dre'en. We haven't quite figured out space travel as your species has, but we are very aware of the possibility thanks to the presence of our savior. Maybe one day we will earn Orbius' trust and he will teach us the ways of travel amongst the stars."

"Thanks. But what about—"

"Mr. LaGrange, I do apologize but I need to run down to check on a few things for the evening services. You and Mr. Ishiro'shea get comfortable, and I will send someone up shortly to escort you both to dinner. I think you will like our local cuisine. Until then..."

The door shut quickly. Duke could hear Vernglet scurry down the hallway at a frantic pace.

Ishiro tapped Duke on the shoulder.

"Yep, I noticed it too. He seemed a bit squirrely about those villagers and their 'jobs.'"

The ninja looked around at their surroundings without appearing to focus on anything in particular in their wholly uninteresting room. Duke knew that he was uneasy—and had been since they met Vernglet Wip and trekked through Dre'en.

"I know, little buddy. Something doesn't feel right. But then again, it might just be that it's been a bumpy ride since we decided to hit up Joe's—and we're projecting our bad luck onto this situation as well."

Ishiro shrugged his shoulders. *He's not going to buy that.*

"I knew we totally should've gone to Goddess Larry's Gin Palace for drinks instead."

His companion smirked. Duke hoped that Ishiro'shea appreciated his attempt to lighten the mood.

"I wonder how this Neprian cuisine stacks up. Can't be any worse than a MechaBurger, right?"

Duke propped Betsy up in the corner of the room and sat down on what he assumed was a bed. The cube-shaped furnishing seemed to combine the roles of mattress and frame —the bottom was plush and buoyant—the top was made of something resembling iron, if the iron had been frozen in the tundra of Garlomb for a thousand cycles and then encased within the impenetrable metal of the blacksmiths of To-To Megro Minor.

"Yeah, definitely not a five-star establishment."

Duke wiggled his posterior until he got as comfortable as he was going to get, then stretched out his legs and placed his hat beside him on the bed.

"A bit better. So what do *you* think is up? Do you think he knows something about the astral anomaly that gobbled us up?"

Ishiro shook his head.

"Really?"

The ninja pointed up at the sky and then proceeded to retreat to a cowering position.

"You know, Ishiro, you're right. He did seem shocked when I mentioned the blob. It's almost as if he was startled— then realized he needed to collect as many facts as possible. But to what end? Did we stumble on—or through, I suppose— some sacred religious wormhole? Seems a bit far-fetched— even for us. All he seems to care about is that damn Orb That Does Stuff and the all-powerful Orbius."

The ninja offered only another shrug.

"Have we considered the possibility that maybe he's just a weird dude? He loves orbs and crops and seems to think that this boring-ass city is somehow the 'jewel of the planet.' Yikes. It's more like a library—but with less sex."

The ninja placed his katana on a stone shelf that protruded from the wall. He walked to the window again and studied the plaza intently.

"After a good meal—well, I guess I shouldn't get ahead of myself—after *a* meal and a good night's sleep..."

Ishiro walked over and thumped the "mattress."

"...fine, after a *horribly uncomfortable* night's sleep, then we can talk to those astronomy priests and figure out as much as we are going to. We can keep an eye out for any funny business and, by midday, we'll be back at the *Deus*. Sound good?"

Ishiro'shea agreed to the plan with a nod of his head. He turned back to the window and continued to study the plaza as the night finally swallowed the last remaining flickers of sunlight.

"So, any clue on what Neprians eat? I have a feeling we're going to be underwhelmed."

CHAPTER 11

PLOOB KALARTI

"I MUST SAY, VERN. I'M impressed. Stuffed and impressed. What do you call this again?"

Duke held up a half-eaten conical fruit covered in minute violet fibers.

"Ah, a personal favorite of mine—ploob kalarti. They can only be grown in southern Neprius. Where I come from—far north of here—we are sadly denied adequate ploob kalarti harvests."

"Bummer. What's this?" A slight gaseous belch escaped the bounty hunter at the conclusion of his question.

"That is roast leg of greattu; a local delicacy as well. It is an agile six-legged bit of fauna—about the height of Ishiro'shea but with horns. They feed off of the ploob kalarti fields—that is why their meat is slightly syrupy but with the right amount of acid to cut the rich sweetness."

"Well, I'm a fan. And it was nice to meet some of the other priests. We were starting to think that you were on this rock alone. They were some good dudes, a little high strung—but, all in all, y'all are a decent lot. What were the twins' names? They were some characters!"

"Twins? Oh, Hoblet and Delix? They are not twins, Mr.

LaGrange. In fact, Delix is considered quite attractive in our race—and poor Hoblet..."

"He relies on his personality, huh?"

"You could say that."

"Well, I liked 'em, nonetheless. A pretty okay crew ya' got here, if you ask me."

"I am so pleased to hear this. Mr. Ishiro'shea, I see that you have not consumed quite the same quantity as Mr. LaGrange. Was everything to your liking?"

Ishiro'shea nodded politely and tilted his plate upward to show the priest that he had finished off the majority of his ploob salad.

"Very nice."

"Did you manage to get us on the schedule with your scholarly cats tomorrow to chat about our favorite little cosmic incursion?"

"I am very glad that you asked. Yes, I did. We will meet with them tomorrow in the late morning at their laboratory. It is merely across the plaza and directly to the right of the Altar House."

"Very good. Oh, how did your last-minute preparations for the evening's event go?"

"Oh, all is well. Thank you for asking."

The rugged playboy tipped an invisible hat.

"My friends, it is time for me to head over to the Altar House for our services in honor of the Orb. I hate to leave you, but you know your way back to your room, I believe. Try and get some sleep. Your journey would tire even the most stamina-blessed traveler."

"Cheers to that, Vern!"

"I will come and get you in the morning."

Vernglet stood up and exited the dining hall.

"Looks like we might've been wrong about ol' Wip. Usually when there is something afoot, the food sucks."

Ishiro agreed.

"Let's just hope those eggheads can help us in the morning."

The ninja nodded and swiped an untouched ploob kalarti for the walk back to their room.

The duo proceeded down the dimly-lit corridor that led to their chamber. It was slightly dank and smelled musty with a dash of concentrated cleaning solution.

"They really should redecorate this joint. The haunted castle craze is so seven cycles ago. I guess they get a pass—they probably don't get a lot of fashion trends from—"

A muffled shriek echoed around the hallway. Both Duke and Ishiro'shea paused.

"That's coming from the dining hall."

Duke lowered his shoulder and rushed the dining room door. *Now this is going to be an entrance!*

The collision was not as loud as he had hoped—and the outcome was definitely nowhere in the vicinity of what he had in mind. With a subdued thud, Duke LaGrange collapsed to the floor of the hallway like a soggy noodle losing a limbo contest. He sat up and cleared his head.

"Well," he grimaced, "what's Plan B?"

Ishiro'shea stealthily glided past the recovering Nova Texan and examined the door intently. The muffled screams that they had heard moments before had stopped as soon as Duke collided unsuccessfully with the door. Ishiro'shea continued to examine it with a surgical focus. He extended his right hand to the octagonal knob, clutched it tightly and turned.

Click. The door swung open.

"It wasn't locked? Suspicious noises and cries for help are almost always behind *locked* doors. Sloppy work from these chaps; if they turn out to be bad dudes, that is.

Neprian criminals have a lot to learn about being sneaky and shady."

Duke's train of thought was interrupted as the dining room came into full view. The table at which they had feasted was mostly cleared away; only a few plates of half-eaten greattu and goblets of an overly-sludgy liquid laughably referred to as "nectar" remained. In the far-left corner, facing the wall, was a Neprian priest. Directly below him, crouched and recoiling, was another life form, much smaller than the Neprian and with a skin tone somewhere between bronze and carroty. It had a single stringy, unkempt mat of hair clinging to the top of its head; but outside of the unusual hairdo, slightly larger ears, and the absence of eyebrows, it looked human. More specifi-cally, it looked like a human child.

The Neprian turned around slowly. His expression morphed rapidly, but Duke caught a glimpse of anger before his gaunt face produced a haunting smile.

"Hello again, Mr. LaGrange. Mr. Ishiro'shea."

"Geezer, is it?"

"Geezu, Mr. LaGrange. Geezu. But very close—you are picking up our assuredly odd-sounding names like a native son of Neprius."

"What—I mean *who* is that?"

"This troublemaker is of no consequence. I apologize for causing alarm."

Duke ignored the Neprian's response and walked toward the child-like creature. Ishiro followed closely.

"Mr. LaGrange, I assure you—"

"Geezer, I wasn't aware that there were other species on this planet. Where do they live?"

Duke knelt down a few paces from the Neprian and the child-like creature.

"Hey there, it's your 'Uncle Duke.' Are you a nice fella?"

"Mr. LaGrange," Geezu interjected, "I must ask you to leave this delinquent to me as it is official priest business."

"Official priest business?"

"Yes, Mr. LaGrange. We are very honored to have you here in Dre'en, but this situation is purely a matter for our clergy."

"Geezer, you're acting a little squirmy now."

"Squirmy?"

"What's the true story with this little guy?"

"There is no story, Mr. LaGrange. Maybe Vernglet can explain it to you at a later date. But I must ask you again to leave."

"No story? Nothing?"

"He hit me," squeaked a voice.

The bounty hunter froze. His brain tried to take in the child's comments and weigh the risks of a plethora of actions that could be taken.

"And I'm a girl, not a 'little boy.' And I'm actually taller than most my age, so I'm not little either."

"Geezer here hit you?" Duke asked.

"Yes."

"You silly mongrel, I am a man of the Orb. I would not strike an inferior life form."

"Inferior? Says who?" asked Duke.

"He makes me work in the kitchen and hits me when I'm not fast enough," the voice chirped again.

"Is this true, Geezer?" Duke drew closer to the priest. Geezu's almost translucent skin was pulled taut against his cheekbones.

"No, Mr. LaGrange. In your short time, you must have a good grasp of us. It is a mere child's prank."

"Liar! Look at this!"

The child rotated her head to the left and exposed the back of her neck. A deep bruise came into the light.

"You little good-for-nothing!" Geezu shouted at the child. With his right hand he reached out and snatched the human-esque creature by the patch of hair on her head and yanked her to her feet. Dirt and dust flew off of her ragged clothing.

"I warned you!" shouted Geezu. "Mr. LaGrange, you have stuck your nose into a matter that does not—"

Geezu hit the floor with a thud more dramatic than Duke's shoulder-first crash into the door. The bounty hunter was pleased; Geezu's face revealed that he hardly felt the same.

"His face was harder than it looked," Duke quipped as he shook his now unclenched right hand.

Duke turned around.

"Holy hedgehogs!"

Two Neprian priests rushed toward him javelin-first. Duke turned and grabbed the closest dining chair; he reared back to swing it—but hit nothing. He looked down.

Both Neprian priests were on their backs, their eyes closed. The lethal javelins lay harmlessly on the floor beside them. Ishiro'shea stood over them in attack position.

"Ishiro! Love ya', man. But what took ya' so long? I would have knocked 'em out way faster."

The ninja pointed to the corner where the girl had been cowering.

"She's gone?"

The door to the kitchen was ajar. *She must've snuck out through there*, the bounty hunter concluded.

"We need to find Vernglet and let him know what went down here. I haven't seen a jail on Neprius, but I'm sure these guys will be thrown in something not-so-nice. Damn these bastards, pickin' on an innocent little street urchin."

Ishiro gave Duke a quizzical stare.

"I guess I don't know *for sure* that she's a street urchin. She looks like one, though. Who knows, maybe she comes from a very respectable family."

Ishiro's stare did not waver.

"Oh right! Why didn't Vernglet mention anything about

folks that look pretty similar to us living on this planet? I hope he has his reasons."

One of the guards began to regain consciousness; his thin arms pressed his torso up, but his knees were still anchored to the floor. He reached for his pointy killing instrument.

Duke's boot struck the guard's face—which, in turn, struck the stone floor with a plop.

"Gettin' rusty, Ishiro?"

The ninja ignored Duke's comment, but the bounty hunter knew his friend would be miffed that the guard had recovered from his attack sooner than he would have liked. Ishiro'shea gracefully floated through the dining hall and out into the hallway.

"Okay, okay. Let's go find Vernglet. He has some explaining to do. His abusive priest buddies. This mysterious kid that claims to be an indentured servant. The fact that it appears there's another race on this planet." Duke counted on his fingers. "What else?"

Ishiro was already outside of the dining hall. He nudged his head in Duke's direction.

"Okay, I'm comin'."

Duke waded through the Neprian bodies and met his cohort in the hallway.

"I guess we finally get to see the inside of this Altar House of the Orb? Let's go chat with Vern."

Ishiro'shea started to head down the corridor leading to their rooms.

"Where ya' goin', Ishiro? The exit out to the plaza is this way."

The ninja mimed a sniper.

"Good call. Probably want to have something more than our bare hands just in case we run into any more of those un-priestly priests."

CHAPTER 12

VANITY KILLED THE NEPRIAN

DUKE AND ISHIRO'SHEA STRODE BRISKLY along the corridor. It led to an unfurnished annex that marked the halfway point between the dining hall and their guest room.

"Didn't think I would have to use Ol' Betsy today. Goes to show ya'."

Ishiro'shea paused. Duke followed suit. He trusted Ishiro's senses.

"Yeah, I hear it too. I think it's down by our room."

Both men slid up against the wall with as much stealth as possible.

"Think they heard us?"

The ninja shook his head.

"Me neither," whispered Duke.

They crept around the corner, out from the annex, and into full view. Ishiro crouched down, making himself as small as possible. Duke remained upright, but his back pressed against the wall as if he hoped to cave the partition in with his weight.

The Nova Texan continued to whisper across the hallway to his compatriot. "These Neprians will taste the explosive thunder of my trusted Betsy soon enough—and it's a taste not easily washed out of one's mouth."

Ishiro froze.

Duke tried to contain it, but a laugh escaped him. "Hey Ishiro, don't you wish you wouldn't have taken that vow of silence now, huh? You miss out on all the great and heroic lines."

The ninja, for the first time that Duke could remember without the aid of alcohol, lost his composure. He hit Duke with a hearty bellow—at least, it would have been hearty if it hadn't been silent.

The sound crackled again and Ishiro's silent chuckle evaporated instantaneously. *That's definitely coming from our room.*

Without a single spoken word, both men charged down the last leg of the hallway. A mere ten paces from reaching the door, two Neprian priests emerged from the confines. One held Ol' Betsy and Duke's laser revolver. The other carried Ishiro's cherished katana.

"Whoa now. Hold up there, boys," yelled Duke, having decided that events had already moved past the need-to-whisper stage.

The priests turned to the duo in surprise.

"Hoblet? Delix? You've got to be kidding me!" Duke howled in recognition. "I thought we were friends, man."

The Neprians looked at each other. *What are the chances that they know how to use those guns?*

"We are not your friends, Mr. LaGrange."

"I can see that now," smirked the bounty hunter.

"And now you are without your beloved armaments. You stand no chance as I see it." Hoblet raised the sword above his head and brought it down with a vicious slashing motion. *Okay, he knows how to use that.*

"What makes you so sure? We took out your spear-toting friends in the dining room without even an iota of effort."

"You will not be so lucky this time."

"Luck?" Duke laughed. "And why's that, fellas? We've beaten up twins before—and in more dire conditions than this. In fact, beating up identical twins is our specialty."

"Twins?" shouted Delix. "We are *not* twins!"

"Whatever. You guys are totally indistinguishable. Right, Delix?" Deliberately, Duke directed his question toward Hoblet.

"That's not Delix. I'm Delix, you... you... you moron of the highest order."

"Ouch. Guys, I'm sure you are unique in your own way but looks ain't one of them. I've seen many twins in my day—let me tell ya', and I've had some good times with twins—but that's a story for another time..."

"We look nothing alike. How dare you compare us like that?" Delix's face turned a nasty shade of raspberry. "I knew Vernglet Wip was a fool. Orbius knew all along that you are nothing more than marauding vagabonds sent to destroy our way of life. You aren't smart enough to possess any worthwhile knowledge. You are going to die by your own prized death toy, Mr. LaGrange. For Orbius and the Orb!"

Delix aimed Ol' Betsy at Duke and pulled the trigger. An all-too-familiar sound erupted from Betsy's inner depths, followed by smoke and the smell of fresh carnage. Blood and innards filled the corridor.

Guess he didn't know how to use a gun.

Duke firmed up his stance, his chest protruding proudly. "See, Mr. Hoblet, vanity is not a good trait. It'll get you killed. That... and holding a gun backwards."

Hoblet was petrified. He was covered in bits that, seconds ago, belonged to his good friend, Delix.

"So, you can do one of two things. You can drop the sword and run away—which I highly advise. Or you can try to fight us—and most likely end up like your friend there. And there.

And over there. And I think some of him is stuck up there as well."

The Neprian placed the sword on the ground, pivoted away from Duke and Ishiro, and limped away with noticeable shakiness.

Ishiro'shea lobbied a grin at his longtime friend.

"Yeah, yeah. I, too, can take advantage of the psychological deficiencies of a weaker being. One might say I'm quite brilliant. Vanity is always a killer—when not in moderation, of course. It proves once again that I'm more than just a handsome face with a ridiculously large gun."

The ninja did not give any sign of agreement. He pointed at the ground a few feet in front of the Nova Texan.

Duke swiped at a large chunk of Delix with his boot; the gelatinous mound of flesh jiggled away to reveal Duke's laser revolver. He picked it up, examined its condition, and slid it into his holster. Then he turned and tugged violently at a musty tapestry that hung from the wall. It crashed down to the floor, landing in a deep puddle of Neprian entrails. Duke was able to keep a tiny piece dry. He knelt down and picked up his old friend, Betsy.

"She definitely needs a scrub down. I think part of Delix is lodged down the barrel. We don't have time to break her down and perform a diagnostic, do we?"

Duke answered his own question. "No. We don't."

He scrubbed Betsy down with the scrap of tapestry to the best of his abilities, and slid her into his back holster. *That feels good.* Ishiro'shea picked up his katana, but he did not conceal it.

"You wanna go to the Altar House now?"

Ishiro gave a thumbs-up.

"Look, Ishiro, I want to smash these bastards as much as the next guy—and find out about these slave children or whatever—but I don't like the odds of us versus the entire city of Dre'en. Stacked deck. I say we go back to the *Deus*. Let's see if these cats will talk when our ship is staring down at 'em. Probably a bit more persuasive."

The ninja sheathed his blade. The sound of footsteps echoed down the corridor.

"Seems like we aren't alone anymore. I bet they heard the explosion. Or Hoblet must've made it to his friends already. My vote is to get outta here *now*."

Duke and Ishiro'shea snuck away into the cool night air of Dre'en and accelerated to a brisk pace along the single road of mirror-like stone.

CHAPTER 13

NINETEEN PACES

"**I** DON'T HAVE A GREAT feeling about this."

Ishiro'shea signaled his alignment with that assessment.

"I'm assuming most nights they don't just leave the front gate open like that. They either wanted us to leave to meet our impending doom—and made sure we weren't slowed down by some pesky wall—or they didn't think we would be in a position to leave this joint—because our doom had already impended upon us. Either way, we're walking into a mess that I don't care to be in."

Once again, Duke's colleague appeared to agree.

"If memory serves, we should be coming up on the *Deus* soon, right?"

Ishiro did not respond.

"Okay, must be talking to myself," Duke muttered. "Let's see then, we've already passed through the gates, we've already passed by the village—oh yeah, come to think of it, that bastard Vern never did tell us where all those cats in the village were working. He conveniently changed the subject when I asked; I did *not* pin him for being as sly as he is. Crafty little devil."

Duke scratched his chin. "But, then again, remember what

Delix said? Vern thought we were here for a reason. Sounds like he might've been the only one that wanted us here—even if it was just a temporary curiosity. Vern's a bit more complex than I gave him credit for, I guess."

Duke caught up to Ishiro.

"Oh yeah, and what about the kid, Ishiro? How can those priest blokes not tell us about another intelligent—or seemingly intelligent—race on this planet, assuming there's more than one little street rat running around." Duke's stream of consciousness rant continued. "And it goes without saying, I doubt there were really any astro-scientists that could provide guidance on the red space blob that brought us here. There's just not a damn thing that's made any sense since we arrived on this rock. And another thing—"

Ishiro halted and stopped Duke with an extended right arm. Without hesitation, Ol' Betsy was out of her Ootrelian home and into Duke's hands.

"Holy hedgehogs!" Duke cried as he gazed across the expanse of terrain before them. "Those sons of bitches."

The trees and foliage around the *Deus'* hiding place had been mown down with the delicacy of a blind bonsai tree caretaker.

"Be careful, Ishiro, they could still be lurking around here."

The two bounty hunters descended a shallow hill and onto the flattened patch of grass upon which, less than a day before, their ship had rested comfortably and out of sight. However, the *Deus* was nowhere to be found. Both men had their weapons drawn.

"This cut here is fresh," Duke said as he examined a brutishly hacked sapling.

His companion pointed at a grouping of footprints beyond the scene of spacecraft abduction.

"Ah, those sure look like Neprian flippers if you ask me.

And there seems to be a ton of 'em. All heading that way—over that hill east of here."

Ishiro'shea gestured beyond the hill.

"Good call. There's probably a way back to Dre'en around the wall. They could avoid running into us down the road back into the city. I guess we head that way and try to catch up with 'em, huh?"

The ninja glanced behind the bounty hunter. Duke swiveled around.

"No way, Ishiro. You're not trying to tell me that they somehow carried our ship through those woods, are you? I'm not buying it."

Ishiro shook his head. *Okay, he's frustrated. Man, of all the sidekicks in the universe, I had to pick the one that doesn't talk. Well, the one that still has his tongue and doesn't talk.* The ninja slapped Duke's shoulder to re-emphasize his observation.

"Okay, okay—what about the forest? Oh wait, I see it. Barely. I think. Okay, yes, I really do see it. Something's definitely flickering in that forest. Movement? You think it's some Neprian leftovers ready to ambush us?"

The ninja crouched down and focused intently on the edge of the forest, densely packed with alien flora.

"Probably just some bioluminescent forest critter," the bounty hunter said, kneeling beside Ishiro. "Maybe this will help. It's getting pretty dark now—not Keltian dark—but dark nonetheless."

Duke handed his compatriot a set of travel-size night vision binoculars from his belt. The ninja did a double take.

"I found them on the *Deus* right as we were about to leave. I thought that they might come in handy. You never know."

Ishiro'shea grabbed them and continued studying the wooded area.

"Anything?"

His partner did not provide any answer.

"I tell ya', Ishiro, I know you want to see what's out there—

and, believe me, so do I—but the *Deus* is *that* way." Duke pointed to the crest of the butte, east of their location. "We don't have time to explore this place. We gotta catch up to those ship-stealing priests and, unless we can ride that thing in the forest and chase down Vern, we need to get going. I mean, I know we're faster than an entire legion carrying the *Deus* and all—but they do have a nice head start."

Ishiro adjusted the vision enhancers to their maximum capability.

"C'mon, buddy, we need to go. And, it's not *that* dark to go max power on those things."

Duke paused for a moment.

"In fact, it seems like it just got a bit lighter? Or am I going crazy? Seriously, it's getting lighter out here. It can't already be morning and, if it is, this is the most rapid ascension of daylight in any planet beyond the Ecclox System. I hate that system; how Eccloxians don't have countless seizures from the frequent day-night transitions, I have no idea. Remember when we went there last time? I think the days were down to about forty-five seconds each."

Ishiro'shea removed the binoculars from his eyes and adjusted them meticulously.

"Yeah, you noticing it too? I guess they have early break-fasts here. I don't remember seeing this when we landed. Makes no difference, anyways—we need to head back, bud. We're losing precious time on the Neprian bastards. And I can't wait 'til I have a chance to bash their heads in."

"Your wait will be shorter than you think," shouted a familiar voice.

Duke and Ishiro'shea turned away from the forest to face eastward. Along the entire rim of the hill were a dozen Neprian priests, torches held high—this simulated sun illuminating the Neprian sky.

"But I don't like your chances," the voice continued.

"Oh hey, Vern! What's happening?" Duke responded,

hoping to throw off the Neprian by not acknowledging the precarious situation in which they found themselves. "Thanks for turning the lights on for us. It was starting to get a bit dark. But I do have a question."

"And what is that, Mr. LaGrange?"

"I seem to have misplaced my ship. Any idea on where it might be?"

"Humorous, Mr. LaGrange. Your ship is now en route to Orbius, the new owner of your interesting spacecraft. I'm afraid this is the end of the line for you," proclaimed Vernglet Wip with the wooden oration of a community theater flunkie.

"What gives, Vern? I thought we were buds—I mean, I also thought old Hoblet and Delix were too, and now Delix is a pile of Neprian goop on a curtain somewhere. You might need to get that hallway professionally cleaned, by the way."

"I figured something did not go as planned. I warned Hoblet and Delix that their plan was foolish. Regardless, Orbius demands this. I am truly sorry, my friends."

The Neprian priests widened their formation and encircled the duo. In almost perfect synchronization, they each attached their lit torches to the business end of their javelins. Their weapons dropped into kill position.

"Vern, not to be a nitpicker, but friends don't attack each other with fire-covered spears."

"Mr. LaGrange—"

"Seriously, what's going on here? I mean—if we are going to be skewered like shish kebabs, at least tell us why. We deserve that. You give us a place to rest, break bread and ploob kalarti with us—which was simply divine by the way— and then kill us? Why not kill us at the gate and take our ship?"

"Orbius has demanded it. He has seen enough from you. I cannot go against his wishes."

"So you *don't* agree with it? You kept us around to see if we were worth saving?"

"Mr. LaGrange, Orbius' will is final. You and Ishiro'shea must be destroyed."

"You really believe that, Vern? Do we look like we need to be destroyed? We are as good of dudes as you're ever going to see in this universe. Surely, you have to recognize that? And we are super fun at parties."

"There is no process for appeal, Duke. I am truly sorry. Maybe the Orb will grant us an opportunity to meet again in an afterlife."

"Sounds like a blast."

"Advance." The Neprian motioned and his squad of priestly warriors marched down the hill toward the bounty-hunting duo. Vernglet Wip disappeared behind the apex and out of view.

"Looks like this is going to happen, Ishiro. Do you think they realize that I've got a gun? Actually, two guns."

Ishiro gave a rapid shrug that constituted a chuckle.

"Going by Delix's sharpshooting expertise, I'm guessing not. This Orbius fella must not be all-knowing after all. Who sends in ten skinny clergymen armed with over-sized tooth-picks against Duke LaGrange?"

The Neprians progressed slowly towards them.

"Okay, stand back, Ishiro. Watch a master at work," Duke said confidently as he placed Betsy back in her holster and dropped his right hand to his side. His fingers twitched as he whispered to himself, "Wait for it—thirty paces out... twenty-five... twenty..."

With an unmatched fluidity, Duke rapidly pulled his laser revolver from his hip and rattled off eleven quick, powerful pulses. Eleven Neprian priests hit the ground—approximately nineteen paces from Duke LaGrange. Ishiro sheathed his katana.

"Where are you, Vern?" shouted Duke. "Come back! Is that all you got? Orbius isn't a god or a savior—he's a bona fide idiot for thinking a handful of priests could stop Duke LaGrange."

There was no response. Silence filled the air.

"I guess this means we go after him and get the *Deus* back?"

Ishiro concurred.

Now an even brighter light crept from behind the pinnacle of the mound to the east. An audible trembling was building steadily. Duke and Ishiro'shea exchanged inquisitive gazes. *This can't be good.* Flame-tipped javelins were first in view. Dozens. Hundreds. The numbers kept growing. Then the drawn and gaunt faces became visible, each set of eyes focused on the bounty-hunting duo. The group kept expanding and their numbers spilled out beyond the ridge to form a wide arc between the twosome and Dre'en. This was not Vernglet Wip and a gang of priests; this was a legion of Neprian Holy Warriors.

CHAPTER 14

CHANGE OF PLANS

FROM THE CENTER OF THE Neprian army emerged another priest adorned in a pewter-colored robe —a very different look to High Priest Vernglet Wip. In the torchlight, his skin matched the color of his attire and his eyes were bloodshot spheres of hate. The headgear atop his cranium was also grander than Vernglet's: greattu horns extended from the sides and multicolored streamers flowed in the breeze. He took a few steps to stand in front of his troops and held aloft a sword with a hilt of bones and a winding blade, half the length of the Neprian javelin. It appeared to be a timeless relic that had dished out its fair share of pain and suffering.

"Vernglet Wip is no longer here, nor is he any concern of yours, off-worlders," boomed a voice richer than that of any Neprian the duo had spoken to so far. "The great Orbius has grown tired of your presence. Your termination will now be enforced—something Vernglet Wip was incapable of performing."

"Tired of our presence? After a day? And we didn't even meet the guy?" shouted Duke. "Remind me not to vacation here next cycle."

"I'm glad that you find humor in your last moments of life, Duke LaGrange. May your laughter bring you comfort during your descent into the afterlife."

"Alrighty, big guy. If you say so. But if you recall, I just laid out some of your minions without as much of a thought—what makes you think that I won't do the same to you and your horde of toothpick-toters?"

The hulking Neprian priest laughed.

"I invite you to dispose of me and my legion, by all means, my off-world friend. Make the first move, Mr. LaGrange. But the subsequent move will be your immediate death."

The fingers on Duke's right hand twitched. His stare hardened. The Neprian's laughter increased in volume.

The bounty hunter pulled his laser revolver from his hip and directed a pulse at the leader of the warrior-priest gang. With an unnerving calm, the muscle-bound Neprian twisted slightly to the left. A soldier collapsed behind the colossal commander, falling face first into the soil with a gaping hole in his chest.

"Your aim seems to have failed you, Duke LaGrange," laughed the brute.

"It won't fail me again."

Duke extended his arm and pointed his gun at the commander once again.

"Attack, my legion, attack. Kill the two off-worlders!"

The seemingly infinite mob of Neprian priests surrounded their superior officer. Duke's next shot disappeared into the mass of charging warriors.

"For Orbius!" The bellow resonated from behind the enemy line. "You fail again, Duke LaGrange."

Ishiro'shea stood in attack position, bracing for the oncoming charge. Duke rattled off pulse after pulse, taking down one Neprian after another.

"Ishiro, they're getting closer and I'm not taking out nearly enough. Any ideas?"

The ninja tapped Duke on the shoulder.

"No way, Ishiro. They *want* to drive us into that forest. You saw the movement earlier—I guarantee that they got a few more uglies in there just waiting for us."

Ishiro seemed agitated. He gestured to the oncoming swarm, now so close that Duke could see the sunken features of their emaciated faces.

"We can take 'em. We've been in worse situations. Remember that one time..."

Neprian javelins filled the air. One of the golden rods struck the ground a single pace in front of the bounty hunter.

"Ok, you win. Change of plans, Ishiro. The forest it is!"

The bounty hunters turned and sprinted toward the dense foliage. The repeated sound of the Neprian spears hitting the soil continued to follow them.

"Damnit, how many of those things do they have?"

A javelin struck just to the right of the sprinting Nova Texan.

"Looks like we got another problem, little buddy," Duke said between deep breaths. "How do we get through this brush? Doesn't look like there's a way in."

Ishiro didn't answer but picked up his pace beyond Duke's ability to match. In a few moments he was three or four body lengths ahead of his companion. The ninja leapt in the air toward the opaque barrier of intertwined branches with his katana pointed skyward. His strike was quick and effortless; the martial artist landed without a sound. The wooded barricade split open, revealing a pathway just wide enough for the two bounty hunters to continue their retreat.

"Thanks, Ishiro. But one more thing..."

Duke stopped a few paces within the forest and let off a few rounds of his laser revolver at the overhanging foliage. Debris crumbled down and sealed the katana-hewn doorway.

"That should slow 'em down a bit. Let's go, we need to put

as much ground in between us and those skinny punks as we can."

They reduced their speed to a heavy jog as they navigated the unfamiliar forest. As they traveled deeper, the remaining light from overhead was swallowed up by the forest canopy.

"Listen, Ishiro," Duke said. He stopped. "Nothing. I don't hear a thing."

Ishiro'shea appeared to focus his auditory senses in order to confirm Duke's assessment.

"Did they give up? I don't hear a solitary branch cracking or a single voice. You know, I *should* be happy about this—but I keep thinking that there could be a reason they aren't following us. Maybe they drove us right into their trap?"

Ishiro unsheathed his blade. Duke pulled his laser revolver from its holster.

"Let's keep an eye out, little buddy. I have a bad feeling— again. Man, I really hate this planet."

Ishiro'shea knelt down and rummaged around a few fallen branches.

"Good idea, Ishiro. I'll cover you while you get us a torch going. I don't think we can go any farther without some light. I don't really want to hunker down now and wait until the morning; those priests might change their minds and follow us in here. But I don't think we can go down the path in the dark either—we'd be sitting ducks."

Soon a flame flickered at the ends of two sticks. Ishiro'shea handed one of the makeshift torches to Duke.

"Thanks. Okay, at least if we get ambushed, we'll see 'em. Gives us a fighting chance, right?"

A gust of wind hit both men in the face; darkness consumed them instantaneously. A heavy canvas screen knocked Duke and Ishiro'shea off their feet and flattened them against the forest floor. Their newly-created flashlights left their hands upon impact and returned to their wilderness home.

"Holy hedgehogs! Ishiro, you okay?" Duke asked in a muffled tone, pinned against the ground by the weighty net.

He didn't hear a response. *Definitely not a great time to have a partner that doesn't talk.*

Ishiro whistled. *Good.*

"Well, I'm glad we had those torches so we could prevent ourselves from walking into their trap, right?"

Duke soon realized it was a bad time for sarcasm.

CHAPTER 15

BLINDFOLDS

"HOW ABOUT TAKING THESE BLINDFOLDS off? I mean, you got us... you win."

Hushed tones and jumbled speech echoed around what Duke believed was a cave of some sort.

"Actually, scratch that request. I'm tired of looking at your ugly priestly mugs. It's bad enough that you morons captured us—I don't think I'm ready to see the smug look on your bony faces."

Their conversations continued to elude Duke's understanding.

"I guess I'm talking to myself here. Well, you guys should feel pretty tough. It only took a thousand of ya' to catch Ishiro and I—not very efficient if you ask me. Pretty piss-poor, in fact."

"Seriously, do you ever shut up?"

The response was tinged with genuine frustration, and sounded nothing like the Neprian voices to which Duke had grown accustomed during his time on the planet. Not even the big ugly warrior priest's.

"Oh, hey there. What's happening, friend?"

"I'm trying to find a gag for you. Your constant gibberish is going to give our position away. No prisoner is worth that!"

"You must be related to that oversized priest dude with the flamboyant hat."

"Why on Neprius would you think that I'm related to General Tsarano Gar?"

"You're the only ones with deep voices. All of your other brothers and sisters—wait, do you have sisters? I didn't see any. Anyways, all of your brothers sounded like puberty was a long-term goal. Kudos for not being a squeaky toy."

"See, I told you!" This new exclamation was a bit more alto than bass.

"Now that's what I'm used to," replied Duke. "Hey, Mr. Priest."

"I'm not a priest, you idiot! I'm a kid. And I'm not a 'mister.' This is how I'm supposed to sound."

"Whatever. Is that you, Vernglet? Hoblet? I know it's one of you lot."

"I told you, Po'l. Both things that I said. Number one—he is not on the side of Orbius. And number two—" The voice broke off into a whisper. "He's an idiot."

"Wait a damn second! Holy hedgehogs! You're that puny street varmint. I knew I was going to regret saving you."

"You didn't save me, off-worlder," cried the kid. "I had those Northerners where I wanted."

"Right. Can you at least take off these hoods now that you know we aren't in with the killer clergy?"

"Absolutely not," replied the deeper-voiced being. Duke assumed this was Po'l. "The Northerners have pulled off sneakier ruses than this, under the guidance of Orbius. You could be part of yet another elaborate setup."

"Po'l!" squeaked the kid.

"Sorry. I'm still going to recommend that we execute them —to be safe."

"We're not going to consider that option, Po'l." The voice was soft yet with a firm confidence.

Female.

"Hello, ma'am," interjected Duke. "My name is Duke LaGrange. Adventurer. Trailblazer. Poet. A true man of the universe. You, my lovely Neprian goddess, must be the leader of this band of warriors. Your speech is that of a leader and a visionary."

The creamy voice began again. "You know what? Maybe we do keep execution on the table."

"Thank you, Ja'a. This guy and his henchman add no value to our cause," exclaimed Po'l.

Ishiro'shea began to rustle in the cage.

"Calm down, Ishiro. You aren't a henchman."

"Po'l, I'm kidding," replied Ja'a. "To be honest, I'm quite impressed. I've never been hit on through a blindfold—by someone that hasn't even seen me."

"You can tell a lot from a voice, my beautiful belle."

"Mr. LaGrange, I said I was impressed—not stupid. Remove the hoods."

"Ja'a, you're acting irrationally. Kid, keep the hoods on!"

"Po'l, I know this is hard for you, but the leaders put me in charge of the capture and maintenance of these two peculiar aliens. Let me do my job."

"No worries, Miss Ja'a! See!" The kid had already removed the hoods, obviously ignoring the barking of Po'l.

Duke scanned his cage. *Primitive.* Then, the kid. *Yep, same little urchin.* Then, who he believed was Po'l. *Athletic, probably could handle himself in a brawl.* Then, Ja'a. *My senses haven't missed a step.*

"Thanks, kid. Well, hello, there. You have to admit, I was spot on about one thing. You're quite the sight to behold. Breathtaking."

Ja'a was slender and lean—but muscular. The exposed skin of her arms, midriff, and face were gently bronzed. Other than her ears—which were slightly too large for her head and shaped like tilted ovals—she looked exceptionally human. *Way better looking than those Hilterians at the bar.*

All three of them sported similar hairstyles; the sides of their heads were completely shaven and the hair that they did sport appeared to grow from a single circular pad on their cranium. The kid's hair was a stringy, discombobulated mess, matching her clothes. Po'l's darker hair was neatly groomed into a perfect circle, no hair longer than half a blade of grass. Ja'a's stretched beyond the back of her shoulders, wound in a tight ponytail—an attractive whip of dirty blonde sass. Of the three captors, she was the only wearing face paint—a silvery-blue pattern that stretched around each eye and continued around her head. The choice of cosmetics highlighted the steely crystal of her eyes. *Stunning.*

"We removed your blindfolds, but that's it. We still need to know who you are, where you come from, and why you're here —at this, undeniably suspicious, juncture in time."

"I'm Duke LaGrange. Adventurer—"

"Please stop. Please. If you say that again, I'll send you straight back to Gar and his men. I'm sure they'll have something a bit more *annoying* than our blindfolds."

The kid chuckled. As did Ishiro'shea.

"Ishiro? Really?"

"Ja'a, he *wants* to go back to Gar. Gar is his sworn master. I know misdirection when I see it."

Have you ever seen anyone cut their own head off? Now that's misdirection, thought Duke.

"I'm not sure they have anything more annoying than this guy!"

"Po'l, please be quiet. We need to see if Duke and his quiet friend provide any insight, or add any value for us."

"Okay, fine. My name *is* Duke LaGrange. This is my sidekick, Ishiro'shea. I'm not sure we have great answers for the rest of your questions."

"Why is that?"

"We were brought here by a giant space blob; a red astral anomaly just gobbled up our spaceship and deposited us neatly in an orbit around your gem of a planet."

"Interesting."

"The skinny priests said the same thing. I'm assuming y'all don't get along."

"For now, we'll ask the questions."

"Fair enough, all things considered."

"Yes, all things considered. So you were sent to Neprius against your will—and then what?"

"Ishiro and I parked our ship—which was stolen by those damn priests, by the way—and walked toward what we thought was civilization. We passed a few deserted villages—" Duke paused. "I'm assuming those are yours? Similar décor to this cave prison."

"Continue your story, Duke."

"Thanks for not calling me 'Mr. LaGrange.' So, we made it to the giant wall and that's where Vernglet Wip met us. He seemed like a good dude—odd, but good. He loved him some Orbius though. And crops. Never understood that. So, he invited us into the heart of Dre'en to meet with some Neprian scholars to help us find out about the weird star thingy that brought us here."

"Seems plausible."

"Ishiro and I were given a room and then we met Vern for a nice dinner. We didn't suspect any funny business."

A grunt came from behind Duke in the cell.

"Okay, I didn't suspect anything. Ishiro never felt good about the whole ordeal. We headed back to our room after dinner and heard some rumbling in the dining room, so we went to check it out. That's where we ran into your diminutive jailer over there being harassed by some Neprian thugs."

"Is that true?"

The female child nodded.

"She escaped and we bashed up some priests. When we made our way back up, our weapons were being stolen by two other pale-faces."

"Your weapons over there?" Ja'a pointed at Betsy, his laser revolver, and Ishiro's katana.

"You got it."

"How'd you survive? We noticed the destruction that these items caused on Gar and his troops."

"They're pretty rad, right? However, our buddy Delix didn't quite know how to use 'em. Betsy's pretty much a point-and-shoot firearm, but you really can't mess up the 'point' part if you're going to nail the 'shoot' half of the equation. Seeing his buddy splattered against the wall must've not sat right with Hoblet—so he vamoosed."

"Lies!" Po'l shouted. "He wants to make us seem like we can't figure out his magic weapon so we ask for his guidance—then he kills us, for Orbius."

"Her name is Betsy."

"You name this bringer of death? I knew it—they're sick, sadistic assassins."

"Po'l, let him finish."

"It was obvious that someone didn't want us here so we booked it back to the *Deus*—our ship."

"You guys sure like naming things."

"When we got there, it was gone. I'm assuming that Vern-glet and his priest friends jacked it. I don't know why, though. Or how. If they can't figure out a gun, good luck with a spaceship."

"It does seem odd. Maybe it was Orbius?"

"Whoever it was, my ship's gone. And before we know it, Vern and his buds surrounded us. I mowed some down with my other weapon."

"What's its name?"

"Actually, it doesn't have one."

"Pity."

"So Vern disappears and that ugly Gar pops up and tells us not to worry about Vern—which I wasn't because we had bigger fish to fry—and he brings out hundreds of his soldiers."

"Why didn't you just shoot Gar?" asked Po'l.

"I tried. But I missed."

"Wait, you blasted an entire group without missing—but can't hit a single target? And a huge target at that. I'm not buying it." He turned to Ja'a. "They're pulling one over on us—if he wanted to hit Gar, he would've."

"As hard as it is for me to admit this, I just flat missed."

"Mr. LaGrange—" Ja'a started.

"Oh great, we're back to 'Mr. LaGrange.' I thought we were making progress."

"I have to agree with Po'l. That part does seem far-fetched. Let's pretend you are telling the truth—continue."

"I *am* telling the truth."

"Go on."

"Gar's army rushed us with their spears and we ran into the forest. I felt we put some space between us and then BAM! We're here with you crazy cats."

"Complete garbage," raged Po'l. "I think this needs to be brought to the council. They'll side with me, I guarantee you, Ja'a."

"I think they can help us," replied Ja'a.

"Me too!" shouted the kid.

"You're both wrong. LaGrange is full of greattu dung. His friend can't even speak."

"You know we can hear you, right?"

"Yeah—and I don't really care. Please just shut up and start acting like a prisoner."

"Oh, Po'l, I think we got off on the wrong foot."

"Ja'a, let's just take their weapons and leave them to die. I can't handle this guy one second longer. I'm sure we can figure out how to use the weapons. I mean, they did—and look at them."

"You heard what he said—the priest tried and he exploded," said the kid.

"Lies."

"What if they aren't lies, Po'l? What if they are the only ones that can master them?"

"Ja'a, do you seriously believe that?"

"I don't know. But based on what we saw, they could be the tools we need to turn the tide against Orbius. It's worth the risk."

"Yeah!" screamed the kid, directly at Po'l. He sneered back.

"Hey guys," interjected Duke. "You think my guns are the secret to defeating Orbius and Gar and his armies?"

"Maybe."

"Y'all are crazy."

"*We're* crazy?" said Po'l.

"Let me rephrase that. Y'all are crazy but you, my good sir, are insane."

"And why is that?"

"Well, it's one thing to think two guns are going to win a war—even if I was operating them—but then to think that we blasted some dudes into their graves as part of some elaborate hoax to get in close with you... that's a whole new level of stupid."

"Exactly what I would expect you to say."

"Fine! Go use it. Shoot me and Ishiro. Do your best, Po'l!"

Ishiro'shea kicked Duke squarely in the back.

"No worries, Ishiro. He won't figure it out. In a few minutes, he'll be splattered against the wall like Delix—and then we won't have to listen to his dumb-ass conspiracy theories anymore."

Po'l flashed a smile at Duke. "Sounds like a plan to me—"

"Po'l, stop! Whether they're who you think they are—or who they say they are—we aren't going to try out their weapons. That is for the council to decide."

"I've had enough of this, Ja'a. I'm not sure whose team you're on—or why you'd side with this murderer and his mute lap dog."

"Po'l, be reasonable."

"You know what? You can stay here with these two, I'll head out and keep watch."

"We've got guys out there."

"Maybe they could use some company." Visibly frustrated, Po'l stormed out.

"Let 'em go, Ja'a," the kid begged. "He's wrong, I know it."

"I hope you're right. I really do."

"She is," interrupted Duke. "But tell me one thing."

"Yes?"

"What exactly are we trying to learn from you? Why are we supposedly playing this epic trick on y'all? Oh yeah, and why are you so pissed at Orbius? I mean, I know why I'm mad at 'em—they jacked my ship and tried to kill me."

"One thing?"

"Okay, maybe three."

"I'm not sure I'll tell you any of that—just in case."

"But Ja'a," the kid responded, "if they are spies working for Orbius—they know all of this."

"Good point."

"Wow, you're a wise little street varmint," commented the bounty hunter.

"Thanks."

"Do you have a name? Or just 'kid'?"

"It's Uu'k."

"Okay, 'kid' it is. So, what's the story here, Ja'a? What's the beef with Orbius?"

Ja'a sat down on a makeshift chair just outside of the pair's cage. Uu'k sat cross-legged to her left, seemingly eager for the yarn that was about to unfold.

CHAPTER 16

RUPTURED EARDRUMS

"I GUESS WE CAN START with the droughts. I remember it quite vividly. My family and I lived outside of Dre'en and, out of nowhere, the weather changed," Ja'a paused reflectively. "Crops began to die. Our villages suffered greatly."

"What caused it? What did your scientists say?"

"Scientists? We had no scientists. We're simple folk, Duke. We farmed—and farmed well. Or so we thought. We handled bad weather in the past but weren't able to figure it out this time. Food dried up and villages began to fight with each other over whatever scraps could be collected."

"Did it affect everyone? Or just the rural villages?"

"Most of us lived the same lifestyle. Even in Dre'en—though it was the center of our land—they ate from the same crops as our village and the hundreds of villages in southern Neprius."

"So, how'd you figure it out?"

"It was so bad that our leaders traveled across the land bridge that connects the north and south to talk with the Northern tribes."

"Northern tribes?"

"Yes, your priest friends. Those possessing the pale skin; they come from the northern land mass."

"I thought they controlled Dre'en? That place seems to be crawlin' with 'em."

"That was not always the case. In fact, until the droughts no Northerner had set foot in Dre'en for countless ages."

"I'm confused," said Duke.

"As I was saying, our leaders trekked northward to meet their high priests—and ask for aid and assistance. However, it was clear that their fate was no different than ours. The extreme weather had ravaged their lands with the same blatant disregard for life. When we arrived, they were welcomed by the council of the Northern tribe to try and solve the horrible situation that had fallen upon the whole of Neprius."

"Did the two sides not speak a lot?"

"No. After generations of warfare, the two tribes settled in different halves of Neprius and swore never to cross the land bridge. Both sides lived up to their end of the bargain; cycles and cycles of life came and went and we weren't even sure if they existed anymore. I'm sure they felt the same."

"Fascinating."

"You haven't heard the fascinating part yet, Duke!" shouted Uu'k.

"Uu'k, I'm getting to it."

"Sorry, Ja'a."

"Unfortunately, 'fascinating' carries a fairly negative connotation in this case. Unknown to most of us in the south and, my assumption, to most in the north, the histories of our two tribes were connected by a powerful source that was beyond our ability to grasp. Only a few leaders on our council knew the truth. To everyone else it was just a legend that you told children."

"Yep," Uu'k added.

"There was a hidden temple near the center of the land bridge," continued Ja'a, "guarded by clergy from both lands—it remained secret for millennia. These guards' lifelong duty was the concealment of this shrine and what was inside."

"I'm guessing this is the 'fascinating' part?"

"Yes, inside the temple was an Orb. An Orb that—"

"Must be respected and controls stuff, right? I've heard about it from Vern."

"In their words, they do refer to it as something like that. In ours, the Orb is referred to simply as Peace."

"Cute. I'm not much into round rocks determining the paths civilizations take. Seems like your people and those wacky nutjobs up north are a bit simple minded. A bunch of utter hogwash."

"Duke, I don't think you understand. This Orb is an ancient relic that, whether you want to believe it or not, helped to end the war between our two tribes. Its power was uncontrollable and unimaginable; both sides stole it from one another and caused more pain and suffering on themselves than their rivals. It led them to a treaty and thousands of cycles of peace. Both tribes decided to build a secure place to house Peace and closed off the land bridge from both sides. Of course this meant that our races would never be in contact with each other from that point on—but it was worth it to maintain a truce. The sheer unharnessed power of this arti-fact kept everyone grounded and put into perspective how puny we really are—and how the death and destruction caused by war over petty differences of opinions was senseless."

"Seems a little harsh. If you realized that, isn't that enough? Did you really have to separate the two tribes permanently?"

"I don't know but, for some reason, they did."

"So, what happened next regarding the dying crops and food shortage?"

"The leaders of both races were perplexed and lacked a solution. They ended up sending the High Priest of the North, his name was Jilarian Togg, and our Tribal Chief, He'j, to the temple and see if the Orb could help save Neprius."

"Did they just walk up and ask it to help? It's a flippin' rock."

"Duke, there is much that you don't know about Peace."

"Fine. Go on. But you're losing me."

"The story goes that He'j and Jilarian Togg retrieved the Orb and sat on the banks of the swamps around the temple for days. Nothing happened. And finally He'j grabbed the Orb and shook it—and shouted at the top of his lungs, 'Bring us someone or something that will make an impact on Neprius and rid us of our plight. Thousands will die of thirst and hunger if you don't help us, Peace. You did it once before— please, do it again. Bring us someone that will end this suffering.'"

"Inspiring. Did he have a speechwriter?" Duke directed this quip at Ishiro'shea, who did not return a chuckle.

"Maybe Po'l was right."

"My apologies. I promise I'll be quiet."

"I'm not sure you deserve the rest of the story, but I will continue."

"Thank you."

"Peace began to glow a bright purple, and tremble, and then hover above the two men. The swamp bubbled fero- ciously. The sky went completely black, with the exception of the Orb."

"Then what?" Duke asked, his interest reengaged.

"Then nothing."

"What?"

"Not for a few days at least. Just as He'j and his men were preparing to leave, reports from the north—near their capital of Sansagon—trickled in of a mysterious off-worlder. They brought him to meet with He'j and Togg. His name was Ot Vangu—of Earth."

"Ishiro, ever heard of him?"

The ninja shook his head.

"Figured. And that's why Vern was so squirrely when we mentioned Earth. What was Mr. Ot Vangu up to?"

"The Orb summoned him."

"Of course it did! You would think if a magic rock wants you to save the planet, it could've got him here a bit faster than a few days."

"Vangu couldn't explain it but it was clear that the Orb had brought him here."

"How were they so sure?"

"He was the person that He'j had asked for. His job back on his home world was to bring vegetation and crops to barren lands. He grew life from nothingness; he brought hope to Neprius. He saved us."

"So all was going so swimmingly. What happened?"

"Both tribes decided to elect Ot Vangu as supreme governor; he was wise and had no bias towards either race. He was a heaven-sent impartial leader."

"No such thing."

"I agree with you there, Duke. For Vangu learned of Peace and became obsessed with it—locking himself in a room for weeks and months and cycles. Both tribes became worried and tried to reason with Vangu. Somehow, during his time as leader of the two tribes, he discovered how to control the Orb—something thought to be impossible. He demanded that both tribes pledged their allegiance to him. High Priest Togg confronted him first—as the story goes, it was in the town square of Sansagon—and Vangu struck him down with one blast of light from Peace. Togg, a proud leader, died in the street as the other Northerners watched in awe. It was clear that the Northerners would not fight Ot Vangu. He gained his loyal followers almost immediately."

"And the Southern tribes? And He'j? Your people?"

"We fought Vangu for many cycles. We were no match for Peace—under Vangu's control, it killed many of my people.

We surrendered. Vangu was not kind to us for resisting and so we were enslaved. My entire race was sent to the mines to dig for stones for his palace; stones used as decoration. We slave and die underground for a frivolous cause—and Vangu just laughs at our peril. He made sure that we would not die honorable deaths."

"What happened to He'j?"

"He died at Vangu's hands. That is all we know."

"A corrupted warlord with a magic rock that enslaves farmers to dig for some home decor—well, it's a new one for Ishiro and I. So, I'm assuming you're part of some sort of ragtag rebellion?"

"Yes. Our numbers are small but not insignificant. The sad fact is that many would rather die in the mines in ten cycles than fight for freedom in one."

"Honey, that's most sentient races. Cowardice is not unique to Neprius."

"Vangu's forces continue to grow—the Northerners worship him as a god. In fact, Vangu and the Orb have become one to them and, thus, Orbius was born."

"I was about to ask about 'Orbius.' It's nothing more than Vangu rebranding himself, huh?"

"Yes. He's successfully taken over the entire planet. Dre'en fell to his followers quite easily and now the few left that oppose Orbius are scattered across the southern landmass. It makes it hard to organize; but we might have caught a break."

"And what's that?"

"You. More accurately, your weapons. They seem to be able to at least challenge Orbius."

"Ah. Yes. My weapons. As much as I love Ol' Betsy, I'm not sure they will be much help against a supernatural orb and its lunatic master."

"You might be right. After all, General Gar managed to elude death. However, maybe we'll be able to master your weapon at a level that you aren't able to achieve."

"You must be kidding, sister. That's as crazy as your story."

"The story isn't crazy. It's true," chimed in Uu'k. "You have to help us!"

"Uu'k, I'm not sure Mr. LaGrange and his friend have any interest in helping us. But maybe the fate that brought them here will be enough to make an impact through the usage of their armaments."

"Fate? It sounds like I got caught up in some of Orbius' manipulating-space-and-time practice sessions with his little magic ball. Not sure if that's fate or really bad luck."

"What's the difference?"

"Touché," replied Duke. "Just wonderful. I would have preferred my chances with Korzo-Tapor and the Robots. Right, Ish?"

The bounty hunter then turned his attention to the child. "Hey kid, you know all of this means that y'all are going to take our guns and leave us here to rot in this cage."

"Ja'a, no! You can't do that! They might be simple, but they did try and help me! I know they're good people that can help us."

"I wish I shared that same optimism, Uu'k."

"So, Ja'a, what if Ishiro and I agreed to help you?" Duke paused as Ishiro'shea kicked him in the back again. "We can help you take out some of the Northerners and get to Orbius. We can strike a deal. Hell, we have to get our ship back anyways to get home. I don't have time to wait around for your lot to invent space travel."

"I'm sorry, Duke. Your weapons are too powerful and we are too few in number. With what I have seen—the General Gar episode aside—if I give you the weapons, you can kill us too easily. There is nothing, outside of Uu'k's belief in you, that can make me agree to that. Our elder leaders maybe—but not me."

A loud scream permeated through the cave. A Southern

tribesman stumbled backward into the room and collapsed. He had a Neprian javelin lodged in his stomach.

"Ja'a! They found us!" screamed Po'l. "One down. We're outnumbered! Ten to one!"

Po'l let loose an arrow from his bow. It whizzed through the cave and out into the unknown.

"Hurry, Ja'a!"

A crackling of rapid-fire 'dings' filled the air as the pointed tips of Neprian javelins crashed against the stone exterior of the cave.

"Hey, guys. I have an idea!"

Ja'a and Po'l both looked back at the smiling bounty hunter.

"Shut up!" Po'l shouted. "Can't you see that we're under attack? I don't have time for your plans."

Another spear entered the opening of the cave hideaway and skipped across the rocky floor before coming to a stop near to the cage that held the two bounty hunters.

"Uu'k, go hide behind the cage! Okay, Duke. What do you got?"

"Seriously, Ja'a? Are you crazy?"

Another javelin whizzed by Po'l.

"Their aim's getting better, ya' know," smirked the Nova Texan.

"What do you propose, Duke? Make it fast!"

"Well, first off—make Po'l apologize."

Ishiro, for a third time, kicked Duke squarely between his shoulder blades. Duke responded with a laugh lacking anything resembling panic.

"What?" screamed Ja'a and Po'l in unison.

"You're insane!" continued Po'l.

"Give me my guns and this will all be over," Duke responded in a calm cadence.

"You just want those guns so you can escape."

"Partly—yes. I don't want to be killed in a cage on a primitive third-rate planet by some malnourished priests with really big needles—so escapin' has crossed my mind. It's kinda funny if you think about it."

"What is?"

"You're worried about us killing you if we escape—but if you would've never caught us, maybe they would've never tracked us here. So, either way—we killed you. Sorry, bud."

"Duke, I want to help you—but this is ridiculous."

"Ja'a, wait a second. Hear me out."

"Hurry, we don't have much time to hear you out," Ja'a responded.

"They're closing in," shouted another rebel from just outside the entryway. "We've taken a few out but we're running low on arrows. We didn't pack to fight off a full squad of Northerners."

"Duke?"

"Okay, you don't trust us, right? Give us a chance. Let us out—give us our weapons. We'll get y'all out of this jam. Or try to, at least. If we survive, we promise to go with you to meet your council and see if we can help your cause. We'll give you a chance to persuade us."

"That's it?" shouted Po'l. "You need us anyways."

"And why is that?"

"You don't know how to get to Orbius' fortress up north—where your ship is."

"True, but—"

"No 'buts'. He's useless, Ja'a. I'm going to end this."

"Slow down, Po'l."

Po'l headed over to a patch of dirt and stones along the inner wall. He kicked aside some of the chunkier rocks and picked up the Widowmaker sonic shotgun.

"Hey, get your hands off Betsy!"

"Or what?"

"Ja'a, look, you better warn him. This is not advisable. If we die here, not only do we, ya' know, *die* but our weapons end up in the hands of your enemies. Even if we ran out on ya', at least our guns'll run out on Orbius' minions too."

"I'm tired of this guy. I'm going to end it." Po'l examined Betsy. "Doesn't look too hard," he muttered. "This is how I saw that moron do it before."

"I can hear you."

"Something like this."

"Is that a question? Not a lot of confidence, huh?"

"Shut up!"

Po'l marched to the cave opening and pressed his back against the rigid wall. Veins protruded from his neck all the way down to his pectorals, which were visible above the rounded neckline of his chest plate. *Dude needs to chill. Never a good idea to operate a Widowmaker sonic shotgun when you're this tense.*

"I know what I'm doing. I'm not one of those Northerners."

Po'l held the gun and pointed it in the right direction. *Okay, he's one better than Delix.* Betsy's butt rested comfortably on his cheek.

"Yeah, I wouldn't hold it that way—"

The roar from Betsy filled every crack and crevice of the cave; the sound waves ricocheted like a pinball in a rubber-lined hallway. Debris fell within the dwelling; small pebbles doing their best impression of a light rain. Duke heard Uu'k's scream from behind his prison. *That had to rupture an eardrum—assuming they have eardrums in those giant head flippers they're sporting. Poor kid.*

Then silence. The athletically-built Neprian rebel lay halfway between the entryway and the makeshift jail cell —motionless.

"What happened in there?" a watchman shouted from just outside the cave. "Tell Po'l to fire again! All he hit was a tree! They're preparing another volley!"

Ja'a slid to where Po'l's body had been launched after his ill-advised handling of Betsy.

"Po'l! Are you alive? Answer me! Please!"

She shook him—no response.

"Uu'k, get me some water. Quickly, child."

Uu'k ran and grabbed a leather pouch and filled it with water. She delivered it to Ja'a, cupping her hand over one ear. *Yep, ruptured. Dumb-ass, Po'l.*

"Is he alive, Ja'a?"

"I don't know. I think so. Answer me, Po'l!"

She lifted his face. One side was completely blackened and seared by the gun; blood flowed steadily from the left side of his mouth. His eyes remained closed, already morphed into deep purple mounds of swelling.

The familiar sounds of Neprian javelin tips hitting the façade returned. The rebel fighters retreated to the confines of their bunker.

"What are you doing? We can't let them in here!"

"Ja'a, we can't hold them off out there. They're picking us off one by one. There's too many."

"What are you saying?"

"Look, Ja'a—we're beat. We have no chance. Let's have our stand and take out as many of those bastards as possible."

"Heroic," smirked Duke.

"No time for your quips! We probably have a few minutes before those priests are on top of us. How many are left?"

"We took out a good number. So, maybe twenty or thirty."

"How many do we have? Just everyone in here?"

"Afraid so."

Po'l moaned.

"He's alive! Uu'k, get some more water! Uu'k? Where are you? Uu'k!"

Two more javelins bounced into the cave.

"Help me move him!"

Ja'a and one of the watchmen helped drag Po'l to the side

and propped him up alongside the walls as he continued to unleash wails of agony.

"Okay, grab your arrows—let's pick them off as they make their way in. One at a time. When we're out of arrows, we'll fight at close quarters. Just like we trained. Understand?"

"Yes, Ja'a!" the soldiers replied in harmony.

"Let's make sure Orbius and his brainwashed lackeys remember us this day."

The five Neprian rebels formed a wall a few paces from the opening. They readied their bows.

"Don't waste a shot—let's drop them all!"

"Where do you want me? Betsy doesn't like hanging out in the back, ya' know."

The bounty hunter stood behind the line with his beloved firearm resting on his shoulder, propped up by his left arm. In his right hand he held his laser revolver. Ishiro'shea stood a step behind him to the right, his sword in attack position.

"How—"

"Ja'a, no worries. We'll take care of this."

"But how—"

Ja'a turned back to face their prisoners' recent residency.

"Uu'k! How could you? How *did* you?"

"Please don't be mad, Ja'a. The keys flew off of Po'l when he tried to use Duke's weapon. I just picked 'em up and let 'em out. I know Duke and Ishiro will help us. I trust them. I just know it!"

"Smart kid."

"They're about to penetrate," shouted a rebel solider, turning the line's attention back to the battlefront.

"No worries."

"So you said," retorted Ja'a.

The first shadow crept across the cave floor—gaunt, emaciated, and possessing an elongated instrument of puncturing prowess. In a fluid dance of muscle memory, Duke sheathed his revolver, transferred Betsy to his right hand, and lined up his shot. She let off a scream of epic magnitude. As quickly as it appeared, the Neprian shadow was no more. Betsy returned to her Ootrelian home.

"Ishiro, that should be enough confusion to take these stooges out. Let's do it."

The two bounty hunters entered the cloud of smoke caused by Betsy's blast, Duke with laser revolver drawn, Ishiro'shea with katana at the ready.

"Goodbye..."

"See ya'..."

"Can't run, buddy," Duke shouted as he rattled off pulses from the laser revolver.

His laughter cut through the gunshots.

"How many is that, little buddy? Twelve? Fifteen? Oh, don't run away, guys. We're just starting to have fun!"

Duke returned to the cave; five Neprians looked at him with stares comprised of equal parts thanks and concern.

"Well, guys, like I was saying—no worries!"

"Thank you," said Ja'a in a tone of disbelief. "We are truly in your debt."

"Even Po'l?"

"Yes, I'm sure Po'l won't question what you did for us today. You saved our lives. I am sorry for doubting your intentions. Please forgive us."

"It was nothing. Okay, it was *something*." He bowed as he accepted their praise. "By the way, Ishiro, sorry that I didn't let any more of 'em make it up here. I know you wanted a piece, too. How many did I get? Twenty?"

Duke turned to face his companion. In place of his emerald-clad ninja friend stood a Neprian priest warrior, battered and bloodied. Hate and revenge filled his pupil-less eyes and a javelin filled his hand—a javelin aimed directly at Duke.

"Not if I get you first," Duke muttered to himself as he reached for his laser revolver.

He did not get the shot off.

The Neprian fell to the cave floor. Ishiro'shea stood next to the corpse, a bloody katana at his side.

"Thanks, Ishiro. I should've known that you'd get yours somehow."

Duke pivoted and faced the Neprian rebels again but his eyes skimmed past their collected gazes.

"Oh yeah, most importantly... Thank you, ya' little street urchin."

CHAPTER 17

MR. SHARPSHOOTER

"I DON'T SEE ANY," SHOUTED one of the rebel watchmen.

"Yeah, but some got away," replied the Nova Texan from the entrance of the cave.

"So?" yelled another rebel, checking for stragglers in the foliage outside of the rebel camp.

Duke shook his head slowly and turned to Ja'a, who was tending to the slowly recovering Po'l.

"Your team— Well, they ain't the smartest, huh?"

"They have heart."

"That organ will put you in some pretty precarious situations if you let it."

"Duke, I fully agree with you—we don't have much time before they come back with an even larger army. And possibly General Gar."

"Bring that jackass on. I'll finish him for good," Duke replied, seething.

Ishiro'shea slapped Duke on the shoulder and kept his hand clamped there in a comforting manner.

"Thanks, bud. I'm just pissed. None of this woulda' happened had I not missed that jerk."

Ishiro repeated his gesture.

"I guess there's only one thing to do now. Pack up and head out."

"And where are you and Ishiro'shea heading?," Ja'a asked. "Though I do hope you consider joining us, I have no right to object. You've truly earned your freedom."

"Even though it took the kid over there to trust me enough to let us out, I'm still going to hold up my side of the bargain. I'll stop by and chat with your leaders; you know what we can do and you know how to get to my ship. Seems an arrangement could be in the cards."

"Thank you, Duke. I do appreciate it."

"That's very kind of you, Ja'a. I don't usually have beautiful creatures like you appreciating me—" Duke paused momentarily. "—except for... ya' know. I mean, I've been known to—"

The bounty hunter was interrupted by the faint garbled cries of Po'l.

"Oh yeah, you. I forgot about you," Duke paused. "And it was glorious," he finished.

"He does add a bit of a wrinkle into our plan of a speedy exit," started Ja'a. "I don't think we have time to build a vessel to drag him."

"Definitely not. Let's leave him."

"Duke! No!" shrieked Uu'k. Ishiro'shea had made his way over to the young Neprian and was doing his best to tend to her bloody ear. "I know Po'l can be mean sometimes, but you can't leave him!"

"Oh, alright."

"I knew it. I knew you wouldn't leave anyone behind," Uu'k said through a giant smile.

"Settle down, kid. We still don't know how we can get 'Mr. Sharpshooter' outta here."

"I'm fine," mumbled Po'l. "Let me up."

"Po'l, take it easy. We'll figure something out."

The Neprian rebel started to lift himself up with the aid of Ja'a.

"Quick, guys. Help me with him."

The other two rebel soldiers in the cave flanked the injured Po'l; he draped his arms behind each of their necks for stability.

"You two think you can get him down to the forest and then keep up with us?"

"We're going to try," said the soldier supporting Po'l's right side.

"Or die trying," whispered Duke to himself.

Ja'a stared at the bounty hunter, clearly having heard his less-than-optimistic retort.

Duke decided to change the subject. "So, how long of a trip is this to see the brains of your operation?"

"A few days, maybe more—depending on whether the planet cooperates with us. We have to travel northwest and trek through most of the southern lands until we reach the coastline just below the land bridge."

"Great. Not to be a downer but, since Ishiro and I've been here, we haven't had the best 'cooperation' from this rock. What are you expectin', Ja'a? More priesties? Scary monsters? Avalanches and cyclones? Giant fire-breathing flying panthers?"

"Oh, I didn't know that you were aware of the grundar."

"Huh?"

"Not many Neprians that grew up on the southern land-mass have ever seen a grundar in the wild; they are native to the northern lands. They're quite ferocious. Most that do see them don't live to speak of their unique observation."

"What are you talking about? What's a grundar?"

"Giant fire-breathing flying panthers. Like you said."

"Did I ever tell you how much I hate this place?"

"The likelihood that we encounter a grundar is slim—there

are so many other annoyances that I'm more concerned about. Most notably, Gar's henchmen."

"Speaking of those smelly punks, we better pick up the pace," Duke reminded the team.

The other two watchmen returned to the cave. Ja'a tossed them their ration bags and some additional arrows.

"Te'o and Ma'n are going to carry Po'l for the first leg of our journey back to the coast. You'll need to carry their bags. We can swap out every few hours."

"Yes, Ja'a," they spoke in concert as they each plucked a second ration bag from the air.

"I don't need their help. I'm fine. Let me walk," Po'l muttered. His words trailed off and mutated into an aching groan. "Where's my sword?"

The tall Nova Texan stepped in front of the two soldiers propping up Po'l. He hunched over slightly and placed his face as close to the injured Neprian's without it actually touching.

"I know you don't like me," Duke whispered, "or trust me. I'm not sure why especially, since I just saved your collective asses. If it was up to me, I'd leave your sorry carcass in this cave to be eaten alive by who knows what horrors live in this forest —but Ja'a and the kid, for whatever reason, want to save you. So, if you would keep the moaning and complaining down to a minimum, it would be much appreciated. If not, I can always give you another go-round with Betsy. You have a whole other side of your face to cave in with your excellent gunmanship."

"Don't lecture me, off-worlder," Po'l countered. "Even if you aren't working for Orbius, that doesn't mean I have to trust you." He pulled one arm from around the neck of the soldier and wiped away some spittle, sprinkled with droplets of blood, from his lip. "In fact, I don't. I don't know your endgame and whether Orbius is involved or not, but I get the sense that you'll screw us over without hesitation to get what you want, regardless."

"Maybe so. But what choice do you have? You need me."

"We don't need you," Po'l said between coughing episodes. "We've been doing just fine without you."

"Oh, you have? Okay, so you got Orbius under control. Let me say, Po'l, you guys do a pretty bang-up job of making it look like you're runnin' around with your heads cut off."

"How are you going to find your ship though? It's probably at Orbius' palace right now."

"Ishiro and I can head north and I feel confident that we can persuade a few folks to point us in the right direction." Duke tapped his right hand against his holster.

"Scaring innocent villagers and threatening them with a weapon? You're such a swell guy. And Orbius is just going to give the ship to you? Why? Because you're such a likable person?"

"And I *need* your band of nitwits with your bows and arrows? *That's* going to help us?" Duke's voice raised from his earlier hushed tones.

"This planet will eat you alive, Duke. And your silent friend."

"Leave Ishiro outta this. What's your real beef with me, Po'l? First, you accuse us of being really committed spies—"

"I don't like you," Pol' interjected.

"Didn't your momma teach you not to interrupt?"

Ja'a wedged her arm between the faces of the two rivals. "Po'l, you are in no position to argue. Duke saved our lives—whether you care to admit it or not. Plus, you're only slowing your healing by bickering. You need to rest. We need you in this fight."

"Yeah, Po'l—listen to your boss," Duke jabbed. "Except for that 'needing' you bit."

"Duke, in all due respect and knowing that we are in your debt for your heroics earlier, Po'l is a great warrior and has been loyal to our cause for a long time. It's important for us—to me—to get him back to our leaders safely. I don't blame his distrust, though I can't say that I ever thought you were a pawn in Orbius' game. The truth is, you *are* an off-worlder and an outsider to our cause. I would be suspicious if he *did* trust you without hesitation."

Po'l managed a wry grin.

"You believe this?" Duke aimed his question firmly at Ishiro'shea.

The ninja returned a glance that Duke knew all too well. *Dammit, he agrees with her.*

"For the last time, we must make haste before we are consumed by Gar and his troops. Those that fled are probably back now and letting Gar know where we're holed up."

Ja'a exited the cave, followed by the two soldiers carrying Ma'n and Te'o's satchels, then Uu'k and Ishiro'shea. Duke stepped to the side and allowed Ma'n and Te'o—with Po'l balanced between them—to leave next. Po'l struggled to keep his head raised; his swollen eyes never left Ja'a as she led the group into the Neprian forest. *Wait a second! He's got a thing for her,* Duke thought to himself. *How'd I miss that? In love with his commander—maybe that's why he's so surly. Can't say I blame him. Whoa, be careful now, Duke.*

Duke descended the natural ramp that led from the cave. He unsheathed Ol' Betsy as he watched the rebels and Ishiro'shea disappear into the opaque Neprian vegetation.

CHAPTER 18

UU'K'S DAY JOB

AS FAR AS DUKE COULD see, sloping grasslands intermingled with abandoned plots of farmland—a far cry from the dense forest that concealed their cave hideaway south of Dre'en. Beautifully translucent ponds dotted the countryside; the stillness gave them the presence of being frozen. Outside of a gentle breeze, basic movement in the southern Neprian ecosystem seemed as if it were an extinct species. Duke couldn't help but feel as if he were walking from one end of a two-dimensional painting to the other.

"This has been quite a boring stroll."

"Boring is good, Duke," replied Ja'a. "That means that we haven't run across Orbius' soldiers or anything else that this country can throw at us."

"You're probably right."

"I know I am on this one. It's been two days and nothing—that's a good two days in my book."

"It's funny if you think about it."

"What's that?"

"Two days ago, you had Ishiro and I cooped up in a cage and thinking we were Orbius' spies."

"Is that why you've been avoiding me? Still upset about that?" asked Ja'a.

Duke tilted the front of his hat up with his thumb.

"No, Ishiro and I were just getting our bearings and, ya' know, taking in this beautiful scenery," he smirked.

"Well, I never thought you two were spies," Ja'a said with a subtle smile. "That was Po'l. But, *ya' know*, you can't blame him."

Duke snorted at Ja'a's gentle mocking, then he flashed a far less subtle smile at the Neprian.

"Oh, I *can* blame him. You aren't entirely without blame, yourself. I didn't see you trying *that* hard to convince your underlings to free us. Thank goodness for Uu'k. You had us locked up—and now you need us to help you. Heck, you need us to help your entire race."

"That's a tad dramatic."

"I don't know."

"Anyways, Duke, we're actually interested in your weapons—you are just an added complexity."

"Don't you mean an added 'benefit'?"

"I know what I mean."

The bounty hunter chuckled. "You're alright, Ja'a."

"I'm not quite sure about you, Duke. You've already had a few moments that lead me to believe that you could be this planet's savior or the final nail in our coffin. I just don't know quite yet."

"So, if I'm hearing you correctly—you think I'm pretty extraordinary."

"For now, let's call it 'interesting.'"

"Fair enough. Not to change the subject—because I *do* love talking about my favorite subject—"

"You?"

"Yes, me. But look over there."

Duke pointed to Ishiro'shea. "Seems that Ishiro and Uu'k are becoming buds."

"That's nice to see. She could use a friend. You know, Uu'k has been quite a valuable asset in the rebellion."

"You're kidding, right?"

"No, not at all."

"You mean because she freed Ishiro'shea and I—and we're gonna save the day?"

"Uu'k has been one of our best sources of local intelligence from inside Dre'en—specifically around the halls of the Altar House. Isn't that where you found her?"

"Close to it. She was near the kitchen in a dining hall. Ishiro and I had just had dinner with Vernglet Wip."

"She was under their employment—or rather, she was being forced to perform menial tasks like cleaning and preparing food."

"She's only a kid, though. How does—"

"Duke, I promise you, she volunteered. Her parents did not survive Orbius' wrath and she wanted to contribute."

"She's a kid."

"No one ever wants to be in a war. No one ever wants a child to be involved in that conflict, especially. Uu'k is special, though. I believe she actually fully grasps the entire concept of what's happening to her people—and knows that she has to sacrifice to have a chance to restore happiness and prosperity to Neprius."

"Ja'a, this is hard for me to swallow. And I've had a Mecha-Burger 8000."

"Ask her. Talk to her. She's an amazing kid."

"Where I come from, we do our damnedest to keep children out of harm and away from violence. We leave that for the grown-ups."

"Have you ever had to save your race from a mad, murderous tyrant?"

"Nova Texas has too many of those to count."

"Seriously, Duke. Our struggle needs every bit of help that we can muster."

"Even if it means putting a good kid like Uu'k's life in danger by spying on insane priests?"

"Yes, even if it means that."

"Ja'a, your methods are unusual—even for me. I do commend the commitment. If you say that Uu'k fully comprehends the likelihood of a violent and grizzly death, I believe you. You haven't lied to me yet. But, wow, what a day job for that little runt."

"Duke, don't take my word for it. Talk to her. Or talk to Ishiro—I'm sure he knows her story by now. It's been two days and I haven't seen her stop talking to him."

"And we know Ishiro's not hogging the conversation."

"True."

"I guess, at the end of the day, looking at it from a practical and functional standpoint—no one would suspect her of being anything more than a kid. Fooled me, that's for sure."

"She was the one that alerted us about you."

"That weasel! She led us into the cage—and freed us. Door-to-door service, I guess."

"We heard about an off-worlder—it had been some time since the last one."

"Vangu."

"Yes, Vangu. And we know how that turned out. We'd heard whispers from our network of sympathizers that a large metal vessel had crashed somewhere near Dre'en. Naturally, we assumed that Orbius had found a way to bring more evildoers from his home world to help him control the rebellion."

"Naturally. Lots of evildoers on Earth."

"We sent out a message to our local spies in and around Dre'en—but no one could get close. I knew Uu'k and her location at the Altar House. I guessed that if Vernglet Wip came out to meet you, he would probably get you to his compound as quickly as possible. I relayed the message through our runner network from where I was stationed south of the city and, luckily, it made it to Uu'k uninterrupted."

"I only saw her for a second—her information couldn't have been that in-depth."

"She has a knack for hearing things that shouldn't be heard. In fact, she let us know that the priests were planning to trick you and abduct your weapons."

"How did the priests recognize my guns? There's nothing on this rock remotely similar."

"Their communication network runs as fast as ours. Probably faster. The Northerners use winged flurn to carry messages over great distances."

"Orbius?"

"That was our thought. We can only assume that they used winged flurn to transport the message all the way to Sansagon—a method we ourselves are trying to master. If he was interested in these items, they must be important."

"And I bet that once we stepped off the *Deus*, accounts of our appearances made it all the way to Orbius and back before we made it to the gates of Dre'en. Vangu must've recognized the descriptions of the guns."

"That's our assumption as well."

"Sneaky troll."

"Uu'k gathered intelligence that day and uncovered a plan to steal what the priests called 'tools of monstrous calamity.' She quickly relayed the message down the network but, by the time it made it to me, you and Ishiro'shea were already heading southbound. A band of us, stationed near your crash site—"

"Landing site. I didn't crash the *Deus*. Duke LaGrange doesn't crash ships."

"—near your landing site, then, moved to the forest where we met you."

"Met? Not the word that I would've used."

"We scouted you and waited to assess the situation."

"We saw you moving about in the forest. Or rather, Ishiro saw you."

"Good eyes. Then before we were able to press on and

introduce ourselves—and offer sanctuary, Vernglet and his troops moved in." She paused. "And then we saw them fall with a thunderous clap. Dead. Immediately, we knew what Orbius was referring to as 'tools of monstrous calamity.' Po'l wanted to charge—but I held us back since I didn't know if you would think that we were friend or foe."

"Smart move."

"When we collected ourselves enough to create a sensible plan, General Gar had appeared with his legion. The rest was a bit of luck."

"For who?"

"Both of us, really. When you and Ishiro'shea started to head toward the forest, our team quickly relocated our snare trap—and, once again by luck, you ran right into it. Lucky for us that we now have the services of someone who could provide a serious advantage over Orbius; lucky for you and Ishiro that you weren't hunted down and murdered by Gar's troops."

"This is assuming that we actually get back to the *Deus*, get rid of Orbius, and get off of this planet."

"I hope those aren't doubts, Duke LaGrange."

"Let's call them 'concerns' for now." Duke grinned and removed Betsy from his holster. He stroked the barrel and patted it gently. "Forget I said anything. I can win a war with this old girl."

"That's what we're banking on."

CHAPTER 19

IF A PERSON HAS A SWORD, DON'T CALL HIM STUPID

"THIS SEEMS LIKE A GOOD place to set up camp," Ja'a said.

The land had hardly changed over the course of the day's march. As the evening approached, an unnerving calm continued to reign over the Neprian landscape. Aside from a gentle hill—the lone grassy mound alongside the level prairie path—it appeared no different than the previous dozens of miles.

"I agree," said Po'l. "Don't anticipate much danger lurking around these parts."

"No offense," Duke replied, "but the most dangerous part of this trip has been the stench coming from 'Mr. Sharpshooter' over there." He nodded in Po'l's general direction.

"What does that even mean?"

"Never mind. But seriously, can we give our friend Po'l a bath tonight? I think I saw a pond a few clicks back."

"Duke—"

"Fine. If you don't mind though, I think I'm going to camp up ahead at the edge of the hill. Your watchmen over there can take a turn being downwind from our fragrantly-challenged friend."

Duke walked up to Ma'n and Te'o, who were still propping up the banged-up Po'l.

"Guys, I feel for ya'—I really do. I've been in the drunk tank at Cyborg Joe's when the toilet broke—for two days—and it wasn't this bad."

"You're lucky that I'm not at my best right now, off-worlder," Po'l snapped back.

"What, so you can hurt yourself again? I don't even have to lift a finger with you, Po'l—you knock yourself out."

"Both of you, cool it." Ja'a interjected before Po'l dared a comeback. "Actually, here's an idea—it's about time to rotate positions. Fresh eyes up front and on the flanks; weary legs in the middle. We're probably halfway to the coast. Halfway to meeting with the leaders."

"And to figure out how Ishiro and I get the *Deus* back," added Duke.

"Of course." Ja'a walked a few paces away from the convoy. "Everyone! Let's call it a day and get some rest."

The entire group save the watchmen came to a stop.

"We're going to shuffle it around now before our final stretch," she shouted. "Everyone's doing great."

Ja'a motioned to Ma'n and Te'o, indicating Po'l. "Guys, can you help him down?"

"Bet you're pretty happy about that, huh?" Duke directed his snippy query at Ma'n and Te'o.

They did not respond.

"Enough, Duke."

"I'm fine, Te'o!" huffed Po'l as he pushed away his fellow rebel. "I don't need your help anymore."

"Don't be ridiculous. You need to rest up. We've got a long way to go before we get to Orbius. We need you—not a shell of you."

"Ja'a, I'm fine. I might be a bit slow when we start again— but I don't need anyone else holding me up. Ma'n, Te'o—

thanks, but I can't ask you to do any more than you already have. I'll heal in due time, being carried or not."

"I don't know how I feel about this, Po'l."

"I'm fine."

"Okay, so you can hang in the middle tomorrow with Ishiro'shea. If you need assistance, I feel better having Ishiro'shea near you."

"I don't need anything from that masked goon who's too ignorant to even speak. He's like an untrained pet."

"Looks like you *do* need him, actually," Duke said.

"What?" Po'l responded.

"Turn around, genius."

Po'l about-faced and his nose nicked the edge of Ishiro's katana—drawn in utter silence and ready to decapitate the Neprian rebel.

"You can't hear on account of having taken a sonic boom from Betsy right in the kisser, you can't walk, you definitely can't defend yourself—I think you *need* all the help you can get," Duke said. "Starting with the fact that you *need* Ishiro to *not* cut your head off."

"Lower your sword," Po'l commanded.

Ishiro'shea did not budge.

"He doesn't like you," Duke sneered.

"Lower your sword."

"Po'l, not sure if you're hazy or what—but we aren't exactly your prisoners anymore. No rinky-dink cage separating us from you. You need to apologize."

"That's not going to happen, off-worlder."

"So proud. But so dumb."

"He's sorry," chimed Ja'a, but Ishiro'shea remained steady.

"Not good enough, I'm afraid. When you insult an Irish-Japanese ninja of the cachet and standing of Ishiro'shea—he was Salutatorian, you know—you can't expect him just to lower his blade because some pretty girl asks him to. Po'l's slanderous jab insulted Ishiro's honor—he's sliced folks in twenty neatly cut ribbons for far less than what your colleague did."

Po'l and Ishiro continued to lock eyes. Pol's brash self-assurance slowly became something resembling panic—or at the least, anxiety. *He knows Ishiro means business.*

"Fine, I'm sorry."

"You're sorry—about what?"

"I'm sorry that I called you ignorant."

"Because you know—what?"

"I know—I know." Po'l searched for the words.

"C'mon, Po'l. You can do it, buddy."

"I know that you are actually quite intelligent."

"Not bad," commended Duke. "So, Ishiro—is it enough? Or should we make him grovel a bit more?"

"Duke, please," Ja'a begged. "Enough. Stop this. You made your point."

The ninja lowered his katana. Ishiro and Duke exchanged glances and then cackles.

"Not funny at all," Ja'a steamed.

"Sorry. 'Mr. Sharpshooter' needed to be taught a valuable lesson."

"And what's that?" Po'l inquired with a tone of annoyance.

"If a person has a sword, don't call him stupid."

The bruises on Po'l's face turned from dark violet to a shining red, signaling his embarrassment. *It's amazing that embarrassment looks the same on so many worlds and with so many species,* Duke pondered.

"Let's change positions before it gets too dark," Ja'a said. "Like I was saying before, Po'l, you stay in the middle until you get your strength—Ishiro'shea will move from the right flank and join you. Ma'n, you take the right flank—where Ishiro'shea was. Te'o, you grab the left flank, where I was. Duke, you can replace Ty'n and Bu'r and be our scout. They'll replace you in the rear."

"Aye, aye captain!" Duke quipped as he performed a half-hearted salute.

"Let's hope they do a better job than you."

"Hey now, you enjoyed my company. Admit it."

"What about me?" squeaked Uu'k.

"Uu'k, you stay by Ishiro'shea, please. In the center. With Po'l too."

"Not a problem, Ja'a. I like Ishiro. He's a good listener."

"Hey, what am I? Erontian Camelcat liver?" Duke whined.

"Duke, no offense, but you're more my 'small doses' friend."

Po'l erupted into laughter.

"Okay, I guess I can't argue with that," replied Duke.

The tension seemed to ease a bit.

"Ma'n, Te'o," Ja'a continued, "take your bows and be on alert. I want you to extend our flank a bit. I know it's been smooth sailing thus far but I want to make sure nothing slows us down before the coast."

"Yes. We'll camp out in our new positions tonight."

"Told you that they wanted away from Po'l and his cloud o' funk."

Ignoring Duke, Ja'a shouted, "Bu'r! Ty'n!" She turned. "That's odd, I only see Ty'n. Duke, I might need you to go up ahead and relay the message to them that we're going to rotate."

"Aye, aye captain... again."

Ishiro'shea slapped Duke on the back. *Fine, I'll stop.*

The skinnier of the two watchmen on scout duty came sprinting back. "Ja'a! I came running as soon as I heard your voice."

"Where's Bu'r?"

"He's up ahead. We're close to his old village; he wanted to see if it was still standing."

"He doesn't know if it was taken over by Orbius?"

"No, he left to join up before they made it out this way. It could've avoided their control—it's a good ways away from any other village."

"It *would* be a nice place to rest—a true rest," Ja'a said, thinking aloud.

"And real food!" shouted Ma'n.

"Yes, that would be quite nice."

"Maybe some ploob kalarti," Duke said hopefully.

"He should be back anytime," Ty'n continued. "He said he was only going to check out a few miles ahead. Then again, that was a good while ago. Regardless, once he sees that I'm not at the post, he'll come back here."

"So not every village is under Orbius' control?" asked the bounty hunter.

"We don't know, Duke. There could be some that survived but they would likely be quite remote. We've been trying to find holdouts to help our recruiting efforts and strengthen our numbers. We just don't have the manpower and resources to engage in battles for every town to land a few able-bodied soldiers."

"But if one was entirely free of Orbius, you'd get supporters without any bloodshed."

"Exactly."

A few moments passed.

"There's Bu'r!" exclaimed Ty'n, pointing beyond the grassy hill.

"He looks excited," Uu'k noticed.

"Or scared," commented Duke.

Bu'r was muscular and broad shouldered—bigger than Po'l but not as athletic in appearance. He was barrel-chested but his bulbous stomach extended beyond his belt. He was the only rebel that Duke had seen that did not sport any hair atop his head—it was completely shaven. He did make up for this lack, though: he sported a well-trimmed beard that extended from each ear to just before his chin. His chin was bare save for a thin patch of hair that extended from the direct center of his bottom lip to the midway point of his throat. *Maybe it's a regional look.*

"He can run for a big boy, huh?"

The hearty-statured rebel decelerated as he approached. "I saw it!" he huffed, out of breath.

"Your village?"

"Yes, Ja'a. Only a few miles away. I know we can help them."

"So, they've been controlled?" asked Ty'n.

"The village was dead but I saw movement around the entrance to the mines. They have to be digging for Orbius' precious mustangsen."

"Mustangsen?"

"The decorative stones that Orbius hoards at his palace in the north. He has our entire village performing these vanity tasks to prove how powerful he is—it's how he controls us."

"Bu'r, I'm sorry. We need to get to the coast. The village is a detour we can't afford right now."

"Ja'a—"

"I'm sorry, as much as I want to help your village—it could derail us from freeing our entire race."

"I'm sorry, Ja'a, but I must go. I simply have to."

"Bu'r, you can't defeat an entire group of village guards by yourself—none of us can."

"Duke and Ishiro can!" exclaimed Uu'k.

"That's right, kid," Bu'r concurred, "the off-worlders can save my village."

"You know, Ja'a," Po'l added, "we could use some fresh soldiers helping our cause. As much as I hate to admit it, the off-worlders do give us the ability to strike quickly and effectively."

"Hold on. Saving villages wasn't in the deal. I was going to go to your secret hideout, talk to your old timers, agree on a plan to get back my ship, and if I save your entire race as part of that plan—so be it. There was nothing on there about freeing villages."

"He's right," Ja'a stated. "We cannot expect Ishiro and Duke to help us."

"Borrowing a phrase from an old robot friend of mine, 'damn skippy.'"

"And I don't think that it's wise. It's too risky and takes us off course. In good conscience, I just can't agree to this. I'm sorry, Bu'r."

"Ja'a, there are people that are being tortured and forced to mine for wall art as their lives slowly slip away."

"Bu'r, I get that. More than anyone, I get that. The horrors that Orbius has enacted on my family would rival anyone's—but, bigger picture, we have to go at Orbius, not his lackeys that oversee rural villages on his behalf."

"It's quite an intelligent move on Orbius' part," Duke interposed.

"Excuse me?" Bu'r grunted.

"What better way to keep the focus off of him by enticing freedom fighters to charge after each and every enslaved village; he's manipulating you emotionally. It's a trap. Even if you succeed and free the villagers—it'd be a Pyrrhic victory at best. He doesn't mind losing meaningless battles because it will help him win the war."

"But what about the recruits? We could triple our numbers."

"Possibly. But my guess is that those that are devoted enough to fight for the greater cause have already joined. Orbius' gamble is a smart one."

"Shut up already, off-worlder. I'm with Bu'r. I will help you save your village," said Po'l.

"Thank you, Po'l. You are a true Neprian patriot."

"Me too!" Ty'n joined in.

"Us, as well," shouted Ma'n and Te'o.

"I'm sorry, Ja'a," started Po'l. "We respect your leadership but we aren't going to let Duke scare us away from helping our people. He just wants to get his ship back—and what he thinks of as an inconvenience, we think of as our duty to the cause."

"Is this really how you all feel?" asked Ja'a.

"Yes," the rebels concluded in unison.

"Ja'a, you're making a mistake," warned the Nova Texan.

"Maybe so, Duke. I'll admit, I don't agree with this plan—"

"Aren't you the commander? Command!"

"Duke, I don't lead that way. That might be the way of your people or others that you've encountered—but I accept the fact that I can be wrong or that I can change my mind. We all have a say and I can see the emotion and desire of my team. That trumps my opinion in this case."

"This is a mistake. Oh yeah, Ishiro and I are sitting this one out."

"Duke, your help would be greatly appreciated."

"Off-worlder, you're in this with us now—you might as well do your part and help us. It will only help you," said Po'l.

"And think of the recruits! We'll have dozens of my fellow villagers—and I know we have some fighters—that will accompany us on our final push to the coast. Maybe even join up on your quest to get your ship back from Orbius!"

"You're sure of that?"

"Yes, without a doubt."

"Sorry if I'm not quite so optimistic. But I guess it does beat hanging out here in what could possibly be the most boring place in the known universe."

Ja'a's eyes caught Duke's. She mouthed silently, "Thank you."

"I do want us to camp here tonight," she said to the team. "We can make our way to the village tomorrow and assess the situation. It can wait a night."

"Yes!" shouted the Neprians.

"Great. Tomorrow the life of Duke LaGrange could end on a world of no importance during a half-baked raid of a farming village controlled by anorexic killer clergy. How's that for an epitaph? Whatever. I'm heading up front to keep a look out tonight—I need to get away from you crazies just in case it's contagious."

"Wait up, Duke. I'll join you," Ja'a stated.

"Ja'a, you aren't going to stay back with Uu'k and I?" asked Po'l.

"You'll be fine. Ishiro'shea will guard you."

"I don't need guarding. It's just—"

Ja'a and Duke headed out toward the scout locations previously occupied by Ty'n and Bu'r.

CHAPTER 20

A GOOD NIGHT'S SLEEP

THE FLAME OF JA'A'S TORCH hissed as she sat at the apex of the knoll. To her left, Duke sprawled out against the downward slope with his arms behind his head.

"Do you really think I should've pushed back harder on the team?"

"Honest answer?"

"Yes."

"Then, yes, I do. I'm a big proponent of leaders leading—and not this democratic, 'it makes us feel good inside' hogwash. If you really feel we should press on to the coast, we should."

"They'll go on to the village whether we're with them or not."

"Let them go."

"I can't, Duke. They're my people. Each one has a role to play and can help us take down Orbius."

"Not if we all end up dead and buried in the mines."

"True—"

Duke interrupted. "Are you scared of 'em?"

"Scared? No. Not at all."

"Are you sure? Po'l seems to carry some weight in your decisions."

"Po'l and I have known each other for a long time."

"He likes you."

"I hope so, we've been friends since childhood."

"No, Ja'a. He *likes you* likes you."

"I don't understand."

"He *likes you* likes you means that he is interested in some amorous recreation. Some physical repartee. Some carnal deviance. Some—"

"I get it. I don't agree—but I get it. We've known each other for so long; he's a brother to me. I just don't see him in that way."

"You probably should tell him, then. Because he sees *you* in that way."

"I think you're mistaken, Duke. Our customs and interactions could be something new to you."

"I doubt that," Duke chuckled. "If there's one thing that I know and have a keen intuition for—regardless of the planet or species—it's lustful intent. Okay, also tracking down fugitives and all-around bad dudes. And I'm pretty handy knocking down any sort of booze. But, lustful intent—I can spot it a mile away."

"That's an interesting skill."

"It's an extremely rewarding skill in many cases."

"Not something that I care to hear about."

"It's got me out of some tight pickles." Duke tried to not make the obvious joke.

"So, you're quite the seduction specialist, huh?"

"I don't like to brag but I've been known to woo a pretty lady or two. Or three. This one time, in the Oscavian Caves—I lost count at seventeen."

"Just because you've had some luck on that front doesn't mean that you have any idea what Po'l's thinking."

"You've had to have noticed, right? He was about to piss his pants after you told him that you were joining me up at the lookout position."

"No, he wasn't."

"Yes, he was. Most definitely. And when we were leaving the cave, he couldn't take his eyes off of you. I don't blame him, after all."

"Duke," she said shaking her head.

"Seriously, he digs you. The question is—do you dig him?"

"No, absolutely not."

"Why? He's a strapping young buck. He's a bit of a meat-head, but he'd help you breed out some little rebels to fight orbs, emaciated clergy, and crap."

"Maybe so, but my love and devotion lies elsewhere."

"And who's the lucky guy?" Duke's voice inflected upward.

"My cause. Destroying Orbius and saving my planet."

"Oh," the bounty hunter responded in a dejected tone. "Well, I guess that's good. Won't get you hot and sweaty and satisfy those pesky carnal needs—but I guess it's a good thing to 'love.'"

"It does the trick."

"You know, this entire you-and-Po'l dynamic also explains why he doesn't like *me*."

"How do you mean?"

"You might not understand since you aren't a guy."

"Try me, Duke," said Ja'a, rolling her eyes.

"He's there playing his game to win you over, right? He might be playing a long game or he might just be a natural meanderer. Doesn't matter. Regardless, out of nowhere, in comes this good-lookin', ruggedly handsome galactic man of mystery."

"Who's that? I must've missed him."

The bounty hunter ignored the playful jab. "It's obvious, if you think about it."

"Oh, it is?"

"Yes, Po'l feels challenged by me—as it relates to winning

you over. He's scared that your heart will not be able to with-stand someone as 'interesting' as me."

Ja'a remained stone-faced. *She's not buying this?*

"I think you might be stretching to reach that conclusion."

"Is that so?"

"Po'l really thinks—or thought—that you were part of Orbius' plan. I really don't think it's anything more than that."

"See, I knew you wouldn't fully grasp this idea. You've got to be a dude."

"Actually, he thinks you are an egotistical, reckless, self-absorbed bastard," Ja'a started, "that—in his opinion—still could be a mindless pawn in a twisted game of power and death initiated by the most heinous murderer that has ever graced our entire planet. How's that for grasping?"

"Ouch, sister. I guess we'll agree to disagree."

"So, is there a Mrs. Duke LaGrange?"

Thank goodness, she changed the subject, Duke thought to himself. *Though it doesn't sound like a real winner either.*

"No. Not really a 'settle down' sort of guy."

"Doesn't that get old?"

"Not if you don't let it. Always keep it moving."

After a brief pause, Ja'a stabbed the bottom of the torch into the soft earth and slid down to relax in the same manner as Duke.

"What about Ishiro'shea?"

"What about Ishiro? I mean, he's my best friend, but he's not my bag if you know what I mean."

"No, not that—what about Ishiro'shea, as in, what's his story? Why doesn't he talk?"

Changing the subject again. Thank you.

"Ishiro and I have been doing our thing for quite some time. He was Salutatorian, you know."

"I'm not sure I know what that means."

"It means that he's a damn good partner. And has the paperwork to prove it."

"That's good. How did you meet?"

"On Earth, actually. A city called New Tokyo in an area referred to as Ireland."

"Was it like Dre'en?"

"Way worse. Way bigger but mostly way worse. It was the center of the largest and most intense turf war in a hundred cycles."

"Why were you both there? It's not your planet, right?"

"See, Ishiro is half-Japanese and half-Irish—meaning his family was divided along the battle lines. His mother was Japanese royalty—or rather a descendent of the most famed samurai warrior in history. So, the one side wanted her as a rallying symbol of the conflict. And Ish's dad was an Irish spiritual leader in New Tokyo—and a famed military strategist. So, it was obvious why they wanted him."

"How did they choose a side?"

"They didn't. They hated war. So, they made it very clear that they were going to remain neutral. Which, as you can probably guess, pissed *everyone* off. Being neutral on Earth is another way to say that you have no friends."

"What did they do?"

"How I understand it is that a young Ish was dropped off at the edge of the city and picked up by a family friend that enrolled him in the local school—the College of Cohorts, Consorts, Co-Conspirators, and Other Assorted Sidekick Types. That's all I know."

"And the not talking bit?"

"He swore a vow of silence upon his graduation; it will be his burden until he finds his parents. They went missing in the conflict—some believe they died, some think they fled and are living it up on an island paradise on some uncharted world."

"I can't imagine."

"In fact, I think it's what bonded us together."

"Are your parents missing as well?"

"Not missing so much. More like dead."

"I'm sorry, I didn't—"

"No need to be sorry. I never knew them. I was orphaned. Dropped off on the doorstep of a brothel and raised by a rogue outlaw and his favorite lady of the evening."

Ja'a appeared visibly flustered.

"At least, she was the madam."

Once again, Ja'a struggled to respond. After a while she managed, "That had to make for an interesting upbringing?"

"I learned a lot. But after Mistress Trixie died, my father—if you want to call him that—left."

"I'm sorry."

"And I think that our unique parental situations made Ishiro and I the perfect team. Every corner that we turn in every new city on every new planet that we visit—there's a bit of us that's hoping that we run into our parents or, in my case, the man that raised me. We both know the odds of that happening but it's still with us. What would we even say, anyways? Especially Ishiro—I mean, does he even remember how to talk? But we get each other. Same wavelength, you know."

"I hope you find the man that raised you. And I hope that Ishiro'shea finds his parents."

"Enough of that. Let's talk about something more upbeat."

"You never did tell me how you met on Earth," reminded Ja'a.

"That's for another day."

"Then what should we talk about?"

"How about how we're going to kill these slave drivers and save an innocent village."

"Right. We need to come up with some sort of plan if we're going to do this successfully."

"Kinda hard without seeing the lay of the land, having an estimate on 'bad guy' count, or really knowing *anything*."

"True. We can survey the village tomorrow from a safe distance, then figure out our strategy. Bu'r should be able to help us. I guess for tonight we can focus on making sure no one finds us out here relaxing and resting up."

"Hey, I'm a mighty fine lookout. Even when it's pitch black and we only have that wimpy torch." The bounty hunter rustled around in a small compartment affixed to his belt. "Oh yeah, I've got these."

He handed Ja'a his travel-size night vision goggles. "Check 'em out! They help you see at night."

The Neprian examined them and placed them over her eyes. *That was natural.*

"These look like our bifocal telescopic sight enhancers—but ours don't work in the dark. These are fascinating. I mean, I'm sure they would be fascinating if there was anything to see."

"True, not the best subject to view, but we can take turns as lookout—just in case we see an oncoming group of nocturnal marauders."

Ja'a reclined onto the yielding grass of the hill with the binoculars still pressed to her eyes.

"I've got another question for you, Ja'a."

"What's that?"

"How close has this rebellion come to overthrowing Orbius? Have there been any wins or progress? Or are we shooting in the dark?"

Ja'a hesitated and sighed. "Do you remember that I spoke of a leader called He'j?"

"Yes, with Jilarian Togg."

"Great memory."

"Thanks. I try."

"He'j was very much the face of our rebellion, as you know. You could say that he was like Ishiro'shea's mother and father—the symbol of our cause and the one leading. He was very close to destroying Orbius."

"How close?"

"He told us that he had a theory about the Orb—but it was

just that, a theory. He couldn't bring himself to have troops go into battle over his hunch so he and a select group of soldiers traveled to Orbius' palace in a stealth manner."

"What was his theory?"

"That's just it, he didn't tell a soul. Not even his companions on the mission."

"Why? Seems like an odd thing to do."

"He said that if he was right or wrong, he couldn't tell anyone. If he was right and failed to kill Orbius, the simple fact that Orbius would know that we are aware of his great weakness would bring greater harm to Neprius."

"Interesting."

"We learned not too long ago that He'j's mission had failed. Orbius killed He'j. Word spread fast. He wanted all of us to know that he'd *personally* ended our great leader's life."

"To weaken the resolve of the cause."

"Yes. He's good at that."

The night continued to curtail visibility but Duke noticed, in the faint glow of the flame, a narrow rivulet of tears on Ja'a's cheek.

The rebel leader's eyes caught his stare. "I'm sorry. It's just that—He'j was my father."

Duke attempted to digest this news. "Why didn't you tell me that before?"

"It shouldn't matter—it doesn't matter. My devotion to the cause is independent of my relationship to my father. Whether he was a significant leader or an enslaved peasant, I would still be where I am now—fighting Orbius with every ounce of energy in my bones."

"I don't doubt that, Ja'a. Not at all."

"Thank you, Duke. That means a lot."

Ja'a rolled onto her side, facing Duke. Her face was illuminated by the torch flame; highlighting her striking features against a backdrop of celestial darkness like a spotlight focused on a single actor standing before a murky theater curtain.

"Good night, my friend."

Duke didn't like the term 'friend.' But he also didn't feel right about what he typically would have done in a moment such as this. Restraint was never his forte when it came to lying next to vulnerable females—but he found a way to dig deep and not act like a total asshole.

He took the binoculars from Ja'a and started the first shift of lookout duty.

The morning light eased its way under Duke's eyelids, ending his peaceful slumber. Along with the light, the dawn brought intermittent clouds of fog that hovered over the expanse of fields. It was slightly cooler than the previous mornings. Duke always enjoyed a breeze, having grown up in the living furnace that was Nova Texas.

The bounty hunter stretched his arms and embraced the day—and the inevitability of having to deal with a village under siege; another roadblock between him and the *Deus*. However, his pessimistic outlook was quickly diverted to one of a more pleasurable connotation.

"Good morning."

Ja'a had been on the last shift of lookout duty. She was already packed and ready to return to the rest of the group. Her long pearwood hair was pulled back neatly and arranged in the style that Duke was accustomed to seeing during their trek. The cosmetic stylings that adorned her face had already been reapplied, albeit with a slightly ashier palette, though they showcased her steely eyes no less than before.

"Good morning to you," Ja'a said softly as she knelt down, adjusting elements on her bow and examining the remaining arrows. "Ready to go save a village?"

CHAPTER 21

UNIVERSE'S BEST RULER

"YOU DON'T THINK I'M EVIL, do you?"

The servant immediately halted his feathering of a trophy proclaiming that the owner was the "Universe's Best Ruler" and stared back at the questioner.

"Of course I'm not evil," Orbius said to himself before the servant could respond.

The Neprian priest exhaled and continued to clean the ruler's assorted awards that accumulated on his shelf.

"I just don't get why these rebels keep trying to resist. Do you?"

The servant froze again. His trembling was more noticeable: he knocked over a framed photo of two orcas trapping a poor sea lion on a floating shard of ice with the caption, "Teamwork."

"Of course you don't. You get it. You see it. You know that I'm the only one that can harness the power of the Orb and prevent it from corrupting the entire planet. Right?"

The priest simply nodded and bowed slightly.

Orbius stood up and walked towards an enormous window that looked out over the whole of Sansagon. The priests—*his* priests—were running drills and distributing weapons. Preparations for battle were underway. Orbius smiled.

He raised his hand and stretched his fingers skyward; his bulky rings scratched one another. Whoosh. An electric purple filled the area and the Orb skimmed across the room at eye level and came to rest in Orbius' palm. He examined it. His gaze lingered.

"What do you think?"

The priest cleared his throat. He looked around the room as if to make sure that the Orbmaster was actually addressing him.

"Yes, *you*. What do *you* think?"

"Almighty Orbius, my lord, what do I think about what?"

"About the current events on our happy little world. Your pesky cousins to the south not seeing the error of their ways and realizing that I'm their savior too. And now rumblings about some flying monsters coming out of the west."

"I do not understand their actions."

"I know, right? Ridiculous."

"Yes, my lord, ridiculous."

"And another thing—"

Orbius' thought was interrupted by the sound of two more servants entering his chamber, pushing a wheeled tray containing plates and glassware.

"Excellent! There better be some greattu under that lid."

The priests stopped and looked at each other. They performed a complete turn and shuffled back through the door. A shrill "We need greattu—fast" was audible from the hallway.

"I love greattu. Maybe the best thing about this planet. What was I saying before?"

"I believe you were questioning the actions of those opposing you."

"And not just me, my good friend. They are opposing *you*.

And your families. And—if you think about it—the entire planet of Neprius." Orbius paused. "They are waging a war against the long-term health and safety of the planet."

"That is very true, my lord."

"You could say that on top of everything, we are eco-warriors."

"You could say that," stammered the servant.

"I know. And I am *going* to say it. Oh, and you missed a spot over there."

The priest doubled down on his dusting.

"But why don't they see it? You see it. Your race sees it. I mean, outside of that Togg character. Why is it so difficult?"

"I think—never mind."

"No, go on—*please* go on." Orbius' demeanor turned to grim concentration.

"From what I hear—you know, the word from around town, if you will—"

"Yes?" Orbius asked impatiently.

"The rebels think that you are the evil that the planet should fear. They think that you are trying to make them slaves."

Orbius' eyes widened and his pupils dilated. He gripped the Orb even tighter and its glow pulsed with the increased tension. The veins in his necked stiffened. The servant cowered.

"Which is, of course, crazy. And why they must be punished," babbled the servant. "Who could honestly think that? Especially after you saved us once from the droughts with your advanced knowledge of harvests."

Orbius relaxed. "That's right. They are crazy. What if I relinquished the Orb and someone who couldn't control it ended up with it? What then?"

"Disaster," responded the servant hesitantly.

"Disaster, indeed. You could end up like Earth. Wars,

feuds, conflict. Every good thing that we created or discovered was overshadowed by greed, corruption, and baseless violence. If it wasn't a gang war driven by races with different values about who knows what, it was two governments fighting over a few extra bits of currency or a few scraps of insignificant land. Did I ever tell you that my lab was fire-bombed by a group of people that felt I was violating the right of plants by testing chemicals on them? Tests that potentially might end hunger throughout our entire planet?"

"No, my lord."

"And then I was stoned by another group of wackos as I was fleeing the burning building. They felt I was infringing on God's will by trying to eradicate hunger."

"I'm sorry, oh great Orbius."

"If that wasn't bad enough, I also avoided a corporate assassination because I switched the brand of chemical compounds that I was using, costing some high-level executive a big payday after he promised his mistress a new beach house."

"Truly a planet with many issues."

"There wasn't a singular power to unite the planet. There wasn't a singular point of reason that could govern everyone correctly. Hell, that's the problem with the whole of the universe, if you ask me. I won't let *that* happen to Neprius. The Orb called me to save this planet—save you and your people—and I will stop at nothing to make sure that I do. If I had the Orb on Earth, I could save that planet too."

"They would all be very grateful, I'm sure."

"You better believe it. I will get enough power in due time —and then I *will* save Earth in the same way that I'm saving Neprius. And then on to another poor planet. And on and on."

"A glorious plan, my excellency."

"It is, isn't it?"

Another knock at the door.

"Yes, it's open. Come in."

"Almighty Orbius. Orbmaster. Savior. The one true—"

"I get it, I get it. What do you want?"
"Vernglet Wip of Dre'en is here to see you."
"Send him in."
"Yes, my lord."
"Oh, and will you check on my greattu?"

CHAPTER 22

WELCOME TO SHUD'NUT

DESPITE THE PIVOT SOUTHWARD TOWARDS the village, the scenery remained consistent. For the short excursion, Duke, Ishiro'shea, and the Neprians traveled together—foregoing their previous positions and adopting a 'safety in numbers' approach. Duke figured that if the climate of the mission changed to one of an unfriendly ilk, Ja'a probably didn't want the lookouts to be on an island without immediate backup. *Sensible*, thought Duke.

"We're close. Can you see the smoke?" asked the barrel-chested Neprian, Bu'r.

"The mines?"

"Yes. See that patch of trees just north of town over there? It'll provide us with some cover as we map out an attack plan."

"Slow down, Bu'r. I don't like the aggressive undertones," snapped Ja'a. "Our goal is to free this village of Northern guards and recruit. We will focus on efficiency and safety—you can't do that with vengeance driving your actions."

Bu'r looked dejected.

"I understand. Freeing my village is enough reward."

"I would hope so."

"Hey Bu'r, what do ya' call this home of yours?"

"Shud'nut."

"Shud'nut' we be focusing on getting my ship back?" Duke deadpanned.

The rebels all glanced at the bounty hunter—obviously, not in the mood for a morning jest. Duke had had a feeling that his quip wouldn't land but the rebels' scowls displayed more anger than he had imagined. Even Uu'k seemed disappointed. *Even Ishiro!?!*

"Sorry, that was in poor taste," the bounty hunter acknowledged.

"And it wasn't funny," added Uu'k.

"Not surprising coming from you, off-worlder," snapped Po'l with a nasty bite.

"It's too early to fight you on this one, Po'l."

"Why are you in such an agreeable mood?"

Duke didn't respond to Po'l's query. However, Ishiro'shea snuck up and slapped Duke in the small of the back.

"What?"

Ishiro'shea's eyes asked a tricky question: *Did you do what I think you did?*

Duke motioned back something resembling a *No, nothing happened* gesture. Ishiro'shea seemed to understand.

"You alive, Duke?" Po'l interrupted. "Are you just going to ignore me?"

"It's a great day to be alive. And with you lot. We're about to save a village—hard to beat that! Right?"

"Right. Okay," said Po'l in a confused tone.

"How about over there?" interjected Ma'n. He pointed towards an open patch of soil blocked from the view of the town by some midsized trees. "This looks like the only cover before we're in plain sight."

"Aren't we a bit worried that—since this *is* the only cover—that the Neprian guards are probably watching it like a hawk?" asked the bounty hunter.

"I think you give them too much credit," said Po'l.

"I don't know. They did manage to take over your whole planet. How's your face feeling, by the way?"

"Yeah, I'd like to see how long you would last against the Orb."

"I've handled a lot worse than a rock filled with magic and mumbo jumbo."

"Calm down. Both of you," Ja'a said soothingly. "We're on the same team."

"Are we?" Are you sure, Ja'a?" asked Po'l.

"You know that we are. Our motivations might differ from Duke's—but our goal is the same. We need you both to defeat Orbius."

Ishiro'shea hopped down into a crouch and slid in front of everyone—he pointed toward the outside wall of Shud'nut.

"Down," Duke shouted at the group. "I see them too, Ishiro. Only three. No wait, four."

The ninja confirmed the latter count and stared back at Duke inquisitively.

"Yep, I agree."

"You agree with what?" asked Po'l in a slightly annoyed tone.

"I agree with Ishiro. He's not a 'what'; haven't you learned your lesson about insulting my friend?"

"Duke," Ja'a interjected, "what does Ishiro'shea have in mind? Do you have a plan?"

"Sort of."

"Sort of?"

"Yeah, sort of. We see four guards—and we're going to dispose of them."

"Yes, but how? What's the plan?" pleaded Ja'a.

"That *is* the plan."

"Ja'a, I told you these two weren't going to help. I have an idea."

"Okay, Po'l," said Ja'a. "Gather round, everyone. What are you thinking?"

"First, if we can distract the guards long enough for Ty'n and Bu'r to flank them—that will set us up for minimal casualties. Ma'n and Te'o can provide—" Po'l stopped mid-thought. "Where are y'all going?"

Duke and Ishiro'shea were already out from their camouflaged hiding spot and in the open field that led right to the perimeter walls of Shud'nut. In a few hundred yards, they would be easily spotted by the guards.

"You know, Ishiro. What if there are more *inside* the walls?"

The ninja hesitated momentarily—then continued toward the village.

"Yeah, best not think about it, right? We got this. Yeah, most likely, we got this."

Duke drew his laser revolver. Ishiro'shea unsheathed his katana.

"So, you think they'll just let us in?"

Ishiro did not blink.

"Probably not."

They continued their brisk saunter towards Shud'nut.

"Duke! What are you doing? You're going to get killed!"

The two men ignored the shouts from behind them; Duke wanted to reply with a snarky comment about Po'l being happy about that potential outcome but he decided against it. *Best be remembered as a brave, albeit stupid, hero than a smartass if this thing goes sideways.*

"Well, they seemed concerned for us but they don't seem to want to join us, huh? Better this way. They would just get in the way."

The bounty hunters were within an arrow's shot from the wall when they were finally noticed by one of the Neprian priests.

"Halt, strangers. Who are you?"

"We're here to clean your jacuzzi," Duke fired back.

"I'm not certain I understand your request," shouted the confused Neprian.

"Ja-cuz-zi," Duke yelled back, enunciating each syllable.

"Hey, have you ever heard of a jack-yoozi?" the priest screamed back to his colleague.

"A what?" the other one began, a jo-kawzi? What's that? Hey, is this some kinda Southern trick? Who are those guys?"

"We aren't Southern Neprian trash, if that's what you're asking each other," Duke called up. He imagined how offended Po'l would be at that comment. He smiled.

"You don't look like a piece of Southern Neprian trash, that's true."

"Why thank you, kind sir."

The priest was still confused. He motioned for his fellow priest to come over and discuss their predicament in more detail. They deliberated, out of Duke's earshot, for a few minutes.

"What are y'all talking about up there?" asked Duke. "That jacuzzi won't clean itself."

"I'm sorry, I'm not certain what you mean by jow-cooli, stranger," shouted back the priest.

"Let us in and I'll show you."

"I think not," returned the second priest.

"But Orbius sent us."

The priests paused.

"You know—Orbius. Orby. The head honcho. Boss man. The Dude of Dudes."

"We know who Orbius is. We need to discuss further."

A third priest joined the brainstorming session.

"Hey there, friend," Duke shouted to the newcomer. He didn't receive a response. "Also, not only did Orbius send us to clean your hot tub but he also told us a super important, highly confidential secret that we must relay to you. It's about the defense of this village. We've received updates from General Gar about the positions of the Southern rebels."

All three priests looked even more confused.

"We will need to consult with one more of our colleagues. He is a direct report to the General."

"Great! Why don't you invite all of the guards in the city? You can all weigh in on how you want your pool cleaned—and on how to handle this top secret intel."

"Strangers, we still don't understand this term, 'jaw-kwayze,' and our colleague is the last of us guards here in this rotting cesspool of a village."

"We could ask Gander Vorv. He's on mine duty."

"Oh yeah, Gander is pretty well-versed in protocol," the other agreed.

Duke and Ishiro'shea exchanged glances and smiled.

The fourth priest was slightly larger than the other three and appeared agitated by this impromptu debate.

"What do you want? What's worth waking me up for? It's bad enough they moved me to this dirty outpost babysitting slaves and away from killing Neprian rebels."

"Sir, we wanted your opinion on a situation."

"What situation?"

"Do you know what a 'ja-zuki' is?"

"What? No. Is this some game that you lot made up? I'm not interested."

"I said that you wouldn't know," said the first priest.

"Maybe I do? Say it again."

"Jow-cootie."

"Use it in a sentence."

"I don't know how."

The fourth priest grew even more annoyed.

"It's just these strangers down there said Orbius sent them to clean ours," the first priest said, and pointed to Ishiro'shea and Duke.

"Hi." Duke smirked and gave a sly wink.

"You morons," exclaimed the bulky priest. "These are the off-worlders that I mentioned."

"Oh."

Four pulses beamed in rapid succession. All four Neprian priests collapsed. Dead.

"Well, they made it easy for us, huh? It was nice of them to let us know that there weren't any more inside—and then huddle up all nice and close."

Duke placed the revolver back in his holster and took out Betsy.

"And now about this door."

He aimed at the wooden door that stood between them and the innards of the city of Shud'nut.

"I hope no one is standing behind it."

Betsy screamed and let off a thunderous emission. The door was obliterated instantaneously. It did not appear to have hurt anyone—in fact, Duke couldn't see a single villager through the gaping hole that now served as their entryway.

"Hey, hold there!"

Duke turned and faced the mines. A Neprian priest was running towards him. He had a whip and was flailing and popping it with ruthless animosity as he charged the bounty hunters.

"Ishiro, this is all you."

The ninja nimbly accelerated towards the oncoming priest with his katana drawn. *Poor Gander Vorv.*

The priest hurled the whip in the ninja's direction, but Ishiro'shea leapt into the air and avoided its impact. He landed soundlessly and, with a simple slash, struck down the slave master. It was quick, silent, and clean. It was ninja.

CHAPTER 23

A SKILLED POLITICIAN

ETWEEN BETSY'S EXPLOSIVE GREETING AND the shattering of a giant wooden door, the villagers of Shud'nut started to appear, presumably in order to see what was going on. Many made their way out from the mines. Others scurried deep within in the village, emerging from dimly-lit storefronts and huts.

"What did you do, Duke?" Ja'a asked as she and the other rebels rushed up from behind.

"We freed the village. You're officially welcome." Duke removed his hat and bowed.

"We didn't say 'thank you,'" Po'l reminded him.

"Oh yeah. Well, you can say it now. No more priests. Everyone is free. And no one got hurt."

"Thank you!" shouted Bu'r. "Ja'a, this is great! Shud'nut is free!"

"Excellent, Bu'r. We need to direct the villagers to the town square and start inquiring about potential recruits."

"Of course," responded Bu'r. "Let's go—they're going to be so happy!"

Bu'r, Ty'n, Ma'n, and Te'o rushed off in four different directions to direct the villagers to the center of the town.

"So—" Duke began.

"Yes?" said Ja'a.

"Do I get a big thank you?"

"You were reckless. And dangerous."

"And successful."

"I suppose," Ja'a muttered as she walked towards a gathering of confused villagers.

"No appreciation from this lot, Ishiro. No appreciation whatsoever."

The two off-worlders migrated to what they thought was the town square, where the inhabitants of Shud'nut had begun to gather around a raised platform, presumably designed for such keynote addresses. Roughly three hundred Southern Neprians filled the clearing with little room to spare. They all appeared to be in a state of shock and bewilderment. Most took a keen interest in the two odd-looking guests that had disposed of five guards and a door without as much as breaking a sweat.

Ja'a ascended to the top of the platform; her feet stood eye level to an adult Neprian.

"Fellow Neprians," she began, "please be calm. I am Ja'a, daughter of He'j."

At this, the crowd immediately ceased all conversation. A hush fell over the audience.

"Thank you. People of Shud'nut, as you know we have been enslaved by an evil in the North—an evil known as Orbius. We continue to fight against him and his followers—and we will defeat him."

Duke was bracing himself for an uncontrollable roar of support, but the villagers said nothing. *Very odd.*

"Thanks to our new friends from a land far from Neprius," Ja'a continued, "you are no longer condemned to this tyrannical slavery. People of Shud'nut—you are free!"

Nothing. *Very odd, indeed.*

"Who are these strangers?" shouted a villager. "Maybe they want to enslave us too." The other villagers seemed to agree with this notion.

"These strangers just saved you from your captors. Isn't that enough to make you trust them?"

"Yes, so they could enslave us for themselves!" erupted another villager.

"Friends! They have saved the lives of our company already on this journey—would they do that if they only wanted to enslave you? They are the allies that we so desperately need in the fight against Orbius!"

"What's in it for them?" shouted another townsman.

"Tough crowd, Ishiro," Duke said to Ishiro'shea as the rumbling sounds of dissent seemed to escalate amongst the villagers.

Ja'a attempted to salvage the discussion. "Our friends have a mutual benefit in the destruction of Orbius. It is their only way to get home. So, please, I'm asking you to join us in our fight. For our people!"

"Why? So we can die with you?"

"You will certainly die as slaves under Orbius. Be part of the solution and free our people!"

Many in the crowd erupted into laughter. Ja'a was visibly shaken by the response.

"*You* are going to defeat Orbius? You and these castaways *—and a kid?*" exclaimed an older male Neprian that stood directly under Ja'a. "You have a kid fighting with you, for the sake of Neprius! The only thing that you bring us is pain."

"Orbius is going to punish us for sure, now," another villager shouted. The crowd seemed to agree.

"Your father couldn't defeat Orbius," the older man continued, "so what makes you think his naive daughter can? This is hopeless. Your interference will cause us greater pain and suffering."

Bu'r climbed to the platform to accompany Ja'a.

"Everyone, I am a son of Shud'nut. Ja'a speaks the truth. We can defeat Orbius."

"A son of Shud'nut brings this calamity upon us. A sad day for us all," the old man said.

"What are we to do, Ye'f?" a villager asked the old man.

"We must ask for forgiveness from Orbius so that we can return to how life was before this intrusion."

"And live as slaves?"

"Better slaves with breath in our lungs than free and rotting in the ground," Ye'f replied.

Duke, still at the outskirts of the town square, found a stone wall and stood upon it. He was not as elevated as Ja'a and Bu'r, but he was high enough to be seen by the entire gathering. He grabbed his revolver and fired it in the air. Silence descended upon the group.

"Hi there. My name is Duke LaGrange. Trailblazer. Adventurer. Poet. A true man of the universe. And I'm here to free you. And I'm here to kill that nasty bastard, Orbius. Don't believe me? Watch this."

Duke rattled off another round of energy pulses that removed parts of the wall with ease.

"Y'all should be thanking Ja'a and her crew."

"Off-worlder, we don't need to hear from you. You helped bring this upon us. There is only one clear thing for us to do." Ye'f turned to face the crowd, as any skilled politician would, and proclaimed, "We must appease Orbius by capturing these rebels and turning them over to him. Maybe he will be lenient in his punishment and, eventually, let us get back to mining with only the lash of a whip to worry about."

There was a short pause. Then the village cheered in unison.

"No, please don't listen. We are giving you freedom," pleaded Bu'r from atop the pulpit. Ja'a looked as if she had been hit in the midsection with a blunt ax.

The crowd closed in on the platform. Duke aimed his revolver at the mass of villagers.

"No, Duke! Stop!" shouted Ja'a. "Don't kill them; they don't know any better. We can't turn on our own people!"

"It appears that it might be you or them."

"Please don't," Bu'r pleaded.

Ishiro'shea hopped up onto the stone wall next to Duke and tapped him on the shoulder. He pointed to the apex of the pole that supported the platform—which was much higher than the actual platform itself.

"Good plan, little buddy!"

"Ja'a! Get everyone on the platform and be ready to make a break for it!"

Duke wasn't sure if the Neprian rebels understood. He fired off a pulse from his revolver—and another.

"Stop!" screamed Ja'a involuntarily.

She looked around and saw not a dead villager, but the large vertical beam behind the platform beginning to shake and sway—and then fall directly into the mosh pit of angry villagers. The townsfolk scattered to avoid being mashed into Neprian goop. The seven rebels, now understanding Duke's intentions, sprang on top of the fallen pole and sprinted to the now-permanently-open doorway out from the town. Duke and Ishiro followed, with weapons drawn. As they cleared the threshold, Duke fired a few more rounds at the top of the entryway. Stone and wood fragments fell, making a temporary seal that kept the mob inside the walls.

"That was close," exclaimed Po'l, collapsing to the ground. It was obvious that he was far from one hundred percent.

"Listen," Duke said.

"I don't hear anything," replied Ty'n.

"That's the problem. Why aren't they following us? I mean, that debris blocking the door won't hold them too long—do they give up that easy?"

Ishiro'shea pushed aside Po'l and Ma'n and darted back

toward the village. He disappeared within the dust cloud made by the impact of the door fragments on the soil.

"Ishiro? What are you doing?" Duke shouted.

"Duke. Oh no," Ja'a moaned.

They all looked at each other.

"Where's Uu'k?" Duke asked, without wanting to hear the answer. "Ishiro!"

Duke and Po'l rushed to follow Ishiro'shea.

"Stay back," Po'l demanded. Ja'a and the rebels didn't argue.

"Okay, you ready? This could get messy." Duke said to Po'l as they reached the pile of fallen stone and wood.

He noticed that Po'l had not recovered completely. "Need help?" Before Po'l could respond, Duke extended a hand. They locked hands and Duke helped the rebel warrior scale the mound.

As they both touched the ground on the inside of the wall, Ishiro'shea appeared with sword drawn and Uu'k on his shoulder.

"Is she okay?" asked Duke.

Ishiro'shea merely winked. With surprising ease, he glided over the rubble with Uu'k.

Po'l and Duke surveyed what was in front of them. They looked at each other. Duke placed his hand on Po'l's shoulder.

"Best we keep this to ourselves."

"For once, I agree."

"Let's get out of here before they see us."

The two left the entrance to Shud'nut and joined their band—now complete again.

"What happened in there?" asked Bu'r.

"Uu'k is safe," Duke replied.

"Did he kill my people?" Bu'r asked in an agitated tone. "Did he?"

Duke was silent as he tried to think of the proper words.

"Uu'k is safe. That's all that matters. Ishiro'shea did what all of us would've done—and he did not go in with violence on his mind."

"But—" started Bu'r.

"That's enough, Bu'r. Let us move on," Po'l said, ending the conversation.

Duke nodded at Po'l. Po'l did not return a reply.

Ja'a approached both men. "Thank you both. And especially you, Ishiro."

Ishiro bowed.

Duke began, "Are you sure this cause of yours is worth it? We just had an entire village try to kill us because they would rather be slaves of Orbius than join your rebellion. That's typically not a good sign."

"I don't know what happened in there, Duke. Truly I don't."

"All you care about is getting your ship back anyways, LaGrange."

Ah, there's the Po'l that I know and love.

"Yes, I'm doing this to get my ship and get off this horrible rock—but are you certain that *you* are on the right side? They seemed pretty content working the mines for Orbius. Maybe he's a steady employer? I'm just a little worried."

"I promise, Orbius is the tyrant that we claim him to be. I'm as shocked by the response of the Shud'nut villagers as you."

"My people. My neighbors. I don't know what happened." Bu'r sat looking into his open palms, his face wet. "I don't why they responded like that. We aren't a big village but we are a proud village." The broad-shouldered rebel paused. "We *were* a proud village. I'm sorry that I made you all risk everything for that."

He looked at Uu'k. Ishiro'shea was still holding her upright; her face was pale and her eyes frozen.

"Most of all to you, Uu'k. I'm sorry," Bu'r sobbed.

The child spy did not return as much as a blink.

"Maybe we can clear things up with our leaders once we get to the coast," offered Ja'a.

"I guess."

Duke was not as optimistic as Ja'a.

CHAPTER 24

UNCLE LO'N

"THIS IS IT?"

"This is where the senior leaders of the cause reside. Yes."

"It's kind of a—" Duke cleared his throat and continued, "—let's just say it leaves a bit to be desired."

"Judging by your tone, I'm assuming that's not a complimentary term," returned Ja'a.

"Doesn't seem like a place from which one would launch a planet-saving rebellion, if you ask me."

"I didn't," Ja'a replied. She picked up the pace and headed under a natural archway created by two trees one cracked into a right angle, the other with a posture crippled by age.

The archway led to a clearing surrounded by a grove of tropical trees and brush. It was dense, but not like the forests south of Dre'en where Duke and Ishiro'shea had first met their Neprian allies. Grass was in sparse clumps on the light tan soil which merged into grainy sand extending beyond the outer rim of trees west of the compound. Duke couldn't see the ocean, but he could hear the waves just beyond their forest wall.

"Can you smell it?" Po'l asked boastfully.

"Is that a rhetorical question?" Duke smirked.

"That's the smell of our beloved aquatic goddess; she who has both nurtured us from the bounty of her watery bosom and has buried men in her darkest depths for them never to return," Po'l proclaimed triumphantly.

Duke and Ishiro'shea exchanged glances.

"He has a way with words," whispered the Nova Texan to his mute friend.

"This perfume means that we are home, we are with our true friends, and we are in her tender care," Po'l continued.

The other rebels stood around him, overcome with pride and admiration. All except Ja'a. Duke locked eyes with her and felt that he could read her mind—and it was telling him not to say what he was about to say.

"You know, Po'l," Duke began. Ishiro immediately covered Uu'k's ears. "Maybe it's different here on Neprius, but if a woman's parts smell like rotten fish and saltwater—maybe she needs to scrub her darkest depths a bit more."

For a split second, Duke was hopeful that Po'l wouldn't quite understand his meaning. He did.

"How dare you insult our land!"

"Technically, I insulted your water."

Po'l, still a bit worse for wear, charged at Duke. The bounty hunter assumed a martial stance—but Te'o and Ma'n caught the lunging Neprian.

"It was just a joke, Po'l. Lighten up," said Duke.

"A poor joke at that," Ja'a interjected as she turned and headed towards the largest of the buildings.

"Ja'a, wait. I didn't mean it like that. It was just a joke." Duke took a step towards her but Ishiro extended his arm and halted his progress.

"Why's Ja'a so mad?" asked Uu'k.

"Your Uncle Duke said something really dumb," he said softly as he knelt down to her eye level.

"Figures," Uu'k retorted.

"Hey!"

"And you aren't my Uncle Duke."

Ishiro was clearly pleased by his small companion's attitude. However, she was soon interrupted by a very angry Po'l.

"LaGrange, I've had it. You may think this is a joke still and you can poke fun at me—I'm man enough to take it—but don't insult the very place that we are fighting and dying to preserve."

"Lighten up, Po'l. I get it."

"I don't think you do. But one day you will get it, oh, you will."

"Is that a threat?"

"Greetings! Welcome, great warriors!" boomed an abrupt interruption. "Old friends, little friends—hello there, Uu'k— and these new friends that Ja'a has delivered to us."

Seemingly out of nowhere, an elderly gentleman appeared before them, accompanied by Ja'a. He had wide shoulders and a stocky build, much like Bu'r but without the bulbous midsection. Duke could tell that he was once a warrior. Or a bouncer. His hair, cut short, was a sparkling white and he sported a neatly trimmed beard. The man's skin was of a darker hue than any of the other Neprians—it had the look of worn leather.

"There is no need to fight amongst ourselves when there are so many out there that deserve to feel the wrath of our fists and the sting of our arrows," he bellowed. His voice was that of a leader that commanded respect. It was clear that Po'l was trying to mimic his swagger. *And without much luck,* thought Duke.

"This is the leader of our cause and a great hero, General Mo'a," proclaimed Ja'a. "He heads our council."

Mo'a nodded slightly. "Just Mo'a, please. A council leader without a council is no leader."

The entire group remained silent as they absorbed Mo'a's comment.

He continued, "Sure, there are council members scattered about—but what do we council? We have no government to oversee. No positions to appoint. We plan raids and sneak attacks against Orbius; that's it. I feel that the only title that I'm worthy of is 'old man that can't accomplish anything.'"

"Pleasure, regardless." Duke tipped his cap. Ishiro'shea bowed in respect.

"Ja'a, tell me about your friends here," Mo'a requested, regaining his jovial tone.

"Po'l, obviously. And I believe you've met Ma'n and Te'o— they served my father."

"Oh yes. It is good to see you again, old friends."

"Yes, great Mo'a," Po'l replied humbly.

"Stop groveling," said Mo'a. "I'm not anyone's king. I'm just the old man that's trying to keep our operation afloat. Nothing more, nothing less. We all have our roles to play and our input to provide. Right, Uu'k?"

Uu'k smiled.

Ja'a continued, "Let me introduce Bu'r of Shud'nut and Ty'n of the Southern Forests."

"Greetings, my good men. Your service is beyond appreciated."

Both men nodded at the Neprian leader.

"And who are these two curious-looking souls standing next to Uu'k?" Mo'a asked.

"These are the off-worlders, Duke LaGrange of Nova Texas and Ishiro'shea of Earth."

"Hey."

The entire crew of rebels cast piercing stares at Duke—or rather, hurled, like an octopus practicing dagger throwing.

"What?" Duke asked, knowing full well that his informal greeting had not been well-received.

But Mo'a only returned a great laugh.

"Duke—oh, it's nice to have someone that's not so stuffy around me!"

The Nova Texan winked at Ja'a. She returned a slight grin.

"My beautiful Ja'a, you know that I have viewed you as one of my own; your father was a brother to me. I miss him every single day—but not as much as our cause does. I fear I lack his leadership—rather, I *know* I lack his leadership."

"Mo'a—" interjected Ja'a.

"Hush, girl. I know my shortcomings. I also know that he would be very proud of you."

Ja'a blushed. It was the first time Duke had seen her so vulnerable.

"And he would be proud of you, great Mo'a. He often spoke of your fighting prowess."

Mo'a laughed. "Something I haven't had in many cycles. And it takes more than swords and arrows to defeat an evil like Orbius."

"He also spoke to me—many times, in fact—about your spirit and conviction. And if I believe in something as strongly and passionately as his friend Mo'a, I would live a richly fulfilled life."

It was Mo'a's turn to blush. His eyes glazed over and he stared at nothing in particular. *He must be caught in a good— no, a great—memory*, thought Duke.

Mo'a jolted from his momentary trance. "That is very kind, Ja'a. Very kind. You've made an old man very happy."

Ja'a bowed her head gently.

"But, sweet daughter of He'j, I have someone else that you might remember even more fondly than my ancient bones."

He pointed to the entrance that led into the base. Leaning up against the frame was an older Neprian male—not as old as Mo'a, but definitely old enough to be Ja'a's father. He was extraordinarily fit for his age; he appeared to be sculpted from hardened mud. His ink-colored mustache curved downward and extended well beyond his chin. Atop his shaven head was a neatly groomed row of thick black hair that stretched from the midpoint of his cranium to the start of his neck, transitioning into a braided mane which fell to the middle of his back. He stepped out of the shadow of the doorway and approached the group.

A smile flashed over Ja'a's face with such power that her cheeks almost exploded. She dropped her bow and sprinted towards the mysterious Neprian. She leapt into his arms and he swung her around with great enthusiasm. His smile mirrored that of Ja'a's.

Duke looked at Po'l. *Surely* he had to be upset at this. But Po'l also sported a grin.

"Hey, who is this character?" Duke bent down to ask Uu'k.

"That's Lo'n," she whispered back.

"Boyfriend? Grandpa? Massage therapist? Who is he?"

Uu'k looked at him, "that's Lo'n."

Unprompted, Bu'r tapped Duke on the shoulder.

"Duke, that's Lo'n. Can you believe it?"

Duke looked around and Ma'n was mouthing to him silently, clearly saying, "That's Lo'n."

The bounty hunter clenched his teeth.

Ja'a turned to everyone—her hand still around Lo'n's waist —and proclaimed, "Everyone, this is Lo'n—"

"I know it's Lo'n! Everyone knows frickin' Lo'n!"

They all turned to face Duke. Ishiro'shea looked at the ground.

"I mean—" Duke cleared his throat. "Nice to meet you, Lo'n. I've heard so much about you."

Duke awkwardly knelt down in an exaggerated curtsy. Mo'a laughed.

"Is that right, off-worlder?"

"But of course. The great and all powerful Lo'n. Your exploits are known throughout the universe. Entire races are sacrificed in your honor every cycle. The mere mention of your name can impregnate certain species. Both male and female. You are a god, my friend, a true god."

Lo'n's eyes locked on to Duke's. Silence fell upon the

group. Not even Mo'a chuckled.

"Off-worlder, I like you!"

The Neprians exhaled audibly and some broke into a light giggle.

"Where did you find this one, Ja'a? And his masked companion?" asked Lo'n.

"It's a long story, Uncle Lo'n."

"So you were He'j's brother?"

"Not by blood, off-worlder. But we were very close. Ja'a was always like a niece to me."

"So you're a fake uncle?"

"I guess. You could say that," Lo'n replied, confused.

Duke turned to Uu'k and smirked. "See, I *can* be your uncle."

Uu'k stuck her tongue out. Ishiro'shea patted her on her head and smiled through his mask.

"Uncle Lo'n, this is Duke LaGrange and Ishiro'shea. They came to us when their ship was swallowed by a giant star portal, as they call it, and then had a run-in with the Northern priests. They escaped and joined us."

"Aren't you forgetting how you captured us and treated us like spies? And how we saved everyone? And then you drug us to some ragtag village and they turned on us? And we saved Uu'k from being kidnapped and sent to Orbius?"

Ja'a looked cross.

"Duke, that is very interesting," said Mo'a. "Sounds like you already have some tales to tell."

"Very interesting, indeed," Lo'n said. "How did you survive these trials?"

"Cunning. Brute strength."

"He has special weapons," Po'l interjected. "His weapons are quite powerful—in fact, Orbius likely wants them to help squash our cause."

"Hey Lo'n, ask Po'l what happened when he tried to operate my 'special weapons.'"

Po'l grumbled.

"I take it that their power is only fully realized in the hands of an expert?" asked Lo'n.

"Yes, you got it, Uncle Lo'n!" said Duke with a large smile. "I like this guy. Where've you been keeping *him?* We could use some enlightened thinking in this crew."

Po'l grumbled even louder.

"Duke, unfortunately, the last stretch of time has not been kind to me. I've just now found my way back to the coast and Mo'a's protection."

"Where were you?"

"Out there taking care of Northerners, huh?" shouted Bu'r. Ty'n and Te'o echoed with their own shouts of approval.

"A few, my proud friends," Lo'n answered, "a few."

"He's being modest," Mo'a chimed in. "Lo'n was on the mission to Orbius' fortress with He'j."

"A mission that failed," Lo'n said in a low tone.

"A mission that was doomed for failure; rushed and ill-planned from the onset," Mo'a retorted.

"Maybe so, Mo'a, but He'j was lost to us. It's our greatest loss since we started battling Orbius and his minions."

"You were with my father?"

"Yes, Ja'a. A very small group of us joined him. We felt it was the only way to penetrate his base and take him out. Even if we mustered a massive army, which you know would be impossible, it would be dwarfed by Gar and his priest warriors. Not to mention the numbers we would lose on the march north."

"Our next attempt will have to be of a similar approach," said Mo'a.

"But this time, we will have their weapons, right?" inquired Ty'n.

"It seems that our new friends have been a great help to us," Mo'a continued, "but what we ask is more than simply fighting off low-level priests. This is not their fight. It is our cause. I don't feel comfortable about potentially leading these two visitors to their deaths."

"Mo'a, I understand your concerns, but these visitors bring us an advantage that we have so desperately been missing. I think they should join us."

"Hey guys, over here. Stop acting like we aren't standing right next to you."

"Apologies, Duke," said Lo'n.

"We make our own decisions. Not to be an ass, but you can't make us do anything."

"Understood," began Mo'a, "and to echo what Lo'n said —apologies."

"Just because you have those weapons," Po'l growled. "You wouldn't be so tough if—"

"Enough, Po'l," demanded Mo'a.

"What about your ship?" chimed Ty'n. "Surely it will be an easier journey with us."

"Holy hedgehogs, can you all just shut up? You're arguing over nothing. Mo'a—appreciate that you're lookin' out for us, but Ishiro and I are planning to come along. Not because of your cause or how cool 'Uncle Lo'n' is—solely because we need to get to the *Deus* to get off this damn planet."

"This makes me very happy," Lo'n announced. "We will drink the finest Neprian wine that the coast has to offer in celebration of our newest ally and the impending trek northward."

"Hear, hear," responded Mo'a.

Ishiro'shea looked at Duke and extended a thumb.

"Finest Neprian wine? You keep getting better and better, ol' Lo'n-y boy," started Duke. "Maybe over a few glasses, you can share with us any weaknesses that you noticed."

"And what else we might encounter," added Ja'a.

"Ah, yes. Both excellent questions. I can tell you are both great leaders. And an unbeatable team."

Po'l groaned. Mo'a slapped him on the back.

CHAPTER 25

NEPRIAN WINE

"WHAT IS THIS STUFF—" DUKE began, "and why did you wait until now to share?"

"I'm glad you like it, Duke," responded Lo'n.

"Easily the best thing we've come across on this rock. There isn't even a close second."

"You surely can't mean that," replied Lo'n. "What about our lovely Ja'a? Surely, this wine falls short when compared to her beauty."

"Shut up, Uncle Lo'n," said Duke, blushing.

"I agree, shut up," Po'l blurted out in an aggressive tone.

Never mind. If it's making Po'l uncomfortable, sign me up.

"I stand—err, sit—corrected, oh wise Lo'n. I've never seen anything as beautiful as Ja'a in the whole of the universe," Duke began rather theatrically. He stood and struck a pose of an actor preparing to deliver the climactic speech of a staged drama. "I've traversed the cosmos and nothing—from the twinkling crystals when the light of the twin moons shine against the caves of Oscavia to the seemingly never-ending skies over Nova Texas, which are the bluest of blues that your baby blues could ever see—would even come close to the radiance of this beloved daughter of Neprius."

"Now *you* shut up," said Ja'a.

"I cannot be silenced! As I look up into the celestial cloak that descends upon us this evening—with only the flickering flames bestowing luminescence upon our merry crew—I can't help but think, why are we so lucky? Why are we so fortunate to have stood in the presence of a beauty that would start wars and topple kingdoms—and the millions of worlds floating above our heads will never be so blessed."

Duke bowed.

After a momentary pause, Lo'n stood up and applauded. Mo'a let loose a laugh that shook the ground. Bu'r and Ty'n whooped and cackled. Ma'n and Te'o applauded. Ishiro'shea rolled his eyes and shrugged his shoulders. Uu'k was already asleep, curled in a ball beside the ninja.

"Seriously, shut up," repeated Ja'a. She took a long sip of her Neprian wine.

"This is ridiculous," Po'l huffed.

"Oh, Po'l, lighten up," said Mo'a.

"No offense, General—"

"I'm not a general anymore."

"Whatever. No offense, Mo'a, but we are on the verge of risking our lives. No, that's not true—we are on the verge of most likely dying for this cause, and we are sitting around getting drunk and listening to this off-worlder spew nonsense."

"Calm down, Po'l. We're just having fun," said Lo'n. "It's good to laugh. There's more to life than war and heartache. In fact, if life was solely pain then why are we fighting to restore it?"

"Hear, hear," said Duke, offering a toast.

"What are you toasting, off-worlder? You have no business here. This planet doesn't need you. This cause doesn't need you or your weapons. I don't need you. Ja'a doesn't need you."

Duke made a mocking pout towards Ja'a.

"I know that you saved us in the cave with your little weapon—"

"My weapon happens to be quite large."

Ishiro'shea slapped Duke on the leg. Po'l ignored the bounty hunter's interruption.

"—and you saved Uu'k from the villagers but we don't need you anymore. You are nothing but a self-centered, egotistical pain in the ass. You are *more* likely to get us killed. It gets a lot more dangerous than peasants and priest soldiers."

"First off, Ishiro saved Uu'k," Duke said under his breath.

"What if we defeat Orbius with these weapons? With *their* help."

"What do you mean, Po'l?" asked Ja'a.

"Do you think that someone that loves himself so much will just walk away without our entire race having to kiss his feet? He will become a tyrant more dangerous than even Orbius."

"Po'l, that's enough!" screamed Ja'a.

"I agree, Ja'a. This is not the attitude and composure of a future leader of Neprius," added Mo'a.

"Neprius has no future if we need his kind to save it. We are defeating a villain with an even greater threat."

Silence fell upon the group.

Duke stiffened his stance, which no longer bore any resemblance to an actor's. He gently placed his wine on the sand as his smile dissipated.

"Po'l, I was just kidding around about Ja'a—well, I mean she is beautiful, but—"

"See off-worlder, you aren't capable of being serious."

"Look, I get it. I'm not part of your cause and, quite frankly, I don't want to be part of your cause. However, circumstances have made it apparent that my cause and your cause are symbiotically linked. I'm not saying you have to like me—in fact, it's been obvious that you don't, ever since you were convinced I was a spy and you almost killed yourself trying to work Ol' Betsy. Guess what? I don't care for you either. You're reckless. All of that's okay with me. But I do need my ship back. And if me getting my ship back helps Ja'a and Uu'k and the guys over there have a better life, that's just gravy. But we stand a helluva lot better chance working together."

"It's obvious that Ja'a and Duke are working together," Lo'n added. "So are you saying that she has poor judgement?"

"No. Well, yes. Maybe. I don't know. I'm sorry all, but I can't continue. Not with him."

"Po'l! You can't leave. We need you," cried Ja'a. "Why are you behaving this way?"

"This cause is my life. I will defeat Orbius alone."

Po'l threw his full glass of Neprian wine towards the sea. The rebel stormed into the central building of the compound, muttering under his breath.

"Well, that happened," said the bounty hunter.

"Duke, I'm sorry, I don't know what got into him," said Mo'a.

"I do, but that's for another day."

"What?"

"It doesn't matter," Ja'a interjected. "We are all tired and have been through many perils already—and we haven't even started the final journey. And the wine might be getting the best of us."

"Yeah, he didn't even have any—"

"Duke," Ja'a continued sternly, "the wine is probably getting the best of us. Right, Duke?"

"Fine."

"I'm going to go talk to him."

"I'll go with you, Ja'a," Mo'a said. "He is my nephew, after all."

"No, Mo'a. I think it would be best if I handled this alone."

Ja'a followed Po'l's path into the compound.

"So wait," Duke began, "we actually have a real 'uncle' here?"

Mo'a, his head hanging, sauntered away from the gathering.

"It's hard to see your kin behave in such a manner," said Lo'n. "Can't help but feel like you have something to do with it."

"He doesn't," retorted the Nova Texan.

"Why do you say that?"

"It has nothing to do with Mo'a—it's Ja'a."

"I'm not following you, Duke."

"Po'l has the hots for her."

Lo'n's face was overrun by an empty stare.

"It means that he's got feelings for her. You know, googly eyes, sweaty palms, heart beating fast. He loves her."

"Oh, that *is* interesting."

"Yeah, and I think that's why he hates me."

"I don't follow."

"Ja'a and I have, you know, gotten along real well and all. He probably feels threatened. I mean, before me, she was surrounded by some real B-teamers." Duke swiveled on the spot to make sure Ma'n, Te'o, Ty'n, or Bu'r weren't looking. "They're good guys and all, but Po'l was the only alpha in the lot, so he never feared them stealing his woman."

"This makes more sense. You might have been the straw that broke the greattu's back. I wasn't aware of this situation and with all of the other pressure that he's under—what transpired doesn't shock me."

"Other pressure?"

"See, Duke, Po'l is Mo'a's nephew—"

"Yep, got that."

"—and is in line, or rather expected, to be the next great warrior-general of the Southern tribes. It has not gone according to plan thus far. He's not even the leader of this band of rebel guerrillas."

"That accounts for his awkwardly dramatic speech when we arrived here. I think its aim was to be inspiring."

"Probably so. Mo'a is a great orator—and has given speeches to troops and townsfolk alike that roused their spirits to the point that they would do anything for him."

"And now the woman he loves is preventing him from achieving his destiny. That's not that uncommon, if you think about it. Women be ruining everything, right?"

Duke playfully punched Lo'n in the shoulder. The meaning of the gesture seemed to be lost on the veteran Neprian warrior.

"Po'l is reminded every day that he will likely never be the great leader that he was groomed to be by seeing someone else control his squadron. And now that I realize that the person that represents his failure as a commander also represents his failure in personal happiness—I see why he acted the way he did."

Duke took another swig of his drink.

"I can sympathize."

"Really?"

"Yes, I once had a 'Ja'a' back many moons ago. She also was better than me at my job. And she also got away. Now she's simply a ghost."

"To lost loves and moving on," Lo'n said, raising his glass. "Now let's rejoin the group before they drink all the wine."

"Cheers to that."

The duo made their way back to the torchlit semicircle. Mo'a seemed to be leading the storytelling.

"Duke, my friend, they were just telling me about your adventures thus far. And the magic that those weapons of yours possess. They say that Betty is quite the eradicator of priest warriors."

"Betsy."

"Oh, yes, Betsy. Can we see this Betsy in action?"

"And the little one," added Ty'n.

"Sure, why not?"

"Ishiro, toss a rock up in the air—and I'll blast it."

The ninja shook his head and pointed down at the sleeping Neprian on his lap.

"Oh, sorry. Anyone? Pick up a stone and throw it as far as you can towards the sea."

"This sounds like fun!" boomed Mo'a.

"I'll take a stab at it," said Lo'n.

He reached down and grabbed a rock roughly the size of his hand. He reared back and chucked the object towards the seashore. As it began its descent back to the soil, Duke relieved his laser revolver from his holster and fired a single shot in the direction of the stone. Direct hit!

"Impressive. What if I did this, however?"

Lo'n grabbed three rocks in one hand and quickly tossed them away from the camp. They sailed in different directions and at different trajectories. Duke, with his gun already in his hand, rallied off three pulses in rapid succession. The courses of all three stones were altered—all direct hits.

"Duke, I see why everyone thinks that you can turn the tide for us," belted Mo'a. "I've never seen anything like it."

"Indeed," confirmed Lo'n. "Now what about this Betsy you speak of?"

"Wait until you see this!" shouted Bu'r.

Duke removed Betsy from his back and presented her as if she were a prized jewel from the royal family of Oscavia.

"See that gathering of trees over there?" asked Duke to Mo'a and Lo'n.

"Yes."

"See how dense it is—almost like a wooden wall separating this area from the water? Be prepared to be amazed and awed by Betsy's singing voice."

He aimed the Sonic Widowmaker shotgun at a dense area of foliage where five or six large trunks appeared to intertwine into a single tree.

"Sing for us, ol' girl," Duke whispered as he pulled the trigger.

The bellow of the firearm knocked Mo'a to his knees. Lo'n seemed shaken by a bad case of secondhand recoil. Both gazed in wonderment at what remained of the trees.

"Duke, I don't know what to say."

"I do!"

Ja'a sprinted toward them.

Not good, thought Duke.

"Are you kidding me? This is a hidden base. Keyword—hidden. If Orbius or Gar or one of their henchmen find this place, our cause is over with, done. Duke, I'm not surprised—"

"They made me do it—" interjected the bounty hunter.

"—But Mo'a? Lo'n? Guys? I'm sure someone heard that... that... sound—someone that's not supposed to hear it. And, on top of that, you woke up Uu'k."

Even Ishiro'shea seemed to side with the enraged rebel.

"The noise reminds me of when," Lo'n started, as if he were in a trance, ignoring Ja'a completely, "a—err—I can't put a finger on it. It's impressive, I must say."

"You're probably thinking about a penguin in a blender—" Duke began.

Ja'a cut the bounty hunter off. "Enough! Of course, when I heard the weapon go off, I immediately assumed that we were being attacked. Then I come out and witness this? A bunch of fools and their wine."

A crowd of Neprians had started to trickle out of the base.

"Nothing to see here," shouted Duke. "Go back in and do your rebelling. Or whatever it is that you're doing in the base."

"This is why I will be joining you, after all," came a voice from behind the irate female. It was Po'l. "Someone needs to make sure this mission doesn't implode."

"And that's you, is it? We don't need you, Po'l. We have Lo'n. He's survived Orbius' fortress once and he will again."

"Thank you, Duke, my friend," began Lo'n, "but we could use everyone to help us overcome the perils of a journey to Sansagon. It *is* quite dangerous."

"Did you not see his weapon, Lo'n?" asked Bu'r. "It can't be stopped."

"I wish it were so. But there are many things that pose great dangers even when you have this Betsy," replied Lo'n. He turned his attention to Ja'a. "I'm sorry, I will take full blame for this distraction. You are right, it was foolish."

"Very."

"Yes, very foolish. Don't blame Duke. I take full responsibility."

"Yes, but it was that moron that fired it," said Po'l, pointing at Duke.

"You changed your mind awfully quick about the mission. What was it? Worried about Lo'n and I becoming best friends and kicking total ass? Or that I might be an evil spy sent by Orbius in what would be the most elaborate and well-orchestrated double cross in history? Or is that I might be getting a bit too close to—"

"Shut up!" shouted Ja'a. "Everyone sit down—and shut up."

The group, including Mo'a, followed her command. Ja'a herself sat down and grabbed someone's wine that was sitting on the ground. She took a big swig.

"Mo'a, I'm sorry. I feel I'm letting you and my father down. And the cause."

"I won't even entertain a thought like that. Your father would be proud of you and what you've become—regardless of if you are the one to drive the stake through Orbius' heart or not. That reminds me—I have something for you." Mo'a headed back into the main building.

Ishiro'shea patted Ja'a on the back. She appeared to find it comforting.

"So, Lo'n, what are we to expect on this journey?" Duke asked in a focused, sober tone. Ja'a's eyes lit up. The rest of the Neprians and Ishiro'shea leaned in and awaited the old rebel's response.

Lo'n took a hefty drink of his wine. "It was not an easy road. That's for sure."

"So what are we talking about? More priests?"

"Yes, we have no idea of knowing how many of Gar's troops we will encounter. Maybe none. Maybe hundreds. My guess is that he has his eyes and ears out, awaiting our approach."

"How would he know?" inquired Duke.

"He knows that you and your unique armaments aren't in his control—so rest assured, he's on high alert. I'm sure he has squads out in every nook of Neprius."

"Okay, aside from an unknown number of skirmishes with those javelin-tossin' bastards, what else?"

"Up first..." Lo'n paused. "The land bridge."

The Neprians groaned collectively.

"I'm guessing that means the land bridge isn't a viable vacation spot," asked Duke.

"Remember when I told you about our warring tribes and how Peace was buried and sealed off in a temple?" said Ja'a.

"Yes, until He'j and Togg recovered it and brought Vangu here," replied Duke.

"Right. The hidden temple is on the land bridge," began Ja'a. "Some guards were sent in to watch the temple. Every decade or so, others would enter the land bridge to assume the same position. However, no one knew if they ever made it to the temple to actually guard it. There was nothing allowed out —no news whatsoever. Not until He'j and Togg led the mission to recover Peace."

"And?"

"There were no guards. The temple could have been unguarded for hundreds of cycles," she replied.

"At least the Orb was still there."

"Yes, that's because they decided to seal off the land bridge. No one in, no one out for generations—except for the guards."

"Sacrificial lambs, it seems," replied Duke.

"But I didn't mention that the bridge was sealed off rather... well, hastily."

"What do you mean?" asked Duke.

"Entire communities were living within the swamps of the land bridge."

"Why weren't they evacuated?"

"I don't know," replied Ja'a.

"So, I'm guessing that these villagers just didn't die out," commented Duke.

"According to He'j and Togg—," began Ja'a.

"They are monsters," interrupted Lo'n.

"Monsters?" asked Ty'n.

"Yes. They've become one with the swamp. They're wild animals—inbred to the point where they are barely recognizable as Neprians, just a grotesque mix of the two races."

"That sounds fun," replied Duke.

"And, what we learned was that they're tired of eating the bounty of the swamp," said Lo'n.

"Cannibals? I hate cannibals," Duke quipped.

"Does anyone *like* cannibals?" asked Po'l in a sarcastic tone.

"We were caught off guard. We lost some of our best men. Those that escaped the swamps alive were lucky."

"Any weaknesses?" asked Ja'a.

"Vegetables?"

Lo'n ignored Duke's comments. "Actually, we did notice that they're nocturnal. We never encountered them during the day. I would suggest swift travel during the day—and being as quiet as possible when the darkness descends."

"Not to be an ass, but why don't we just build a boat and sail around this strip o' death? Seems like the logical thing to do."

"It is logical," responded Lo'n. He paused. "But—"

"Here it comes."

"Orbius has already thought of that. He has guards along the coast in boats. And he's sunk the few that we maintained in the South anyways."

"Right. That officially sucks."

"It's not ideal, no. He's forcing us to go directly through the swamp."

"Smart. And they can get down here much quicker with control of the sea."

"Yes."

"Damn. So with these swampfolk running the land bridge, did they take over the temple?"

"Oddly enough, no. Something about the temple spooked them."

"Not sure what would spook an undead swamp monster," said Duke.

"I think He'j knew. He never told us why, but he said that re-entry into the temple would be certain death. Neither he nor Togg ever mentioned the reason. He'j was not prone to exaggeration and, coupled with the fact that the cannibals didn't take it over, that was good enough for us. We all assumed that traps were in place to protect the Orb and that they remain still. Traps that only He'j and Togg knew or that they placed on their exit."

"Or maybe something worse," added Po'l.

"I hate to agree with Po'l," Duke began, "but, in my experience, it's *always* something worse."

Po'l looked shocked.

"What else, Lo'n? Let's say we get past the flesh-craving inbreds... What's next? I'm assuming they'll have a welcoming party in charge of guarding the northern entrance to the wall and making sure no one gets in. Or, in our case, gets out."

"It is heavily guarded."

"Great."

"But, I'm not too worried about that."

"Why? Because of Ol' Betsy?" Duke said with a grinning confidence.

"No. Because I know where the gaps are. It's a bit rougher terrain but they leave it open because—"

"Let me guess," interjected Duke, "because they don't think anyone could make it through whatever is on the other side."

"Yes. We would have to go through the heart of the swamp."

The Neprians exchanged glances without saying a word.

"So instead of just having to avoid these cannibals, we're going to break into their house, urinate on the living room floor, and try and leave without being caught?"

"I'm not sure I follow but, yes, it will be a trickier proposition."

"Is that how you and my father got through?" Ja'a asked.

"No, not exactly. He'j remembered a passage from his trip with Togg that was clear—however, it was blocked up after we got through. But to our knowledge, they never added support to the area that marks the end of the swampland. Togg said it was pointless and Orbius—once again, to our knowledge, hasn't any reason to go against that thinking."

The bounty hunter stood up and paced around the group. He tipped the brim of his hat. "Let's say we get through the cannibal-infested swamp and beyond the wall—without having to fight through the priests. Then what?"

"It's a long trek to Sansagon. The direct route is mostly grasslands. Not a lot of hiding; we'll be exposed. On the positive side, there aren't many towns or outposts that could spot us. We will probably have to deal with a few scouting parties, but I don't think that will be our biggest concern."

"And that would be?"

"Grundar."

"Oh, right. I forgot about the damn grundar."

"You don't think we'll actually come in contact with them, right?" asked Ja'a.

"Probably not. You never know."

"Have you seen them?" she asked.

"No."

"No one here has seen one? And yet we are freaking out over a potential attack?"

"Yes."

"I think someone might be pulling one over on ya'. I mean, invisible beings forcing you to do and not do certain things based on extreme consequences—pretty sure that's a relatively common annoyance in most every developing civilization."

"Grundar are very real, Duke."

"Believe what you want to believe. If we're lucky enough to avoid these mysterious, magical flying kitty cats, is it a straight shot to the fortress?"

"Yes."

"And can we get in?"

"I believe so. Our theory—that a small unit can penetrate Orbius' base—is sound. We could never win all all-out attack, even if we had greater numbers."

"Did you actually make it in last time?" asked Po'l.

Lo'n looked around at the group. "No."

There was some mild grumbling amongst the team. Even from Ja'a.

"Hey, he's been closer than any of us," Duke started, "and he witnessed He'j make it through. Tell 'em, Lo'n."

"You're right."

"So what happened on that mission?" inquired Po'l.

Lo'n looked at Ja'a.

"Ja'a—"

"Go ahead, Uncle. I can handle it. I know my father was killed at the hands of Orbius—it's something that has petrified my heart—so the details of your attempt won't change anything. We need to know what you know, if we are to have any chance at success."

"Very well." Lo'n cleared his throat. "Our party was about the size of this one. As we descended upon the fortress, we decided to split up and search for weaknesses around the entire perimeter. Unfortunately, most of us discovered guard units. We fought valiantly. He'j found a way in—through an underground tunnel—and came back to tell us. He discovered me engaged in a brutal fight with three priests."

"What happened?" asked Bu'r.

"He'j helped me defeat them. We quickly went to the defense of our other comrades... but were too late. We lost everyone. Then He'j told me to do something that I regret to this day."

Lo'n bowed his head.

"It's okay, Uncle. Go on. Please."

"He told me to go back to the coast. I needed to tell everyone that there was a way in—a natural tunnel system that originated from a cave north of the base. If we both attempted entry and failed, the cause would have to start over from the beginning. He said the knowledge was greater than both he and I."

Lo'n hung his head. A tear ran down Ja'a's cheek.

"And so I left him," Lo'n continued. "I left him there to die. I can't help but think that I could have saved him; that we could have defeated Orbius... together."

"But Uncle, if my father's fear came true, and you both were killed, we wouldn't know that there's a way in."

"However," Duke began, "since He'j made it through—"

"They probably have sealed off that passage. Doubled down on any weakness," Po'l said, finishing Duke's thought.

The rebels looked around at one another. No one said a word. Their gazes focused on Lo'n as they awaited his response.

"My gut tells me that it's still open."

"And why is that?" asked Po'l.

"He'j didn't go in that way. He discovered it, yes, but he didn't use it."

"What?"

"He felt that if I could bring back a party—armed with the knowledge that I had gained about the fortress—it would be better than this one single shot. We could send a troop or two through the tunnels and then a few to do exactly what he did."

"And that was?"

"Walk right up to the front door and knock."

"But why?" Ja'a cried. "That would've been suicide. My father didn't have a death wish."

"No, but he cared about this cause more than anything and he knew that he wasn't destined to be the savior. That honor—that destiny—would fall to someone else."

Ja'a began to weep softly. Ishiro'shea put his arm around her.

"I made my way back to the coast—but, as you know, that took me much longer than I had hoped."

"What caused the delays?"

"Traveling alone with no food and in enemy territory is not easy. I had to scavenge and—I hate to admit this—steal from villages along the way."

"Did you have any run-ins with Gar's men?"

"Yes, I evaded capture once, just east of the Valley of the Grundar."

"And the cannibals?"

"I was lucky. I traveled by day, and at night they paid me no interest—or did not pick up my scent."

"I'm glad you made it back, for one," started the bounty hunter, "and I feel you give us the edge we need to take down Orby, Gar, and whatever else is up in that fortress."

"For the *Deus*, right?" added Po'l.

"Yes, for the *Deus*, of course," Duke replied. "What else would it be for?"

Ja'a began to laugh. Ishiro slapped him on the leg.

"Now Duke, if I didn't know any better, it seems that you might be coming around on this idea of helping out the cause," added Lo'n.

"I'm here for one reason and one reason alone—"

"Yourself," Po'l said, again finishing Duke's thought—this time using a word selection he personally wouldn't have chosen.

"Well..."

"Ja'a, I'm so glad that I found this," interrupted Mo'a.

Saved by the Mo'a.

"What, Mo'a?"

Mo'a extended his arm and in his hand dangled a long chain necklace. The interlocking rings were thick and clunky and appeared quite heavy. They were an odd mix of silver and black; almost like matted pewter. On the chain hung a pendant, lighter in color but chunkier in design. It was a half circle with a jagged edge down the center. It seemed to be part of a two-piece emblem, missing its complementary half.

"What is this?" asked Ja'a.

"This is something that your father wanted me to give you. He gave it to me before he left for Sansagon. I have no idea what it is, what it means, or anything. It's nothing of value—it's made from regular mustangsen. And I have no idea what the emblem means. I've never seen it before."

"Did you ask him when he gave it to you?" inquired Duke.

"No, Duke, I did not. He was so very adamant about making sure she has it, I thought it might have some special meaning, like a family heirloom."

He handed it over to Ja'a. She examined it.

"I have never seen this before."

"I have," began Lo'n. "Your father wore the other half. He said it was good luck because he knew you would eventually wear the other half. The pendants formed a perfect circle— and, even though they were broken, they would be whole again. He believed it symbolized the Neprian struggle. The planet would be whole again. The mustangsen also served as a constant reminder of Orbius' greed and evil—for it's the very material that our brothers and sisters are dying in the mines to recover for his own vanity."

Ja'a placed it around her neck. Her tears evaporated and resolve hardened her expression.

"Thank you, Mo'a. This means a lot. More than you will ever know. And thank you, Lo'n, for that story. When we defeat Orbius, I will find my father's half and restore it—just as we will restore this planet."

The Neprians cheered. Duke and Ishiro'shea raised a glass next to their new comrades.

"Let us enjoy these drinks. Tomorrow, we head north!"

CHAPTER 26

MISSED MEETING

"MAYBE WE SHOULD'VE TAPPED THE brakes on that ninth bottle of wine, huh?"

Ishiro'shea raised his arm groggily and signaled a thumbs-up in the slowest of slow motion. His hammock rocked a bit... then some more... then the ninja was deposited face-first onto the hard stone floor.

"Not very ninja-like, little buddy."

Duke splashed some water on his face, sat back down on the slab of weathered padding that constituted a bed, and covered his face with his hands.

"Seriously, I think we might've hit it too hard—especially the day before an extremely long walk."

Ishiro repeated his earlier gesture—this time from a position face down on the ground.

"At least the room's an upgrade over our last Neprian accommodations."

"Off-worlders, you ready? We're all meeting in the main hall." The voice passed by the doorway and faded. *Shut up, Po'l.*

"We'll be there," Duke shouted, but he knew it was hopeless that Po'l actually heard his response. He then turned to

Ishiro. "Are you kidding me? They want us now? Do Neprians not get hangovers?"

Duke closed his eyes.

The pattering of feet continued to fill the hallway outside their room; a symphony of voices followed. Duke picked up his sidekick by the arm and propped him up against the door frame.

"Look alive, Ishiro. Let's just hope this is a quick strategy session. I mean it's not like we won't have days of walking... and walking... and walking to discuss how we're going to hide from cannibals and hide from flying panthers and hide in tunnels. Damn, our entire game plan is to walk and hide. Anyways, let's not keep 'em waiting anymore. They probably can't even start the meeting without us."

The duo left their room and made their way down a narrow stone corridor. A torch protruded from the wall every few paces so that the hall was adequately lit despite having no windows. The two exchanged stares with rebel soldiers and other assorted followers of the cause as they passed; it was obvious that these people knew more about Duke and Ishiro'shea than vice versa.

The bounty hunters followed the sounds of commotion and turned right halfway along the corridor. They entered a vast circular public space; hundreds of Southerners navigated the room in rapid crisscross patterns without colliding with one another. Chatter, laughter, and animated discussion filled the room. Both men had to cover their eyes—the intense light was a drastic change from the torchlit halls. Duke looked up to see that the entire ceiling was a glass dome.

"Hey you!" Duke shouted at a group of what appeared to be soldiers. They ignored him. "I said, hey you!"

All four turned around in unison.

"Yes, Duke LaGrange of Nova Texas," one replied.

"How do you know who I am? Never mind, don't have time for it. Where's the great hall?"

The quartet laughed. "This is the great hall."

"That lying ass, Po'l. He said to meet him in the great hall. He thinks he's so funny."

"I saw Po'l moments ago," began another one of the soldiers, "but he was heading into the main hall."

"Are you serious? It's way too early for this. Can you at least show me how to get to the *main* hall?"

The soldier pointed to an oversized wooden door at the side of the room.

"It's just on the other side of that door. When you enter, there's a hall—on the right is the hatchery for the winged flurn; keep following the hall and take a left immediately following the mail room. After a few paces you will see two spiral staircases—take the one of the left. The one on the right goes to the arts and crafts center."

"Where does the one on the left go? The opera house?"

"No," replied the solider, "that's on the other side of the base."

"Of course it is."

The rebel continued, "But follow the right staircase down and you will see the door to the main hall."

"Thanks."

"Good luck."

"We might need it."

They followed the instructions to a tee, Duke only stopping to ask the hatchery attendant if he could order a bucket of fried flurn. The attendant did not find it humorous.

Duke looked up at what had to be the door to the main hall, on the basis of the humongous placard that read: *Main Hall.*

"Sorry we're late!"

The room was empty, with the exception of Lo'n and Ja'a.

"Hey guys, you missed our chat."

"I see that."

"We leave after we all have a bite to eat. Sound good?"

"Not really. What's the plan?"

"I can fill you in on the way."

"Hopefully we won't have to use these too often," Lo'n said, hoisting a curved saber that was almost as tall as Ishiro'shea. *Impressive.*

"Hey, buddy," Duke said, nudging Ishiro. "Sword envy?"

The ninja ignored him.

"Okay, well then—where's the grub?"

"Ishiro'shea! Duke!" screamed a juvenile voice. It was Uu'k. "You can't leave without saying goodbye."

Duke glanced at Ja'a and mouthed, "Not going?"

"Uu'k is going to stay here with Mo'a," Ja'a replied. "She has earned some time away from Dre'en and from adventure. Also, she expressed interest in learning how to handle a sword."

Ishiro'shea knelt down beside Uu'k and they embraced.

Duke patted her on the head. "See you soon, Uu'k."

"You better. I want Ishiro to teach me some of his sword tricks."

"I'll do everything I can to make that happen, kid."

"Thanks."

"Now can I get an 'Uncle Duke' before we leave?"

"No."

Lo'n laughed and handed Uu'k the hilt of his saber. The blade clinked against the ground with an excruciating sound. It was obvious that the Neprian child did not quite yet possess the physical strength to hold the sword aloft.

"It will come with time, Uu'k. If we hurry—and if Ja'a says it's fine—maybe we can do a quick beginner's lesson before we have to leave."

Uu'k rushed out in her excitement to learn from the Neprian swordsman.

CHAPTER 27

A COUNTER-ORB?

THE TREK FROM THE REBEL hideout to the entrance of the land bridge was a day and a half—at a brisk walk. Of the nine travelers, only Bu'r seemed to struggle with the pace. Lo'n, despite being the oldest, appeared to be affected the least. Duke's earlier challenges to acclimate to the fresh air were behind him. *Maybe I could get used to this whole non-pollution thing,* he thought. It reminded him of his youth on Nova Texas. The good parts, at least.

The wall itself was an ominous structure that could be seen miles away, rising above the forest. It was nothing like the divider that ran outside of Dre'en—it was more archaic, more primitive. Boulders made up its base—they decreased in size as they moved skyward. The top of the wall curved out and was laced with sharpened wooden pikes, presumably to annoy would-be breachers.

From the coast, they had mostly traveled through uninhabited areas of forest and field, but the last few miles had been on a cleared path from one of the villages to the land bridge. The road led directly into a narrow archway in the wall—the only potential entryway visible from their location.

"I was kinda expecting some guards," remarked Duke.

"Wouldn't the Northerners want to prevent y'all from gaining access to their home?"

"They don't feel it's necessary," replied Lo'n.

"That bad, huh?"

"Unfortunately. They don't think we would risk trying to make it through the swamps and whatever else might be there."

"What about those guys gettin' out? Maybe they could go terrorize some priests and help us out."

"That would not be a good thing, Duke. You don't want these guys out of the swamps. But, luckily, they won't."

"What do you mean?"

"They are part of the swamp. It's their home and they won't venture far from it."

"How can you be certain?" asked Duke.

"Yeah, how can you be sure?" echoed Ty'n.

"Once we get inside the wall, you will see. There are hundreds of these beings—maybe thousands—and they only live in the swamp. They haven't even moved out to other areas around it. Their homes—if you want to call them that— blend into the muck; they are truly one with their ecosystem."

"I hope we don't have to see—but I get your point," Duke replied. "And the swamp runs all the way to the northern wall?"

"It's concentrated near the wall. In fact, we probably won't even smell the swamp until the end of our first day."

"How far is the walk?"

"Walk? Duke, we will be going a bit faster than a walk."

"How far is the jog?"

"We should cover the majority of the land bridge in a full day. I think we should camp near the temple—which, I hope, will spook the swampfolk. When daylight hits, we will go as fast as we can until we hit the exit. Even though the cannibals won't be out during the day, the terrain is tough. Other creatures lurk there—and the path won't be as easy as what we've experienced thus far."

"Kinda figured that," smirked Duke.

"Any more questions?" Lo'n asked the group.

"Are you sure you'll know the way to the hidden temple?" inquired Ma'n.

"Yes. When He'j and I crossed, we marked a path—I'm hoping the markers remain. If not, as long as we get to the swamp, we can follow it to the wall."

"My man, Lo'n! We're lucky to have run into you!" Duke extended his arm to give Lo'n a high five; Lo'n did not reciprocate the gesture. Duke assumed the Neprian didn't know what a high five was.

"Wish we could say the same about you, off-worlder," grumbled Po'l.

"Guys, let's get focused," said Ja'a. "This is going to be a perilous journey. Let's do everything in our power to avoid these creatures and get through the swampland intact."

"So, how do we get... in?" asked the Nova Texan.

"Open the door, moron," heckled Po'l.

Duke walked over to the archway and gave the door a firm push. It slowly creaked open.

"Don't even bother locking it, huh?"

"It was sealed from the outside—on both ends—until He'j and Togg excavated and discovered these doors," explained Lo'n. "And since securing the walls isn't high on Orbius' to-do list, they just remain unlocked."

What's with this planet and not locking doors?

The road that led to the archway stopped abruptly on the other side. For as far as the eye could see, a maze of branches dominated the landscape. Twisted, tangled, intertwined—the work of a hundred cycles worth of unimpeded growth. *This is an old forest,* thought Duke. No intuitive paths could be identified—it was just wooden chaos.

"How do we, um, get through this mess, Lo'n?"

"By enduring a lot of scrapes and scratches, my off-world friend."

"Great. What about—"

Ishiro'shea jumped to the front of the line and hacked away with his katana. Branches fell with far less noise than one would expect. He slashed and cut as he marched forward.

"One step ahead of me, little buddy."

"Not a bad idea," added Lo'n. He removed his saber and joined Ishiro'shea. They hacked through the forest in unison, clearing enough space for the party members to pass through with ease.

"Once we get out of this—which shouldn't be much longer —we should see our first marker. From there, it's a relatively treeless run until we get to the temple and set up camp."

"I'm all for that."

Amidst the foliage was a solitary scrap of orange cloth flickering gently in the breeze, fixed to a lonely branch jutting out from a thorny bush. *Marker number one.* The bounty hunter squinted and focused his sight up ahead—another dot of orange.

"What do you think is so bad about that place?" Duke asked Ja'a, pointing at the parts of the temple that peeked out from the mangled trees.

"I'm not sure—probably some traps so that no one else would successfully enter again. Like Lo'n said."

"That doesn't make sense to me."

"What do you mean?"

"If he took the Orb out, why would he waste his time placing traps until after he returned it? Why would he add obstacles for himself when he came back to seal it away again?"

"Maybe—"

"Maybe," Duke interrupted, "there's something else down in that temple."

"Don't be foolish," interjected Lo'n, who had overheard their conversation.

"Think about it, Lo'n. There has to be something in there that He'j wanted to keep a secret."

"Probably, for good reason," added Ja'a.

"Yes, Ja'a is right. He'j only had the best interests of his people. If there is something down there, we don't want to, nor can we afford to, encounter it."

"I don't doubt that *at all*—but what if it's something that can help us? Maybe He'j was being overly cautious."

"Like what?"

"What if there's another Orb?"

The group engaged in a collective gasp. A drawn-out hush permeated the camp.

"I don't think that's the case," said Lo'n, breaking the silence.

"But why?"

Ja'a began, "If my father felt there was any way that a person, creature, artifact, or other thing could help the cause— he would have explored it. He certainly wouldn't have told his most trusted friend to stay clear of it at all costs."

Lo'n smiled and nodded in Ja'a's direction.

"I think it's worth a visit," proclaimed the bounty hunter.

"No!" shouted Lo'n. "Duke, when daylight hits we are going to make it through the swamp and into enemy territory. We are so close—why would you risk everything on something that can be avoided?"

"Curiosity."

"Haven't you heard that curiosity killed the humpback tyorf-gella?"

"I can honestly say that I have not—but I get where you're going with it, Lo'n. But what if there is something useful in there? What if—"

"Enough. This cause isn't going to be dictated by 'what ifs' and 'maybes.' We have a mission," Ja'a said with conviction. "We need you and Ishiro'shea to help us—and I know you need us to get your ship back—but as mission leader, I forbid you to go into that temple."

Duke's mouth hung open. *She has guts, that's for sure.*

"Isn't it enough that this temple is providing us a shield—for whatever reason—from the beasts that lurk mere paces away?"

"I get it—don't look a gift horse in the mouth, right?"

Ja'a offered only a blank stare. *Probably didn't get that one.* "I don't know, but you shouldn't question it."

"If your father hadn't been the one to issue the order, would your judgment be as ironclad?"

"What does that mean?"

Ishiro slapped Duke.

"Answer me, what does that mean?"

"Ja'a, you would do anything for this cause—so why refuse to open a door that could help us?"

"Because my father told us that door shouldn't be opened —and I would trust him until the end of our planet."

Duke could sense her blood beginning to boil. *I should back off*, he thought. But Duke liked to ignore his thoughts.

"What if your father was... mistaken? What if the end of your planet will only be prevented by what's in that temple?"

Ja'a stormed towards Duke, her eyes burning.

"I'm in charge and the final command is to stay away from the temple. Got it?"

"What if I don't—"

"What if you don't follow my orders? Is that what you were going to say? You don't have to. You're right. We don't control you. But good luck getting to the wall at night through the swamp. Without a team. You'd be good as dead. Or you could go back south—away from your precious ship. Have at it! Good luck!"

Silence fell over the group again—this time even more suffocating.

"You're right. I'll stop. You're in charge. I will follow you to my death, oh fearless leader of mine," Duke said in a snarky tone. He removed his hat and bowed.

Ja'a turned away without responding to the bounty hunter's demeaning gesture; she grabbed a large branch and drove it into the ground at a low angle. She started to shape a pointed tip near the end with an arrowhead.

"Get back to work, everyone. Those that aren't shaping pikes to give us a barrier, start working on fire pits. We only have a few more moments until the night is upon us. Our meaningless discussion ate up precious time—"

"And if we don't get these fires lit and pikes sharpened, we could be the ones that are 'ate up.'"

"Nice one, Lo'n," Duke said as he bunched dry pieces of tree debris into a pile.

"Duke," Lo'n whispered, "I get it. Don't tell Ja'a but I've also wondered what lies in that temple—and why he was so adamant about it. But this is not the time. If we can get off the land bridge without losing anyone—that would be amazing. He'j and I weren't that lucky last time."

"What do you think is in there—honestly?"

Lo'n paused. "Ja'a doesn't know this about her father but he didn't trust many. He trusted Mo'a, me, his late wife—but that's about it. There could be something in there that's really powerful but which he felt could complicate the situation if it fell into the wrong hands."

"So maybe another Orb? Or a counter-Orb?"

"Possibly. I think if it was an indestructible creature that was to be left undisturbed—he would have told us. I think if it was a set of traps—"

"Which is what you originally said," interrupted Duke.

"Yes, if it was a set of traps, He'j probably would have told us. So, the fact that he wasn't open about it—even with his trust issues—leads me to believe it could be something more complex."

"Something that if not discussed in the proper context could be misconstrued or manipulated."

"Exactly."

"Like another Orb!"

"Well—"

"Well, I guess it doesn't matter. I'm not going to betray Ja'a."

"You must really like her, Duke."

"She's not too shabby. For a Neprian," said Duke. "And I do respect her. Anyways, I appreciated the chat, Lo'n."

"Who has first watch?" shouted Ja'a as she drove another pike into the ground. Duke and Lo'n exchanged looks, ending their clandestine conversation.

"We do!" Duke replied, raising his hand.

"I'm not so sure that's the best idea."

"You don't trust Ishiro'shea and I? When have we ever broken your trust?"

"True," Ja'a answered. "But—"

"I'll take the first watch with them," interjected Po'l. "They won't do anything stupid on my watch. Nothing more than usual, at least."

"I can live with that," replied the rebel leader.

"I'm a bit offended," returned Duke directly to Ja'a. "After all we've been through."

The commanding Neprian paid no attention to the bounty hunter's comment.

"Now let's finish our camp and hope we have an easy night ahead of us."

<hr>

The dozen or so mounds of crackling fire provided ample illumination; Duke would be able to spot an encroaching swamp cannibal from a decent range. *They won't get to fifty paces from the camp before I could pick 'em off*, he thought to himself.

The night was silent—as was the swamp. No moans. No groans. No growls. Nothing resembling grotesque man-eating swamp creatures seemed to be lurking about, waiting to pounce on the sleeping Neprians. He shifted his legs and backside upon his rock seat and tipped up the brim of his hat. He twirled his sidearm by the trigger guard.

"So, looks like we might make it outta here without running into those flesh-gobblers."

"It's still early, off-worlder," replied Po'l. "I think you should probably be more on guard, like your talkative friend."

Ishiro'shea had his katana unsheathed as he crouched behind a row of pikes.

"He's somewhat of a worry wart."

"You aren't worried at all?"

"Nah, I think we'll be alright. With me, Ishiro, Ol' Betsy, Lo'n, and this guy here," Duke said, twirling his laser revolver with even more pizzazz, "we can take care of anything."

"You know there are a few more of us here, too."

"Yeah, we'll be fine despite that."

To Duke's surprise, Po'l chuckled. *Has he finally snapped?*

"You know what—that was a solid joke. I'll give the devil his due."

Po'l extended his hand and Duke reluctantly shook it.

"How much longer do we have in this shift, you think?" asked the Nova Texan, not expecting an answer. He stood up and walked around the perimeter.

"Everything okay?"

"Outside of losing the battle to boredom, I'm just peachy. It's been a weird day."

"Because Ja'a got pretty annoyed at you? That was quite amusing. She made you look like a scolded child. Actually,

Uu'k would've put up more of a fight than you," Po'l said with a grin.

"Hey, watch it. That's big talk coming from a guy that got beat up by an inanimate object."

"Not my brightest moment."

"I hope not."

"But back to today," Po'l said in a more serious tone, and at a lower decibel level. "Do you really think there's something in the temple?"

"No need to start it up again. I'm done talking about that. I said my piece and Ja'a—"

"Shut you up."

"Kinda. She was furious."

"Seriously, do you think there's something in there?"

"No... yeah... yes, probably... maybe... I don't know."

"Was that a yes or a no?"

"Honestly?"

"Yes, honestly."

"I can't believe I'm telling you, of all people, this—but I do think it's a little strange about how cryptic Ja'a's dad was about the whole 'Don't go in there no matter what' mumbo jumbo. If it was that bad, wouldn't you tell someone so they would definitely know to avoid it? I would. So yeah, if you twisted my arm, I think there's something in there."

"I see."

"But no matter what it is, it's not worth angering Ja'a again."

"I agree with you."

Duke sat back down and leaned over until his nose was almost touching Po'l's.

"Say what?"

"I agree with you. I think there's something powerful and dangerous and potentially useful in that temple. I bet it's the same reason the cannibals don't go near it."

"You agree with me?"

"I don't know if there's another Orb as you suspect—but a system of booby traps doesn't seem like something that would keep away flesh-craving sub-Neprians for ages."

"Exactly, right?" exclaimed Duke. "The story doesn't jive."

It was as if Duke's past quarrels with Po'l were distant memories; he spoke in a voice befitting a lifelong friendship.

"Not at all," Po'l concurred.

A moment later, the bounty hunter spasmed as he caught himself in his own excitement—his body unconsciously rejecting Po'l's agreeable tones.

"Nope. Never mind. Not going to do it."

"What if—"

"Stop, don't want to hear it. Not gonna do it. No way."

Ishiro'shea must have overheard, which was hardly surprising given the quietness of their watch. He walked over and glared at his longtime friend. *He must know when I'm about to do something stupid*, thought Duke.

"Hear me out, Duke," Po'l pleaded. "Everyone here is asleep. We can all make a quick dash in and take a look around. If there's something in there, we can take it—or leave it—"

"Or kill it."

The bounty hunter started to squirm; he *wanted* to side with Po'l. *Why is this so difficult?*

"We do have to chance the fact that there aren't any traps —at least traps that we can't overcome," Po'l continued. "But I'm willing to risk it. If there's something that can help us out against Orbius, I'm willing to die for it. I know it's against Ja'a's wishes, but it's worth the sacrifice. Lo'n is in agreement as well. He told me."

Ishiro'shea was shaking his head and pointing at the sleeping rebels.

"Oh yeah, good call, Ishiro. Who's gonna stand guard in case we get attacked by the children of the oozy lagoon?"

"I didn't think of that," Po'l said. "I'm definitely going in—how about Ishiro'shea?"

"Not exactly the best alarm system if something did happen. Also, if we go missing, it might be more difficult for him to explain where we went than one of us."

"Good point. Do you want to stay?"

"I can't. If there is something in there, Betsy will want to greet 'em. And you aren't... well... qualified to handle her."

"Fair point. Never mind then. There's no way I'm not going. I have to find out what's down there."

"Listen here, Po'l, I love this new attitude—we'll need it for when we cross Orbius' path—but the only way that makes sense is for Ishiro and I to head in and you stand guard."

"I hate that. Are you sure?" asked Po'l in a pleading tone.

"Yes. Right, Ish?"

The emerald-clad ninja threw his hands in the air in what could only be construed as more than mild disagreement.

"So you're out too?" Duke asked Ishiro'shea.

The ninja silently sighed in response. *He's in.*

"Great, let's make this quick," said Duke. He turned towards Po'l. "Thanks. I appreciate this. We'll be as discreet as we are fast. In and out and we'll report back if our suspicions are correct. For the cause!"

"And your ship, right?"

"Yes, and our ship."

CHAPTER 28

A GARDEN FERTILIZED WITH COTTON CANDY

"THIS SHOULD JUST ABOUT DO it."

Duke rammed Betsy's butt end into the temple door. The giant slab moaned and opened inward. It was completely black inside.

"Voila, little buddy. Yeah, He'j set an intricate system of traps but yet forgot to lock the front door? My ass."

Duke pushed aside the vegetation that had grown to the point of almost covering the temple entrance. He struggled with a particularly stout branch that had fallen as the door swung open.

"He could've at least cleaned up the front porch. Some help?"

Ishiro'shea removed his sword and sliced the stubborn branch into three neat pieces that dropped to the ground.

"You ready to do this?"

Ishiro'shea nodded.

"Ja'a is going to be so pissed," Duke began, "unless we bring back something of value. And she'll still probably be pretty pissed. So let's be fast, quiet, and productive."

Ishiro ignored his friend. Duke remembered that he was, after all, talking to a ninja.

Duke continued to talk, now more to himself than Ishiro'shea. "I guess if there isn't anything of value to get, we're just going to have to take it from Ja'a."

In response, Ishiro'shea grumbled.

"Fine, *I'm* going to take it from Ja'a. I'll take the heat. I'm already kinda in the doghouse."

Duke lit his makeshift torch. Ishiro'shea followed suit as the bounty hunters stepped inside the ancient dwelling.

The flames illuminated what could be best described as nothing. *Kinda anticlimactic*, thought Duke. The room was cavernous; the walls, floor, and ceiling were all constructed from goliath stone rectangles, all equal in size. There were no ornaments hanging from the walls, no furniture, no dead bodies, and no tasteful rug to pull it all together. It was empty. It was nothing. Well, basically nothing. The lone exception was on the wall opposite of the entry. One of the bricks was marked with sloppily-applied white paint streaks.

"You think that means something? Of course it does. Lift me up."

Ishiro'shea didn't budge.

"Okay, fine. I'll lift you up."

Duke knelt down and Ishiro'shea placed his thighs on the Nova Texan's shoulders, straddling his neck. Duke struggled but made it to his feet with his companion on his shoulders, as if they were about to play a game of especially demented chicken fighting.

"Make this quick!"

Ishiro'shea pressed his hands down on the top of Duke's hat to restore balance.

"Holy hedgehogs! Watch the hat!"

Duke was barely done speaking when Ishiro nimbly vaulted up so that his feet replaced his straddled legs on the bounty hunter's shoulders. He stood completely erect; Duke grabbed his ankles for additional support, though it was likely unnecessary.

"Can you get it?"

Ishiro'shea reached out and pushed the brick. Nothing. He slapped it with a bit more force. Nothing.

"Hit it harder!" yelled Duke.

Ishiro'shea wiggled his ankles, signaling Duke to let go.

"Maybe I can shoot it?"

But Ishiro'shea sprung from Duke's shoulders and, in midair, connected with a swift kick to the direct center of the stone. He landed on the ground without the slightest of noises. The stone rattled momentarily. The wall began to slowly suck the brick inward. Sparks danced as the slab scraped against its neighbors.

"A heads-up would've been nice, Ish. You coulda dislocated a shoulder."

The rattling increased at a rapid rate—the entire wall vibrated. It sounded as if an entire truckload of chains had been dropped from a two-story building. The vibration escalated.

"This can't be good."

Clouds of dust bellowed from the ground at the base of the wall. The shaking became more intense and the wall began to ascend.

"Or it can be—amazing!" exclaimed Duke.

An entrance to a cave had been exposed. It was pretty standard as far as cave entrances went—not as ostentatious as those in Oscavia, but not as menacing as the Great Tunnels of Zyrma Chuk'nik. But it did feel ancient. And it was dark—as all good caves are. Duke stepped beyond the threshold and extended his torch.

"Nothing. I can't see a damn thing in here."

The light provided almost no help in distinguishing the depth or height of the tunnel; if his feet hadn't been firmly on the ground, Duke would have believed he was floating in the abyss of deep space. He knelt down, holding the light as close to the ground as possible.

"If He'j did set any ambushes here, we'd be goners. I haven't been in something this dark since—"

Duke broke off suddenly. He gripped Ishiro'shea's forearm.

"Hey, wait a second. You smell that? Tell me you smell that?"

There was no response from the ninja—as per the norm.

"It smells—" Duke struggled for the right word. "Pleasant?"

He released his grasp on his friend's arm.

"Like—" Duke again had difficulty coming to terms with his thoughts. "—fresh cut flowers."

Caves, on the whole, usually lived up to the stereotypes—dark, dank, musty, spooky. This one was dark, yes. Spooky, a bit. But dank and musty, it was not. Duke tilted his chin upward and expanded his nostrils as wide as possible to soak in the enjoyable fragrance. Ishiro'shea did the same, after pulling down the portion of his mask that covered his nose and mouth.

"It's like a garden that's been fertilized by cotton candy."

Duke waved the torch in front of his face, aiding his navigation from one wall of the cave to the other as he searched frantically for the source of the odor. Ishiro'shea followed suit.

Something's not right, the bounty hunter thought to himself. *It doesn't feel right. It smells right—in fact, it smells wonderful. But too wonderful.*

The two men continued to search in the darkness, pressing their hands against the rocky corridor walls. The blaze of the torch flame barely provided enough visibility to see an arm's length in front of their noses. The darkness seemed to suppress the flame, winning the eternal battle of shadow and light. As they moved down the path, the glow from the torch became even fainter and their visibility was reduced to mere inches. Still the pair trekked on. Even though he couldn't see Ishiro'shea nor would the ninja break his vow of silence to say it, Duke knew what was going through his companion's mind:

We probably shouldn't have done this. But Duke pressed on stubbornly. And Ishiro'shea accompanied him faithfully.

"I think we're gonna find something big like an Orb. A real game-changer. You know the story—rain and rainbows, darkness and dawns, Erontian saké and freshwater mermaids. We're gonna turn a corner and see the light at the end of tunnel."

Duke wasn't wrong. But the bounty hunters did less of turning a corner and more of falling down a steep, jagged incline—landing with a thump as they hit an equally jagged rock pit. But, on the bright side, they did see a light in the distance.

"Told you."

Duke stood up and brushed off the dust and debris from his clothes using his hat.

"We should probably check it out, right? I can feel something. Something big. I can't wait to see Ja'a and Lo'n when we come back with the saving grace of their cause. Hell, even Po'l."

The ruddy glow was only the length of a standard spacecraft from where they had fallen. It was flickering irregularly. As the two approached the source of the light, they could see it was emanating from an extremely tall archway, reaching a height equal to the entrance into Dre'en but much less welcoming. There was no door or gate. The two off-worlders entered.

"Halt!" boomed a monstrous roar. "You are trespassing on private property and holy ground."

Duke drew his laser revolver. Ishiro'shea readied his katana. The massive beast that sat before them, its legs crossed within a brightly lit chamber, didn't even pay attention to the flashing of armaments.

"Getting pretty brave, aren't you, swamp maggots? Take this—"

The gargantuan creature—as tall as four Jungafallowians

and as stout as the entire Trampling Death Robots welded together into one humongous musical nightmare—thrust a glass bottle in their direction with his right hand. His other hand was firmly placed on a bulbous pump. Duke fired. The shot hit the monster's left bicep. It was as if the giant didn't even notice it. Before Duke could rattle off another pulse, the monster squeezed the pump. A cloud of pink translucence filled the room, caking Duke and Ishiro'shea in a chalky dust that smelled like... fresh-cut flowers fertilized with cotton candy.

"Did you—" Duke said between coughs, "—did you just douse us with perfume?"

"What?" bellowed the beast in a thunderous voice.

"I said, did you just spray us with perfume? I shot you—and then you make us smell better?"

"You can speak—intelligibly?" asked the monster.

Duke caught eyes with Ishiro'shea and began, "Well, I can."

"The other one, is he your pet?"

"Well—" Duke began. Ishiro'shea threw a glance as sharp as his katana back at the bounty hunter. "No, he just doesn't speak."

"But how is that you can stand this?"

The beast held up his glass holster containing an electric pink fluid.

"It's quite nice, actually."

"Oh no. I will now have to kill you and think of a new way to keep you pests out. This worked for so long," he muttered dejectedly.

"Wait, what? No. Hey, we aren't pests. Who do you think we are?"

"You come from the swamps, right?" the brute said. He finally seemed to notice his wounded arm. He placed some pressure with his hand and it seemed to stop bleeding almost immediately.

"You think we come from the swamps? No, I'm from Nova Texas. Outer space. Far, far away from this rock. Ishiro'shea here is from Earth."

"Outer space? You swamp creatures are gaining a sense of humor, I like that. Maybe next—who knows? Soufflés?"

"We are *not* from the swamp!"

"You seem pretty annoying—which is a trait of the people in the swamp."

"Yes, but we don't have the most important trait."

"And what is that, swampy?"

"I don't know—how about living in a swamp?"

The giant laughed and the vibrations shook the walls. He placed the perfume canister down gently and then stood up. His muscular frame filled the entire space of the room. His skin was a muted orange and he wore no clothes outside of a strategically placed loincloth made of a furry substance. Duke did not want to find out how he came across this piece of clothing—nor how long he had been wearing it. Bulky gauntlets adorned his wrists and ankles.

"Before I kill you, can you at least tell me what compelled you to explore my home? Call it basic curiosity. To be honest, I haven't seen one of your types in a while."

In the full light, Duke could see that the monster had two large lower canines that extended beyond his lip so that when he spoke, Duke thought he was going to put his own eyes out.

"Okay, first off, we aren't from the swamp. We came here to look for something."

"What exactly is it that you are seeking?"

"I'm not entirely sure."

"Not very convincing, swamp man."

"See, there's a war going on. We're trying to help the southern Neprians take out this guy named Ot Vangu."

"A war going on? Outside my home? I haven't heard any troops or battles or anything of the sort. I think you're making this up, pond dweller."

"Enough with the names, alright? I'm telling you the truth. We are camping out here, next to the swamp—"

"Swamp! I knew it," the giant roared and reached for a wooden club to his right. He raised it.

Duke grabbed Betsy from his back and uncorked a frustration-filled load. The club splintered and fell limply to the floor. The echo from the explosion drove a stake directly into Duke's eardrum.

"Hey, that's a neat gadget. What do you call it?"

"Her name is Betsy," Duke screamed, still trying to regain his hearing.

"I like Betsy. And I don't think a swamp man would have a toy like that."

"You finally believe me?"

"Trial period. But tell me again—why are you in my lair?"

"Look, Mr. Giant—wait, what's your name?"

"Let me think about that. No one has asked me in so many cycles—I'm not exactly sure." The behemoth looked a bit embarrassed. He then snapped back and said in a proud belt, "They used to call me the Keeper."

"The Keeper of what?"

"Of the Sphere of Power."

Duke and the ninja exchanged glances.

"A sphere?"

"Yes."

"Of power?"

"Yes, that's what I said, you odd little thing."

"So, it's an orb?"

"Sure, if you want to call it that. It's around here somewhere."

The Keeper turned and began to rummage around the floor of his lair. Bottles of his potent perfume, bulky canisters, and odds and ends—all of an ancient patina—were tossed and hurled in the air. Clinks and clanks echoed throughout the chamber.

"Nothing of value, it seems. A bunch of junk. Most of it's that mustangsen garbage," Duke said to Ishiro'shea.

Ishiro'shea narrowly avoided being impaled by what could only be described as a hat stand for someone with a cranium the size of a galactic Winnebago and a deeply-rooted affinity for headwear.

"Ish, are you hearing what I'm hearing?" the bounty hunter asked, dodging a gravy boat hurled at a hazardous velocity. "I knew there was another Orb! Oh man, the looks on their faces. I can't wait. Can't believe they doubted our hunch."

"Where could it be now?" the Keeper mumbled to himself.

"Let us help," the bounty hunter said. "How about we look over here?"

"No, it's not over there."

"Are you sure?"

"Yes."

"How about over here?"

Duke and Ishiro'shea ascended a dozen steps that led to a platform full of another hodgepodge of useless objects. They began to dig through the heap of artifacts.

"Be careful. Some of those are pretty important."

"To who?"

"I can't remember, to be honest, but I know they're pretty darn important."

Duke and Ishiro'shea continued to discard the items at a rapid pace and with a blatant disregard for the preservation of the artifacts.

"Okay, no spheres, orbs, or balls—or anything that could be misconstrued as roundish in nature—up here. Just a bunch of knickknacks."

Duke kicked the mound. Items spilled over and hit the floor with ringing clanks.

"When's the last time you saw it?" he asked.

"I don't know. It's hard to keep track of time in this place."

"All of this junk and not a single clock to be found," Duke muttered to himself.

"Was it before or after you gave the other sphere to He'j and Jilarian Togg?"

The Keeper halted mid-toss. He looked perplexed.

"What other sphere? And who's Hodge and Jilarpian Targ?"

"Seriously, big guy? The two dudes that borrowed the first sphere. You know, to save the planet and all that."

The Keeper began to laugh. "Oh, I get it, a joke to lighten the mood! Very funny. Next you're going to tell me that they make a toilet compatible for over eighty species. I haven't laughed like this in a good while."

Duke and Ishiro'shea did not laugh. It was a few moments before the Keeper realized. His hooting ceased abruptly.

"You're aren't serious—are you?"

"Dead, unfortunately. They came here not too long ago—maybe a few cycles back—and borrowed the Orb. I mean the Sphere of Power."

"Not to my knowledge, they didn't."

"That's what I was afraid of," Duke said in a dejected tone.

"What?"

"I think you might have been robbed."

The Keeper let out an audible sigh and plopped down, legs crossed, causing a slight tremor in the room.

"Not again," he said.

Duke and Ishiro'shea slapped their foreheads with the palms of their hands in unison.

"I'm slightly afraid to ask—but what do you mean, 'not again'?"

"Sit down, my diminutive pals."

"It's that bad?"

"Afraid so," huffed the monster. "I am the Keeper of the Sphere of Power—a job that I take very seriously."

"Uh-huh." Duke expected the worst.

"But it's a job that I might not have been the best choice for. I'm a mover and shaker, deep down. I want to be out there —you know, doing stuff."

Ishiro'shea proceeded to sit down and prepared himself for a lengthy yarn. Duke followed suit, albeit less gracefully.

"Did you know that I was once an artist?"

"Considering we literally stumbled upon you a few minutes ago... No, we weren't aware of that amazing piece of trivia."

"I was. I dabbled in a lot of media—I liked mixed media; some found objects here, some painting there, maybe even a touch of sculpting. I was quite good. Had a few retrospectives at the local museum, way back when."

The bounty hunters had no response to the rambling biography, but Duke tried. "Not to interrupt what I'm sure is a fascinating trip down memory lane, but we have to get back to our friends soon—so we would appreciate getting back on track."

"Right, of course," apologized the beast. "So, I wasn't the best for the job. But, as the only remaining member of my race —really, of any race from the time of my people—I felt it was my duty to prevent the same calamity that ended our reign on this planet. Then, there were these two creatures that came in —two distinct races, it seemed—"

"Whoa, stop! What two races?"

"See, my new friends, my time on this planet goes back to when the mountains were but pebbles and the seas mere puddles of rain. When the—"

"We get it," Duke said cutting him off, "you're old and have been here a long time. Continue."

"Right. But even before that, my race cultivated this planet and built a society of caring and prosperity and progress—and, eventually, exquisite art. Did I mention my retrospective?"

"Yes."

"One day—and I'm not sure where or who or when—but

one day, our people discovered the Sphere of Power. It allowed us to do things that we never could before. It helped us clear mountains for roads and save villages riddled with disease and grow the best ploob kalarti for our festivals. It was all-powerful."

"And then what?"

"Like all things that grant you power without having to earn it, it corrupted the minds of my people. Cycles turned into hundreds of cycles and into millennia. Control of the Sphere bounced from one tribe to another. Death and madness permeated the land. Eventually, we assembled into two tribes and the war raged on. Near the end, the two factions didn't even resemble each other—the sphere had manipulated our minds and altered our physical appearances. Even I have been affected—my current state does not reflect how we once were. But we battled our former brothers, now heinous and ghastly and terrorizing the skies on the backs of demons. We were shorter but stronger and hurled boulders at them as they swooped down to skewer us with fire-covered spears."

"Near the end, you say? What happened?"

"The races destroyed each other. Death prevailed. Unharnessed power rendered the powerful powerless." The Keeper took a deep breath and a solemn expression erased his earlier scowl. "And left in this wasteland was myself, my house, and the Sphere."

"How did you survive?"

"Not really sure, to be honest. When the weather started to change and chaos seemed to replace normalcy, I retreated here and remained for cycles. Eventually, I returned to the surface and there was nothing. As I started to explore... there, in an open field, was the Sphere. Needless to say, I decided to take it—it's not like *more* harm could be done. I think part of me thought I could control it."

"And I guess the story ends with the fact that you couldn't?"

"Actually, no. I took it home and it responded to me. Right away. I sat right here, where we are now, for ages, trying to better control it. Become one with this power that eradicated my entire family, my entire race. It didn't seem inherently evil —and I didn't feel evil as I bonded with it. I definitely didn't feel like going out and starting a war even if there had been someone to start a war with.

"Ages passed as the arrow of time points in but one direction—memories of my people, the festivals, and even my art retrospective became very distant."

"Obviously, not too distant," Duke chimed in.

"Not *too* distant, no, but they started to feel like a dream. I must have been with the Sphere for a thousand cycles—or two or ten—when I was startled by a simple knock on the outside of my house. It was a duo of odd-looking creatures—about your size—the first living creatures that I had seen in many cycles. Needless to say, they assumed that I was a monster and lobbed pointy objects at me. I finally settled them down and invited them in. We talked for hours. They explained that their people had been the original race on the planet—of course, I chuckled and politely corrected them. I didn't want to say it, but I think they evolved from the parasites that survived the wars. I told them about the Sphere and the history of the planet—they seemed particularly interested in the Sphere, almost mesmerized."

"Let me guess what happens next—they stole the Sphere?"

"That predictable, huh?"

"I had a feeling."

"I'm not sure what exactly happened after that, but sometime later two different people from these two races came to me. This time they had the Sphere with them and asked me to keep it with me forever. They said it was the only way to prevent their races from killing each other—I could sympathize with that, and wished my people would have thought of it. They offered to guard my home, even send soldiers to protect it. I appreciated the gesture but, as you can see, I could've defended it myself in battle. I let them 'guard' me."

"They also blocked off the entire land bridge that connects the northern land mass from the south," added Duke. "You've been isolated here for another thousand cycles. Just you and this swamp—and the swamp people that have evolved from whatever was left here when they blocked off the bridge."

"And now someone stole it out from under my nose—again. I wonder who—and why?"

"It was the same race that gave it back to you for safe keeping. They are called Neprians."

"Why would they do that?"

"To save the planet. They were experiencing a great drought and famine—and entire villages were being wiped out."

"That's rich," smirked the Keeper. "It took me countless ages to be able to control it—as much as it would let me—and they think they're just going to summon it to do their bidding? It's just going to start to glow and then prepare a fancy dinner for everyone?"

The Keeper was visibly upset. "I wonder why they didn't just ask me? Probably knew I would just say no."

"Probably. And it's probably a bit difficult to explain to the masses that a giant monster has been watching their precious Orb for countless ages. Even a bunch as gullible as these Neprians."

"True," the Keeper continued, "but I wish I could have told them about its true power. It has a mind of its own. If it winds up in the hands of someone evil, it will be an instrument of death and annihilation."

"Yep, already there, big guy. They asked it to help with their crops and it brought a being from across the universe that could make the crops grow again. He fulfilled his job—but, instead of leaving, he became consumed with learning how to control it. The people of the North became his army and he enslaved those in the South that resisted."

"What is his name?"

"He goes by Orbius."

"Not very original."

"Agreed."

"Sounds like he probably could've taken over this lot without the Sphere."

"Agreed, again."

"So, can he control it?"

"From what we hear—yes."

"And how do you fit into this story, my new friends? Since you are not from this planet of Neprius, as you call it."

"A bit of bad luck. Orbius' tinkering led to the Sphere sending an astral portal near our neck of the woods—and we happened to get consumed by it. Because of his unchecked insanity with this magic rock, I'm stuck here instead of enjoying some Glyptodian Summer Ale at Cyborg Joe's."

Ishiro'shea perked up at the mention of Glyptodian Summer Ale.

"I see. And you aim to help these Neprians defeat Orbius."

"And get our ship back."

"Ah yes, I assumed there was something else too. Needless to say, it is imperative that you bring it back soon. Otherwise, this Orbius will destroy Neprius—whether he means to or not."

"No offense, Keeper, but you've lost it twice now. Not sure if bringing it back makes a ton of sense. Is there a way to destroy it?"

"Destroy the Sphere of Power? It is without a doubt inde-structible, my spacefaring comrades." The Keeper seemed a bit miffed at the question, and their lack of faith in his "keeping" abilities.

"Okay, so we'll get it and bring it back to you."

Duke glanced over at Ishiro'shea. *Unless we figure out something better.*

"I promise I won't lose it this time."

"Great."

"Let me see if there's anything that can help you in your attempt," the Keeper said as he picked through his mound of decorative homeware and miscellaneous décor. "You probably don't need a spatula, do you?"

"I doubt it. How about a bottle of your perfume? A smaller bottle, of course. We have a trick that we want to play on a friend of ours that doesn't bathe as often as he should."

"Not a problem, take two."

Duke snatched a pair of ornate glass containers and affixed them to his belt.

"Many thanks, Keeper. I hope we see you again soon."

"If not," the Keeper replied, "I fear the planet will be no more."

CHAPTER 29

FIGHTING THE SWAMP

"GUYS, YOU WON'T BELIEVE WHAT we just—" the bounty hunter shouted. Then, immediately, he froze. Ishiro'shea followed suit.

Their campground was unrecognizable, turned into a warzone infested by proto-humans covered in leaves and mud and moss; sluggish and lumbering. Their gaseous body odor was so putrid and thick that it appeared as an opaque cloud of green above their heads. Their ghastly faces were reminiscent of the Melted Skin art movement made popular by Treglor of Phleg-Mem—especially the early cycles. It was clear that the swamp people of the land bridge were not scared of the temple or, at least, anyone camped in its shadows—and they appeared to be pissed off.

Duke and Ishiro'shea hustled down an incline towards the scuffle. Duke immediately rattled off a few pulses, striking three creatures squarely in their heads. All fell to the muddy bank with a squish.

Duke pivoted sharply at the feeling of a moist, cold weight on his left shoulder. His eyes locked with the swamp being— but only one eye returned the gaze. The beast's other eye socket was not where it should have been—it sat squarely in

the middle of his left cheek as if it had slowly migrated southward. The grotesque appearance immobilized Duke.

"Gross."

The cannibal opened his mouth to reveal mangled, mud-
colored teeth sharpened to fine points. The stench was unbearable. He lunged at Duke as he clamped down his jaws; his
ferocious bite snapped mere inches from Duke's right ear. The
bounty hunter shook himself out of his trance and threw a
right jab to the monster's face. It pushed the cannibal back a
few paces but didn't seem to do any harm. Duke swung again
and connected to the stomach region. This had even less effect.
The cannibal reached out with both arms and grasped Duke
by the neck. He proceeded to lift the Nova Texan in the air;
Duke hung on to the creature's wrists to slow down the
choking process. A swift gust of wind passed Duke's face and
he fell to the ground. Landing right next to him was a rotted,
pock-marked appendage. He looked up. The monster was
without his right arm.

"Thanks, buddy."

Ishiro gave a quick nod toward the cannibal, who was
seemingly unaware that he lost his arm but very aware that he
lost his prey.

"Tough bastard," Duke muttered as he lifted himself onto
one knee. He spun his laser revolver out of his holster and let
loose two shots into the belly of the beast, who dropped to the
ground with a groan.

Ishiro'shea was slicing and dicing his way to the center of
the camp; Duke was blasting and punching a parallel path to
the same destination. A few short moments of carnage led
them to the pikes that they had placed as a temporary fence.

"Can you let us in, Ja'a?"

"And take down our last line of defense?" interjected Po'l.
"Are you serious?"

"You're going to leave us out here to die?"

"If that's what's necessary."

Ja'a barked orders at Ma'n and 'Te'o; they dropped their bows and ran to the perimeter of the fence where Duke and Ishiro stood fighting off encroaching mutants. Ma'n hoisted his ax above his head and crashed it down upon the base of a pike. It crumpled to the ground. He repeated this two more times, creating a space large enough for the two off-worlders to enter the safety of the camp. However, it was also big enough for swamp cannibals to follow them in.

"Thanks, Ja'a," yelled Duke. "I knew you wouldn't—"

"No more talking. Simply, no more. You left us out in a bad place, Duke. Your fun adventure left us without a lookout and much needed support."

"Wait, Po'l said he would look—"

"Don't blame this on Po'l. He's been asleep in the camp ever since you went on lookout," Ja'a said. She sent off two arrows into the mass of swampfolk in rapid succession. "You and Ishiro'shea were on duty... and now—this!"

Po'l, you little rat.

"Can you believe that, Ishiro?" Duke asked as he dropped five more raiders. "I thought these guys were scared of the temple?"

"It appears that I was wrong," replied Lo'n.

"No kidding," retorted Duke.

"I promise you, Duke, the last time that I was here—with He'j—we figured that the temple held some sort of power over them. We used it as a shield."

"Maybe they saw you in the temple and realized that it couldn't be that bad if *you* would go in," interjected Po'l.

"Thanks for screwing us over, Po'l. And I thought we turned a corner. We need to have a chat one of these days."

The moans of the approaching monstrosities continued to escalate. Their numbers appeared to be multiplying, with more emerging from the murky river all the time.

"We're running short on arrows," shouted Ty'n from the far end of the camp. He dropped his bow and pulled out his duo of daggers. He began to jab and poke at any body part, or anything that resembled a body part, that made it through the openings between the sharpened fence posts.

"Same here," shouted Te'o. "Need some help now!"

A section of three pikes parted and a steady stream of cannibals were poised to enter the inner confines of the camp.

"No you don't!" shouted Lo'n. He sprang from another part of the perimeter and swung his saber down on the torsos of the first monsters to penetrate the fence. He swung his over-sized blade at the mutant force with elegant aggression.

"Impressive," Duke said in between shots. "You starting to feel a bit jealous *now*, Ish?"

The ninja ignored his companion and continued to keep the horde at bay with his own nifty swordsmanship.

"Duke, I could use you right now," Lo'n shouted. The numbers appeared to be getting the best of him.

"We need help over here now," cried Po'l.

"Breach! Breach!" bellowed Bu'r.

"Over here, too!" screamed Ma'n.

"Not to be a backseat general, Ja'a, but I'm not sure how much longer we can hold out. Two of these bastards are coming in for each one I send to his maker."

"Duke's right," Lo'n confirmed. "What's the plan?"

More portions of the fence were rendered useless as the cannibals swarmed the campsite. Ja'a did not offer a response.

"I can't hold them much longer," groaned Lo'n as he cleaved off two of the creatures' heads in one swing. "Ja'a?"

"We need to leave the swamp," Ja'a exclaimed.

"I think we're aware of that," Duke countered.

"Everyone, fall back. Over here, near the fire. Duke—give us as much cover as you can."

"Yes, ma'am," he shouted. He unleashed a rapid-fire salvo from his laser revolver as he walked backward toward the group.

"What's the plan, Ja'a?" asked Po'l urgently.

"Grab your weapons—as many as you can carry but won't slow you down," Ja'a shouted, calmly and with confidence. *Much different than Shud'nut,* thought Duke.

"Everyone good?"

After a smattering of affirmations, Ja'a continued. "We're going to break through their ranks and head north through the swamp, along the bank. We're going to run until we hit the wall. I know it's going to be challenging—but it's our best bet to get out of here."

"Is this even possible?" asked Bu'r.

"It's possible," confirmed Lo'n. "That's the path that we were going to take anyways, the same one He'j and I followed —now we will just do it a bit faster. And at night."

"Great. Not to be a downer but how are we going to break—"

"When I say 'now,' stop firing," Ja'a said, interrupting the bounty hunter as if he'd never started speaking, "I will cover you as you get Betsy ready. Fire her into the north part of their lines. It should give us an opening—then we fight our way through until we get behind them. Then run."

Never going to work.

"Let's go!" shouted Ma'n.

"Alright!" screamed Po'l.

"Great plan, Ja'a. Your father would be proud," Lo'n added.

Idiots.

"Stop, Duke."

He holstered his laser revolver and removed Betsy from his back. The encroaching mass continued to advance. Ja'a released two arrows that struck the two closest cannibals in the middle of their faces, dropping them instantly. She grabbed a handful of arrows and reloaded her quiver.

Betsy roared.

An entire section of swamp cannibals collapsed.

Betsy roared again.

More toppled over each other.

"Fight until you're out the other side. Then run north to the first clearing."

The Neprian rebels charged in, Lo'n leading the group.

"Stay between us, Ja'a," shouted Ma'n and Te'o as they surrounded her with their axes. "Your bow won't be much use in this scrum."

Duke stored away Betsy and retrieved his revolver. He followed Ishiro'shea into the smoke-filled clearing. Rapidly, he volleyed off pulses at anything with a feculent odor. The sounds of his comrades' voices were drowned out by the sounds of limbs being severed or blown off and splashing into the gloomy waters. He hoped the limbs didn't belong to any of those comrades. The cannibals screamed and moaned but Duke wasn't sure if that was from dismemberment or just their general disposition. He didn't want to wait around and find out.

"Duke, you're the last through," Ja'a screamed from a clearing ahead, alongside the bank of the swamp. "You, Ishiro'shea, and Ty'n need to make a break for it!"

"Don't need to tell us twice!" Duke pivoted and ran, a few paces behind his much speedier ninja companion. He turned to his left, "Hey Ty'n, don't run so close to the swamp—that's where—"

Out of the corner of his eyes, Duke saw the cannibal leap from the water and grab Ty'n's ankles. The Neprian rebel hit the ground and rolled onto his back. The monster dived on top of Ty'n in an attempt to smother him—but he received a dagger in the throat.

"Get up!" shouted Po'l from up ahead. "They're heading towards us."

Duke stopped and dropped two more of the cannibals that were closing in on Ty'n. He made his way out from under the deceased creature and started to head to rejoin the team.

He increased his pace to a full sprint—partly to get away

from hundreds of flesh-craving aberrations, partly to beat Ishiro'shea.

"Okay, made it. What are we waiting on?" Duke huffed.

Bu'r pushed Duke aside and charged back into the oncoming horde.

Ty'n was back on the ground again. Two more cannibals halfway submerged in the swamp held his legs down. One had a dagger in the forehead but still appeared to be keeping the rebel at bay. Before Duke could blink, one dove on top of Ty'n. Then another. And another.

Ty'n was no longer visible.

Duke went to fire his gun, but halted.

"Bu'r, come back here," screamed Lo'n. "It's too late. You're going to get killed!"

Bu'r swung his mace at the pile of swampfolk covering Ty'n's body. He knocked down two at a time—but he made no gains. His face was red but his eyes were focused. He killed more cannibals in that burst than he had the entire day. But they kept coming.

"Die! Die! Ty'n, can you hear me? Die!" Bu'r cried, still swinging.

"We don't have long before we're back in the same situation that we were in a few moments ago," Lo'n reminded Ja'a.

"Somebody has to get Bu'r, right?" asked Te'o.

Duke began to fire his revolver at the massive blob of mutants. He picked his march up to a jog.

He looked back at the rebels and screamed, "Holy hedgehogs, are you morons? Run!"

"But Duke?" shouted Po'l.

"Run! Damnit, run!"

Duke heard the splashing of puddles and the squishing of mud against boot soles. It became distant and faint very quickly.

Duke was now behind Bu'r.

"It's time to go back," Duke said calmly in between shots

from his revolver. "Nothing you can do here, nothing you could've done."

The barrel-chested Neprian did not respond. He just kept bashing and clubbing. Cannibals fell to the left and right of him. But they kept coming.

"Ty'n wanted to free his people. You can't help him when you're dead."

"Ty'n's not dead!" shouted Bu'r, his eyes red and wet.

"Bu'r, he's dead!" Duke countered as he pushed back cannibals with more pulses.

"Leave me alone! Go! Let me fight!"

"You're letting down Ty'n. You're letting down Shud'nut. You're letting down everyone. Don't be selfish."

Bu'r let out a deep roar and swung his club in an elongated looping motion, crushing four skulls in the process.

He turned to look at Duke. Pain riddled his gaze. Tears covered his upper cheeks. His stare said it all. He knew it was time to go.

"For Ty'n." Bu'r started to sprint north.

"About damn time," Duke said to himself as he followed Bu'r into the deeper part of the swamp.

After a lengthy sprint, Duke could finally see the rest of the party up ahead. They were all sitting around a twisted tree, breathing heavily.

"I'm sorry, Bu'r," began Ja'a in a soothing tone before the distraught Neprian had any time to catch his breath. She placed her hand on his shoulder. They stared into each other's eyes for a moment, then the husky Neprian sank to his knees. He wept loudly.

"Ty'n fought valiantly. Your friend will be remembered with great reverence. Be proud of that, Bu'r."

"That skinny bastard wasn't supposed to die like that," Bu'r cried. "He deserved better. It's my fault."

"Enough. You've seen great men and women die for the cause—and innocent people, too. Ty'n knew the risks and he wanted to make a difference. We need you alive to make sure that we *do* make a difference. Do you understand me?" Ja'a's tone grew more unapologetic, more direct. "We will honor him by ridding Neprius of Orbius and his rule. We can't do that without your help."

"Yeah, I've never seen an ass-whuppin' like you put on those guys back there," Duke added. "Quite impressive, if you ask me."

Bu'r looked up at the off-worlder. He wiped the tears from his cheeks.

"Thank you, Duke."

Lo'n stepped in front of the bounty hunter and nodded at Ja'a.

"I know we've been through a lot, but I must urge us to press on. And fast. They won't stop following us. What they lack in foot speed, they make up for in perseverance."

"We don't have to make it through the swamp—just until daylight. They won't chase us in daylight. And that's fast approaching," Ja'a clarified.

"Exactly. We need to put as much distance between us and them—and when the sun comes out, they'll return to the swamp."

"Let's hope we don't have another 'They won't come near the temple' moment again."

"I couldn't agree with you more, Duke."

The morning light began to peek through the clouds above the land bridge—and, thankfully for Duke, it was only a short run. Traversing an entire alien continent—no matter how small—by foot was pushing his limits to begin with; having to run a marathon at the midway point was not his idea of a good time. *Still, the swampy atmosphere of the land bridge was preferable to the cleanliness of Dre'en*, he thought.

"Much better," Ja'a said as she stared up at the rays of light. "We should take some much-needed rest before night falls again."

Cheers erupted from the group—especially Duke. The northward march continued along the tributary; all members made sure to keep their distance from the water to ensure that Ty'n's fate wouldn't be replicated.

"How are we doing, Lo'n? We should be close, right? Does this look familiar?"

He did not respond.

"Lo'n?" asked Po'l again.

"I'm not sure. We followed the swamp until it hit the wall—that's what I remember. But this vegetation—"

"Yes?"

"I don't recall seeing it."

"Great!" shouted Po'l as he threw his hands in the air.

"Everyone stop for a second," Ja'a commanded, "and let's give Lo'n a chance to collect his thoughts. You followed the river to the wall, right? And we've been doing that."

"I'm sorry, but this doesn't seem right. In our haste fleeing from the cannibals—I think we might have gone down a different path than the one He'j and I took."

"But we *are* heading north, right?" asked Ma'n, looking up at the sky.

"Yes."

"That's good at least," said Po'l. "I say we just push on north. Right, Ja'a?"

"I'm sure there's more than one way to get to the wall," added Te'o.

"Yes, but I don't know what lies in front of us down *that* path."

"How close are we?" asked Duke. "Approximately."

"I really don't know."

"We couldn't have steered off course too much. I mean, it wasn't that long of a jog."

"I tend to agree with Duke," said Ja'a. "Chin up, Uncle Lo'n. Whatever is ahead of us, we can handle."

"I'm more worried about what's behind us," chimed Duke.

"So, does that mean we are on the march again?" asked Po'l. "Or can we rest?"

"I think we should push on—just in case we are farther away than I remember."

"I agree," said Ja'a.

Her statement was met with grousing from the group.

"Are you sure?" asked Po'l in a pleading tone. "It's been a pretty taxing trip. Between the sneak attack and Ty'n—"

"Ja'a's right," interjected Bu'r, surprising everyone.

"Are you sure you can continue?" asked Po'l. "You've had a worse day than any of us."

"I think we should go. While it's light outside. I don't want anything else to happen to us."

Ja'a smiled back at Bu'r. He blushed and returned a nod. On that exchange, the entire group picked up their weapons and started to jog northward—but stopped as they approached the gargantuan patch of foliage that first alerted Lo'n that they weren't on the same path as he had previously trekked.

"Left or right?"

"I guess I should make that call, huh?" answered Lo'n. He pointed his saber to the left.

"Sounds good to me," added Duke.

And the group was on the move again.

"So far, so good, huh?"

"Seems that way," replied Lo'n.

"I would consider getting out of the swamp to be good," smirked Po'l.

"I don't disagree with Po'l," added Ja'a. "Lo'n, any feeling on how much longer?"

"I'm sorry. I don't know. But it can't be much farther to the wall. At least I don't think so."

"We do have daylight on our side," said Ma'n, clearly searching for a silver lining.

"I'm afraid that might not be the case."

At Ja'a's statement, the group halted immediately. She pointed ahead of them. To their left remained the ever-present swamp; to the right, the thick dense forest. The light pierced through the sparse canopy overhead, illuminating their path. However, the road seemed to end. The forest and swamp merged together with only humps of solid ground peeking up from the fetid muck as if they were tiny islands amidst a great sea. Even worse, the canopy's coverage became much less sparse—in fact, it became a shield against the sun's rays. They would have to enter a realm of pure darkness during the middle of the day.

"Weapons out. Let's light some torches. Only enough to see," Ja'a barked. The team followed her commands promptly —even Duke.

"Surely there's another way," muttered Te'o.

"We don't have time to turn around and try another path. We push on."

They picked up the pace as they entered the swampy forest. The last few shafts of light petered out as the water began to cover more and more of the muddy terrain. Even the trees seemed to become more twisted and sinister. The concentration of the odor increased—the smell of death and rot was so potent, Duke felt it might crush his lungs. His eyes stung.

The rebels hopscotched from dry patch to dry patch, trying to avoid watery missteps. They didn't want to find out what the noise from an echoing splash might waken. They had already lost one valuable team member to this swamp. Losing another was not part of the plan.

"This isn't getting any less spooky."

"Scared, Duke?"

"No, Po'l, but—"

Ja'a silenced them with a simple shush.

"Stop," she whispered. "Be alert."

"Holy hedgehogs," Duke said, mimicking Ja'a"s whisper.

Eyes appeared within the foliage along their right flank. Then subtle gurgles. The limbs of the dying trees rattled. Heads started to bob out of the swamp in front of them, behind them, all around them.

"We're surrounded."

The swampfolk started to mobilize on their right—the others held steady.

"This isn't some primitive brawl. They're coordinated," noted Duke.

"Hold still, keep your weapons drawn," commanded Ja'a. "If we move, we go in one direction—straight ahead and try and outpace them."

"The water is going to slow us down—it won't be a simple footrace like before," corrected Lo'n.

"It's our best bet."

Lo'n concurred with a look of defeat.

"Look, they're moving. Over there," said Ja'a.

The swamp creatures on the right flank parted to allow other creatures to advance towards the rebels. These two mutants carried torches and what appeared to be clubs rendered from the sturdy swamp trees. However, these fire-bearing swamp men stopped well before the group.

"Guards," said Duke.

"Of what?" asked Po'l.

"Him."

Emerging from behind the line of cannibals was a creature nearly two heads taller than the largest mutant that they had fought off. He was draped in a cloak of mud and leaves and barbed branches. Moss seemed to cover his entire cranium, dripping down from his forehead and over his eyes. Glimmers of mustard-colored eyes peeked through. It was if he was a living extension of the swamp itself. It was clear that he was the Alpha King of the Swamp.

He stared directly at Duke. It was as if he knew that Duke was not like the others. He then raised his hand above his head and closed it, clenching his fist.

The arrow that Ja'a loosed was swift and struck the Alpha King squarely in his wrist. It did not exit the mutant; he looked at the arrow resting lifelessly in his flesh. He then pulled it through his body slowly. The King roared with laughter.

"He means business," said Duke.

The King dropped his arm and the legions of quasi-humans screamed and grunted in unison. They charged. Duke's first pulses didn't make it to the King, clipping the guards instead.

"Run, everyone!"

Ja'a made it only a few paces before she encountered an impenetrable roadblock of mutant cannibals.

"Looks like another dogfight. You ready, Ish?"

The ninja nodded back at his companion.

The mutants closed in.

"Or maybe not," said Duke slyly. He pushed Ma'n and Te'o aside and proceeded to the front of the line. He put away his revolver.

"Little buddy, if this doesn't work and you get out of here —tell the Queen that she owes you a few drinks."

The Nova Texan strutted to the barrier of swampfolk nonchalantly, sporting a nervous grin.

"So," he started. "Someone told me that you might want to try a free sample of our latest fragrance."

The monsters returned blank stares.

"He's lost it," chimed in Po'l.

Duke grabbed the perfume bottle and sprayed a few puffs in the general vicinity of the beasts. They paused—then let out glass-breaking shrieks of agony. Many fell immediately to the ground and contorted in pain. Others dove back in the swamp. However, this clearly angered the other mutants surrounding them but out of the radius of the perfume spray. They pushed on.

"Okay, you can go now," Duke said to the group. He sprayed more perfume, clearing a way for the rest of the party.

Almost out.

"They're still coming," shouted Lo'n.

"You'll need to run faster, then."

The King himself was now approaching the group, keeping pace—it was clear that he knew how to traverse the shallow waters better than the rebels.

"Glad I grabbed another one," Duke said to himself. He threw the bottle up in the air—high above the head of the King and the most aggressive pursuers. One blast from his pulse pistol shattered the bottle—creating a dense perfume mist that fell on their heads. Some of the cannibals dropped like flies; others turned and ran in the opposite direction of the escaping Neprians.

Duke and Ishiro'shea headed toward the group. The sprint seemed like a blur, but the two covered more ground than they thought.

"The wall's just up here," shouted Lo'n. "It might be a tough climb."

"No time for that," returned Duke, now caught up. "I'm done with this swamp."

Betsy 1, Wall 0.

One by one, the members of the group climbed through a gaping hole in the wall and landed on the drier surface of the northern land mass.

"So, Duke, where did you get that—spray?"

"Long story. Remember the temple? Yeah, we met this guy."

CHAPTER 30

NICE TO SEE YOU AGAIN

"THAT'S QUITE A TALE," LO'N said. "Don't you think?"

He looked towards J'a.

"Yes, quite." She spoke softly, as if she was still contemplating what Duke had told her.

"I don't believe it," Po'l said forcefully. "Not for a solitary moment do I believe that. He'j wouldn't steal anything."

"He might," Ja'a began, stunning Po'l, "if he thought it was in our best interest."

"And who *wouldn't* be freaked out by a giant monster guard? Introducing himself probably wasn't high on He'j's ol' 'What should I do now?' list," Duke reminded them.

"True." Ja'a paused. "But to the more pressing issue. There's no excuse for abandoning your post and leaving us in a very precarious situation."

Duke had no retort.

"I think he's making it up," Po'l started again, "so we'll think his nighttime escapade that left us vulnerable to those cannibals wasn't for nothing."

"How do you explain the perfume?" asked Duke.

"Po'l, we don't have time for this now," Ja'a said. "It's a lot to digest. We've put a good distance between us and the swamp so I don't see us having to deal with this 'Keeper.' But it's all very interesting."

Ja'a picked up her pace and moved to the front of the group, lock step with Ma'n and Te'o, before anyone could blink. She motioned the pair away and proceeded to take on the scout position independently.

"You believe me, right?"

"Most definitely," said Lo'n. "There are many things in Neprius that I don't understand—that *we* don't understand—especially when it comes to that Orb. And *that* swamp. I'm just glad he gave you that fragrance. Dumb luck or not, we owe you yet again."

Po'l grew red in the face. Duke shot a smile in his direction.

"I'm sure it won't be the last time either. We're making good time now that it's open land ahead of us, but we still have a few more days trek to get to Sansagon."

Now Po'l's face was the shade of the astral anomaly that brought the bounty hunters to Neprius in the first place.

The group journeyed for the better part of the day. The landscape of the northern land mass resembled that of the south, with its long sweeping grasslands and low sloping hills. *Equally as boring*, thought Duke. The only difference was that the terrain was dotted with unique rock formations, the likes of which Duke had never seen. Massive boulders jutted out of the ground at odd angles—some as gargantuan as the *Deus Ex Machina*, others not much bigger than Duke himself. Their jagged edges made it appear like lodged spear tips from a race of ancient titans that would have made the Keeper seem pocket-sized. Regardless, they were everywhere. Some standing alone, others in clusters.

Ja'a must have trekked a great deal farther than Ma'n and

Te'o's previous scout position: when she approached the group she was sweating and trying to catch her breath. She inhaled deeply.

"Up ahead—" She hunched over, hands on her knees. "—priests. They're tailing someone."

"Who?"

"Not sure. They weren't on lookout, they were definitely following someone."

"Any guesses?"

"My guess would be a runaway."

"As in someone that escaped the mines?" asked Duke.

"Yep."

"How many did you see?"

"Just two. I'm assuming they're tracking a lone runaway."

"I don't think there are any mines around here, so they must've made it pretty far," said Lo'n. "And to send two armed guards... Seems like overkill for a single runaway."

"Maybe it's someone of importance," Po'l said. "Or at least someone that would join our cause. Surely, if they made it this far, they are a force to be reckoned with."

"Let's go," said Duke. The rest of the group turned to him, appearing shocked. Even Ishiro'shea did a double take.

"So, you didn't want to help out the villagers at Shud'nut—but *this* is fine? Blindly going off course to track down a mysterious escapee?" asked Po'l.

"Or maybe they are just tracking down lunch?" added Bu'r.

"Sure, I mean, you said it yourself—they could be important," Duke replied. "If they can help us, let's do it."

"Because you want your ship back?"

"Whatever the reason, I'm saying I'm in."

Duke looked at Ja'a. She didn't acknowledge him, her eyes fixed on the ground.

"I don't like this," said Po'l.

"Oh, the ever-trusting soul," Duke said with a groan. "I always took you for a 'shoot first, ask questions later' type of guy. Maybe I misread you. I mean, if they need two guards to take down this runaway, they might be too dangerous for you anyways. I *did* see you struggle with those cannibals back there."

"Enough!" Ja'a barked, cutting Po'l off before he could lash out. "Thoughts, anyone? Productive thoughts."

Duke smiled at Po'l.

"How off course?" inquired Lo'n.

"Probably an hour or so. Without knowing how far behind they were from their prey, it's hard to tell," replied Ja'a.

"Doesn't seem too bad," Duke said. "I'm still for it."

"Me too," Bu'r chimed in.

"What do you think, Lo'n?" asked Po'l.

"I think we should press on. The risk isn't worth the addition of one member of the group. And what if it's a child or someone injured? Are we prepared to leave them and push on?"

"Wouldn't a child or an injured person only need a single tracker?"

Lo'n continued, "I say that we maintain our course and focus our efforts and energies on Orbius."

"Lo'n, my good buddy, I'm going to have to disagree with you. I say we take the chance—it's only a few hours, after all. If they can't help us, then we free them and let them travel with us until we can safely drop them off. Or if they want, they can continue on their merry way—they're obviously heading somewhere. It's worth the risk, to me."

"We are wasting precious time arguing!" screamed Po'l.

"He's right," said Ja'a, prompting a smirk from Po'l. "Let's vote. There are eight of us, so I'll abstain to allow a majority."

The group circled around their leader. Softly, she said, "Those that want to track these priests and see who—or what—they are pursuing, raise your hands."

Duke shot his hand up first. Bu'r followed. Ishiro'shea was next. Ma'n and Te'o stared at the ground.

"I'm sorry, friend, but it looks like you lose this round," said Lo'n.

"Actually—" started Po'l.

Po'l stood with his hand raised. Duke felt as if his intestines had just exploded. It was obvious that Po'l seemed to enjoy shocking the bounty hunter—even if it meant siding with him.

"Very well," the elder Neprian sighed. "I don't agree with this. But if we can make it quick, there's no harm, I guess."

"Okay, this way," ordered Ja'a.

"If we double-time it, maybe we can get there before they catch him," added Duke.

"Or her," said Ja'a.

"Or it," countered Duke. "But let's hope it's not an *it*. I hate *its*."

***

"Exactly what I feared," said Lo'n. He remained hunched behind one of the jagged rocks protruding from the Neprian landscape. "A waste of our time. If we pick it up, we can make up a ton of the ground that we lost before night hits."

"Are you kidding me?" Duke shouted, only to be met with an aggressive "shhh" from the group. "You know who that is, right?"

"Yes," Lo'n replied, less than enthusiastically. The others seemed to come to the same conclusion.

"That's Vernglet Wip. He knows stuff. Important stuff. And, if he doesn't tell us this important stuff, I want to make sure his skull is properly smashed in for setting us up and getting us into this mess."

"We came here to free someone being enslaved for no reason and who could potentially help us in our quest," Ja'a said. "I'm sure this Wip character deserves everything that he gets—and those two guards seem like they can do an adequate job. Now let's go."

Duke looked at Ja'a. Her glance in return offered no insight into what she was thinking. The others tried not to make eye contact.

"Guys, he knows *stuff*. We can get information out of him and, if he doesn't, then Ishiro can slice him into neat little pieces. Win-win."

"He knows stuff? What stuff?" Lo'n chirped back, in a tone of frustration.

"He knows where his ship is," Po'l added. "He only cares about that, remember?"

"You're right. He probably does know where the *Deus* is. And the Orb. And weaknesses at Orbius' place. And the easiest route in and out. He made it this far before getting caught. Well, I guess he isn't caught *yet*."

Duke peeked out from behind a particularly odd-shaped rock formation. The rebels remained hidden from the scene that was unfolding below; safely behind a cluster of the unusual rocks at the ridge of a slight incline nearly a hundred paces away from the trackers. Duke assumed that they were out of earshot—as long as they spoke with their "inside voices."

"Okay, he's caught now," Duke corrected himself with a huff.

The two Neprian priests had Wip backed up against a boulder. Their spears were mere inches from his face.

"C'mon guys! We came this far, let's at least see if we can get something from him. What do we have to lose?"

"Lives," Ja'a replied calmly.

"Fine, I'll go alone. If I die, no big whup. You guys can run away and keep pursuing Orbius. I'll even leave Ishiro'shea for you as a parting gift."

Ishiro'shea shook his head.

"I knew this was a bad idea," Lo'n began, "even if rules are rules and the majority won. Bad outcomes—even when following the rules—are still bad. I simply cannot stand for us risking anything to help a runaway priest. Nothing he can do is worth this. It's a total waste. I say we leave now. No, I demand it."

"But then we can't pick his brain—no matter how warped it is. *That* would be a total waste. There's no point to any of this if we don't at least try to see if we can get something useful from him," professed Duke.

"The point is that this is *pointless*," Lo'n hissed.

"Calm down for a second. Let's think about this," Ja'a said.

"No," Lo'n roared. "This is ridiculous."

"Hey," Duke started, "no need to—"

"I demand that we leave," Lo'n repeated.

"Friend, let's take a deep breath—" Duke replied.

"Ja'a, tell them to go," Lo'n continued, without acknowledging the bounty hunter.

"Duke brings up a good point. He might know something," said Ja'a.

"Unbelievable. 'Something.' 'Stuff.' That's all you got." Lo'n stood up and headed back towards their original path. *Based on their expressions, this is a Lo'n that no one has ever seen before,* surmised Duke. *Especially Ja'a.*

"Lo'n!" screamed Ja'a.

The subtle, indistinguishable murmurs of the priests' voices suddenly stopped. Ja'a immediately realized what she had done.

That was not an inside voice.

"Who goes there?" shouted one of the trackers.

"Help!" screamed Vernglet Wip. "Help me!"

"Shut up, Wip. Who's behind those rocks?"

"Me," shouted Duke gruffly. But it was Ishiro'shea that slowly stepped from behind the rock and into plain sight. The ninja moved his mouth under his mask, giving the impression that the words were his own.

"Stay there! Hands up. You are now the property of Orbius, Orbmaster of the Orb."

"Okay, I give up. Please don't hurt me. I'll lie on the ground and be a good little boy," Duke bellowed from his unseen location. Ishiro'shea gave him a venomous stare and then proceeded to lie down on the ground—behind the first row of boulders.

One of the trackers made his way to Ishiro'shea, face down in the dirt.

"Who is he?" shouted the guard that remained with their prisoner. "A rebel?"

When the guard was a few paces from him, Ishiro'shea sprang up and darted back behind the rocks.

"Stop or—"

The guard never saw the club coming. Bu'r's swing had the force of ten Neprians and dropped the priest with ease.

"Hey, what's going on? Did you let him escape? I know I should've gone," shouted the other tracker. "Stay there, Vern."

"Idiots. Lather. Rinse. Repeat," whispered Duke. "Okay, get ready. He'll be here in five... four... three... two..."

BLAMPH! The second tracker was out.

"Good job, Bu'r," congratulated Duke.

Ja'a chased towards Lo'n.

"Ja'a, let him blow off some steam. We have a chance to get some... answers, maybe," Po'l said optimistically.

She didn't hear him. Moments later, they were interrupted by a familiar voice.

"Thank you! Thank you! You saved me!" came Vern's high-pitched voice from his place of would-be capture. "I can't thank you enough. What can I do to repay you? Whomever you are?"

"Not sure you want me to answer that," Duke said as he

stepped out from his hiding spot and positioned himself in Vernglet's line of sight.

The Neprian priest's face sunk within itself before it sank into his hands. Duke interpreted the next sounds as some sort of Neprian curse words.

CHAPTER 31

A THUD IN THE NIGHT

"**Y**OU'RE GOING THE WRONG WAY," squeaked Vernglet Wip. He squirmed, trying to find a comfortable position amidst his roped bonds. "Right into Orbius' central army."

"Shut up, priest," barked Po'l. "You're lucky we kept you alive."

"A massive mistake in my estimation," said Lo'n gruffly. It was clear that he was still angry about the decision, but he was now calming visibly.

"He might come in handy, still," pleaded Duke. "We just don't know yet."

"You said he would have information—and did he?" asked Lo'n.

"Not as such," started Duke, "but—"

"No, he's now a liability. I went along with saving him, but he's of no value. And he's evil. Orbius' stooge," said Po'l. It was clear the tide of his opinions was shifting in Lo'n's direction.

"I don't think he would have sent two trackers to bring him back if he was totally loyal to Orbius," added Bu'r.

"Yes," chimed in the prisoner. "Like I told you, I was being sent back to Sansagon to my death for being a traitor."

"Convenient story. Maybe Orbius knew we would take you in—and you are supposed to sabotage our mission," said Lo'n.

"That does make some sense," murmured Po'l.

"You love your conspiracy theories," jabbed Duke.

"I don't believe his story about going against Orbius' wishes for the greater good of the planet," Po'l said defiantly. "I don't think he has the spine for it."

"You all know what Orbius has done to your people. But look what he's done to mine. We are no less slaves than you. Maybe we lack actual chains—but we also lack free will. Is it that hard to believe that one of my kind has come to realize this?"

"Yeah."

"Yep."

"Totally."

"You set yourself up for that, Vern," said the bounty hunter, "but I see where you're coming from. Don't get me wrong, I'm still royally pissed—but I get it."

"It's true. Gar knew it. He saw it in me. He ordered my imprisonment. He claimed that I gave you an out—that day in the field where your ship was—set you up to kill our troops and flee. I didn't know that he brought an entire legion with him."

"Utter nonsense. Surely you can't believe this drivel," groaned Lo'n. "Ja'a, let's cut our losses and leave his carcass to rot in the sun."

He held up his saber mere inches in front of Vernglet's face.

"Lo'n, no. I don't know if I believe him but he doesn't have any weapons and doesn't pose a threat. I think we should continue on, and an answer will present itself."

"He's slowing us down."

"I don't think that's the case."

"As long as we don't listen to him, I'm fine. He would love

for us to follow his directions and bring us right to Orbius' warm embrace."

"That's where you're heading now," Vernglet pointed out.

"For now," Ja'a began, "we will listen to you, Lo'n. You know these lands and how you made it to Orbius last time."

"That's a mistake—"

"It might be wise to keep your mouth shut," said Lo'n, raising his sword again.

"Hey now, chill. He can hang back here with Ish and I. We'll watch him. I still have some questions for him."

"Fine."

Lo'n stormed to the front of the group. Ja'a looked back at Duke and locked eyes. He couldn't figure out if she was confused or angry—or simply disappointed in how her "uncle" was behaving.

Vernglet seems to bring out the worst in people.

Duke whispered to the priest, "You gotta help me out here, Vern."

"What do you mean?"

"They really want to kill you."

"But isn't the enemy of your enemy your friend?"

"Not if that person is a slimy Neprian priest with a long history of enslaving their people."

"Fair point."

"Is everything that you said true?"

"Yes."

"We are walking directly into the jaws of Orbius' army?"

"Directly. I've been running from his clutches for some time now. I know."

"I don't know why I'm trusting you, after you sold us up the river back in Dre'en. I mean, not cool, dude."

"I had no choice."

"I'm willing to entertain that notion. Thoughts, Ish?"

The ninja looked Vern up and down, from toe to head. He glanced back at Duke and shrugged.

"Helpful."

The fabric on Ishiro's mask tilted upward. He was smiling.

"How long do we have until we meet them head on?"

"A day. Maybe a bit more."

"Not much time. It's getting dark, so maybe we can sleep on it and come up with a plan to at least consider the fact that you might not be part of some complex orchestration by Vangu. Oh man, can you imagine Po'l if there *is* a conspiracy? He would be unbearable. And we would likely be dead."

"I will continue to think of ideas, Duke."

"So, are you sure you don't know anything else about the *Deus*?"

"Just what I told you. Orbius was very interested in it. I'm guessing he is going to use it as a weapon—another means of controlling us."

"Maybe. Not sure he could fly it—it's a bit finicky. And I definitely know he couldn't teach your lot to drive it." Duke paused momentarily. "No offense."

"None taken."

"And it's just at his fortress?"

"I wasn't with the group that delivered it to him."

"One last thing, Vern. This has been bugging me."

"Yes?"

"Don't take this the wrong way, but why does Orbius care so much about you? It doesn't seem like you know the inner workings that could help bring him down. One traitor doesn't win a war."

"But it can lose a war."

The bounty hunters looked at each other. *What the hell does that mean?*

"He fears that my resistance—and his inability to publicly punish me—"

"You mean kill you."

"Most likely, yes. His inability to dispose of me will spark rebellious thoughts that are buried deep in our people. I know

Ja'a and her people don't view us as capable of standing up for something—but it's there. Somewhere. Our servitude to Orbius without even a hint of defiance has been our lowest point. Some of us recognize this and refuse to let it happen again."

The bounty hunter scratched his chin.

The troop marched on as night fell over the Neprian landscape. Ja'a directed them to a dense collection of rock formations surrounded by a few rogue trees.

"See those formations ahead?" asked Ja'a. "Forward lookouts can post up there. We can camp under these with a single scout on the other side. Any volunteers?"

"I'll take the forward lookout," said Te'o.

"I'll join him," huffed Lo'n.

"Okay, and I'll watch the back first. Vern can come with me, too."

"I think he should be up front with us, Ja'a. I know you're a great warrior but two trumps one if he does decide to get feisty," remarked Lo'n.

"I can handle it."

"I know you *can*. But it's not wise."

"I agree with Lo'n," interjected Po'l. "It's logical."

"You and logic have met?" snapped Duke.

"Enough," said Ja'a. "Unnecessary, but I will yield to the group. And to logic."

Lo'n turned to Vernglet. "Don't even think about trying any of your priestly trickery. I'll behead you before you can say Orbmaster of the Orb."

He grabbed Vern roughly by his rope cuffs and led him to the lookout position. Te'o followed.

"Good night."

"What is it, Ishiro?"

The ninja was kneeling over the Nova Texan, peering out into the dead of the night.

"It's nothing. Go back to bed."

The mute martial artist tugged at Duke's shoulder again and pointed. Off in the distance a faint flicker of light was losing a battle against the ominous darkness.

"That's just Lo'n and Te'o. You're losing your touch. You're better than that. Now go to bed."

Ishiro'shea tapped Duke again—this time with more force.

"Hey!"

The ninja pointed to his ear.

"Listen to what?"

Ishiro pressed his palms down, signaling for Duke to shut his trap.

"Fine," Duke said, and waited. "Nothing. You're hearing things."

A subtle thud. Duke stood to attention.

"Okay, I heard it that time. You don't think—" He paused. "No. Vern *did* set us up? It's a trap? That means—holy hedgehogs, that means Lo'n and Te'o are in trouble."

Ishiro'shea started to sprint nimbly in that direction.

"Wait! Should we tell—nope, answered my own question. We need to ambush this bastard and any friends that he might have brought along to help. They'd smell Po'l a mile away."

Ishiro'shea pointed to the large rock barrier behind their campsite.

"No, I think we need to leave Ja'a out of this, too."

The duo ran towards the lookout position with as much stealth as they could muster. *Ishiro'shea's much better at this,* thought Duke. The terrain was flat, so their path weaved from rock to rock to whatever piece of the Neprian topography would provide cover.

"There it is again," whispered Duke as he slunk behind an oversized boulder angled into the Neprian soil. "There might be an entire band of priesties waiting on us."

They continued on.

"One more hiding spot before their camp—and it's pretty well covered. If we need to snipe them from there, we should be fine. Let's go."

The collection of stones was to the east of the scouting location. It had a slight incline that reached a pinnacle at a point almost as high as the hill where Lo'n and Te'o were camped with Vernglet Wip. It was the perfect spot for reconnaissance—*super secretive* reconnaissance at that. The pair crawled silently to the apex of the formation and laid belly down. They could hear the crackling fire from a torch stuck in the ground.

"I don't see 'em. Too late?"

Ishiro'shea pointed.

"That's... that's Lo'n. Hey—" Duke started to scream for Lo'n's attention but Ishiro'shea quickly covered his mouth and shoved him down. Duke mumbled unintelligibly through Ishiro's hand. It wasn't a particularly nice comment.

After a few moments, the ninja and the bounty hunter rose again to survey the area. Ishiro'shea pointed at another person. On the ground.

"Is that one of Vern's henchmen?" Duke said softly. "Did Lo'n take him out? That would make this much easier."

He examined the figure more closely. "No," he whispered to himself.

Lo'n scanned the area, standing over the prone body. Ishiro'shea threw Duke's head down to the surface of the rock again.

More mumbles.

"That can't be," Duke said as they hid on the downward slope of the rock. "That can't be," he gulped, "Te'o?"

Ishiro'shea nodded in affirmation.

"Lo'n was too late. They got to Te'o. We should definitely go give him backup."

Duke leapt to his feet at the summit of the hill. Ishiro'shea tried to stop him, but the bounty hunter was undeterred.

"What the—Look, Ishiro."

Duke drew his laser revolver and rushed down the rock face. His companion followed suit, katana drawn.

"Duke, Ishiro'shea," Lo'n huffed as they approached. "I'm glad you're here. As I had feared, Vernglet Wip was leading us on the entire time. This was all a ruse. His fellow priests tracked us down and attacked. They killed Te'o. I was able to fight them off and they fled. I knocked him out and was about to finish him off."

He pointed at Vernglet Wip's motionless body.

Lo'n's saber was hoisted high in the air with his right hand. Te'o's ax hung at his side, gripped in his left hand. The priest was slowly coming to.

"Drop the sword."

"What?" the aging rebel asked, staring in confusion. "This cancerous wretch killed Te'o. Who knows how many are on their way now."

"None," Duke said emphatically.

"Excuse me?"

"None. There aren't any that are coming for us. At least, none directly caused by our friend Vern here."

"What are you talking about, Duke?"

"Don't play dumb. I watched you drag Vern's body and drop it next to Te'o."

"Your eyes mistake you, off-worlder."

Ishiro'shea took a step toward Lo'n with his katana at the ready.

"Hold, Ish. We saw you drag the body. I get it. You didn't want to slice him into two Vernglets and have to drag the blood and entrails over here—we woulda seen through that. Po'l probably woulda seen through that."

"You're wrong."

"Why'd you do it?"

"Do what?" he pleaded.

"You know what. And drop the sword."

Duke aimed his gun directly at the rebel's chest. Lo'n paused, breathing deeply.

"I can't do that," Lo'n said, his voice changing from confusion—or a poor performance of it—to one of cold calculation. "This guy here has to die. And then you and your friend have to die. You shouldn't have come here, Duke. Orbius might have only imprisoned you, but now you'll have to be silenced."

"Orbius?"

"You know so little of this land, off-worlder. Orbius is our only hope. Our savior. The only one that can control the Orb. He'j was foolish—and he paid for it. I had to make sure that he wouldn't be in the way anymore. And now, you. You are in the way. This fruitless rebellion is in the way."

"Haven't you heard the old saying about absolute power?"

"The Orb *is* the absolute power—and Orbius is our buffer from its evil magic. He is our guardian."

"Why does a savior need to enslave people to mine for jewels and rocks?"

"Non-believers must be punished. If they stop Orbius, our planet is doomed."

"He's not very all-powerful if he's worried about a few disorganized farmers. You honestly believe what he's saying?"

"I do. It's the truth."

"And you know this how?"

Slight movement came from under Lo'n's foot. A groggy Vernglet Wip moaned and tried to roll onto his back.

The Neprian turncoat did not answer Duke's question.

Lo'n lobbed his saber at Duke. Duke fired.

CLINK!

The sword fell to the ground; next to it, Ishiro's katana. Lo'n crumpled to the ground on top of the wounded priest.

"I did *not* see that coming," Duke said to no one in particular. He walked over and helped Ishiro'shea move Lo'n's body off of Vern. "Man, could really use an anthropomorphic musk ox from one of the moons of Gartosh at a time like this."

"What... what happened?" asked Vernglet.

"Not really sure. But let's just say that I'm going to be making the case that we seriously consider your navigational recommendations."

Vernglet stared at Te'o's dead body. He glanced to Lo'n's.

"Orbius has many spies. He plays many angles."

"This one was a strong hand," Duke began, "I have a feeling that this is going to be harder than I thought."

Ishiro'shea picked up his sword.

"Thanks, Ishiro. I *really* owe you this time."

All three turned as a slowly accumulating rumble crept up behind them. *Everyone's awake.* Duke turned to his compatriot.

"How are we going to explain this to Ja'a?"

Ishiro'shea's expression offered no helpful suggestions.

The group stampeded towards them. Ma'n led the way, presumably due to the worry that if something went wrong, his lifelong friend Te'o was likely affected—and this was, of course, precisely the case. Po'l was next—his enthusiasm likely relating to blaming Duke for the entire mess. Bu'r followed. Ja'a came up last, since she had been stationed furthest away. Duke could see the dread on her face—she was probably in the process of calculating the worst possible outcomes.

"Whoa! Same team! Same team!" shouted Duke as Po'l aimed an arrow at his nose.

"Are we?" Po'l countered with equal force. "What happened?"

"No, no, no," cried Ma'n as he finally noticed Te'o's body a few feet from where they stood. He rushed over and slid to the ground. He felt his pulse. It was very clear that Te'o had not survived the massive slash wound across his chest.

"Ma'n," Duke started, "it was—"

"Shut up, off-worlder!" Po'l said, cutting him off. He

stepped a few paces closer to the bounty hunter. Duke and Ishiro'shea had put away their weapons to prevent the situation from looking any worse. Bu'r scrambled over to Te'o's body and consoled the clearly heartbroken Ma'n. Duke overheard him mentioning "Ty'n" and "honor" and "courage."

"What happened?" barked Po'l. "Tell me. Now."

"What do *you* think happened? Lo'n wasn't who we thought he was."

"You expect us to believe that? You're partners with him, right?" Po'l said, nodding in Vernglet's direction. "It was an elaborate setup. This entire time."

"Not this again. Really?"

"We're to believe that Lo'n, one of our greatest warriors and comrade of He'j, is a traitor? And that he killed one of his own? You've lost your mind, LaGrange. Or you think we are just that stupid."

Duke gritted his teeth. *Not going to say it.*

"Look—"

"No, you look. You killed Lo'n. You killed Te'o."

Ja'a had finally arrived and stepped in front of Po'l. She signaled for him to drop his weapon. She knelt down and examined Lo'n's body. She traced her finger to the wound. She wasn't crying, hysterical, or even sad. She wasn't emotional. *Odd.*

She rose and locked eyes on Duke's, cold and steely. She gave him nothing. She then walked to Te'o's slain body and put her hand on Ma'n's shoulder. She repeated the action with Bu'r. Her eyes fixated on the slash mark that had clearly been the death blow to her former ally. There was a sense of eeriness about the entire situation. No one moved or spoke. Ja'a walked back to stand directly between the two off-worlders and Po'l.

"Tell me. From the beginning. Leave nothing out."

Po'l began to speak, but she halted his response with a

simple glance. During her mediation, Ja'a was not going to suffer emotion.

"Not now, Po'l. I want to know what happened. Or at least what Duke is going to *tell* us the story is. Let's start with why you are here."

The bounty hunter cleared his throat and started.

"Ishiro'shea heard something. A noise. I thought he was crazy—especially when he pointed in this direction. But then I heard it too."

"How did that not wake us up?" Po'l blurted out, to Ja'a's visible dismay.

"Let him finish. Do not interrupt again."

Scolded, Po'l's face sunk in on itself. Duke enjoyed it.

"I don't know. It wasn't a loud noise by any means. Just a soft thud. No screams or shouts."

"Go on," said Ja'a.

"Right. Then we both snuck over here as quietly as possible. We hid on the top of that rock over there." Duke pointed at their recent stakeout locale. "Then we witnessed everything. Most everything."

"And that is?"

"Lo'n standing over Te'o's body. Blood dripping off his saber."

"That doesn't prove anything." It was Bu'r, still consoling Ma'n, who interjected this time. His tone was more curious than angry.

"Like I was saying," Duke continued, "Lo'n stood over Te'o. Then he started to walk over to Vern who was passed out —or rather, knocked out—a few paces away. Right over there. Then, what put this whole thing together was that Lo'n started dragging Vern over to Te'o's body. Ish and I showed up just as he was about to deal the death blow—making it look like Vern did the deed."

"And that deed was?"

"Vernglet's conspirators came in and killed Ma'n before Lo'n fought them off and they fled."

"But why knock the priest out first?" asked Bu'r.

"It would have been easy to tell that he killed him first and drug the body. Especially if it was a messy death."

"Even if this was all possible, why? Why would Lo'n risk this to kill the priest and Te'o?"

"It was just Vern that he wanted to kill."

"But why?"

Duke and Ishiro'shea looked at Vernglet and signaled for him to tell the story.

"Because I knew Lo'n was working for Orbius."

"That's it, Ja'a," snapped Po'l. "I've had enough of this. I mean it this time. Lo'n going crazy and killing people, I'll buy that. A cunning trap from this sleaze—I'm very likely to buy that. I could even give you the craziness of this weak little bastard breaking free and killing Te'o under Lo'n's watch. But I'm not going to sit here and let you believe that Lo'n was a traitor."

Po'l stormed off to the rock that Duke and Ishiro'shea had recently used to spy on Lo'n.

"Why didn't you say anything?"

Vern took a deep, chesty breath and retorted, "Would you have believed me?"

"No," Ja'a answered honestly.

"And that's why Lo'n wanted to leave you or kill you initially," chimed in Bu'r. "He knew that there was a chance—albeit a slim one—that you could convince us."

"Right," answered Duke.

"This is a lot," Ja'a began. "I don't know what to think. No, I do know one thing. Our friend Te'o deserves a proper burial. That is not to be questioned. Let's dig and honor him. He gave his life for the cause. Maybe in this darkest hour some clarity will present itself."

The entire group—*sans* Po'l—started to dig. Even Vernglet Wip.

"Po'l," shouted Ja'a. "Please come help us honor Te'o."

"I'm not going to dig a grave for one of our own alongside his murderers. A priest that sent countless droves of our people to their enslavement and two off-worlders that likely helped him—that's not what Te'o would have wanted. You all taint his honor."

"Be reasonable."

"I am, Ja'a. I very much am. My time with this group is done. I'm going to follow Lo'n's path and kill Orbius myself. I can't stand being part of this embarrassment—this disgrace—any longer."

"Po'l—" Ja'a pleaded.

"I should've left when we met with Mo'a, back at the base. I let you talk me into this—but not anymore. Not now."

He turned and walked away.

Ja'a began to go after him but Bu'r grabbed her arm. "He made his decision."

"And it's a decision that proves that I've failed as a leader."

CHAPTER 32

VALLEY OF THE GRUNDAR

"DO YOU HAVE TO KEEP him tied up?" Duke asked Ja'a. "I mean, we are following *his* directions—so you have to trust him to some degree."

"I'm not sure that I can ever fully trust a priest. You're new to Neprius and haven't witnessed all that they've done to our people."

"But it was under the threat of death by Orbius."

"That makes no difference. They could've resisted. They blindly followed evil. Even if Vernglet is an outlier, it doesn't excuse him from the monstrosities that he allowed for cycles. I will have a hard time trusting everything that he tells us."

"Baby steps?"

"Yes, baby steps. In time, I hope that I will conclude that he is honest and true and there aren't any sinister motives. Until then, he remains tied up."

"But we follow his directions?"

"Yes."

"Sorry, Vern. I tried." Duke shouted back at the Northerner.

"Her points are valid and understandable," responded Vernglet. "In time, I hope that they see my true colors."

"That's what I'm afraid of," chimed in Ma'n. "We haven't had the best of luck regarding people's true colors as of late."

The group pressed on. Now down to only six—including the quasi-prisoner, Vernglet Wip—they did not have a scout or flanks, and traveled in a single huddled mass. As they pressed northwest, following the priest's guidance, the landscape began to slowly change. Increasingly, the sprawling grasslands were dotted with giant angled stones. On the horizon, bluffs sprouted up in the shadows of a mountain range that seemed to touch the sky.

"The Valley of the Grundar," Vern said, pointing at the first set of rocky cliffs. "There is a passage that leads through to the valley. From there, we can approach Orbius without detection—or, at least, reduced chances of detection. It's only a two-day march."

"The valley is safe?"

"Safe from Orbius' men—yes. Other than that, I cannot guarantee anything."

"That's reassuring," said Bu'r.

"It's the best that we have," responded Ja'a. "If we push, we can make it to the passage and into the valley long before nightfall."

"I'm not camping out there, Ja'a," shouted Ma'n. "What if the legends are true? What if there are actual grundar?"

"Not this again," interjected Duke.

"Then we need to push harder and make it through the valley and en route to Orbius."

"I'm okay with that!"

The rebels picked up their pace. Ma'n and Bu'r moved ahead of the others, clearly spooked by the thought of the flying fire-breathing felines. Ishiro'shea remained at the back with Vernglet, who was having trouble moving faster due to his arms being bound behind his back.

Duke turned to Ja'a. "How do you think Po'l's doing?"

"I'd rather not talk about it. I hope he finds his way to Orbius safely. That's all that I can say."

"Understood. Can we at least talk about Lo'n?"

"What about him?"

"Ja'a, I didn't see a speck of emotion from you when everything went down. Surely—"

"I'm fine. A leader does not let emotions dictate their decisions. It was obvious what happened."

"It was?"

"Yes, it doesn't make sense as to *why* he would do it—but I know he did it."

"Don't you feel betrayed?"

"He was the closest thing that I had to a father outside of my own. Of course. However, I feel worse for my father. His best friend not only betrayed him, but tried to send his daughter into the clutches of the very thing that he fought against. I don't want to know what he would think now."

She clutched her necklace. Duke could see that sadness was trying to break through her defenses.

"I've been around this universe too many times to count, but I've yet to find a leader so dedicated to their cause as you. I mean it. No joke. I know we haven't seen eye-to-eye on everything, but—"

His rare and heartfelt plea was interrupted by a shout from Ma'n. "Is that the passage?"

"Vernglet?" asked Ja'a.

"Yes. We go through that opening and within moments the sky will open up and we will be standing in the Valley of the Grundar."

Ja'a turned to Duke. "Thank you."

She then picked up her pace and took the command position as they approached the cave.

As Vernglet had predicted, the walk through the passage was short and uneventful. And it did open up to a valley—and quite dramatically. Duke estimated the valley was the size of the whole of Dre'en. The mountainous cliffs surrounded the lush landscape. Greens, yellows, and whites adorned the beautiful palette; the valley seemed untouched by even the primitive level of civilization elsewhere on Neprius. It was picturesque and, more importantly, quiet. The lack of life was almost unsettling.

"It's a direct route to the other end of the valley," said Vernglet. "There is another passage—not too dissimilar than the one we just left. That will put us out due west of the base. When we near the village of Horteyaya, we can take a northern route to avoid Orbius' many eyes and soon we will see the fortress."

"Thank you. And I do believe that I owe you this." Ja'a walked to him and drew out a single arrow from her quiver. The priest winced involuntarily, but Ja'a grabbed his rope bonds and sliced them off in one single motion with the edge of the arrowhead. The priest exhaled.

"You haven't led us astray and I want to show you trust. Our people have battled for so long that trust will be the hardest gift to bestow, but I want to start that process now. Here. With you. We are both children of Neprius and we can never heal unless we both see that."

Vernglet Wip bowed in appreciation.

"Enough of this—let's go kill us an Orbmaster!" Duke said, twirling his laser revolver on a finger. "How about it, guys? Let's do this!"

His attempts at rallying the troops fell flat. "Hey Ja'a, tell me about the grundar again? Winged fire-breathing panthers, right?"

"Yes, that's the legend. Though I've never seen—"

"I think you're wrong."

"Wrong about what?"

"They're *big-ass* winged fire-breathing panthers that look *really* pissed off—oh yeah, and you're about to see one."

The entire group turned to see what Duke had witnessed.

Landing without a sound was a massive flying cat. The saber-like teeth that protruded from the upper jaw were each about the length of Duke's arm.

As one, the group drew their weapons.

"It's a grundar. A real one," uttered Bu'r in amazement. "I can't believe it."

The beast let out a deafening growl. *Perfect murder machines,* thought Duke. *Almost beautiful, if you take out the whole "likely to kill us" part.*

"Hold fire," said Ja'a. "It could be scared of us. It probably hasn't seen a Neprian before."

"It doesn't look too scared," replied Duke. "And it looks like we're about to meet its friends."

A dozen more grundar were flying from the cliffs on a direct path to them. They landed, encircling the rebels and providing no exit.

"Back to back, everyone!" shouted Ja'a. "Hold steady."

"If they really can breathe fire, we're about to be toast. Literally," Duke added. "Great, another one. And it's really, really big."

A final grundar descended from the sky. It was a grundar a head taller than the next largest. But the major difference was that it carried a passenger. A not-friendly-looking passenger.

Duke had wondered if he appeared gargantuan only because he was sitting atop the majestic beast—but he was quickly proven wrong. When the grundar rider dismounted he stood twice the height of the tallest human. His face was almost skeletal in appearance, gray skin pulled tight against his bones, but his frame was muscular. His eyes were pupil-less; as if someone had stuffed a pair of polished onyx stones into his eye sockets. Somehow, though, they contained life and emotion. The weathered shroud that he wore matched the color of his eyes and its tatters and rips flowed in the air upon his descent. He carried a staff of warped wood, almost the size of a young tree, and marked with wounds inflicted by combat and time.

The rebels kept their weapons drawn. The grundar rider snarled in his displeasure, showing jagged teeth that could cut iron.

Two of the grundar parted as he approached the encircled band of warriors. Duke fired his laser revolver impulsively. The giant raised his left hand and deflected the energy pulse. Not even a scratch.

"You guys are getting more and more daring."

There was a slight hiss to his voice.

"Wait... what?" Duke blurted out. "What are you talking about?"

"I didn't think that your leader would send you into *my* valley."

"This seems familiar," Duke whispered to Ishiro, recalling the Keeper's confused insistence that they were swamp cannibals.

"Our leader?" asked Ja'a.

"The one that stole the Orb and is trying to bring the end to life."

"Wait... what?" Duke said again.

"Enough of your stalling. Girls, ready to pounce..."

"We are not the warriors of which you speak," Ja'a proclaimed. "We are trying to *stop* him. We are trying to destroy the Orb."

The grundar were growing restless.

"Nice try," the grundar rider said dismissively. "I've seen your types. And I know that *he* is your leader." He pointed.

Vernglet looked genuinely shocked.

"What? Vern?" Duke blurted out. "He's actually our prisoner. Well, sort of. He *was* our prisoner."

"A prisoner that sports no bonds or chains?"

"Good eye. I can explain that," replied Duke, with a touch of embarrassment.

"Your people must have a very liberal interpretation of 'prisoner.' He looks like all of the others—digging and mining and destroying. I knew it was only a matter of time before you made it to my valley."

"I assure you, Master of the Grundar, I am no leader. And these people speak the truth," began Vernglet. "My people—my former people—follow the orb-stealer. I'm afraid he is unstoppable with the power that it brings him."

The rider seemed to consider Vernglet's claim.

"Nice try, again. You are but six. Am I to believe that you are going to take down this Orbmaster? And his army?"

"His name is Orbius."

"Cute."

"We are going to try," proclaimed Ja'a.

"You are a feisty one. Are *you* the leader?"

"Yes, and, kind sir, if we were part of this horde, do you think that the Orbmaster would have sent only us six to capture the Valley of the Grundar?"

"Very good point." He scratched his cheek with a spindly finger which ended in a hooked nail.

"But how did you learn that this Orbmaster knows of my existence? I've been in this valley for ages without a single interaction from your kind. Or yours." He pointed at the priest.

"It's clear that you've been in battle."

She motioned towards a grundar with a gash on its right front leg, then at another with a cut between its eyes.

"You are quite observant and correct, leader."

"My name is Ja'a. From the Southern landmass. A long way from here. My people were enslaved by Orbius. We are fighting back against him and his army. We want to be free again. We want Neprius—this planet—to be free again."

"And us two, we're from outer space," Duke said, trying to imbue the term "outer space" with mystic spookiness.

It was apparent that the grundar rider was not shocked or impressed by the concept of cosmic life.

"I'm Duke LaGrange," Duke concluded weakly. "This is my compatriot, Ishiro'shea."

"Is that so?"

"And sorry about shooting you earlier. Habit."

"Wait, was that thing that you hurled at me supposed to be a weapon?"

Duke opened his mouth but at first nothing came out. He cleared his throat. "Sorry, anyways."

"Why are you fighting Orbius?" asked Ja'a.

"He has the Orb—and therefore he has the ability to levy uncontrolled carnage to my valley. The Orb only brings destruction. My friends and I are not ready to see our home destroyed again. We will eventually have to face this Orbmaster. I was in battle with a garrison southeast of here, until I heard that someone had entered the valley."

"You were battling an entire garrison by yourself?" Ma'n blurted out.

The rider gazed at Ma'n and then nodded.

"How did this Orbius get hold of the Orb? I thought it was lost to time; its stories and legends all but evaporated with the ancient races. With *my* race."

"It was stolen," Duke jumped in, "from the Keeper."

"The Keeper?"

"Yes, the only other thing on this planet that's as big as you. He was guarding it in his temple."

"Oh, wait—do you mean Toby?"

The rebels looked shocked.

"Toby?" asked Ma'n.

"Now that makes so much sense," said the grundar rider, appearing more relaxed. He repositioned his staff to support his weight. "I can't believe he's still around. I'd like to give him a piece of this!" He raised a fist. "Calling himself the Keeper, huh? If there's one thing that he's not good at, it's keeping things. You know he's lost it before, right? And he's not much good at finding things either, I guess."

"Yep, he told us. He also told us that he was the only thing to survive the destruction caused by the Sphere of Power. So how do you know him?"

"That's not entirely true," the grundar rider said, ignoring the question. "Maybe near his home, he was the only thing to survive. The sphere sunk much of the land to the bottom depths of the sea."

"That explains the narrow land bridge," added Ja'a.

"But a few pockets of survivors remained—mostly in secluded areas. Not sure if they are still around, to be honest. I doubt it—that was a long time ago. Even we have expiration dates. I stayed in the mountains and started to breed grundar. It seemed like the best thing to do. I mean what else was I to do? An art retrospective? This is my seven thousand, three hundred and forty-eighth litter here."

He turned to his cats. "And my favorite!" he added in a playful tone.

The grundar purred joyously. The rebels collectively relaxed.

"You know about the people that gave it back to him after he lost it, then?"

"I do. Peculiar race that came out of nowhere. I blinked— couldn't have been but an age or two—and we had civilization again. Primitive, albeit, but civilization. Hadn't made it to the soufflé stage yet."

"You knew they had the Orb—and that's what was causing the war?"

"I did not—not until I saw them give it back to Toby and block off the land bridge. Their skirmishes didn't make it to my lands. I would occasionally scare an ambitious explorer in the valley but, other than that, I ignored them entirely. Had I known sooner, I would have tried to destroy it then. But Toby seemed to do a better job that time around. Until this latest fiasco. So this Orbius character stole it from good ol' Toby?"

"Actually, my father stole it from him," Ja'a replied.

The rider seemed taken aback by this tidbit of information. "This is getting really juicy now. Do tell," he said eagerly.

"Don't you have a battle to go back to?" asked Bu'r.

"They'll wait. Go on," the rider said, waving away Bu'r's comment.

Ja'a proceeded to fill the grundar rider in on the droughts, He'j and Jilarian Togg, the arrival of Duke and Ishiro'shea, and Lo'n's betrayal. Vernglet explained his role in the tale. Duke talked about his conversation with Toby.

"That's quite a yarn. I'm actually inclined to believe it. It's too ridiculous to make up. And Looloo over there seems to like you. I trust her."

The winged grundar nudged her nose into Bu'r's back, knocking him down. She licked the top of his head.

"So what should we call you?"

"I am Fazeek, Shepherd of the Grundar. But you can call me 'Shepherd of the Grundar.'"

"Not where I thought he was going with that... but okay," whispered Duke to Ishiro'shea.

"Shepherd of the Grundar," began Ja'a in a formal, almost regal, voice, "do we have your permission to leave your valley and try and stop Orbius?"

It was obvious that Fazeek loved the formality—and the fact that it was referred to as *his* valley.

"By all means," he responded. "But to truly be part of this, we need to get you to this Orbius a bit faster than your tiny legs can carry you."

He whistled and six of the winged beasts approached and submitted for mounting. Looloo leapt eagerly to Bu'r's feet and knelt down.

"I guess we go bareback," remarked Duke. "Anyone else feel a bit uneasy about this?"

The bounty hunter looked around. All of the others were already on their grundar and hovering above the ground. Duke hopped on, then was jolted back as the cat leapt to the sky to join the others.

"My new friends—we have two goals. Destroy this Orbius. And find a way to destroy the Orb. It will not be easy. I will rejoin my loyal menagerie south of Orbius' hideout and try and eliminate his main force. My lovelies will take you to the location of your desire—and then they will return to me and our battle."

"How do we tell them?" asked Ma'n.

Fazeek looked perplexed.

"With words."

"They understand us?" questioned Bu'r.

"Of course," Fazeek replied.

The rebels all looked at each other. Duke didn't know if he believed Fazeek.

"And what about saddles?" asked Bu'r. "You don't expect us to ride—"

"Bareback, yes," said Fazeek.

"So, you're telling me that these monsters are just going to let us hop on their backs and fly away; all the while, we are supposed to be skilled enough to balance without any saddles right out of the chutes?" questioned Bu'r again.

"Not if you refer to them as 'monsters' again," replied Fazeek.

"This seems like a tall task," added Ma'n.

"Oh, I'm sure you'll figure it out," said Fazeek. "You seem like an intelligent lot." He sharply pivoted his oversized grundar and darted into the wide sky.

The group of rebels stared at each other again, this time with downward turning lips and scrunched brows.

What just happened?

"Well, you heard the man," Duke began, breaking the silence. "Vern, where are we going again?"

"The outskirts of the village of Horteyaya."

"Okay, Mister Grundar—"

The cat bucked.

"Miss Grundar?"

It meowed, affirming Duke's correction.

"Take us to Horteyaya."

Nothing. The feline turned to Duke with a look of confusion on her face.

"She doesn't know what we've named these places," Ja'a reminded the bounty hunter. "Try this."

She cleared her throat.

"There is a village west of Orbius' fortress. You know the fortress that I speak of?"

The grundar loosed a throaty growl.

"Can you take us to the westernmost rim of that town—and make sure no one sees us?"

The grundar exchanged roars of varying decibel levels, relaying Ja'a's message. They flapped their wings in unison; the squalls generated from the motion almost knocked the riders from their steeds. They leapt into the Neprian clouds as they headed towards Horteyaya—or wherever it was that the grundar thought Ja'a had commanded them to go.

CHAPTER 33

CAMPS

THE FLIGHT OF THE GRUNDAR was actually pretty smooth, all things considered. It wasn't executive platinum on a galactic cruiser—but it wasn't coach on an Oscavian Cavehopper, either. For his first foray into feline flying, Duke scored it a solid B+. The team waved goodbye as the majestic creatures vaulted into the night air soundlessly. With a single flap of their silvery wings, they were propelled beyond the bounty hunter's range of visibility to become one with the starry backdrop.

"We don't have much time," urged Ja'a. "If we are to go around Horteyaya and into the shadow of Orbius' fortress, we need to move swiftly. And silently."

No one countered her order. *Why would they? She's right.* The grundar had travelled speedily—and had certainly been superior to the alternative of walking—but the evening was already reaching a mature stage and they had ground still yet to cover. The team crested the hill that had hidden their descent. They lit no torches for fear of being seen. The light from the nearby village would have to suffice. For now.

The slinking and slouching reminded Duke of too many recent events—from the grasslands outside of Dre'en, to the hallways of their hotel imprisonment by the Neprian priests, to the witnessing of Lo'n's ultimate betrayal. He wasn't a fan. He was almost looking forward to a straightforward confrontation with Orbius. Even if his Orb controlled everything and must be respected.

The village of Horteyaya wasn't walled like Shud'nut. *Maybe walls are a Southern thing,* pondered Duke. The individual dwellings seemed to be larger and more rugged than the tiny huts outside the city walls of Dre'en; they were boxier with clean lines and smooth edges. Cubes with a slender rectangular door. All were the same color, height, and shape. Not the elegant kind of simple; the boring kind of simple. It was as if they were mass-produced. Duke wondered if anything from Toby's art retrospective could have brightened these places up.

"A typical Northern settlement," whispered Vernglet over Duke's shoulder. "It reminds me of home."

"A bit on the—" Duke searched for the word. "—simple side, don't you think?" It was difficult for him not to call them "drab." Or worse.

"Why would we want our quarters to be exciting? Isn't the point to provide a place to sleep in and keep the elements out?"

"I guess. In many cultures, beings put their own individuality into their houses. Different colors they like. Big paintings on the walls. Swimming pools. You name it. It's been done. I heard that Sprinkles has a taxidermied three-headed ice wombat in his bathroom."

"I don't know this Sprinkles but it sounds interesting. However, I like these abodes. Call me old-fashioned."

"Have it your way."

Ja'a halted the company as they approached a clearing. It looked similar to the area outside of Shud'nut, with one major exception. Wooden pens taller than two Neprian priests were scattered outside the entrance of a cave.

"The mine," said Vernglet as he pointed into the mouth of the cave.

Duke ignored him. He couldn't help but fixate on the goings-on *in* the pens. In the wooden coops were Neprians. Dirty, unwashed, hygienically-unsound Neprians. Each one covered in mud and indistinguishable muck; their hair matted to the point it looked like it was carved from stone. On their faces were downtrodden, vapid expressions, vacant eyes barely ever looking up from the equally filthy pen floor as if eye contact was a capital offense. Sadness didn't do it justice. Down-on-their-luck was way too nice. They were simply beaten.

"Ishiro, are you seeing this?"

"What did you think we meant when we said we were slaves to Orbius?" asked Ma'n, noticing Duke's shock.

"I thought they took a few of you down in the mines for manual labor. A few guards here and there. Not ideal, but not *this*."

"Maybe in Shud'nut," said Bu'r. "It's a Southern town out of the immediate sight of Orbius. They're going to be much more *by the book* here in Horteyaya."

"They don't want Orbius to stop by for a quality control check and see anything that could be misconstrued as leniency," Vernglet chimed in. "That would be very bad for all."

Duke sat crouching behind a bush, his mouth agape. Sure, he had heard of this type of treatment. But a few paces away, he could see it. Hear it. Smell it. It made him sick.

He reached for his pulse pistol. Vernglet stopped his hand. "This is not the way."

"What are you talking about? Look at 'em."

"I know. If you shoot now, you will spoil the plan. You will take a few lives and save a few. But Orbius will know that we are here. The element of surprise is our greatest ally."

"How can you let this happen?" Duke's emotions caused his voice to increase in volume. Ishiro'shea tapped him on the shoulder; Duke returned his voice to an acceptable level. "How can you let your people do this to other living things?"

"I am guilty, Duke. I cannot run from what I've done or—or, more accurately but no less damning, what I let happen. Orbius has corrupted us all and the servitude to his rule has clouded any chance at rational thoughts from my people. I cannot defend this, nor can I expunge my past—I hope my small part in this cause will at least show that some of us are capable of changing. I wish for a time when that will be important, because it will have meant the demise of Orbius." Vernglet's face twitched and his eyes flickered.

His voice waned. "I don't deserve a second chance for everything that occurred under my watch in Dre'en. It shouldn't have taken a trip to Sansagon for me to realize the full extent of what was happening. But it did. And if I can help you stop this, then maybe I did something right in this life. And the next generation of Neprians—both races—will have a chance to live in peace."

Overhearing the conversation, Bu'r interjected. "I wish my friends back home could see this. They wouldn't have treated us the way they did."

Ishiro'shea put his arm around the beefy rebel to comfort him. Duke could tell that Bu'r carried the weight of his people's rejection, and that it was slowly crushing him.

Three priest guards emerged from the cave carrying wooden rods longer than the javelins that Duke was accustomed to seeing in the hands of the Northern folk. The last third of each pole was dotted with sharp tacks and barbs. Not enough to kill, but more than enough to produce the desired outcome of the prodder.

"No," Duke said to himself.

The priests inserted the rods into the pens and began shouting. The slaves squirmed and tried to move but they were packed in so tightly that they ended up falling over each other and being subjected to more pokes and slices. The priests increased the frequency and the force of the strikes and, with each violent episode, they increased the width of their smiles. Despite their confinement, the prisoners still lunged for an unattainable freedom, scratching and clawing their fellow detainees to flee the reach of the pointed tip of tyranny.

It was impossible for Duke to separate the pain-riddled screams of those being caught with the javelin's point from the agonizing groans from the slaves being crushed by their fellow prisoners. It was a single amorphous bloodcurdling wail that burrowed deep into Duke's mind.

Vernglet's expression mirrored those of the prisoners. He looked at the ground.

"I hope you see now why my decision was to leave and separate myself from Orbius' influence. I was in Dre'en for far too long. Setting up altars and having kids clean pots and pans was much different than what I experienced here."

Duke wanted to understand. Vernglet wasn't *that* good of an actor. He also knew the timing was suspicious and made for textbook spy work. However, he gave the priest the benefit of the doubt. He just hoped it was more than simply proving Po'l wrong that was driving his faith.

They trekked until the sun began to turn the northern sky a radiant orange. The sounds from the mines were but a faint memory, but Duke knew it would take much longer to erase the images of what he had seen in Horteyaya. As they continued, their surroundings provided less and less cover.

"There. Do you see it?" said Vernglet, pointing to a ridge on the horizon. "That's directly outside of Orbius' palace. Beyond the hills is a steep decline into a ravine. In that ravine is the fortress—and farther out is the heart of Sansagon."

Ja'a turned to her team. "We made it. Now we must finish this."

The team cheered—but not too loudly.

"Let us all rest before our final push. Vernglet, you have

led us honestly and without deceit. We are grateful. Now, we must ask you for one last favor."

"Yes, noble Ja'a of the Southern landmass."

Duke rolled his eyes at Vernglet's incessant formality.

"Help us strategize a way to enter Orbius' fortress and dispose of him before he can use the Orb to wreak havoc upon us."

"I would be honored. And I happen to have an idea."

Before Vernglet could continue, a black speck appeared in the sky to the south. It was growing and growing—or rather, it was getting closer. It wasn't long before it was easy to see what it was—a grundar.

"Surely they didn't change their mind and are coming back to eat us?" asked Duke.

"There's only one, so I doubt that," replied Ja'a. "And, it looks like it's carrying something. Or someone."

"It appears much too small to be Fazeek," chimed in Vernglet.

"And Fazeek doesn't ride his cat like he's taking a nap," said Duke. "Whatever is on that flying feline, it's unconscious."

"Fazeek could be unconscious. Or what if he's dead?" retorted Vernglet.

Before Duke could answer, the huge cat hit the ground with a plodding gallop and came to a halt a few paces before the group. It lowered its body to the ground. From its back rolled a beaten, bloody body. The thud sounded painful. The living corpse looked up.

"The bastard was right," the injured passenger said through bruised and swollen lips.

Po'l.

"Quick, get him some water," shouted Ja'a.

Ma'n and Bu'r rushed to the injured Neprian's aid.

Duke walked over to the grundar and placed his hand on its nose. It purred softly.

"Thanks, girl. You did good. You don't know how happy I'm going to be to hear Po'l admit he was wrong."

The purr rose to a muted roar and then the grundar was off the ground and heading back towards the battle.

Po'l was sitting upright, downing liquid from Bu'r's canteen. "I just flew on a grundar. And there was some giant skeleton that said he knew you. And Orbius' army... it's... heading south. Lo'n was leading us right to them."

"Wait a second," interrupted Duke.

"Yes?" moaned Po'l.

"So you *were* wrong about Vernglet?"

"No time for this, Duke," hissed Ja'a.

The Nova Texan extended a hand and helped Po'l to his feet.

It can wait.

"Good to have you back, old friend."

CHAPTER 34

SMUGGLER'S DOOR

"VERN, WE TRULY COULDN'T HAVE done this without you."

"I'm glad to help, Ja'a. This passage through the ridge and around the ravine isn't even known to most. It was a smugglers' tunnel long before Orbius rose to power."

"It must be the tunnel that He'j mentioned," remarked Bu'r.

"It is not," countered Vernglet.

The rebels' faces contorted with confusion.

"He'j did not find this tunnel. Nor any tunnel."

"I don't understand," said Ja'a.

"Lo'n was deceiving you. In the off chance that you didn't fall for or survived him leading you into the teeth of Orbius' invasion force, you would have been sent into a side entrance that was already laid with a trap and a dozen-plus soldiers."

"So He'j—"

"Yes. He'j *did* try to go in through the front door."

"Suicide," whispered Duke to Ishiro'shea.

"He was a fierce warrior," said Vernglet.

The group fell silent, absorbing the priest's words.

"So this smuggler's tunnel," said Duke, attempting to refocus the conversation, "it drops us right into the fortress?"

"For the most part. It opens up into an attic chamber of a supply closet, just off one of the halls leading into the throne room."

"Great. I'm guessing that Orbius will be there, in the throne room?" asked Duke.

"That is the most likely scenario," replied Vernglet.

"And soldiers? Will this supply closet be guarded?" asked Duke.

"I don't remember it being attended."

"But you don't know for sure," noted Po'l.

"No."

"I think it's a risk that we have to take," replied Ja'a.

Everyone nodded in agreement, including Po'l.

The voyage through the cave system was unexciting. Its lack of use was apparent. Pools of stagnant water dotted the uneven path. A few holsters for torches jutted out intermittently from the passageway; Duke lit each one as they moved farther along. Surprisingly, they encountered no smugglers' traps. Duke thought this was odd—but then again, it was odd that Vernglet knew of a secret passage into Orbius' fortress that the almighty Orbmaster wasn't aware of. The bounty hunter began to talk himself out of believing Vern, but then thought better of it. His internal struggle grew fierce. *I've been on Team Vern from the get-go—best not abandon him now.*

Time was hard to determine in the darkness of the tunnel, but Duke thought it was likely still in the early part of the morning when they approached a cylindrical room that marked the end of the passage.

"Wrong turn?" asked Duke.

"If you want to get into Orbius' house uninvited and without him knowing, Mr. LaGrange, then this is definitely not a wrong turn."

Duke puzzled over the convoluted response for a moment, then replied, "Good."

Vernglet Wip approached the wall and then began to caress it.

"It's here somewhere," he said to himself. "I think it's right—"

A loud click echoed through the chamber. A panel, until now hidden in the stone, swung open.

"—here," concluded Vernglet.

He grabbed a ladder from within the opening, placed it on the cave floor, and started to unfold it. It appeared to Duke that it was the perfect height to reach the top of the room. *But then what? There isn't a door, or at least a noticeable one.*

The priest struggled to bring the ladder upright.

Po'l limped over, still suffering from his wounds sustained during the battle with Orbius' army, and helped Vernglet lift the ladder and lean it against the cave wall.

"Thank you. It's heavier than I remember."

"Wait, Vern," began Duke. "Were you a smuggler? I thought you were a farmer before becoming a priest."

"I had many jobs before I served Orbius. Bringing in goods that were misguidedly outlawed by Togg's government to Sansagon for purchase was one of them."

"So... a smuggler?"

"I preferred 'merchant of exotic and hard-to-come-by goods.'"

"You continue to surprise me."

"I also sold crop insurance for a time."

"Not as surprising."

"Okay, now what?" interjected Ja'a, cutting off Duke's conversation with the former smuggler.

"My apologies," said Vernglet. "Memory lane can be quite the detour."

"Is there an opening beyond our sight?" asked Ma'n.

"It's beyond everyone's sight. You have to activate it with a special code."

"I'm not following," said Po'l.

Duke was about to offer a retort that would have assuredly been ill-received, but Ishiro'shea tapped his shoulder forcefully. *He's probably right*, thought Duke.

"At the top of the room, where the wall meets the ceiling, there is a small inset. It won't be visible until you're up there—it's well-hidden from anyone that might have accidentally stumbled into the caves. You have to know *where* to look. I positioned the ladder so that when you ascend, you will be led right to it."

"Then what?"

"Inside are five circular holes and a pile of brightly-colored pebbles and stones. You must place the stones in a certain pattern. The door will unlock. Then you have to remove them in another particular order and the door will open. It will remain open for exactly the time it takes to sing 'Sansagon the Beautiful.'"

"How long is that?" asked Duke.

Vernglet broke into a rendition of the patriotic tune. It wasn't the Nova Texan planetary anthem, but it was catchy.

"Okay, so we have about a minute and a half," Duke said to Ishiro'shea.

"What's the pattern?"

"It's pretty easy to remember, Ja'a. It's a red stone, two blue, another red, and a yellow. If you are reading it from left to right."

"Red, blue, blue, red, yellow. Got it," said Duke. The bounty hunter started to climb the ladder. He looked back at the group. "Come on now."

"Once we're in the attic of the supply room, we're in. There isn't a way to open the door from that side. That's one of the reasons it has remained hidden from Orbius."

"Got it. Once we're in, we're in," Duke shouted back as he

continued his ascent. "Let's go, everyone. We have a tyrannical maniac to squash."

Bu'r and Ma'n followed the bounty hunter, then Ja'a and Ishiro'shea. Vernglet brought up the rear.

Duke made it to the top and felt around the surface of the wall. Sure enough, there was a small inset panel about the size of his laser revolver. He readjusted his position so that he could see inside the cubbyhole. As Vernglet had described, there was a pile of colorful rocks—some even looked like jewels. *Typical smugglers*, thought Duke. There were also five tiny craters, each the size of one of the rocks.

"I see it, Vern," Duke shouted. "Wouldn't a button have been easier?"

"Buttons can be accidentally pushed. This requires previous knowledge that had to be acquired."

Vernglet's voice lowered as he uttered the word "acquired"—likely harkening back to his days as a smuggler.

"Makes sense, but my hand barely fits in here. Okay, red, blue, blue... uh..." Duke stopped to think.

"What happens if you place the stone incorrectly?" Ja'a said to Vernglet.

"The ceiling opens up and boiling oil is dropped down over the ladder. Instantly transforming those on the ladder into a gruesome, mangled, gnarled—"

"We got it," Duke screamed. "Red, blue, blue, red, and YELLOW."

"Yes."

A loud click resonated throughout the cavern.

"Great, it's unlocked," said Vern. "Now remove them in this order—yellow."

"Okay, yellow removed."

"The first red that you placed," continued Vernglet.

"Done."

"Both blues at the same time. Then the last red."

"Here goes nothing," said Duke with a quaver in his voice.

A squeaking shriek and a whoosh of air followed. A soft light filled the room. It was a light from *another* room—on the other side of the now-open door.

"We're in, my friends," exclaimed Duke.

"Careful," Ja'a reminded the group. "We have no idea what's in there."

Duke crawled through. The room was empty and quite cramped.

"No way we're all fitting in here," relayed Duke. "What next?"

Vernglet responded from inside the cave. "There is a door at the far end of the attic floor. Open it and you should be able to fall right into the supply room. It shouldn't be exposed to the hallway; we should be hidden."

Duke followed the orders, traversing the restricted attic crawlspace until he discovered a hatch. He opened it and dropped directly into the supply closet, as Vernglet had described. *That was easy.*

The others followed suit. Ishiro'shea and Vernglet were the final two to make it to the attic door. As the ninja hit the supply closet floor without a sound, the door suddenly opened, exposing the group to the hallway—and to a dozen priests with javelins pointed at them.

"General, we have intruders!" screamed a guard in a high-pitched, nasal tone.

"Vern!" shouted Duke.

There was not a response. Then a whoosh and click. *The smugglers' door.*

Duke could sense Po'l's smug "I told you so" from the back of the supply room. He thought that was the worst feeling in the world—but then was reminded that the dangerously sharp spears being thrust in his general direction might hurt a bit more.

CHAPTER 35

FOR THE GOOD PART OF NEPRIUS!

THE ARROW FLEW MERE INCHES from Duke's ear and struck one of the guards in the chest. Duke's reflexes kicked in and he rattled off a few pulses. Most landed effectively. The guards retreated a few paces, providing the rebels with a little more separation from their assailants.

"Quick," Ja'a commanded. "Let's get out of this damn deathtrap of a room!"

The group sprinted down the ornate hallway until they reached a grand foyer sporting equally grand doors at its terminal point.

"Maybe that's the throne room," said Ja'a.

Bu'r and Ishiro'shea tried to open the door, but it wouldn't budge.

"Move," shouted Duke. He drew Betsy. She shook the entire hallway. The doors splintered and collapsed inward. *Orbius knows we're here now.*

"Even better than a throne room," said Ma'n. "The armory."

The sound of the footsteps of Orbius' troops were growing louder. Their approach was rapid.

"Let's prop these doors up. They should provide some cover," Duke said to Ishiro'shea.

The bounty hunters began to form a rudimentary barricade. Bu'r noticed their efforts and quickly joined in. Po'l, Ma'n, and Ja'a started to grab as many projectile weapons as they could—javelins, arrows, spiked stones, skins filled with flammable oil—and stockpiled them behind the makeshift barrier.

"This should make for one hell of a final stand," Duke said to Ishiro'shea.

"Who said this was our final stand?" Po'l interjected. "Our business is unfinished. A trap by that wormy priest won't stop us."

"*They* might have something to say about it being our final stand," Duke said. He pointed Betsy's barrel towards a horde of javelin-toting priest soldiers.

"A mere delay."

"I appreciate the optimism, Po'l. And, just so we can get it out of the way—I'm man enough to say it—"

"Say what?"

Duke knew that Po'l was aware of exactly what the bounty hunter was about to say. He wanted to milk it. *That bastard.*

"About Vernglet and—"

"Yes?"

"I never thought this would be the last word uttered in the life of Duke LaGrange, adventurer, trailblazer—"

The footsteps came to an abrupt end.

"Rebel trash and off-world scum." The voice was booming. It sounded like fresh death. Tsarano Gar. "I'm surprised that you decided to drop in on us like this. More courage than I thought."

"I'll give it to you, Gar," Ja'a responded, "your spy fooled us. But there's a massive chasm between placing us in this trap and actually stopping us."

Gar did not respond immediately. He looked around, almost confused at Ja'a's retort.

"Fine. Whatever you say, rebel. Prepare to die as your father did, begging for forgiveness."

The general released a throaty baritone laugh.

Duke could hear Ja'a gritting her teeth.

"But before you put up this annoyance of a resistance, remember that whatever you do now will affect what I do to this ingrate."

The general reached behind two of his soldiers and yanked out a ratty-haired Neprian child—gagged and tied.

"Uu'k!" shouted Duke.

Ishiro'shea's teeth were now grinding even louder than Ja'a's.

"How?" asked the bounty hunter.

"Lo'n," replied Po'l, his voice full of defeat.

Duke drew his gun and aimed it at Gar's head.

"Kill me and this puny accident of a life will be skewered."

Before Duke could respond, he felt a body leap past him.

"Come back, Ma'n!" shouted Ja'a.

The rebel hurdled the barricade and charged the entire Neprian line, his bow drawn. He sent arrows into flight toward the mass of soldiers without breaking stride.

Gar held the soldiers from advancing. He shoved Uu'k back and she disappeared behind the ranks.

Ma'n threw the bow down as he approached Gar. He drew his ax. Two soldiers stepped in front of their commander and were chopped down in a single motion from the irate rebel. His momentum carried him to Gar and he came down with a powerful stroke. However, his ax was halted in midair by Gar's twisted sword.

"Weakling," shouted Gar passively.

Ma'n countered with another swing, but again it was blocked by Gar's blade. Gar reached out with his free hand and clamped down on Ma'n's throat. The rebel struggled and dropped his ax as he gasped for air. Gar's death blow was quick but he held the blade firm so that the other rebels could see and digest what had just happened. With a slight shrug, Ma'n's corpse slid off the sword and fell limp to the floor.

"Attack!" screamed the general as he sank to the back of the line.

The soldiers stormed the rebels.

Between Duke's marksmanship and the constant barrage of deadly projectiles lobbied from behind the barrier, the priests weren't immediately successful in breaching—but their numbers never dwindled. It was a constant flow. And though Duke could keep shooting forever, the rebels' other ammunition was running low.

"We can't hold them off much longer," said Po'l. "And Gar is getting away with Uu'k."

"And pretty soon Orbius will turn up—with the Orb," added Bu'r.

"At least I could get a shot at him," said Duke.

"Orbius is not that careless," reminded Ja'a. "He won't put himself in harm's way—especially since we aren't posing much of a threat at the present."

"So, basically, this *is* our last stand?" questioned Duke.

"If Uu'k has been kidnapped, then Mo'a must have pieced together Lo'n's betrayal," Ja'a said, changing the subject. "They will be working on another mission as we speak."

"Or those that abducted her with Lo'n's help already destroyed the base and everyone in it," Duke replied grimly, "and we *are* the last hope."

"I refuse to believe that."

"They've been pretty successful thus far in one-upping us," countered Duke. "They stole Uu'k from right under our noses; a betrayal from one of the trusted rebel brass."

"And your priest friend," added Po'l.

"Yes, and Vern. I'm not making myself immune from anything. I was fooled, the same as you."

Po'l seemed surprised by Duke's honesty. And then he lobbed a javelin into the chest cavity of a charging priest.

"I refuse to believe it. I have faith in Mo'a."

"We don't have much left," screamed Bu'r.

"Here, Ishiro, catch." Duke tossed his pulse pistol to the ninja. Ishiro'shea dropped the bow and arrow that he was using. Duke took Betsy from her holster. "At least we'll have two things rockin' when they run out of arrows."

Betsy cleared the hallway. Duke let loose another shot, pushing back the line even more. He smiled. Ishiro'shea discharged pulses into the cloud of smoke.

"As long as this door provides cover, we can do this all day. They have to run out of soldiers at some point. Right?"

Before Duke could receive an answer, a booming crack rang out. Duke and Ishiro'shea, being the closest to the door, were thrown to the ground about halfway into the room.

Duke looked up. The door that had served as their barricade was shattered. The culprit was a javelin nearly quadruple the size of the ones carried by the priests. Emerging from the cloud of dust and debris was a gargantuan mounted crossbow, pushed by four priests. The rebels were now fully exposed, and the priests accelerated in their advance.

Ishiro'shea leapt to his feet and threw Duke the pulse pistol in the same motion. He drew his sword. The meaning of the gesture was clear: if he was going to die, it would be with his sword in his hand. Duke spun the revolver on his finger and slid it into his holster. He drew Betsy. If this was going to be his last day, he would spend it with his true love. The Neprians followed suit. Bu'r, Po'l, and Ja'a drew their weapons and readied for the horde that was sure to overwhelm them.

"This should take a few out!"

Betsy sang. Smoke and the smell of burnt death filled the hallway. But the pattering of feet didn't wane. The mounted crossbow continued to roll towards them.

This is how it's going to end. On a two-bit planet in an

unknown sector of the universe. Definitely not going to have a parade in my honor, Duke concluded. This was *not* how the bounty hunter drew it up.

During the course of his career as one of the best-known bounty hunter–playboys in the universe, Duke had been charged by many violent entities, so he knew the anxious feeling right before he engaged in mortal combat. When his enemy was a few paces away, he would tense up and visualize the first few moves that he planned. Maybe an offensive attack, or a counter to what the assailant was likely to do. Against a massive blob of assailants, it would be all firepower until the lights went out. He aimed Betsy at the direct center—at the group toting the rolling crossbow.

"For Neprius!" shouted Ja'a.

"But only the good part!" added Duke.

The rebels began to scream—an organic and primal sound. Worthy of a last stand.

Oblong faces, gaunt and bony, emerged from the cloud. Duke tensed.

And then they were gone.

An entire side wall collapsed on top of the soldiers. The roar of the charging mass was silenced in a mere flash. A chunk of rock lay on top of dozens of soldiers. The others that stood behind the disaster area looked shocked, then readied themselves for another charge.

"What just happened?" asked Duke, wiping dust from his eyes. There was no response.

Stepping from outside and onto the makeshift stage created by the fallen wall fragment was Fazeek. And his grundar. And the grundar's grundar friends.

"I thought I would come lend a helping hand," Fazeek shouted. "And paw. Attack, my lovelies!"

Looloo roared.

The grundar pounced and growled. The priests mostly screamed. And ran.

Fazeek turned to the rebels. "Well, don't just stand there. We've got this handled. Go get that Orb!"

"Thank you, Shepherd of the Grundar," proclaimed Ja'a, rather regally considering the circumstances.

Fazeek turned his back to them and entered battle, waving his staff and striking down the much smaller soldiers effortlessly.

"Thoughts on how to get to the throne room that Vern spoke of?" asked Duke. "I bet Orbius is tucked away in there... unless Vern was lying to us about that as well."

"With Uu'k, too," added Po'l.

Ja'a hesitated. It was clear that she didn't know.

"We can't follow Gar's route since that will lead us right through the skirmish," said Duke. "And Fazeek doesn't seem like someone that would enjoy us meddling in his business. Maybe. No..." He caught himself. "Well, maybe..."

"What?"

"This."

Duke took aim at the side wall of the ammunition room. He fired Betsy.

Once again the bounty hunter was making his own doorway. Betsy fired again. And again. The gaping hole connected to another hallway. It was empty. No guards; nothing.

"I say we go that way," Duke said, pointing into the vacant hall.

There wasn't another option. They all sprinted into the open area, then stopped to assess their position.

"The hall looks like it wraps around to the right up ahead," said Ja'a. "Maybe it circles back to the direction that Gar was heading with Uu'k."

"Makes sense," chimed in Duke.

"In agreement?"

"Yes!" called Po'l and Bu'r. Ishiro'shea nodded.

They all made their way down the passageway, following it as it wound to the right. Before long Duke could see that they were heading in the correct direction. At the end of a long, narrow corridor was another decorative entrance—not as big as the ammunition keep, but more detailed. It appeared to be made of mustangsen and dotted with a jeweled design befitting a crazed dictator. Only two guards stood outside, both holding golden javelins.

"I'm thinking that's our destination."

Duke unleashed his pulse pistol and dropped both guards.

"Let's go meet this Orbius and his pet rock."

CHAPTER 36

JUST A VILLAIN

THERE WASN'T EVEN A LOCK on the door. *How very Neprian.* The doors swung open and hit the wall with a ringing clang.

The capacious dwelling was so large that Duke had trouble finding the perimeter walls. The entire village of Horteyaya could have crammed into it with room to spare. From what Duke could see, the walls were gray, with a metallic tint. In the center of the room was a maroon and yellow rug that stretched from the entrance to a set of four steps that led upwards to an immense and gaudy throne. Sure, there were a few stones here and there—but mostly it was roughly sculpted mustangsen, matching the walls.

Standing at the bottom of the steps was General Tsarano Gar. His monstrous claw was gripping the back of Uu'k's neck. Her wiggling and writhing did not appear to faze the Neprian general. His other hand held his drawn, twisted sword, its business end facing the visitors. Extending from the throne, like wings on either side, was a contingent of priest warriors. They looked like the foot soldiers that the rebels had encountered in their march towards Sansagon, save that they wore additional armor around their chests and bulky helmets that covered the majority of their faces. Their javelins were drawn and they each held a circular shield in their left hand that seemed to reflect the remnants of light that emanated from the lanterns that hung from the ceiling.

Standing in front of the throne was a human who sported a cloaked robe of deep red accented with bright yellow. Around his waist was a rope that served as a belt. His hood was down, revealing a very ordinary face. No scars. No facial hair. No demonic eyes or fangs. His skin was a milky-cream color, with noticeable creases and age lines. *He's a bit on the ordinary side,* thought Duke, *especially for a ruthless tyrant and murderer.* The more Duke contemplated it, the more Orbius' nondescript nature started to freak him out. *So ordinary that he is terrifying.*

Orbius raised his hand, seeming about to speak.

"I see why you have so many mines," began Duke. He could tell that the Orbmaster was irritated. Duke thought that he probably had an opening line planned for such an occasion. The bounty hunter loved ruining plans. "I mean, this entire place is mustangsen. Not the most decorative material out there."

"What about it?" Orbius spoke.

"Nothing, just that a good interior design firm could make a killing on this planet," added Duke.

"I see."

Orbius' voice matched his appearance—bland. It wasn't overly masculine or feminine; it didn't fill the room, nor was it meek or inaudible. He raised his hand again, pointing into the far corner of the chamber. Duke squinted but saw nothing outside of a towering curtain, approximately the length of a spaceship.

"Guards, a little help," said Orbius in an agitated tone. Three ran over and started to tug on a cord that also hung down from the ceiling. It matched the cord on Orbius' waist but with much more girth.

"Sorry, my friends," started Orbius. "They were supposed to be over there for the grand reveal."

"The grand reveal of what?" asked Po'l.

The spaceship-length curtain was a perfect size for what it covered—a spaceship. The *Deus Ex Machina*, to be exact.

"Your ship!" shouted Bu'r. Oddly enough, Duke didn't say anything. He tightened his grip on his gun.

"You don't look shocked, bounty hunter. And why is that?"

Before Duke could answer, Po'l blurted out, "Why do you have this ship in your throne room? I thought the point was to use it to terrorize our people and escape to other worlds."

Orbius did not answer. It was as if he knew that the gears were turning inside the Nova Texan's head.

"He doesn't want the *Deus* to go anywhere. Terrorize your people, yes, but not by flying it over settlements and blasting his way to obedience."

"I don't need your ship to terrorize these primitives."

"I don't understand," said Bu'r.

"It's what the *Deus* is made of, huh?" said Duke. "You want to harvest it as you would any mine. It's made of your precious mustangsen."

"How many more pieces of decor does he need?" chimed in Po'l.

"I thought it was quite a coincidence. I mean, think about it—the most monumental slab of mustangsen in the known universe happens to end up on my planet in the middle of my final conquest of these rebellious twerps. Sure, you probably don't call it 'mustangsen'—but it is, you know."

"Hard to believe, indeed," Duke said, barely managing to squeeze the words through his clenched teeth. He turned to Ishiro'shea and whispered, "I guess it can get us *into* trouble as well as out? We should totally write a review if we make it outta here."

"I still don't get it," said Bu'r.

"He's not mining the mustangsen for decorative purposes," began Duke.

"No," Ja'a interjected, "he's using it to control the Orb."

"What?" asked Po'l, as confused as Bu'r.

"Yep," said Duke. "The rings on his fingers, this room, the *Deus*—heck, even the mounds of junk in the Keeper's cave—all of it was mustangsen. It somehow controls the Orb."

Ja'a looked down at her chest.

"My necklace."

"Very good. You aren't as stupid as you look," said Orbius in a congratulatory manner. He bowed sarcastically.

Duke thought for a moment. "Your father had a necklace like that as well, right?"

Before Ja'a could answer, Orbius cut in.

"Yes, your father," he rolled his eyes. "What a nuisance! He thought he could challenge me, overtake me. He started all of this, you know? He asked for help and the Orb summoned *me*. He thought he could alter it all by barging in and trying to summon a worthy adversary for me. And guess what? He failed. Miserably. The Orb brought you two."

Orbius pointed at Duke and Ishiro'shea and giggled. Duke tried to wrap his head around the fact that the Orb selected him and Ishiro'shea to save the planet. And it was He'j that had requested it, wearing the other half of the necklace that Ja'a wore at this very moment. *Heavy stuff.* He decided that he liked it better when he thought that it had been merely random chance and an insane maniac's practice sessions at dimensional portal manipulation that had sucked them into the astral anomaly and deposited them on this cursed rock.

"Yes, girl, your father failed. And then I killed him. Struck him down like I have so many of your friends. And like I will do to your annoying rebellion. Kind of sad, if you think about. I mean... sad for you. It's actually pretty great for me."

"It's not over," Ja'a insisted.

"Oh, but it is, my flower. It is."

Po'l broke through the line and charged at the throne. Orbius waved his hand and motioned the guards to halt the angered rebel. Po'l slashed down the guards with his sword. Gar released Uu'k and started to head towards Po'l.

"Halt, General. No need," said Orbius, without any trace of fear.

He held his hand high. An object floated upward at a leisurely pace from behind Orbius; when it was an arm's length above his head, it stopped and hovered. The sphere glowed a radiant violet, and tiny fragments of electricity pulsed around its outer shell. Sporadically, the pulses would halt, revealing the sphere's cloudy interior. It was The Orb That Controlled Everything and Must Be Respected.

Orbius manipulated his fingers in a calculated manner; the mustangsen rings danced. A beam shot out and crashed in front of Po'l. The explosion sent Po'l into the air with a velocity that defied the laws of normal physics. He was thrown across the room and crashed into the side of the *Deus*, then met the floor with the sound of shattering bones. A muffled scream escaped Uu'k's gag. *No one could have survived that,* thought Duke.

Orbius laughed. "Just a sampling of what I can do."

He's pleased with himself.

"You mean what the Orb can do," corrected Duke.

"It's all the same to you, bounty hunter," said Orbius. "Now put down your weapons and kick them over to me, or you will end up like your friend with the broken spine over there."

"Why should we?" exclaimed Ja'a. "You're just going to kill us anyway."

"I will squash your rebellion, yes. I will throw you into the mines—especially you, bounty hunter—but I won't kill you. I'm not a tyrant."

Orbius looked disappointed that no one appeared to agree with this sentiment.

"And, you my radiant daughter of He'j, I do need a queen. Or at least someone that is somewhat attractive. I mean, I can't even tell the male Northerners from the female Northerners. Am I right? My hometown wasn't exactly known for beautiful women—but this is another level. Then again, Newark had its other benefits."

He trailed off into self-reflection before regaining his train of thought. "I'm being serious. I had one servant pegged as a guy—a cycle later, she's pregnant."

No one shared his joviality, but it did make Duke curious about Vernglet's gender. He hoped that he hadn't insulted him/her by defaulting to masculine pronouns.

"I would rather die than have any part of this," Ja'a said boldly.

"No you wouldn't," replied Orbius. "Dying looks quite painful, if you ask me."

"You will have to kill me. I won't go to the mines and I definitely won't stand by your side."

"Such vigor. I like it."

Duke looked over at Ja'a. In a low voice, he said, "Drop your weapons. As long as you're alive, there's hope. It will give Mo'a additional purpose. As bleak as the prospects of the rebellion look, Mo'a will always try to rescue his best friend's daughter from enslavement."

"What's that?" asked Orbius, trying to make out what Duke and Ja'a were saying. "Oh yeah, I almost forgot. If you don't, I'll have Gar slit this puny wretch's throat right in front of you."

Uu'k squirmed, but not as much as Duke would have expected. *She's tough. She's a spy, after all.*

"Fine," Ja'a huffed. She dropped her bow.

Duke knelt down and put both of his guns on the floor. Ishiro'shea followed suit with his katana and Bu'r with his mace. They kicked them all to the Neprian guards. They were officially weaponless.

"I totally should have led with the kid," said Orbius to himself.

"Hey, Ot!" yelled Duke. For a brief moment Orbius seemed taken aback at the use of his real name. It was doubtful that his priestly servants referred to him as anything other than Orbius, if they were even that informal.

"Why yes, Duke LaGrange, bounty hunter and failed rebel. Go on."

"So," began Duke, ignoring Orbius' insult, "what's the plan?"

"Why should I tell you 'the plan', bounty hunter? I mean, that's like Villain Mistakes 101."

"True. But you aren't *just* a villain. You're a villain with a magical Orb. That has to give you some leeway, right?"

"I suppose."

Gar looked back and snarled at Orbius.

"Simmer down, General," Orbius said. "We have this under control. You have the girl under control, right? That's our ticket. Their weapons are on the ground. We're good."

"So, the plan. What do you get out of running this one-horse primitive planet? Is it just ego?"

"Ego?"

"Yeah, or is this payback from being pushed down on the jungle gym at recess?"

"Compelling. But no. You're going to be disappointed by my answer."

"Try me."

"I'm actually the good guy. The one that is on the side of right. The light side. The hero. The protagonist."

Duke didn't think the joke was funny. Then he realized that Orbius wasn't joking.

"The Orb could be in far worse hands than mine."

"You're enslaving an entire race. You are aware of that, right?"

"A race that wants to free the Orb from my possession—

and, in turn, it would end up in worse hands. Probably. Therefore, the Southern Neprians are necessary casualties for the greater good. You see, I'm the only one that can control the Orb—and if I control it, it's not doing any damage."

"No damage!" screamed Ja'a. "Have you seen what you are doing to my people?"

"Refer to my last comment, sweetie," replied Orbius. "Stop resisting and the pain will stop. I never understood why you challenged me in the first place. These guys didn't."

It looked like Gar was trying to muster a smile.

"You know," Orbius continued, "I'm not trying to control you or your people. Just protect them."

"From what?" asked Duke.

"I told you, bounty hunter—worse things than I."

"Any names?"

"No one has stepped out from the shadows yet, but that's how the universe works. A great power is discovered or built or acquired—and eventually the most evil and sinister entity ends up with it. Maybe that's you, Duke LaGrange. Have your rebel friends thought about that? As it goes, tragedy ensues until balance is restored. Look at Earth. He knows what I'm talking about." Orbius pointed to Ishiro'shea. "You're from New Tokyo, right?"

Ishiro'shea did not move a muscle.

"The Orb is power that can't be harnessed by anyone other than myself."

"Or someone else with access to a ton of mustangsen," challenged Duke.

"I'll admit, it helps control the Orb. It's my remote control, so to speak. But, I am *one* with the Orb now. It's part of me and I am part of it. It called me here to bond with me. I'm the one it chose as the savior of this planet."

"It also chose us," Duke said with a smirk.

"Ah yes, it did. I thought about that when I heard that you

had landed outside of Dre'en. I thought about it a lot. But, it was quite obvious to me."

"It was?"

"Yes, Duke LaGrange, it was. The Orb wasn't going to send someone to actually challenge me or overtake me, definitely not that—it was going to send someone that would prove so useless that they would actually crush the rebellion for me. The rebels view you as their best shot at taking me down. Coupled with all of the traitors that I already have—like your old friend, Lo'n—your demise will destroy all hope that's left."

"Pretty self-centered view, wouldn't you say?" asked Duke.

"I would not say. See, old He'j just asked the Orb to send help. He didn't say help for what. I killed him before he could elaborate any further. So the Orb did send help—help for me. Help to stop this futile cause that's killing more people than necessary."

Ja'a, Duke, Ishiro'shea, and Bu'r all exchanged glances. *It isn't totally insane to consider Orbius' rationale, thought Duke. Could the Orb have known what He'j meant? Does it really want to quash the rebellion so it can spend more quality time with this nutjob?*

"So, if we stop the war and surrender," began Ja'a, "and acknowledge that you are the one true master of the Orb and should reign over Neprius—"

"Yes," Orbius said eagerly.

"—you will free my people from the mines."

Orbius thought about this and started to speak, but caught himself. He pondered a bit more. Gar peered back to make sure that his boss had heard the question.

"No."

"What?"

"No. I still need mustangsen mined. Duke's ship should help for a bit but it won't last forever. And, if you think about it, you kind of deserve some punishment for this annoying resistance."

"Then—" started Ja'a.

"Yes?"

"Then we won't surrender. You will have to kill us now."

"This is growing very tiresome. Fine, if you really want to die, I can make that happen. This will be as painful as it was for your father."

The Orb ascended even higher above Orbius' throne and pulsated with even brighter colors. It spun faster and faster as it prepared to strike the rebels.

The blast was blinding and deafening.

But Duke was in one piece. He looked around. So were his companions. The blast didn't look or sound like the one that had hit Po'l.

Duke scanned the room looking for the source of the burst. His eyes panned to Orbius' throne. The Orb was no longer hovering in the air—it wasn't anywhere to be seen. General Gar and his guards had been displaced by the explosion but appeared to be alive. Orbius, though, wasn't visible.

Duke swivelled his head again, towards the *Deus Ex Machina*. In the cockpit was a barely visible silhouette. The figure was thin and boney, with a head too big for its body. *Vern.*

"Nice shot, Vern!" shouted Duke.

How did he do that? He doesn't know how to work a space-craft—he's a primitive, thought Duke.

The Neprian priest poked his head out from a side window.

"Did I hit it?"

"You did good, Vern. Impressive shot," yelled Duke.

"It just told me what to do—it's like it knew that I needed to save you. And there was no other way. As in, no other reasonable way to survive. None whatsoever. You were goners."

"We get it, Vern," said Duke. He turned to Ishiro'shea. "Saved us again. Maybe we leave a slightly better review now."

Just as Duke finished his thought, another noise filled the throne room. The *Deus* fizzled and shook and the light in the cockpit dimmed. It was powering down.

"So it *is* still broken. Its timing is impeccable," said Duke to his ninja companion.

Emerging from behind his throne, Orbius was regaining his composure and shaking off the proverbial cobwebs. The blast had knocked him off of the altar and down to the floor but he didn't appear injured.

"What just happened?" he screamed. "And where's the Orb?"

No one responded.

The bounty hunter continued to scan the room. There was no sign of the Orb, nor was there any sign of Orb shards, fragments, or shrapnel; there was nothing that said that the Orb was destroyed.

"Is that Vernglet Wip?" Orbius asked General Gar. The general was struggling to his feet with Uu'k still in his clutches. "I thought you disposed of him. Who cares? Guards! Kill him."

The guards charged the *Deus*. The remaining guards surrounded Orbius. One of them grabbed Uu'k and passed her to the Orbmaster. Unfortunately, the rebels' weapons were still very much out of reach.

CHAPTER 37

GIVE ME BACK MY SPHERE

FOUR JAVELIN-TOTING GUARDS STORMED the doors of the *Deus*. Duke could see the panic in Vernglet's eyes. The lifeless ship had no other option than to accept the inevitable breach. Duke, Ishiro'shea, Bu'r, and Ja'a stood next to each other—too far from their weapons to retrieve them without having to deal with Gar and the rest of the armed soldiers. However, Orbius seemed preoccupied with the attack on the *Deus*.

"You will pay for that, Wip. Not smart, man, not smart." Orbius paused and regathered himself. "Where is my Orb?"

"Destroyed," shouted Duke, diverting Orbius' attention from the *Deus*.

"Destroyed, you say? If it is, then this has no chance of working."

Orbius twinkled his fingers, rubbing the mustangsen rings against each other. Nothing. He did it again, nothing. For the third attempt, he completed the motion with a clenched jaw and progressively reddening face.

"No chance of doing what, Ot?" Duke smirked.

The Orb sped from an unseen location in the corner of the

room and into the tyrant's clutches. Orbius turned his attention back to the quartet of rebels.

Shit.

"Now, while my minions take care of that traitorous rat in the ship, I get to finally dispose of you. Despite the brief delay, this should be fun. For me, that is."

Orbius laughed maniacally.

First thing that he's done that's worthy of a true supervillain, thought Duke.

The soldiers began prying Vernglet from the cockpit of the ship. He was grabbing anything that he could, to no avail.

"I'm going to fry you after I deal with your friends here, Wip," said Orbius, though his eyes remained squarely focused on the four rebels.

The soldiers released Vernglet, unnoticed by Orbius. They also released their footing from the platform that they had scaled to capture him. They crashed to the floor.

Standing beside a confused Vernglet Wip was a bruised and battered Po'l. The metal pipe—clearly a piece of the *Deus'* exterior that had dislodged itself when it ceased operations—was covered in Northern blood. Orbius *did* notice this.

"Seriously, how many lives does this guy have?" asked Duke to his cohorts.

"How cute. You aren't dead. Whoop-de-doo. I just get to kill you *again.* Yay for me." Orbius sounded a bit annoyed, like a child receiving an extra chore just as they are almost finished with their original list. He pivoted towards the ship and raised his hands. The Orb began to spin even faster. *Po'l won't be able to survive this,* Duke concluded. *No one would survive this.*

The wall to the left of the throne exploded. Stone fragments consumed the entire room.

Despite the echoing boom, Orbius' voice could be heard above the noise. "What now? Seriously, what now?"

In the frame of the newly-created door was the outline of something big. Huge, in fact.

"You have my sphere."

Out stepped Toby, hulking and ticked off. Orbius had not expected to see a mountainous creature asking for his Orb once the dust settled, that much was clear, but to his credit he didn't panic. He appeared calm, if not a bit frustrated by the continued interruptions. Duke was impressed again with his villaining. *Not bad for a glorified gardener*, he thought.

"I think you are mistaken, my ogre friend," replied Orbius, wiping the dust from his face and hood. "This is *my* Orb!"

He motioned towards the Keeper. The Orb emitted a beautiful beam of light in the direction of Toby, who raised his forearms to shield the impact. The ray deflected off of his gauntlet and was redirected to the ceiling, greeting the surface with a crash. Parts of the ceiling fell to the floor.

"Impressive. I see your gauntlets are made of mustangsen."

"I guess," bellowed Toby, obviously not understanding the significance of the construction material. "Now, give me back the Sphere."

"I don't think—"

Orbius wasn't able to finish his sentence. He dove back to avoid the swing of Toby's gargantuan club, which sent three guards into the air and deposited them on the other side of the room. Toby swung again, cracking the throne in half. The soldiers surrounded him and heaved their javelins. He didn't seem to like that very much and demonstrated his irritation by crushing them with blunt force aggression.

During the chaos, Uu'k broke free of Gar's hold and sprinted towards the rebels. Gar followed suit with his sword drawn. Ishiro'shea made a course to intercept the grizzled Neprian general.

"Bu'r, get Uu'k to safety," screamed Ja'a.

Bu'r obliged, snatching her up and heading towards the

Deus. Po'l and Vernglet were already down from the platform and hiding in its shadows, searching for usable weapons.

Tsarano Gar swung at Ishiro'shea with his sword but the ninja eluded it with a swift forward roll. The general turned and swung again—another miss. Ishiro'shea countered with a powerful kick to the chest. Gar was stunned but didn't lose his footing. He stabbed at Ishiro, but again came up empty. His frustration took the form of a vitriolic growl. Ishiro'shea took the offensive and leapt at Gar, but Gar blocked the strike and countered with a clubbing fist to the ninja's jaw. Ishiro'shea tumbled a few steps behind Gar. He still clutched his katana.

"Behind you!" shouted Duke. "Behind you!"

A Neprian soldier approached the ninja from behind with his javelin aimed to kill. Gar charged from the front. Ishiro'shea turned and ran towards the guard. Then, mere moments before the Neprian performed his death blow, Ishiro'shea dove to the ground feet first in a slide. He tripped the guard, who crashed face first, dropping the javelin. The rampaging Gar halted to avoid colliding with the fallen guard, who was now rolling with increased velocity. Gar returned his attention to Ishiro'shea. He swung—but the ninja, having grabbed the free javelin, blocked the swipe with the midsection of the shaft. It snapped in two under the power of Gar's swing. Ishiro'shea fell on his backside.

"So much for that, off-worlder!" roared Gar. He raised his sword and sent it crashing down upon Ishiro'shea with all of his power. Ishiro'shea moved.

The sword was stuck. Gar tried to remove it, his muscles flexing and tensing as he struggled to dislodge it from the floor.

Ishiro'shea was quick. He leapt from the floor and appeared almost to hang in the air. In one motion, the point of the shattered javelin struck Tsarano Gar across the bridge of the nose. He shrieked in pain.

Sprinkles didn't even have it that bad, thought Duke.

Gar released his sword and stumbled backwards. Another

javelin tip ripped through the general's backside and exploded through his chest. Then it was pulled back through his chest cavity. He collapsed to the floor, lifeless.

Vernglet stood above the body, holding a bloody javelin taken from one of the would-be captors that had yanked him out of the *Deus*.

"I never liked that guy," he proclaimed.

"Quick," Ja'a shouted to Duke. "Betsy! While the guards are distracted!"

Distracted, was of course, an understatement. Pummeled would be a more appropriate term, considering the power of Toby's club.

The bounty hunter hustled and dove at Betsy. He quickly checked to see if she had survived all of the falling debris. *Looks good enough.*

"Not so fast, Duke LaGrange," proclaimed Orbius. The Orb was floating above him—though not as high as it had been previously—and once again it was spinning and glowing. "Your fun is finally at an end. I'll deal with that brute in a second. You, I kill now."

"Don't I even get an overblown sinister dialogue before I go? That would be fitting, considering I'm Duke LaGrange, after all." He paused. "You know, adventurer, trailblazer—"

The blast was quick and exact. It burst from below Orbius' neck and into the wall behind Duke.

Ja'a sat with the laser revolver in her hand.

"At least someone on this planet can shoot!" said Duke.

He could hear Po'l groan from across the room.

As Orbius' flaccid body fell, the Orb crashed to the floor. It stopped momentarily and then slowly rolled towards the bounty hunter as if it had a mind of its own and high-end rear-wheel steering. No fizzling. No sizzling. No lights or clouds. Only what appeared to be an ordinary round glass ball with the power of sophisticated and seemingly spontaneous locomotion. Duke picked it up and examined it.

All fighting had ceased. The Keeper stopped his bashing of skulls and looked at Duke inquisitively. Ja'a kept her gun drawn. The remaining soldiers stared at the bounty hunter, still gripping their weapons. Bu'r positioned Uu'k behind him. Po'l moved to provide additional cover. Only Ishiro'shea seemed to react what Duke would refer to as "normally."

Duke stood up and held the Orb above his head.

"Behold, puny peasants! I am now one with the Orb! I am Orbius... Junior!"

Nothing.

Then a laugh permeated through Ishiro'shea's mask. Uu'k joined in. The rebels all gave a deep collective sigh. Toby and the Neprian priest soldiers seemed confused.

"Here you go!" Duke nonchalantly tossed the Orb to the Keeper. Toby caught it and placed it in a satchel that hung from his hip.

"Thank you," he said. "And, I've decided that I'm almost certain that you and your friends aren't swamp people."

"Thank you," replied Duke. "I guess."

He turned his attention to the priests. "Oh yeah, you lot. Drop your weapons."

The guards all dropped their weapons. They didn't seem too unhappy. One even smiled.

"What'd I miss?"

Fazeek entered through the Toby created opening on the back of his favorite grundar.

"Oh hey, Toby. Long time," Fazeek said, not successfully hiding his true feelings regarding the Keeper. He glanced at Toby's satchel, his eyes squinted. His gaze shifted to Duke, then to Ja'a, and finally back to the Keeper. "You think you can keep it this time?"

Toby didn't sneer back as Duke had anticipated. "I think so. But I could use some help, old friend."

Fazeek's expression changed to one of genuine surprise. It then morphed into a wry smile.

"Sure. Not many old-timers like us around."

Duke walked over to Ja'a and extended his hand. She shook it gently.

"Your dad would be proud."

Ja'a hugged him tightly.

CHAPTER 38

FORTY-EIGHT MINUTES

"**I** WAS COMING TO THE realization that this day would live only in my dreams," bellowed Mo'a. "However, here we are. Orbius is gone. And it's the daughter of He'j, my best friend, that accomplished this." He drew in a deep breath as his eyes moistened. "I am very proud of you, Ja'a. And your father would be as well."

"I already told her that," Duke whispered to Ishiro'shea.

"Great Mo'a," Ja'a began as she rose from her seat at the circular table. "My hope is to focus on the future of our planet. Yes, Orbius is gone. The mines are empty. But cycles of battle and death leave us with two strained peoples and much work to do."

She looked at Vernglet Wip; he nodded in her direction.

"Yes, Ja'a. We are aware," said Mo'a. "Once we heard the news, we started to discuss the next steps to rebuild a Neprius that represents peace and coexistence. The first question is what to do with the Orb."

"Hey there, big Mo'a," Duke interrupted. "That's been taken care of."

"What do you mean, Duke?"

"No offense to you and the council, but we went ahead and made those preparations back in Sansagon."

Mo'a looked irked. Duke could tell that decisions of this magnitude weren't typically made unilaterally.

"Ja'a, is this true?"

"Yes," she responded without hesitation. "There was only one logical decision. Even transporting the Orb back here to our base would have been too risky."

"I see," Mo'a said unconvinced. "What has happened to the Orb, to Peace?"

"It's back in the hands of the ancient Keeper."

"The beast that you spoke of? The one that lives in the old temple in the swamp?"

"Yeah, his name is Toby," added Duke.

"Didn't he lose it? Twice?"

"He did, Mo'a," said Ja'a. "But he has help this time around."

"Help?"

"Yes, the Shepherd of the Grundar has promised to monitor the skies above the Keeper's lair."

"Interesting. I'm not sure what I think about this arrangement."

"They've put aside their differences to forge a powerful symbiotic union."

"We hope to do the same," said Vernglet Wip. Duke noticed that it lacked its usual nasal whine.

"I see."

Mo'a contemplated the news. He placed both hands upon the table and leaned forward. He slowly peered up and made eye contact with all of the attendees. Bu'r. Ishiro'shea. Po'l. Ja'a. Duke.

"A wise move."

A collective gasp of relief came from around the table.

"A wise move befitting of an empress."

Ja'a's smile dissipated and shock consumed her elegant profile.

"Mo'a?" she queried.

"Yes, Ja'a. You may have made the decision of how to protect the Orb from harming us without our input—but this, we are adamant about, and will not accept counterarguments."

The room was silent. Duke stood. Ishiro'shea followed suit. They raised their glasses of Neprian wine.

"To Empress Ja'a!"

Everyone in the room cheered. Vernglet Wip walked over and hugged the newly-appointed monarch.

"Not a lot of paperwork required to be an empress here," Duke muttered to Ishiro'shea.

The ninja nodded.

"Once I heard the news of Orbius' downfall," shouted Mo'a above the congratulatory cheers, "I went ahead and planned a bit of a celebration. I hope that's okay, Ja'a. It won't have the scale of our past ceremonies naming dignitaries and rulers, as we were short on time to plan. And, to be honest, we've never had an empress before."

"That explains the lack of paperwork," added Duke to Ishiro'shea.

"So, I'm afraid it will just be a big party."

"Cheers to that!" Duke added.

"I'm honored, Mo'a. That is, if I accept this position."

"If?" questioned Mo'a. "Ja'a, the people of Neprius *demand* it."

Ja'a continued, "As part of this celebration, I do have one order of business that must be addressed."

"Go on."

"I will only take this responsibility if Vernglet Wip—the *honorable* Vernglet Wip—is named the Ambassador of the North."

"Vern, you hear that?" Duke said, slapping the gaunt

Neprian on the back. "They called you honorable. Who would have thought that?"

"Are you sure, Ja'a?"

"That's *Empress* Ja'a," Duke reminded Mo'a.

"We're going to work on that title also," added Ja'a. "Empresses are only in fairy tales."

"Title aside, are you sure that you trust this priest to help in the rebuilding?" asked Mo'a.

"Mo'a, had Vernglet not risked his life and shot the Orb down from Duke's ship, we would have been destroyed."

"Yeah, you pulled a fast one on us, Vern!" Duke said to the priest. "We thought you sold us up the river."

"I knew I was no help in combat, so I fled—if I had said something, you wouldn't have believed it anyway. My only hope was to sneak into the throne room. Luckily, the ship knew what I needed to do."

"Well played, ol' Vern."

"And Mo'a, it will take both races to rebuild our planet. No one understands that more than Vernglet Wip."

Mo'a thought hard about Ja'a's request. His temples contracted and his brow wrinkled.

"You are right, daughter of He'j. It is a great idea."

"I would be honored," Vernglet Wip said, bowing to the elder Neprian rebel. He then turned to Ja'a and repeated the gesture. "Empress Ja'a—or whatever designation that you choose for yourself—may we begin healing the unnecessary wounds of conflict."

"How about president?" said Duke. "President Ja'a—has a nice ring to it."

Ishiro'shea kicked him.

"Oh yeah, bad track record with those."

The Neprians were stone-faced.

Duke attempted to get the conversation back on track. "Now, about this party..."

The coastal compound came alive as the moon shimmered across the crashing sea. Brilliant colors and exotic smells permeated through the base. Southern Neprians danced and hugged and drank. Many came up to Vernglet and embraced him with the same emotion that they did Bu'r or Po'l. Vernglet seemed genuinely happy. He told them all that the real hard work lay ahead but that they would undo the evil of Orbius' reign. He eventually found a handful of partygoers intoxicated enough to want to engage in this deeper sort of dialogue. Most just hugged him.

A thick meathook of a hand landed on Duke's shoulder. The bounty hunter turned around to see Bu'r.

"How's the wine tonight?" asked the broad-chested rebel.

"Not bad, not bad at all."

"Thank you, Duke LaGrange of Nova Texas. We couldn't have done this without you and Ishiro'shea. I believe the Orb did summon the right people."

Duke blushed and quickly gave Bu'r a big "Nah." He proceeded to change the subject. "What's next for you, my friend?"

"I'm going to return to Shud'nut. It's my home and they need my help. It won't be easy. I'm sure they are embarrassed about how they acted."

Duke couldn't help but think of how the citizens of Shud'nut would react after seeing what Ishiro'shea had to do to get Uu'k back. *Bu'r's job will definitely not be easy.*

"That's very noble of you. I'm sure that if you decide to stay here, the brass will shower you with honorary titles and all of that stuff."

"Maybe. But with Ja'a in charge, I think they have it under control."

"You're probably right."

"I just wanted to thank you. I probably won't see you

again, off-worlder." Duke noticed Bu'r's sly grin as he used the term. "And I wish you the best in your return home to the stars."

The bounty hunter raised his glass of wine, then clinked it against Bu'r's.

"To Ty'n. His sacrifice was a worthy one."

"And to you," Bu'r said, fighting back a tear. "Thank you for helping us make it a worthy one."

Ja'a ascended to a platform constructed in the middle of the open plaza. Vernglet and Mo'a flanked her. Fire-tipped pikes surrounded the stage. The Neprians began to coalesce around the platform, raising glasses and cheering. Mo'a stepped to the forefront and calmed them down.

"Everyone, I present you, Ja'a, the first empress—" He looked at a scowling Ja'a, "—or similar designation as yet to be ironed out—of Neprius."

The cheers turned into roars, then halted as Ja'a began to speak.

"My father loved our planet. He died trying to do what we did—end the reign of an evil ruler. A ruler that sent us to the mines to be whipped and beaten as slaves, killing us if we resisted. But let's not forget, he enslaved our neighbors to the North as well. He corrupted their minds with fear and forced them to harm us—or die. I beg you all to not hold grudges against our fellow beings. It will be hard, I know that. Death and suffering are not easily forgotten. But we must try. We will not have a single, harmonious Neprius unless we can all forgive and move on."

The crowd applauded. Vernglet smiled.

"This gives me much hope. But as my good friend, Vern-glet Wip, has reminded me—the hard work still lies ahead."

Her tone turned from hopeful to reflective. "I could never even attempt to thank and honor those that sacrificed their lives and health for our cause. However, I do want to mention the names of those that accompanied us and did not make it back to enjoy this moment. I want to be very clear—we would not have survived without their efforts. The noble Ty'n of the Southern Forests held off voracious swamp cannibals so that we could make it through to the North. The honorable Te'o fell victim to an unexpected traitor, whilst doing his job, providing us a lookout as we traversed the hostile lands leading to Sansagon. And the courageous Ma'n. He challenged an entire squad of soldiers, as well as Gar himself, to save a child. Please honor them and all others by doing your best to make Neprius a better place. A place that they died for."

Organically the crowd raised their glasses as silence overcame the entire plaza.

"Thank you," Ja'a continued. "And to those that did make it back. The great warrior, Bu'r of Shud'nut!"

Cheers erupted.

"His mace and passions carried us through many perils. You all know Po'l—his bravery is unrivaled."

More cheers.

"He escaped death's grasp on countless occasions."

Duke rolled his eyes.

"He provided our band with a warrior's spirit. I hope that he will accept my offer to continue the legacy of his uncle Mo'a and lead our army—though I hope that we never need to use it."

Po'l received pats on the back and handshakes from all of the attendees around him.

"And, lastly, to our new friends from the stars. The silent Ishiro'shea—I've never seen a fiercer soldier. His lack of words is made up for by his actions, which speak volumes of his character."

Duke put his arm around the neck of his ninja companion, "Attaboy! I never knew I worked with a real life hero."

Ishiro'shea returned the snarky comment with an elbow to the bounty hunter's ribcage.

"And to Duke LaGrange. Adventurer. Trailblazer. Poet. A true man of the universe."

Duke tipped his hat. Ja'a, the new leader of Neprius, returned a smile.

"Enjoy tonight," she concluded. "Tomorrow, we welcome a new Neprius."

The loudest cheers of the evening filled the seaside air as Ja'a left the platform and returned to the party.

"Ishiro, we did good. I think."

Ishiro'shea responded with a thumbs-up. Like a flash of light, reminiscent of the ninja himself, a smallish figure affixed to Ishiro's left leg.

"Ishiro!" shouted Uu'k, not releasing the hug. "Before you leave, can you teach me some more sword fighting? Today was fun!"

Ishiro'shea knelt down and examined the wooden training sword he had given her earlier in the day. He gave her a thumbs-up.

"Thanks! See you in a bit! And thanks to you too, Uncle Duke."

The child spy sprinted off into the crowd and disappeared.

"Uncle Duke. Finally."

Ishiro'shea took his turn and extended his arm around Duke's neck.

"Okay, okay! But don't teach her *all* of your tricks—she's pretty salty. For a filthy street urchin."

Uu'k scrunched her nose at Duke, then smiled. Ishiro'shea nodded and followed the child spy's path to the perimeter of the party.

Duke examined the wine in his glass against the moonlight. He slurped down the last remnant.

"Need a refill?"

The voice was beautiful. It sounded the same as when he heard it blindfolded in a cave south of Dre'en.

"Your highness."

"No need for that, Duke."

"Thanks for the mention in the speech."

"You know, I didn't always know where you stood."

"Join the club."

"But I always knew where I wanted you to stand."

"I don't follow."

"I could tell—even during those early attempts at flattery— that you had a heart."

"It's what keeps me alive."

"No, our cause. Our group. Me. We—*I* needed someone with passion to fuel our cause. We needed a heart."

"I wasn't so sure after Shud'nut."

"I wasn't either, if I'm honest. And you challenging that was a good thing."

"You sure didn't act like it."

"You can be an ass. I'm still not entirely over you leaving us in the swamp solely to scratch the itch of curiosity."

"Fair point. But, you have to admit, Toby did prove to be a useful ally."

"But don't miss my meaning, Duke LaGrange, I'm very appreciative of everything that you have done. Whether it was for the cause, or to get back your ship. It doesn't matter. We couldn't have accomplished what we did without you."

"Thank you."

"One more thing before you leave our 'primitive, two-bit world' as I believe you called it."

"Something like that," Duke said, blushing.

"Do you remember that night on the hill?"

"I do."

"You told me about—how did you put it? Pesky carnal needs?"

"I did? I mean , yes, I did."

Ja'a grabbed Duke's hand and led him to the *Deus Ex Machina.*

For the next forty-eight minutes, the Nova Texan experienced a different side of Neprian culture and, specifically, a different side of this gorgeous and giving Neprian female.

It was a side that he very much liked.

He was pretty confident that he had the best time at the party of anyone there.

The rat-a-tat-tat knock on the exterior of the *Deus* woke up both Ja'a and Duke. They looked at each other and exchanged smiles.

"About last night—" started Duke.

"Duke, you don't have to say anything or expect anything. It was what it—"

"I was just going to ask how I did?" he interrupted.

Ja'a grinned as she turned her head away. He heard a discreet laugh from the attractive Neprian.

"I'll take your silence to indicate a job well done."

"Duke," Ja'a began, "I have to admit—it was like nothing else that I've experienced."

"That's what I like to hear."

"I won't challenge you on your prowess in that department, but I'm truly sorry if I led you on or took advantage of you. The long journey, you being thrown into my life and my cause, the emotions, and everything else just bubbled up and it seemed like the right thing to do. And it was everything that I needed—passion, escape, connection, pleasure. I hope it was enjoyable for you as well."

"Wait a second. You used me?"

"Duke! No, no. That's not what I meant."

"Sure sounds like it," Duke retorted.

Ja'a struggled to find her words.

"I'm yankin' your chain."

Ja'a responded with a blank stare.

"Oh, right. It means I'm just messing with you. In fact, I

appreciate anyone that can take advantage of Duke LaGrange. If anything, I'm impressed."

"That's not what I did. I acted on impulse—but I find you very—"

"Ja'a," Duke said, cutting her off. "You don't need to explain yourself. I'm a big boy. And it was enjoyable for me. A moment that I won't forget."

His tenderness seemed to catch Ja'a off guard.

"You know my place is here," she said.

"I do. I've never doubted that. And you know my place is—"

"Out there," Ja'a said, finishing his thought. "But I do want to give you something."

She removed her necklace and handed it to Duke.

"No way. That's a gift from your father. I couldn't."

"You helped me realize my father's dream. And this could help you get home."

"I'm sure there's enough mustangsen here on the *Deus*. I mean it's *made of* mustangsen."

"It would make me feel better. I want to give you every opportunity to get back to your part of the universe."

"It's an honor." He draped the necklace around his neck— it was a little snug but it didn't choke him.

The pounding noise increased in volume and frequency.

"Okay, Ishiro! We're coming."

Duke and Ja'a descended to the entrance closest to the incessant knocking. The door opened.

"Oh, it's you Po'l," said Duke, somewhat surprised and unsure of the impending reaction.

"Duke," he began. "Good morning."

"Good morning to you," Duke responded tepidly.

"Ja'a, I had a feeling that I would find you here. I need to tell you something."

"Do we need to go somewhere private?"

"No need. I wanted to tell you that I'm not going to take you up on your offer."

"What?" Ja'a asked. "But this is your chance to become our general. It's been your dream."

"It was. I've learned a lot. My eyes have been opened to all that I *don't* know. I've been a fool." He faced Duke. "Not everything that I've done was foolish—but more than I care to admit. I still have my doubts about you, LaGrange—but not about you being a traitor or a liar. Just about you being anything other than a giant ass."

Duke grinned.

"Not the first time that I've been called that in—well, since last night."

Po'l looked confused but continued. "Ja'a, I'm honored to have received your trust but my path is much different than yours. You have been my greatest friend and I know that you will bring peace to our planet."

Ja'a stepped towards Po'l and kissed him on the lips. His eyes widened. She pulled him close and embraced him as a brother. "I love you, Po'l. I hope you find what you're looking for."

"I will."

Duke heard a child's voice in the distance. Ishiro'shea and Uu'k approached. Ishiro'shea had his katana drawn; Uu'k did not have her wooden training sword—instead, she had a simple but very much real dagger. They parried back and forth as they shuffled towards Duke, Ja'a, and Po'l.

"It looks like you're taking to this naturally," Ja'a said to Uu'k in a maternal tone. "Maybe you will be a general one day."

"Ishiro'shea's the best teacher ever!"

"Already migrated to an actual blade?" asked Duke.

Ishiro'shea gave a thumbs-up to Duke as he continued to fend off Uu'k's swipes and swings. She stopped and withdrew her dagger. She gave Ishiro'shea an elongated embrace.

"Thank you, Ishiro'shea. Good luck getting back home. And come visit again."

Ishiro'shea returned the embrace.

"I guess it's that time," Duke said, regretting the cloud of sadness his statement cast over the gathering. "Time for us to hit the road and for you to rebuild your planet."

"I almost forgot," Ja'a said. She rummaged inside a beat-up leather satchel. She removed a bright purple glass Orb.

"Ja'a! Why? How? What?" Po'l stammered and struggled to pick which question to ask first.

"Po'l, it's okay," she said reassuringly. "The Keeper, Fazeek, Duke, and I made the decision. The Orb needs to leave our planet for us to have a chance to rebuild without the worry of its corruption—but we don't want people thinking that it has escaped. Both of the ancients have decided to go along with the ruse. In fact, it was Fazeek's idea."

"Yeah, I don't think he trusts Toby," Duke added. "Can't blame him."

"Also, it will give Duke and Ishiro'shea a better chance to get home. If it deposits them somewhere other than their home, then they can always try again until it gets it right."

"And we have a place in mind that it will be safe."

CHAPTER 39

CYBORG JOE'S, REVISITED

"M R. LAGRANGE, CAN I GET you another Glyptodian Summer Ale?"

"No thanks, Earl. I'm more in the mood for—"

"Whisky?" asked Queen Joe.

"How'd you know?"

"Lucky guess. That was quite the tale. Who would have thought that damn red blob would have led you to such an adventure?"

"I have a feeling that *you* did."

Queen Joe sunk below the bar and appeared with a dusty bottle of Earth whisky. She did not respond to Duke's comment. She placed five glasses on the bar top and slid them along, the first four stopping in front of the desired patron at even intervals. The fifth remained in her hand.

"To adventures," said the Queen, "and restored mojo."

"Definitely to restored mojo," added the bounty hunter.

Duke clinked his glass with Ishiro'shea's. The ninja sucked up the shot in a flash. Duke swivelled in his chair, facing the patron to his right.

"And to Po'l," proclaimed Duke.

The Neprian nodded and drank the whisky.

"So what's mojo? And what's this drink?" asked the Neprian.

"Your new friend has a lot to learn," added Joe.

"What better place than at Cyborg Joe's?" exclaimed Duke.

"Very true. And I think Lilly is eager to help. She seems to like him."

Duke looked along the bar. The anthropomorphic musk ox from one of the moons of Gartosh was batting her eyelashes at the rebel. The Neprian responded with an expression of fear and horror.

"Hey Lilly," said Duke, "Good to see you again."

"Thanks for the whisky," she replied.

Duke raised his glass and downed the brown liquid. He turned back to Queen Joe. "What's been going on since we left? How'd everything shake out with Sprinkles?"

"I haven't heard from the Robots in a while," she replied. "I think they were arrested on Jungafallow IV. But we just repaired the ceiling last week. So—let's keep Betsy quiet, please."

"Sounds good."

"Oh—someone was asking about you the other day."

"Who?"

"Prince Korzo-Tapor."

"That guy? He tried to kill me, you know. All because of the Robots."

"Are you sure?"

"What else could he have been pissed at?"

"You are Duke LaGrange, remember."

"True."

"But he was asking a lot of questions. Earl was pretty coy, but the prince *did* press."

"What did he do?"

"He ended up using a portal. Probably to gamble."

"Ah."

"But—"

"But what, Queen?"

"Soon after, someone that you know *very well* also used the same portal. Mazilda Cloax."

Duke was silent. His face lost emotion. He extended his glass to Queen Joe and she refilled it without hesitation. He sucked the whisky down aggressively.

"I'm done with portals."

"Probably a wise move," said Queen Joe. She returned the now much lighter bottle of whisky to a cabinet below the bar top. A faint purple glow rose from behind the bar. Her eyes met Duke's. "Don't worry, it will be safe."

"Who's Mazilda Cloax?" asked Po'l.

"You know how I'm the renowned bounty hunter?"

"So you say."

"She's better."

"She? Is she the one—"

"Another time, another place, my friend," Duke said, cutting off Po'l. "Now we have to teach you how to survive Cyborg Joe's Grill N' Go & the Why Not Saloon. If you can make it here a night without being killed, you'll be just fine out in the universe."

Duke pointed at the MechaBurger 8000 sitting before the Neprian. "Lesson one. Don't eat that."

"Why not?"

"Trust me. Earl, are you trying to kill him?"

"I'm sorry, but he ordered it."

The Glyptodian barkeep removed the plate as Po'l took another sip of his Erontian saké.

Duke picked up the menu and ordered two soufflés.

A booming thud rattled Po'l, causing the Neprian to spring to his feet.

Duke laughed. He looked down.

Ishiro'shea was out cold on the barroom floor.

"Lesson two. How to pick up women with a drunk space ninja."

THE END

THANK YOU

I hope that you enjoyed *How to Pick Up Women with a Drunk Space Ninja*. If so, I'd love for you to join my newsletter at DukeLaGrange.com.

Don't forget that the adventures of Duke and Ishiro'shea continue in Book II…

How to Win at Pit Fighting with a Drunk Space Ninja!

Available in Print and E-Book.

ABOUT THE AUTHOR

©JAY KEY 2018

JAY KEY knew at a young age that he wanted to be the world's first professional wrestler turned fraternity president turned digital media executive turned Society of Vertebrate Paleontology-approved blog writer turned science-fiction comedy author. At various points, Key called Dallas, San Francisco, and Los Angeles home—but it wasn't until a move to Chicago that writing professionally became a reality. Authoring a serialized version of *The Adventures of Duke LaGrange* and a popular blog on the paleobiological accuracy of dinosaurs in pop culture, Key used that momentum to complete *How to Pick Up Women with a Drunk Space Ninja* in 2017. It debuted with Star Wheel Books in 2018.

Jay now lives in a suburb of Dallas-Fort Worth with his wife, Shelley, their daughter, Finley, and their French bulldog, Olive.

twitter.com/ofamesozoicmind

instagram.com/jaykkey

facebook.com/starwheelbooks